Palgrave Studies in the Enlightenment, Romanticism and Cultures of Print

General Editors: **Professor Anne K. Mellor** and **Professor Clifford Siskin**

Editorial Board: **Isobel Armstrong**, Birkbeck & IES; **John Bender**, Stanford; **Alan Bewell**, Toronto; **Peter de Bolla**, Cambridge; **Robert Miles**, Victoria; **Claudia L. Johnson**, Princeton; **Saree Makdisi**, UCLA; **Felicity Nussbaum**, UCLA; **Mary Poovey**, NYU; **Janet Todd**, Cambridge

Palgrave Studies in the Enlightenment, Romanticism and Cultures of Print will feature work that does not fit comfortably within established boundaries—whether between periods or between disciplines. Uniquely, it will combine efforts to engage the power and materiality of print with explorations of gender, race, and class. By attending as well to intersections of literature with the visual arts, medicine, law, and science, the series will enable a large-scale rethinking of the origins of modernity.

Titles include:

Scott Black
OF ESSAYS AND READING IN EARLY MODERN BRITAIN

Claire Brock
THE FEMINIZATION OF FAME, 1750–1830

Brycchan Carey
BRITISH ABOLITIONISM AND THE RHETORIC OF SENSIBILITY
Writing, Sentiment, and Slavery, 1760–1807

E. J. Clery
THE FEMINIZATION DEBATE IN 18TH-CENTURY ENGLAND
Literature, Commerce and Luxury

Adriana Craciun
BRITISH WOMEN WRITERS AND THE FRENCH REVOLUTION
Citizens of the World

Ildiko Csengei
SYMPATHY, SENSIBILITY AND THE LITERATURE OF FEELING IN THE EIGHTEENTH CENTURY

Peter de Bolla, Nigel Leask and David Simpson (*editors*)
LAND, NATION AND CULTURE, 1740–1840
Thinking the Republic of Taste

Elizabeth Eger
BLUESTOCKINGS
Women of Reason from Enlightenment to Romanticism

Ina Ferris and Paul Keen (*editors*)
BOOKISH HISTORIES
Books, Literature, and Commercial Modernity, 1700-1900

John Gardner
POETRY AND POPULAR PROTEST
Peterloo, Cato Street and the Queen Caroline Controversy

George C. Grinnell
THE AGE OF HYPOCHONDRIA
Interpreting Romantic Health and Illness

Ian Haywood
BLOODY ROMANTICISM
Spectacular Violence and the Politics of Representation, 1776–1832

Anthony S. Jarrells
BRITAIN'S BLOODLESS REVOLUTIONS
1688 and the Romantic Reform of Literature

Jacqueline M. Labbe
WRITING ROMANTICISM
Charlotte Smith and William Wordsworth, 1784–1807

Michelle Levy
FAMILY AUTHORSHIP AND ROMANTIC PRINT CULTURE

April London
LITERARY HISTORY WRITING, 1770–1820

Robert Miles
ROMANTIC MISFITS

Tom Mole
BYRON'S ROMANTIC CELEBRITY
Industrial Culture and the Hermeneutic of Intimacy

Nicola Parsons
READING GOSSIP IN EARLY EIGHTEENTH-CENTURY ENGLAND

Jessica Richard
THE ROMANCE OF GAMBLING IN THE EIGHTEENTH-CENTURY BRITISH NOVEL

Andrew Rudd
SYMPATHY AND INDIA IN BRITISH LITERATURE, 1770–1830

Erik Simpson
LITERARY MINSTRELSY, 1770–1830
Minstrels and Improvisers in British, Irish and American Literature

Anne H. Stevens
BRITISH HISTORICAL FICTION BEFORE SCOTT

David Stewart
ROMANTIC MAGAZINES AND METROPOLITAN LITERARY CULTURE

Mary Waters
BRITISH WOMEN WRITERS AND THE PROFESSION OF LITERARY CRITICISM, 1789–1832

Esther Wohlgemut
ROMANTIC COSMOPOLITANISM

David Worrall
THE POLITICS OF ROMANTIC THEATRICALITY, 1787–1832
The Road to the Stage

Palgrave Studies in the Enlightenment, Romanticism and Cultures of Print
Series Standing Order ISBN 978–1–4039–3408–6 hardback 978–1–4039–3409–3 paperback
(*outside North America only*)

You can receive future titles in this series as they are published by placing a standing order. Please contact your bookseller or, in case of difficulty, write to us at the address below with your name and address, the title of the series and the ISBN quoted above.

Customer Services Department, Macmillan Distribution Ltd, Houndmills, Basingstoke, Hampshire RG21 6XS, England

Sympathy, Sensibility and the Literature of Feeling in the Eighteenth Century

Ildiko Csengei

palgrave
macmillan

First published 2012 by
PALGRAVE MACMILLAN

Palgrave Macmillan in the UK is an imprint of Macmillan Publishers Limited,
registered in England, company number 785998, of Houndmills, Basingstoke,
Hampshire RG21 6XS.

Palgrave Macmillan in the US is a division of St Martin's Press LLC,
175 Fifth Avenue, New York, NY 10010.

Palgrave Macmillan is the global academic imprint of the above companies
and has companies and representatives throughout the world.

Palgrave® and Macmillan® are registered trademarks in the United States,
the United Kingdom, Europe and other countries.

ISBN 978-1-349-33904-4   ISBN 978-0-230-35917-8 (eBook)
DOI 10.1057/9780230359178

This book is printed on paper suitable for recycling and made from fully
managed and sustained forest sources. Logging, pulping and manufacturing
processes are expected to conform to the environmental regulations of the
country of origin.

A catalogue record for this book is available from the British Library.

A catalog record for this book is available from the Library of Congress.

10   9   8   7   6   5   4   3   2   1
21 20 19 18 17 16 15 14 13 12

Transferred to Digital Printing in 2012

For my parents

Contents

Acknowledgements

This book started as a PhD dissertation at the Faculty of English, University of Cambridge. I revised it for publication during my tenure as an R.A. Butler Research Fellow at Pembroke College, Cambridge. I am grateful to Corpus Christi College for funding my first visit to Cambridge and then for being my home during my postgraduate years. I am also thankful to Pembroke College and Newnham College, Cambridge, for accepting me into their fellowship and for providing an ideal environment and resources for writing, thinking and research.

There are a number of colleagues, mentors and friends who have offered feedback, support and encouragement from the inception of this project until its completion. Without their input this book would not exist in its current form. First of all, I owe a very special debt to Mary Jacobus, who supervised my PhD dissertation, for her patience, devotion and skill; I am grateful to her for having been a supportive professional presence from the very beginning to the present day and a most conscientious reader of earlier versions of these chapters. Her energy, enthusiasm and continuing support has always been a source of inspiration to me. I am also greatly indebted to Peter de Bolla, Simon Schaffer and Tilottama Rajan for reading earlier versions of the manuscript, and for offering helpful feedback, constructive criticism and tremendous amounts of support and encouragement over these years. I am very grateful to Tamás Bényei for having been an inspirational scholar and mentor and for starting me on this career path many years ago. I am also indebted in various ways to Jennie Batchelor, Fiona Brideoake, David Collings, Philip Connell, Markman Ellis, Joel Faflak, Chris Geissler, David Hall, Krisztina Hamara, Paul Hamilton, Daisy Hay, Simon Jarvis, Jacques Khalip, Nigel Leask, Sally Ledger, Sam Mather, David McCallam, Dean Mobbs, Donald Morse, Lesley Murdin, Mary Newbould, Rosemary Parkinson, Nicola Parsons, Thomas Pfau, István Rácz, Michael Reeve, Bede Scott, Ágnes Simon, Jasmine Solomonescu, Neil Vickers, Orrin Wang, Ross Wilson, David Witzling, Mark Wormald and George Yeats.

I am grateful to my colleagues at the Faculty of English, University of Cambridge, Pembroke College and Newnham College, for providing a research-friendly and intellectually vibrant environment. The collegiate system, which fosters interdisciplinary discussions, definitely left its mark on my thinking; I learnt a lot from the events of the Centre for Research in the Arts, Social Sciences and Humanities (CRASSH) and the fascinating table conversations I was fortunate enough to have had at various colleges with colleagues working in a variety of fields. I would also like to say thanks to my students at Cambridge for keeping my mind open to many acute observations, fresh perspectives and challenging questions pertaining to eighteenth-century sensibility.

I am indebted to the speakers and participants of the 'Sympathies and Antipathies: Altruism and Emotional Response Across the Disciplines' conference, held in 2009 at CRASSH in Cambridge, for all the thought-provoking discussions; my thanks go in particular to Fay Bound Alberti, Carolyn Burdett, Thomas Dixon, Christopher Frith, Loraine Gelsthorpe, Emma Mason, Ayesha Nathoo, Marianne Noble, Keith Tester, Sylvana Tomaselli, Arne Johan Vetlesen and Margot Waddell. I am especially grateful to my colleague and the conference's co-organiser, Paul White, for his friendship, collegiality and the countless wonderful conversations on sympathy in the Cambridge University Library's tearoom that kept me thinking and kept me cheerful.

I would like to thank Mieke Bal, Dominick LaCapra and the faculty and participants of the School of Criticism and Theory at Cornell University in 2003 for giving me the opportunity to integrate new perspectives into my thinking. I am especially grateful to Anne Birian, Alain Schorderet, Cecilia Kapoor and Apostolos Lampropoulos for sharing their knowledge and friendship. I am also indebted to the organisers and participants of the numerous other conferences and workshops that I attended whilst working on this project. I am especially thankful to the British Society for Eighteenth-Century Studies for offering annual opportunities for intellectual exchange with fellow-minded eighteenth-century scholars, and to Gavin Budge and Frank O'Gorman in particular for introducing me to the work of the society as a graduate student and having me as a committee member for many subsequent years.

For their financial support I would like to acknowledge my debt to the Cambridge Overseas Trust, Corpus Christi College, the British Federation of Women Graduates, the Master and Fellows of Pembroke College, Cambridge, the Butler family, the Leverhulme Trust, the Newton Trust, the Faculty of English, University of Cambridge, the Principal and Fellows of Newnham College, Cambridge, CRASSH and the Wellcome Trust. Without their generous assistance, it would not have been possible for me to bring this project to completion.

The librarians of the Cambridge University Library, the British Library, the Bodleian Library, Oxford, and the Wellcome Library have been immensely helpful and patient with my requests. I am particularly grateful to the staff of the Cambridge University Library's Rare Books Room, Reading Room and West Room, where most of my research was done and where the majority of these pages were written. My special thanks go to Bruce Barker-Benfield, Senior Assistant Librarian at the Department of Special Collections and Western Manuscripts at the Bodleian Library, for helping me find my way around the Abinger Collection when Godwin's papers were still uncatalogued, and for his continuing assistance with my queries during the reorganisation and cataloguing process.

Some parts of this book have previously been published as journal articles. Sections from Chapter 2 appeared as 'Sensibility in Dissection: Affect, Aesthetics, and the Eighteenth-Century Body in Pain', in *Hungarian Journal of English and American Studies* 9.2 (2003): 148–73 and are reproduced here with the permission of the *Hungarian Journal of English and American Studies* and its editor, Donald E. Morse. The material of Chapter 3 was published by the MHRA as '"I Will Not Weep": Reading through the Tears of Henry Mackenzie's *Man of Feeling*', in *Modern Language Review* 103.4 (October 2008): 952–68. Parts of Chapter 4 appeared as '"She Fell Senseless on His Corpse": The Woman of Feeling and the Sentimental Swoon in Eighteenth-Century Fiction', in *Romantic Circles*, Praxis Series, Romantic Psyche and Psychoanalysis, ed. and int. Joel Faflak (December 2008), http://www.rc.umd.edu/praxis/. The material of Chapter 5 was published as 'Godwin's Case: Melancholy Mourning in the Empire of Feeling', in *Studies in Romanticism* 48.3 (2009): 491–519, and is reproduced by permission of the Trustees of Boston University. I am grateful to the editors and the anonymous reviewers for all their comments and suggestions on these articles.

The author and publishers wish to thank the following for permission to reproduce archival or copyright material: the Bodleian Libraries, University of Oxford, for permission to quote from the Abinger Collection; Cambridge University Press for permission to quote passages from Adam Smith, *The Theory of Moral Sentiments*, ed. Knud Haakonssen (Cambridge: Cambridge University Press, 2002) and Julien Offray de la Mettrie, *Machine Man and Other Writings*, trans. and ed. Ann Thomson (Cambridge: Cambridge University Press, 1996); Oxford University Press for permission to quote passages from Elizabeth Inchbald, *A Simple Story*, ed. J. M. S. Tompkins (Oxford: Oxford University Press, 1998); Jason Aronson, Inc. for permission to quote from *The Work of Hanna Segal: A Kleinian Approach to Clinical Practice* (New York and London: Jason Aronson-Rowman & Littlefield, 1981); the University Press of

New England, Lebanon, NH for permission to quote several passages from Jean-Jacques Rousseau, *Julie, or the New Heloise: Letters of Two Lovers Who Live in a Small Town at the Foot of the Alps*, trans. and annot. Philip Stewart and Jean Vaché (Hanover and London: The University Press of New England, 1997).

Every effort has been made to trace rights holders, but if any have been inadvertently overlooked the publishers would be pleased to make the necessary arrangements at the first opportunity.

I would like to acknowledge the support of those close relations whose existence made all the effort and hard work worthwhile. I owe a very special debt to my husband, Tim Hosey, for his constant, loving presence and for having been the voice of reason throughout my years of work on feeling. And I am greatly indebted to my parents, Lajos Gyökér and Aranka Szabó, and my brother, Tamás Gyökér, for their unconditional love, sympathy and sensibility, and for surviving my long years of absence and finding ways to bridge the geographical distance by their continuing support and encouragement. My knowledge of the practicalities of emotional response would not have been the same without their loving letters, cards, phone calls and visits to England. I dedicate this book to them with love and gratitude.

Finally, I would like thank the editors and anonymous reviewer at Palgrave Macmillan for their careful reading of the manuscript and for their enthusiasm for my book. I am grateful for their invaluable comments and suggestions. In particular, I would like to thank Nick Brock for his copy-editing, and Ben Doyle and Paula Kennedy for their impressive professionalism, prompt editorial work and their support of my book project from the early stages to publication.

Introduction: Sensibility from the Margins

I

This study aims to explore the factors that make it possible for self-interest, cruelty and violence to become constitutive aspects of the ostensibly benevolent, philanthropist ideology of eighteenth-century sensibility. It undertakes to investigate the darker side of sensibility by focussing on the question of emotional response. In literary and cultural criticism, sensibility denotes a cultural trend of emotional upheaval, a cult of sympathy and compassion that extends to all areas of life roughly between the 1740s and the end of the century. This book understands sensibility to be a specific way of expressing, writing and reading affectivity that is determined by the crisis and transformation of such historical and social factors as the development of new models of human subjectivity in science and medicine, philosophical ideas of innate benevolence and sympathy, political and sexual revolution, and the rise of the novel, together with the emergence of a largely female, middle-class readership. But rather than taking this complex cultural phenomenon as a given (as in outlining a coherent 'age' or a 'culture' of sensibility), this book will look at the ways in which sensibility in the eighteenth century is produced and reproduced in various fields of life, art and culture as an inherently ambivalent, two-sided discourse.[1]

This study will investigate the various ways, loci and materials through which sensibility comes into existence as a textual, literary and aesthetic mode of representation. Its contention is that sensibility is controversial and ambivalent from the start; it is constructed of feelings, ideas and concepts whose repressed dimensions are present at its very heart, and whose margins and extremes are also illustrative of its formation. Therefore, in order to investigate how sensibility is produced

1

as a culture of emotions laden with ambivalence and negativity, I will aim to explore the margins of sensibility, which are formative of this upheaval of benevolent emotionalism and humanitarianism. I argue that the key to understanding the ambivalence of sensibility lies within the nature of emotional response, which in this period implies complex processes from a mechanically-imagined transmission of feeling to imaginary identification. Exploring in detail the ways in which affective response operates in the period will be a key aspect of this project. While this approach makes feeling analytically focal, its broader implications are ethical and political: it helps us see how sensibility could be appropriated for conflicting political views such as abolitionism and anti-abolitionism, or the ideals of the French Revolution and their culmination in the Terror.

The material includes eighteenth-century literature, philosophy, medical and political writing, as well as memoirs, familiar letters, personal notes and papers, mostly from the second half of the century. Apart from core literary texts of sensibility, such as Rousseau's *Julie, or the New Heloise* (1761) or Henry Mackenzie's *The Man of Feeling* (1771) and works by its most central philosophers (Shaftesbury, Francis Hutcheson, David Hume and Adam Smith), I also consider recently edited material such as Sarah Fielding's *The History of Ophelia* (1760), along with late eighteenth-century critiques of sensibility by Mary Wollstonecraft and Elizabeth Inchbald. The last chapter makes extensive use of William Godwin's unpublished papers, letters and diary. Although the focus of my research is sensibility in Britain, my investigation also extends to influential continental ideas and debates that create the ground for the emergence of sensibility as a controversial phenomenon, including the work of the Swiss physiologist Albrecht von Haller, the French materialist thinker Julien Offray de La Mettrie, and the philosopher and novelist Jean-Jacques Rousseau. Different kinds of texts – literary, political, medical and philosophical – will be treated here as equally important agents in the production of sensibility, to be analysed and read in their own right.

This book will show how the ambivalence of affective response plays an important part in the multifaceted critiques targeted at various aspects of sensibility throughout the period, including its symptom-language of tears, sighs and swoons, as well as the assumptions of transparency, virtue and disinterested sympathy related to this symptom-language. The attacks on sensibility during the eighteenth century were diverse and seemingly inconsistent with one another. Their authors represented a variety of standpoints and a multitude of – often-conflicting – backgrounds and political agendas. Some saw sensibility as a threat, because it could be excessive and could operate impulsively, while others complained that sympathy was selective, because moral impulses do not work all the time. Writers such as Oliver Goldsmith and Henry Mackenzie warned against the threat posed by the spontaneous and uncontrollable flow of sentiment, while others – including George Canning – ridiculed the two-faced nature of the cult of sensibility and castigated the tendency to shed tears for the trivial while simultaneously ignoring urgent social issues. In response to the too-good-to-be-true, transparent and virtuous feminine morality advocated by Richardson's *Pamela* (1740), Henry Fielding's *Shamela* (1741) challenged the disinterestedness of authentic female emotion, and Hannah More – in 'Sensibility: A Poem' (1782) – targeted the equivocal 'drapery' of 'exclamations', 'tender tones', and 'fond tears'.[2]

Throughout the period women's relation to feeling and to the symptom-language of sentiment was a persistent ground for concern. Novelists from Sarah Fielding to Mary Wollstonecraft experimented with the sentimental genre to convey resistance – often from within the tradition of the novel of sensibility itself – to oppressive social conventions and expectations. Critical voices became particularly strong towards the end of the long eighteenth century. In her *A Vindication of the Rights of Woman* (1792), Mary Wollstonecraft openly critiqued sensibility for being an institutionalised culture of weakness made fashionable in order to appeal to women, but the cultivation of which could bring about their own social enslavement. By being educated into sensibility, she argued, women were made slaves to their senses, neglecting the development of skills that could be more useful and empowering for women's social existence.[3] Jane Austen satirised sensibility on similar grounds; in *Sense and Sensibility* (1811) the excess of sentimental delicacy is seen as a threatening condition from which woman needs to recover, and in *Persuasion* (1818) the forever-indisposed Mary Elliot – a victim of sensibility as well as the reader's ridicule – is already very far from the idealised, fashionable mid-century nervous heroine. But medical writers of the eighteenth century also warned about the pathological side of sensibility, claiming illness to be one of its darker repercussions. Like creative writers, philosophers and political theorists, physiologists of the period were much intrigued by the fashion of cultivating sensibility. As Anne C. Vila puts it, taken to an extreme, 'increased sensibility yielded not greater refinement of mind and heart, but the serious and blameworthy prospect of "falling ill from feeling too much"'. And illness was indeed a dangerous margin of sensibility as it could turn a culture of sociability into one of solipsism and isolation. 'That is', writes Vila, 'the same vital élan that seemed to inspire people to practise such crucial virtues as compassion and benevolence might instead trigger a physically grounded solipsism utterly incompatible with sympathetic social interaction.'[4] A culture of feeling was thus only a step away from a culture of feeling bad.

The chapters will unravel these diverse – and sometimes contradictory and self-contradictory – critiques of sensibility according to their specific targets and find answers to the reasons for their emergence in different eighteenth-century contexts. My investigation will look closely at the question of emotional response and its discontents, exploring the problematic and often-dysfunctional operation of key other-regarding responses characteristic of discourses of sensibility. I use 'feeling' and 'emotional response' somewhat broadly here, to denote the many ways in which the eighteenth century understood reactivity to stimulus, including its cognitive, sensory, nervous, muscular and moral components. I adopt this generic use for now, aware that one cannot equate our current understanding of 'emotion' and the diverse eighteenth-century terminology that included such period-specific concepts as the passions, affections, sentiments, irritability, sensibility and sympathy. Rather, 'emotional response' and 'feeling' are used here to encompass the specific eighteenth-century phenomena denoted by diverse early concepts. Some of these concepts (including sympathy, irritability, sensibility and later developments like empathy) will constitute the focal points of this book and will be explored in detail.[5]

Samuel Johnson defined 'sensibility' in the mid-eighteenth century as 'quickness of sensation' and 'quickness of perception'. While this does not (yet) seem to imply the variety of meanings and cultural fields that come to be encompassed by sensibility's connotations and cognates over the course of the period, Johnson's definition of the adjective 'sensible' already reflects this cultural diversity. By 'sensible' he meant a range of qualities that included perceptibility by the mind and by the senses, the 'quality of being affected by moral good or ill', as well as 'having quick intellectual feeling'. The colloquial, 'low use' of the word interestingly coincides with how we understand the word today, that is, by 'reasonable, judicious, wise'.[6] As Johnson's definition shows, eighteenth-century sensibility was a cultural phenomenon that pertained to all aspects of human existence, addressing especially the meeting points of mind, body and morality. When exploring the ambivalence of sensibility the book's chapters look more closely into each one of these aspects; accordingly, Chapter 1 deals with sympathy as a moral response, whereas Chapter 2 looks at feeling in the context of the body's materiality. Chapters 3, 4 and 5 are devoted to literary texts, exploring affective response in its interaction with the body and the mind. Our journey through the philosophy, medicine and literature of the long eighteenth century will seek out particularly those moments where sympathetic response proves difficult or simply fails to operate.

II

The definition of eighteenth-century sensibility has always been a challenging endeavour. Looking into the literature of the period and the criticism written about it, one finds oneself in an embarrassment of riches. Definitions abound, though the concept is generally agreed to imply a belief in natural goodness, benevolence and compassion, and it is often associated with a cult of feeling, melancholy, distress and refined emotionalism.[7] To some extent, the proliferation of meanings and definitions has to do with the prevalence of this concept in most fields of eighteenth-century life and culture.[8] Scholarship has described sensibility as a period marker, a cult of emotionalism, a culture of women, and even a political and ideological tool. Moreover, it is often noted that sensibility has a readable, language-like quality. Important studies by Janet Todd and R. F. Brissenden describe eighteenth-century sensibility as a system of meaning frequently referred to as 'the language of the heart', with its own distinctive vocabulary and collection of signs and bodily symptoms. Critical writings on sensibility have investigated the historical transformations and connotations of sensibility and related concepts. This vocabulary of sensibility contains recurring elements with specific period- and context-related meanings. Debility, innocence, heightened emotionalism and floods of tears are natural and desirable for persons of sensibility, both male and female. Blushing, fainting, swooning, crying, handholding, mute gestures, palpitations of the heart – symptoms with an emotional content – make frequent appearance in the writings of the period.[9]

Here I will undertake to explore how the meaning of sensibility was generated and informed by issues that literary scholarship and cultural history have tended to consider less central to their investigations. This book will aim to tackle the extremes where sensibility is barely distinguishable from the most intense experiences of pain and the moments of so-called 'insensibility', where heightened feeling slips into lack of sensation, as in the agonies of torture and the sentimental swoon. In an attempt to explore sensibility from the margins, my book will complement exclusively nervous interpretations of sensibility – a dominant view in medical and literary history. Sensibility as an eighteenth-century cultural phenomenon pertained to all aspects of the study of man. One of these aspects was medical, which context is predominantly explained in today's scholarship in terms of the period's intense physiological interest in the nerves as well as nervous states and disorders. G.S. Rousseau, one of the first scholars to explore the interconnections between the literature of sensibility and medicine, argues that the medical roots of sensibility can be traced back to the work of Thomas Willis in the 1660s. Willis was a seventeenth-century English doctor who worked out what we would now call a detailed neurophysiology of the brain. Willis identified the brain as the centre of the soul and claimed that it depended entirely on the nerves for all its functions, including sensory impressions and, consequently, knowledge. Medicine had been aware of the connection between the brain and the nerves before Willis, but the fact that he placed the seat of the soul solely into the brain had a serious impact on contemporary thought. Rousseau argues that Willis's idea was so important in the seventeenth century that it accounted for the welter of speculations about the structure of the nerve, including arguments about its possible solidity or hollowness. 'Without this knowledge', writes Rousseau, 'it is impossible to account for the intense interest after the Restoration (but not before) in nerve research, and consequently the preparation for sensibility as an emotional state of mind.'[10]

In the course of the long eighteenth century nerves came to be the centre of medical interest, and therefore they also constitute a frequent discussion point for the scholarship that deals with the medical context of sensibility. Drawing on Rousseau's argument, Barker-Benfield explores how nerve theory was widely disseminated at the beginning of the eighteenth century through the work of Newton and Locke, entering large-scale public circulation through Addison and Steele's *Spectator* and the literature of sensibility, including the work of James Thomson and Samuel Richardson.[11] Barker-Benfield explores how the vocabulary of the nerves filters into the literature of the period and analyses the literary representations of gendered nervous illness based mainly on the influence of George Cheyne, Samuel Richardson's doctor and correspondent.[12] Because of his popularity amongst his contemporaries and his influence on Richardson, Cheyne often features prominently in the scholarship that deals with the early physiological context of sensibility; as Barker-Benfield claims, 'Cheyne seems to have been Richardson's primary source for the version of the nerve paradigm injected into his novels, and thereby into the mainstream of sentimental fiction.'[13] But there has been influential research further exploring a broad spectrum of medical literature dealing with the nerves throughout the period. John Mullan looks at nervous disorder with a particular emphasis on hypochondria, melancholy and hysteria, and draws attention to the narrow boundary between sensibility and nervous illness. Ann van Sant is particularly interested in the discursive, rhetorical characteristics of the language of the heart and the nervous system in physiological and literary texts, and Anne C. Vila focuses on the frontiers of medicine and literature in a French Enlightenment setting and explores the medical foundations of sensibility in its broader European context.[14]

An important consensus of scholarship appears to be the understanding of the cultural movement of sensibility in Britain in terms of a shift towards a mainly vitalist perspective that came to be predominant in Scottish medicine in the latter half of the eighteenth century. As Christopher Lawrence claims, the growing interest in sensibility in the period was interrelated with changing physiological views on the operation of body, mind and soul, primarily as a result of the work of the Edinburgh physiologists Robert Whytt, Alexander Monro II and William Cullen. Their work represented a shift away from a Cartesian, dualist notion of body and soul – a notion that served as the basis for the mechanistic views about the body advocated by the leading Leiden physiologist, Herman Boerhaave, and his followers. With Robert Whytt Scottish physiology made a move towards a monistic system, where the soul dominated all the vital functions of the body. In this view sensibility and its agents, the nerves, became a dominant object of enquiry.[15] The work of Whytt contains the roots of a psychosomatic approach to 'nervous' illnesses which cannot simply be explained by any organic cause. Yet, as Hubert Steinke emphasised recently, the physiology of the eighteenth century is not entirely focused on the nerves.[16] While nerves are undoubtedly crucial for understanding sensibility as a cultural phenomenon, there is more to the physiology and psychology of the period than this already widely explored preoccupation. First of all, this book would like to shift the focus of scholarship to highlight the vicissitudes of mechanist and materialist veins of thought that persist on the margins of a predominantly vitalist culture of sensibility throughout the eighteenth century. I am particularly interested in exploring the place of the reactive body and its movements within the context of feeling, which used to be a potentially problematic and slippery territory for most eighteenth-century thinkers.

In *Sympathy, Sensibility and the Literature of Feeling in the Eighteenth Century*, therefore, the concepts of irritability and sympathy – as the site of physical, moral and emotional response – will gain an important position alongside the concept of sensibility, and there will be further investigation of their contribution to the moral, medical and political ambiguities inherent in the cult of other-regarding feeling. The notion of irritability – a precursor of Brunonian excitability – was introduced into the mainstream of eighteenth-century experimental medical research in the 1750s by the Swiss physiologist Albrecht von Haller. As defined by Haller, irritability was a reactive force innate in the body's muscular tissue, explaining both movement in the living organism and the post-mortem contractions that can be observed in dead bodies and severed body parts. Irritability was a muscular reflex and entirely the property of matter, whereas sensibility (the capacity for feeling) was the property of the nerve and ultimately of the soul. While Haller kept these two aspects strictly separate, the Edinburgh physiologist Robert Whytt brought motion under the governance of feeling, making the 'sentient principle' the centre for all sensation and motion.

However, in the wake of Descartes the binary of body and soul was brought into a different kind of unity by materialist thinkers. They argued that capacities traditionally attributed to the soul such as feeling and thinking could also be explained through the operations of matter. While in France Descartes's philosophy led to the exploration of its potential materialism, in England it was the materialistic implications of John Locke's empiricist philosophy that generated debates and led to further philosophical and medical investigations. In France, materialism reached a full statement with La Mettrie's idea of the man-machine; in Britain, such a bold and open claim was not articulated. Reactions to Locke's argument, however, were frequently based on the fear that man would be viewed as a piece of clockwork.[17] Where materialism in early and mid-century Britain took a more cautious path than it did in France, mechanism had several defenders; moreover, as we shall see in Chapter 1, mechanical terminology surfaced in the writings of many contemporaries, regardless of the authors' philosophical or religious views. In the 1740s, David Hartley – the theorist of the vibrating nerve – openly voiced mechanistic views.[18] His theory, however, was far from the full-blown materialism of La Mettrie; on the other hand, materialist ideas persisted in the work of Joseph Priestley in the 1770s and the late-eighteenth-century radicals, including John Thelwall, William Godwin, Erasmus Darwin and Thomas Beddoes.[19]

Traces of mechanist and materialist thought and vocabulary surfaced continuously – and often inadvertently – in a variety of eighteenth-century works, thereby largely complicating any unified understanding of a 'culture of sensibility'. As I will argue throughout this book, these ideas constitute a – for the period – more troubling line of thought within the discourse of sensibility, opening up a space for sociopolitical critique and for resistance to violence and to dominant structures of power. Part of my book's intended shift of focus to the margins of sensibility is the discussion of the concept of sympathy with emphasis on exploring the diversity of its long eighteenth-century conceptualisations and connotations. Sympathy in the period did not only refer to a moral and emotional response and a social bonding force; it also denoted all forms of harmony, correspondence, communication, and even magnetic attraction.[20] In addition to this, however, the mechanism of sympathy could also function as a dangerous contagion of bad feeling and a disruptive force. The history of sympathy is marked by extensive transmission between fields, from astronomy to medical theory, and from moral treatises to the novel. Here I will examine disparate yet often interconnected notions of sympathy that coexist – and often work against one another – throughout the eighteenth century. These notions include a mechanistic and magnetic attraction, a communication or transfusion of feeling, the sympathetic bond, and forms of imaginary identification.[21] Despite this diversity, the focus of the scholarship that deals with sympathy tends to be restricted to one or other of sympathy's many connotations. The notion of sympathetic identification – associated mainly with the philosophy of Adam Smith and sometimes with the work of David Hume – is often prioritised mainly in literary scholarship; on the other hand, magnetic, mechanistic and materialistic conceptualisations are more or less missing from the scope of our philosophical awareness despite their predominance in the majority of texts featuring sympathy from the seventeenth century to the present day. Here I would like to open up the meanings of sympathy and explore the rich variety of its conceptualisations in the course of the eighteenth century. The history of sympathy, I contend, is therefore a history of interaction, and it should be understood in terms of a complex web of interrelationships between several aspects of its meaning. This diversity of meaning, I will argue, was – and remains – an important source of sympathy's morally and politically charged ambivalence.[22]

Instances of mechanical and magnetic sympathy such as Sir Kenelm Digby's weapon salve from 1669 that was thought to attract magnetically particles of blood, the Neoplatonic notion of planetary sympathy or the idea that growing grapes facilitate sympathetically the fermentation of wine in cellars all resist an understanding of sympathy solely within an economy of human feeling. Yet, as many eighteenth-century thinkers, including Shaftesbury, Francis Hutcheson, David Hume and Adam Smith, sought to define sympathy within a framework of passions, affections or moral sentiments, issues that pertain to these categories of affective psychology also left their mark on sympathy's eighteenth-century conceptualisations. As Thomas Dixon argues, 'passions', 'affections' and 'moral sentiments' featured repeatedly in the writings of seventeenth- and eighteenth-century Christian clergymen, preachers, philosophers and literary figures. According to the classical Christian model, claims Dixon, passions and affections were movements of the soul. However, the conceptualisation of these notions in the works of influential Christian writers gradually incorporated more secular arguments and mechanistic ideas.[23] In *Passion and Action* Susan James traces the large-scale re-thinking of the passions in seventeenth-century philosophy. James points to a larger trajectory of mechanisation, and a consequent understanding of the passions within more mechanical models of the body and mind in the work of philosophers including Descartes, Malebranche, Hobbes and Spinoza.[24]

The management and control of the passions and emotions has been a recurrent concern throughout their long history. Albert O. Hirschman's *The Passions and the Interests* deals with this long-standing preoccupation, exploring how different ways of controlling the passions go hand in hand with the birth of capitalism in the early modern period. Hirschman follows through how, throughout their long history, the passions were to be repressed, harnessed (that is, transformed from something disruptive into something constructive), or set against other, more acceptable passions in order to be controlled. As Hirschman argues, while the Medieval period saw money-making pursuits in terms of the sinful and despicable passion, greed or avarice, the modern age witnessed the reinterpretation of these pursuits as desirable, innocuous and even honourable – as part and parcel of a western culture of politeness and gentility. Hirschman traces the history of the dynamic in which the passions were set against – or in fact blended with – the 'interests'. While interest originally denoted the totality of diverse human aspirations, by the seventeenth century its meaning narrowed down to the semantic field of material, financial interest. Because of this shift, 'one set of passions, hitherto known variously as greed, avarice, or love of lucre, could be usefully employed to oppose and bridle such other passions as ambition, lust for power, or sexual lust'.[25] During the time of Hobbes and La Rochefoucauld self-interest came to be seen as the main motor force of all human actions. Hirschman understands the re-evaluation of the passions in the work of eighteenth-century philosophers such as Shaftesbury, Hutcheson and Hume against this prioritisation of the interests during the preceding century. Passions came to be rehabilitated in the works of eighteenth-century moral philosophers; benevolent, other-regarding passions were celebrated, and the view that the world is governed exclusively by self-interest came to be disputed.[26]

Thus, it is important to bear in mind that the question of the passions and their management and control by the individual tends to be embedded in a larger social and economic framework. The interconnection of the personal and the sociopolitical was an important aspect of eighteenth-century affective terminology. According to Annette Baier, the eighteenth-century category of 'character' reflected the way in which 'a person manages her different and often conflicting passions'. For Hume, character was a matter of habits and beliefs that do not change easily; it was 'the outward expressive face of that inner nature, which helps determine the role a person plays among other persons, and the reputation thereby acquired'.[27] William Reddy's concept of 'emotional navigation' reflects the sociopolitical embeddedness of feeling. His concept refers not only to the management and control of emotions but also to a wide array of emotional changes – including emotional suffering – the self has to undergo during the dynamic of maintaining as well as shifting one's life goals in the face of external circumstances. Enduring political regimes, he argues, always establish a normative order for emotions, in other words, an 'emotional regime'. In Reddy's account, eighteenth-century sentimentalism was a form of emotional navigation in response to restrictive social constructions – in other words, a product of the period's emotional regime.[28]

A number of monographs have focussed specifically on the involvement of eighteenth-century sensibility with the realm of the political. In *Radical Sensibility*, Chris Jones reads sensibility as a concept which, in the 1790s, could form part of both a conservative and a radical ideology. Brycchan Carey explores sensibility in the context of British abolitionism and notes that the rhetoric of sensibility was used in the arguments of both pro-slavery and anti-slavery writers.[29] Amit S. Rai offers a critique of sympathy in late eighteenth- and early nineteenth-century British discourse by reading abolitionist and missionary writing in the context of mainstream Enlightenment texts.[30] In *The Politics of Sensibility* Markman Ellis argues that the sentimental novel is the site of political debate related to gender, race and commerce in the period, and he claims that these novels participate in what he calls a 'politics of sensibility' through their appeal to the reader's emotion.[31] While Ellis's book focuses on how the sentimental novel engages with urgent political issues of its time, my study is interested in the way in which a text's appeal to the reader's emotion is realised in the actual process of reading. I will explore the terrain of affective response and the micro-level of individual and group psychology at which sensibility – and its politics – is produced. My focus is on personal and interpersonal affective experiences that underlie acts of reading, interpretation and sentimental encounters – bearing in mind the important political, ethical and social consequences of the workings of feelings which colour these processes. These concerns permeate our current interest in the affective structures of the reading process itself.

III

The flip side of sympathy is multifaceted and often politically charged. It can include self-interest, cruelty, solipsism, social disruption, and even medical and analytic professionalism. We shall see that the boundaries of sympathy are fragile, and the reaction that a certain stimulus is meant to elicit is often hard to control. While not the subject of detailed exploration in this study, laughter, for instance, can also reveal the darker side of sentimental sympathy. Mirthful response is seldom light and innocent; it can get very closely – and often imperceptibly – bound up with violence and cruelty. In his biography of Sir Astley Cooper, Bransby Blake Cooper cites an anecdote about John Thelwall, which reveals the fine line that divides sympathetic from comic response. According to the anecdote, Thelwall gave a lecture 'at Coachmakers' Hall, or some similar institution' about the evils of the slave trade, 'a topic calculated no less to call forth his own powers of eloquence than the interest and sympathies of the audience':

> After vividly painting the horrible sufferings to which the slaves were subjected, he proceeded to describe a mask which he said they were forced to wear, and which was so constructed that, whilst it permitted them to breathe, and perform the duties of their preoccupation without difficulty, it at the same time prevented the possibility of any indulgence being afforded to the cravings of their appetite. Having, with some minuteness, given an account of this instrument, he suddenly drew one forth from a place near him, and fitted it to his face. The effect of this theatrical experiment was not such as he had anticipated: for instead of exciting expressions of horror and pity

at the sufferings of those to whom he stated such as apparatus was applied, a conviction of the absurdity of his account seemed at once to rush into the minds of his audience. His stratagem was accordingly received with shouts of laughter, and he himself, on removing the mask, was greeted with showers of hisses. He had overshot his mark. Disconcerted, for a minute or two he remained absorbed in thought, when, as if doubting that he had mistaken the object of these expressions of disapprobation, he again covered his face with the mask, and turned to the audience. This only served to renew the laughter in an increased degree, and this time, when he removed it, the vehemence of the hisses rendered quite clear to his mind the cause which had provoked them. Different feelings at once took possession of him; – his face flushed with anger, and with a quivering lip he remarked, 'You are perhaps aware that the only quadruped which makes the noise you are now making, is – the goose.' This unfortunately-worded rebuke, Mr. Harrison informed me, literally convulsed the people present with laughter, amid the peals of which the meeting broke up, and the lecturer himself, abashed by his own lapsus, hurried from the scene of his disgrace.[32]

While Thelwall is ostensibly the butt for satire, the cruelty of this comic anecdote is double-edged: on the one hand, it exposes a young radical who strives to draw attention to social injustice at the very point where his enterprise can slip into failure. It points to the fact that the alleviation of suffering that takes place abroad depends largely on the volatile feeling of sympathy and one's rhetorical ability to produce a moving representation in one's home country. The object of the audience's mirth is the rhetorician, who, by putting on the muzzle intended for the torment of slaves, makes himself vulnerable in front of the people. The comic response Thelwall's rhetoric induces in his audience is far from what the seriousness of the topic would deserve. His gesture of wearing the mask diverts the audience's attention from the horrors of slavery to Thelwall's own loss of control, which leads to his loss of rhetorical power over his viewers, turning an intended scene of sympathy into one of bad feelings: humiliation, anger and frustration. At the same time, however, the case of the slaves – the urgent social issue at stake – gets silenced in the confusion of feelings by the gesture that foregrounds the speaker's awkwardness instead, which silencing makes the slaves the ultimate victims of the sadly comic exposé.

As Chapter 3 of this book will point out, however, mirth induced by the intention to evoke sympathy and a general shift in the tragic–comic axis also pertains to a larger, diachronic process: a change of taste, which came to be increasingly manifest towards the end of the eighteenth century and the beginning of the nineteenth. The success of Henry Mackenzie's *The Man of Feeling* at the time of its publication in 1771 and the subsequent ridicule of its tearful scenes only a few decades later well illustrates the transformation of the way in which audiences related to sentiment. The process through which the mixed, ambivalent feelings associated with sensibility increasingly came to be seen as overtly problematic by the end of the eighteenth century is part of a larger process in which sentimentalism and the cultivation of feelings continued to elicit critical (often ironic or satirical) treatment. An attitude of detachment from emotional, sentimental literatures is in harmony with this change. Unlike in the eighteenth century, an open display of tears is seldom seen in today's western cultures as a sign of moral feeling and innate virtue; instead, such displays of emotionality tend to signal vulnerability and are therefore frequently bound to remain hidden, deemed out of place or viewed with scepticism. The free expression of one's feelings and the display of troubling emotions are meant to be contained within clearly negotiated boundaries.

In *Sentimentalism, Ethics and the Culture of Feeling* Michael Bell draws attention to our distrust of and simultaneous – unacknowledged – reliance on feeling. Bell explores the progress of our problematic view of sentimentality from the eighteenth century through the Victorian period and modernism until the late twentieth century; an important goal here is to unpack the characteristic estrangement from feeling in modernist discourses.[33] Also, scenes that evoke emotional response are increasingly the target of scepticism in a world dominated by the media. Luc Boltanski claims that modern viewers of suffering have to negotiate complex dilemmas and anxieties. Distant suffering as represented by the media introduces suspicion about the desires and intentions behind these representations, and even about the very existence of the victims we view. Boltanski argues that this uncertainty increased over the past few decades along with an increase in the quantity and intensity of the spectacles of suffering shown.[34] Daniel Heller-Roazen attributes the modern experience of emptiness, isolation, feelinglessness and depersonalisation to the fading of the 'inner touch' – a sense which makes us aware that we are feeling and sensing. The pre-Cartesian idea of 'sentio ergo sum' and the common sense (by which we sense that we sense and feel) had been a frequent object of philosophical and medical enquiry since antiquity. Today, however, we increasingly live in a world of insensibility, claims Heller-Roazen, where 'unfeeling faces and bodies' 'fill our screens, our books, and our newspapers with ever greater force'. Contrary to the excesses of sensibility in the eighteenth century, some of the characteristic pathologies of our age are caused by feeling too little.[35]

Until fairly recently, literary criticism has reflected these processes by the marginalisation of literatures of feeling. Despite the popularity of the literature of sensibility in the eighteenth century, the study of sensibility is a relatively recent phenomenon; monographs with specific interest in sensibility and sentimentalism have appeared mainly since the 1970s, and sentimental novels gradually re-entered the literary canon in the last two decades or so. On the one hand, this renewed interest in sensibility can be seen as part of the recent revival of the study of feelings and emotions in a variety of fields, starting arguably in the sciences, and including, among others, the disciplines of literary criticism, philosophy, psychology, psychiatry and the neurosciences. In the field of literary studies, the professionalisation of literary criticism and the birth of modern literary theory in the twentieth century brought about an – at least intended – withdrawal of affective response from literary analysis and interpretation. With the growing production of literatures of sensibility in the latter half of the eighteenth century the reception of a work was to a great extent determined by the ability of the text (or its author) to move its readers; however, emotional response was largely exiled from academic practices of reading with the emergence of New Criticism and formalist-structuralist theories in the twentieth century.[36]

In the text-based approaches that dominated the scene of literary criticism roughly until the 1970s, affective response carried in itself the potential threat of subjectivism; as William K. Wimsatt and Monroe C. Beardsley put it, critical judgement based on feeling can result in an 'affective fallacy' or, in other words, 'a confusion between the poem and its results (what it *is* and what it *does*)'. Affective fallacy 'begins by trying to derive the standard of criticism from the psychological effects of the poem and ends in impressionism and relativism'. And the outcome of this process is that 'the poem itself, as an object of specifically critical judgment, tends to disappear'.[37] Wimsatt and Beardsley do not, of course, deny that emotion has a place in literature. This, however, cannot be found in the literary work's immediate effect on its reader. Unlike in the eighteenth century, emotions are 'not communicated to the reader like an infection or disease, not inflicted mechanically like a bullet or knife wound, not administered like poison, not simply expressed as by expletives or grimaces or rhythms, but presented in their objects and contemplated as a pattern of knowledge'. Through its tropes and images, literature functions as a tool by which cultural and period-specific emotional contents are carried on throughout the centuries. Poetry makes emotions perceptible even when its objects 'as simple facts of history' have 'lost emotive value with the loss of immediacy'.[38]

Emma Mason and Isobel Armstrong have recently voiced concerns about the erasure of emotional response from our academic practices of reading, arguing that dominant academic practices cut themselves off from direct affective engagement. As Mason and Armstrong emphasise, historical approaches facilitate detachment, and the experience of emotional response is thus excluded from serious academic discussion. In other words, feeling is understood in its historicity but not in its experience.[39] Reconciling the obvious tension between critical, historical detachment and the immediacy of emotional response is the challenge this study would like to take up. I would like not only to argue for the place of feeling in critical analysis and historical research but also to uphold the importance of history in the study of feeling. History provides a useful framework for understanding both the contextual particularity and the continuity of feeling, telling us why coming to terms with specific feelings that could be experienced in the eighteenth century can be meaningful and important for apprehending our present historical moment. Feeling is not, as Hegel would have it, 'an indefinite dull region of the spirit' or 'an empty form of subjective affectivity'. But nor is history something that merely offers 'empty cases in which the affairs of the world are packed'.[40]

Bearing in mind George Santayana's well-known claim that 'those who cannot remember the past are condemned to repeat it', one could argue that there are valuable lessons to be learnt from the specific case of the rise and fall of eighteenth-century sensibility, where a revolutionary ideology fuelled by a sentimental view of man showed its dangerous and even fatal side.[41] As Chapter 3 intends to show, an eighteenth-century reading technique based on emotional response could function as the means of drawing the reader into this very ideological framework, precisely through tearful scenes of reading. Our age similarly produces texts that compel us to absorb cultural practices and values by directly appealing to our tears or our feelings. Recent research in neuroscience, social psychology and moral philosophy raises new questions and offers new evidence regarding the operation and nature of sympathy, empathy, altruism and emotional response. These issues are especially urgent today when we are increasingly attentive to the powers and pathologies of emotional life and to the ways in which different forms of media, literature, and art affect and manipulate our feelings, and as we seek to understand human motives that result in individual and collective evildoing such as mass murder and genocide.[42]

The pressing question of whether it is possible to relate present-day ethical consciousness and political decision making to a humanitarian, enlightenment ideology that has more than once showed its dangerous face can only be addressed with an attention to both emotional response and its historicity. It is important to understand how the ambivalent values and feelings characteristic of eighteenth-century sensibility might still live on today and remain formative of our ethical, political and psychological outlook. As R.F. Brissenden avers, we are, in many ways, the inheritors of eighteenth-century sentimentalism – the era which produced important documents such as the 'Declaration of the Rights of Man and the Citizen' and the 'American Declaration of Independence' and forged the roots of modern secular humanism, of liberal democracy, and of radicalism.[43] I would like to argue that it is exactly because of its urgency that emotional response needs, so to say, special treatment, which involves not only an attentiveness to its immediacy but also an effort to understand it in its historicity. Therefore, the agenda of this book is to promote an investment in exploring continuity between distant contexts and the application of the knowledge gained thereby. Exploring eighteenth-century sensibility in its historical and theoretical relatedness to later forms of affective response is the method this book will follow.

IV

Sympathy, Sensibility and the Literature of Feeling in the Eighteenth Century aims to encourage its readers to think about the eighteenth century in terms of a framework that links up sensibility and sympathy with the history of psychiatry and psychoanalysis. As it connects eighteenth-century medical, philosophical and literary discourses with the ideas of Freud and his successors, it remains constantly aware of – and informed by – later developments in psychology and psychoanalysis that pertain to the history of emotional response. In this way, this book will set sensibility in the context of a broader history and theory of feeling than is usual in existing scholarship. Two ways of questioning operate in this study: whilst performing contextualised readings of individual texts, the book argues for the necessity of establishing relations between eighteenth-century and modern ways of understanding feelings and the human mind. This methodology is closely linked to the larger questions that my investigation of eighteenth-century sensibility could hardly avoid raising. When it comes to affectivity we will find that our enquiry will often point beyond the immediate boundaries of this specific historical period, and that a strictly contextual understanding is not always sufficient for explaining the workings of feelings and their ambivalence. I argue that the typical symptoms of sensibility such as fainting, crying and melancholia form part of a complex psychopathology that often reaches beyond the concerns of contemporary medicine. My book deals with affects, symptoms and conditions that cannot be understood merely from the 'nerves, spirits and fibres' of the eighteenth-century mind and body.[44] Whilst paying attention to an earlier historical period, the book points to previously unexplored connections between eighteenth-century sensibility and a variety of later developments. I read with an awareness of the theoretical and historical relation between forms of eighteenth-century knowledge of the human mind and later discourses of the psyche.

This study will envisage the age of sensibility as part of a long history of feeling, where connections and continuities can be found in the ways in which feelings have been experienced, expressed, conceptualised and studied from the eighteenth century to the present. The first chapter will start sketching a framework for this long history by outlining conceptual continuities. I will examine how interpersonal affective exchanges were formulated around the concept of sympathy in the eighteenth century by philosophical, physiological, political and literary discourses, and will explore how such intersubjective affective experiences were reformulated in various disciplines from the nineteenth century to the present. Continuities will be traced through concepts such as empathy, identification and transference, leading our inquiry through the theories and practices of various fields, including psychoanalysis, psychology and philosophy.

Interestingly, however, the experience and the study of feeling often go hand in hand in this long history. Modern sciences of the psyche (including psychoanalysis, psychology, philosophy and the neurosciences) have developed ways of systematically investigating what feelings and emotions are, how and where they are produced and how they operate – just like scientific psychologies did in the mid- to late eighteenth century. But this book also deals with the controversial place of feeling in the study of feeling, in other words, whether and to what extent it is possible to experience or to put aside one's own affective reactions during a scientific study of feeling (as seen, for instance, in Freud's essays on psychoanalytic technique, in the psychoanalytic literature on counter-transference, and in Albrecht von Haller's eighteenth-century study of sensibility, where the language of sentiment manifests itself despite Haller's attempts at professional detachment). Feeling frequently infiltrates discourses designed for the study of feeling, whilst literatures of sensibility often involuntarily perform a study of feeling in their turn. William Godwin's letters and diary entries written around the time of Mary Wollstonecraft's death and Julia Kristeva's psychoanalytic work, *Black Sun*, are at the same time both discourses *on* and *of* melancholia. They set out to work through a loss or to understand the feelings of mourning and melancholia, whilst simultaneously producing the language of mourning and melancholia in their turn.

Thus, eighteenth-century discourses of sensibility (whether philosophical, scientific, literary or political) are all productive of various languages of feeling, which will be explored through rhetorical analysis. But such discourses often reflect critically on their own involvement in the culture of sensibility itself, thereby performing the study of feeling (as we will see, for instance, in Henry Mackenzie's and Mary Wollstonecraft's works). My analysis will also extend to various affectively charged eighteenth-century practices and their literary representation, including reading, bodily reactions, scientific experimentation and the act of mourning. In this respect, my understanding of psychoanalysis, alongside other modern sciences of the psyche, is similar. I do not aim to treat psychoanalysis as a methodology for approaching distant texts and early affective phenomena. Rather, I understand psychoanalysis as a clinical practice which produces feeling, and which is centred around interpersonal relationships that are often charged with forms of affectivity, including empathy. At the same time, the literature of psychoanalysis – like the eighteenth-century literature of sensibility – is a rhetorical construct subject to critical analysis and interpretation.

The links between eighteenth-century psychologies and philosophies of feeling and modern discourses of the psyche will often inform the textual analyses given here. At the beginning of the twentieth century psychoanalysis developed a language and a methodology specifically aimed at understanding emotions and their ambivalence. This understanding can, to some extent, shed some light on the problematic structure of feelings throughout their long history. But I must emphasise that it is certainly not my aim here to treat psychoanalysis as a storehouse of knowledge that would – anachronistically – explain eighteenth-century phenomena.[45] My aim is to argue the relevance – whilst bearing in mind the historic specificity – of chronologically distant discourses, which are distinct, yet interconnected, segments of a long history of emotional response. I approach eighteenth-century texts with the assumption that discourses in which sensibility is produced gave an early language to emotions, unconscious contents and repressed forces long before Freud developed his terminology. The eighteenth century produced the first modern discourses of the psyche. Literatures of sensibility and of psychoanalysis ask a number of similar questions regarding feeling, mind and human behaviour, and about the possibility of expressing feeling through language. They share an interest in a physical symptom-language that hides and reveals emotional states and aberrations. Beside their common concern with pathology, discourses of sensibility and psychoanalysis develop ways of apprehending other people, which process is heavily determined by other-regarding feelings. This study will also draw attention to the healing role of sympathy (and the place of language in this process) in eighteenth-century discourses of sensibility, which role has not yet been explored in literary criticism.

But there are a number of differences between the emotional practices characteristic of eighteenth-century sensibility and those developed by psychoanalysis. Psychoanalysis advocates a technique of abreacting repressed emotions and channelling repressed material into conscious, verbal presentation. Emotional practices of sensibility, on the other hand, drive emotions into the very institutions which assist in their repression, while often using social conventions subversively for the communication of transgressive and socially unacceptable feelings. While sentimentalism is a form of emotional navigation, as Reddy would argue, the practice of psychoanalysis makes us aware of the systems of emotional navigation (psychoanalysts would call these defence mechanisms) we have developed. For instance, my scrutiny of the typical sign language of sensibility (tears, sighs, fainting, palpitations, distraction bordering on madness and female indisposition) is thus similar to Freud's method of uncovering the underlying reminiscences, discontents, traumas and suffering that produce the symptoms of neurosis, formed under the duress of contemporary social prohibitions. But literary texts often challenge eighteenth-century medical knowledge, and sometimes they even point beyond the explanations psychoanalysis had to offer more than a century later. Thus, invoking psychoanalysis in the eighteenth-century context of sensibility will also function as a productive counterpoint; the discrepancies between the two periods' conceptualisation of emotion, expression and interpreting otherness highlight historical specificity, while providing a perspective for understanding both sensibility and psychoanalysis in the larger context of the history and theory of feeling and interpretation.[46] Eighteenth-century discourses of other-regarding sentiment and psychoanalysis aim to develop adequate ways of interpreting what is essentially and irretrievably other. The fact that such readings are unavoidably coloured by emotions and driven by processes of identification is both the crux of the ambivalence underlying sensibility and a major concern of psychoanalysis when it deals with issues such as transference or intersubjectivity.

Sympathy, Sensibility and the Literature of Feeling in the Eighteenth Century consists of two parts: the first deals with eighteenth-century philosophies and physiologies of feeling; the second discusses the literature of sensibility in the light of the questions raised in the first part of the book. The chapters examine forms of affective response typical in discourses of sensibility such as sympathy, irritability, crying, fainting and melancholy. In addition to providing histories of concepts and ideas such as sympathy and irritability, the chapters also offer symptomatic case studies, tracing the ambivalence of emotional response in different aspects of life and culture, including the act of writing and reading, literature, philosophy and medical experimentation.

Chapter 1, 'Philosophies of Sympathy', deals with the two-sided, uncanny nature of sympathy, a central concept of sentimental morality. It explores how enlightenment concepts of sympathy evolved in a way that made it possible for diverse and often-contradictory critiques to be voiced against sensibility in the eighteenth century. The chapter carries out an investigation of concepts of sympathy in their transformations throughout the period. My contention is that the ambivalence of other-regarding sentiment is related to the coexistence of disparate notions of sympathy and their problematic conceptualisation. The chapter will investigate those moments where carefully constructed theories of sympathy testify to the failure of the operation of this feeling. I show how lack of sympathy is inscribed in the very construction of sympathy and how such instances of dysfunction are linked to larger concerns about defining human subjectivity and consciousness.

I will begin by following through the emergence of sympathy into a core concept of eighteenth-century moral philosophy in the context of the period's debate on human nature. The first section will pay particular attention to the ways in which mainstream eighteenth-century moral theorists, including Shaftesbury, Hutcheson and Hume, accounted for the dysfunctions of other-regarding sentiment. Here I will bring into my discussion magnetic and mechanistic notions of sympathy, whose history reaches back to earlier, seventeenth-century explanations of attraction. The surfacing of magnetic and mechanistic notions of sentiment in the period, I will argue, conveyed anxieties related to the disruptive – and politically threatening – force of excessive feeling. Passions in the crowd were communicated through the mechanisms of sympathy, resulting in panic, enthusiasm and violence, but the same force of sympathy was imagined by enlightenment thinkers to be a powerful means of social cohesion and a moral force that constituted the foundation of self and society. The mechanism of sentiment will be further explored in the analysis of Henry Mackenzie's 'The Story of La Roche' (1779), where Mackenzie envisions a form of religious sentiment whose potentially disruptive force is channelled into a bonding and healing capacity. The section on Adam Smith's theory outlined in *The Theory of Moral Sentiments* (1759) will explore the solipsism of sympathy based on imaginary processes of identification. Here the recognition of the other as other becomes the very point where sympathy, as a form of identification, breaks down. Paradoxically, however, the healing force of sympathy is grounded exactly in this solipsistic structure. The final section of this chapter argues for a long, and in many ways continuous, history of sympathy. It will explore the legacies of sympathy in therapeutic methods and practices from the late eighteenth century to the present, tracing the conceptualisation of interpersonal affective relations from mesmerism to psychology, psychoanalysis, philosophy and the neurosciences. This section will seek continuities between enlightenment notions – and dysfunctions – of sympathy and later concepts, including empathy, transference and identification.

Chapter 2, 'The Feeling Machine', explores how sensibility and its definition can become inseparable from violence and cruelty. The chapter will also reflect on how cruelty can be motivated by the same impulse as sympathy: the desire to understand the feelings of the other. I shall begin by exploring the political use of eighteenth-century physiological theories through a reading of Daniel Isaac Eton's 'King Chaunticlere; or, the Fate of Tyranny', a story that was published in Eaton's *Politics for the People; or, Hog's Wash* (1793). The politics of the body's reactivity will be further discussed through the debates surrounding the guillotine, showing the uncanny fusion of the humanitarian ideology of sensibility and the violence of the Terror. While Chapter 1 looks at the ethical aspects of feelingful response, this chapter explores physical reactivity in eighteenth-century medical writings on mind, body and soul. The chapter focuses specifically on three seminal participants of a large-scale eighteenth-century debate on the human subject. It offers readings of Julien Offray de La Mettrie's *L'Homme machine* (1747), Albrecht von Haller's *A Dissertation on the Sensible and Irritable Parts of Animals* (1752) and Robert Whytt's *Physiological Essays* (1755), with particular attention given to the ways in which sympathy, affectivity and their lack surface in their discourse. The chapter will also reflect on how the lack of sympathetic emotional response emerges in medical experimentation as a component of scientific neutrality and empirical professionalism.

In the philosophy of Hume and Smith sympathy is the basis of human moral behaviour; however, the work of the materialist La Mettrie seems to suggest that it is exactly the moment when sympathy breaks down that distinguishes humans from the rest of the animal world. I will look at the production of sensibility as an aesthetic discourse in the work of the Swiss anatomist Albrecht von Haller and the Edinburgh physiologist Robert Whytt. The analysis will focus on the body as it is made into a site of signification and a readable construct that, though it eludes language, is forced back into language, often by violence and cruelty. Albrecht von Haller comes to a definition of the sensibility and irritability of the body through a series of experiments that consist in dissecting live animals. He defines sensibility as a capacity for feeling pain, and he therefore makes sensibility visible through the animal's 'evident signs of suffering'. His method of definition, based on the foreclosure of sympathetic response, creates a traumatic text that is structured by symptomatic fissures. Despite its erasure in the process of experimentation, however, affect re-emerges in the tropes of the medical text. The final section, based on my reading of a collection of familiar letters from the time of the Seven Years' War, aims to show how a space is opened up by the victim's point of view for the reader's emotional response, drawing attention to the ethical imperative carried by the tropes of sensibility.

Chapter 3, '"I Will Not Weep": Tears of Sympathy in Henry Mackenzie's *The Man of Feeling*', builds on the controversial notion of sympathy discussed in the first two chapters and deals with tears, the main sentimental signifiers of authentic emotional response. Tears, while they could indeed be signs of truthful emotional reaction, were, at the same time, a means by which a culture established its ideologies through the affective responses of the individual. In this chapter I will trace the way in which Mackenzie's 1771 novel, *The Man of Feeling*, self-consciously enacts the reader's education via the culture of tears. *The Man of Feeling* is said to be the most tearful novel of the eighteenth century, yet, I argue, its affectivity should not be taken for granted. Harley, always identified as the overly sentimental hero of the novel, is sometimes surprisingly tearless at potentially moving moments of his story. His sentimentality is created in front of our eyes by those who read and narrate him, drawing the reader of the novel into a similar, mimetic mode of interpretation. The mind of Harley is constructed like a mirror – alluding to the philosophical constructions of the feeling subject as imagined by David Hume and Adam Smith – which reveals more about those who read him than about Harley himself. Harley's mind not only reflects, but also improves the complexions of those who look into it. In this way, he is never the subject in question, but instead brings about a shift of focus, turning both narrator and reader into men of feeling. I will argue that the 'man of feeling' consists in an always shifting perspective; it is an emotional lens, a technique of reading rather than a pre-existent character-type. The tears of the man of feeling always mark ambivalent moments of sympathy. Through evoking the context of Oliver Goldsmith's *The Vicar of Wakefield* (1766), Laurence Sterne's *Sentimental Journey* (1768) and Sarah Fielding's *The Adventures of David Simple* (1744), the chapter argues that the sympathetic responses of the man of feeling, while giving opportunity for otherness to manifest itself, also help to maintain social hierarchy and existing power structures, thus questioning the possibility of intersubjective encounter.

Chapter 4, 'Women and the Negative: The Sentimental Swoon in Eighteenth-Century Fiction', explores the apparent bodily signs of irritability and sensibility in the context of sentimental fiction. I read typical signs of female sentimental emotional response in novels, including Sarah Fielding's *The History of Ophelia* (1760), Jean-Jacques Rousseau's *Julie, or the New Heloise* (1761), and Elizabeth Inchbald's *A Simple Story* (1791). The female sentimental repertoire of psychosomatic fainting, silences, sighs, palpitations and states of mental distraction is frequently taken for granted, but rarely thoroughly explored by scholarship dealing with the culture of sensibility. In this chapter, I read these typically feminine manifestations of sensibility in terms of the discontents of eighteenth-century female psychosexual existence and self-expression. As I will argue, these often pathological manifestations – sometimes called the vocabulary of sensibility – figure limitations on the possibilities of feminine utterance. These psychosomatic symptoms are rooted in a complex network of affective, social and sexual factors. The chapter mainly, but not exclusively, focuses on the loss of consciousness, speech and sensation – perhaps the least understood and most neglected, but often just as telling symptoms of sensibility. They strike at moments of emotional and sexual importance; they simultaneously empower and disempower, endow with and deprive of the wished-for experience; they let the female speak and silence her at the same time. Many eighteenth-century novels use this repertoire to reflect covertly on the pathology of social repression by exposing sensibility itself, in the form of the 'woman of feeling' as its symptom. I will analyse literary depiction of the female psyche in moments of excitement and usually of sexual intensity, and I will approach psychologically induced states of consciousness and unconsciousness by means of a theoretical framework that connects eighteenth-century medical explanations with psychoanalytic ideas of negativity.

Chapter 5, 'Godwin's Case: Melancholy Mourning in the Empire of Feeling', deals with the famous eighteenth-century literary case of William Godwin's mourning for his dead wife, Mary Wollstonecraft. This chapter explores how sensibility is produced through an inherently ambivalent process: the vicissitudes of identification burdened with the survivor's simultaneous love and hatred. The publication of Godwin's *Memoirs of the Author of a Vindication of the Rights of Woman* in 1798 had an adverse effect on Mary Wollstonecraft's reputation. Despite Godwin's respect and good intentions, the book – with its honest account of his wife's sexual affairs, suicide attempts, and unorthodox religious ideas – scandalised contemporaries, and was an inevitable blow to the feminist views associated with Wollstonecraft's life and work. Even friends like Southey were disappointed and accused Godwin of a 'want of feeling in stripping his dead wife naked'. Roscoe condemned him for mourning her 'with a heart of stone'. While in our time successful critical attempts have significantly restored Wollstonecraft's significance and incorporated her works into the study of literary and cultural history, Godwin's mourning has not yet been fully understood. What does it mean to mourn 'with a heart of stone' a person one deeply loved? How is it possible to demonstrate a paradoxical 'want of feeling' under the influence of the most powerful emotions? Through tracing the immediate affective response to Wollstonecraft's death in Godwin's literary activity, this chapter argues that the growth of affectivity as seen in Godwin's *Memoirs* and unpublished letters, papers and diary is the result of a complex and emotionally ambivalent psychological process, 'melancholy mourning'. The controversial image of Wollstonecraft presented in the *Memoirs* is a further product of Godwin's language of melancholia. Godwin's case reaches beyond the boundaries of the eighteenth-century understanding of melancholia, raising questions that point towards the ideas of Freud and his successors. His mourning – as registered in his writings – offers an alternative case study, which in many respects differs from, and poses new questions to, existing psychoanalytic views.

In the course of this book I hope to have explored the ways in which sensibility is produced as an inherently two-sided discourse that allows for an ambivalent morality to emerge in the eighteenth century. This morality often depends on processes of reading and interpretation and it poses difficulties for the eighteenth-century subject in the encounter with otherness, when this encounter is already self-centred. The ethics of sensibility always remains interconnected with the ethics of reading – a process burdened with powerful and potentially conflicting feelings. The emotions invested in reading hide complex processes of identification, disturbing the boundaries of subjectivity and transforming self and other. Hearing the voice and the plea of the other, providing adequate means for self-expression, and recognising otherness beyond reading, feeling and identification are the common challenge faced by both the ethics of sensibility and the ethics of psychoanalysis. Apart from psychoanalysis, however, our investigation will also extend to more recent discourses of the psyche in today's philosophy, psychology and the neurosciences, where the still unanswered mysteries of human consciousness are further pursued. I hope that *Sympathy, Sensibility and the Literature of Feeling in the Eighteenth Century* will encourage future enquiries into the ways in which we are revisiting the ethics of sensibility in our present ways of feeling, interpreting and relating to others – making sensibility and its ideology matter for us today in – and beyond – its historic specificity.

Part I
Philosophies and Physiologies of Feeling

Part I
Philosophies and Psychologies
of Teaching

1
Philosophies of Sympathy

Scholars have often emphasised the involvement of the discourses of sensibility and sentimental philanthropy with the realm of the political. As Markman Ellis argues, the sentimental novel was a means of moulding the emotions of the reader, as well as addressing urgent political issues of the time, such as social injustice and slavery. The sentimental novel's articulation of such concerns was an attempt to reformulate social attitudes to inequality through the cultivation of humanitarianism and sensibility.[1] According to R.F. Brissenden, the French Revolution put into practice the humanitarian ideals grounded in the belief that man's capacity to act morally is related to his physical and psychological responsiveness to the impulses around him, that is, his sensibility. A belief existed that if individuals could freely exercise their natural sensibilities, they would act in a philanthropic spirit. Such ideas, as Brissenden writes, could serve as the basis for the launch of the Revolution, a general plea for human rights, the movements for the elimination of torture, and the abolition of slavery.[2] However, such a belief in the ideology of sentimental philanthropy was shaken by the end of the century. This attitude is well illustrated by the attacks of the *Anti-Jacobin*, a Tory satirical review of the 1790s. George Canning, one of its authors, writes critically of the Goddess of Sensibility:

> Mark her fair Votaries — Prodigal of Grief,
> With cureless pangs, and woes that mock relief,
> Droop in soft sorrow o'er a faded flow'r;
> O'er a dead Jack-Ass pour the pearly show'r; —
> But hear unmov'd of *Loire's* ensanguin'd flood,
> Chok'd up with slain; — of *Lyons* drench'd in blood;
> Of crimes that blot the Age, the World with shame,
> Foul crimes, but sicklied o'er with Freedom's name [. . .][3]

Canning's untitled poem is published in the same issue of the *Anti-Jacobin* as Gillray's famous caricature, 'The New Morality', which depicts the Goddess of Sensibility crying over a dead bird with a volume of Rousseau in her hand, while resting one foot on the decapitated head of Louis XVI.[4]

The multilayered flip side of human altruism was continuously critiqued and dissected throughout the eighteenth century, and the scepticism regarding the cult of sensibility was frequently targeted at its core values: benevolence, sympathy, pity, and similar forms of other-regarding sentiment. On the one hand, many accused philanthropic impulses of operating selectively, according to the dictates of one's interests.[5] In Marivaux's novel *The Fortunate Peasant* (1735), for instance, the humanitarian acts of the ambitious protagonist, Jacob, are motivated by self-interest. He demonstrates sympathy in the presence of women who can help his career but heartlessly abandons Genevieve, the poor servant girl who would hinder his social advancement.[6] The selective operation of sympathy became an urgent political issue after the French Revolution. The conservative attacks by Canning and Gillray imply that the values of sentimentalism allowed one to shed tears over the trivial whilst neglecting the larger, social tragedy brought about by the ideology of sensibility. Interestingly however, while the lack of sympathy was perceived as morally problematic, the excess of disinterested feeling was also seen as threatening to the integrity of self and society. Throughout the eighteenth century, a number of literary writers (including Sarah Fielding, Henry Mackenzie, Oliver Goldsmith and Mary Wollstonecraft) voiced concerns about the consequences of other-regarding feelings operating impulsively and irrespective of who their object really is. Excessive sympathy, they thought, could bring poverty and destruction to the man and woman of feeling. The study of sensibility in the field of medical science also reveals the ambivalent relationship between sensibility and moral feeling. Albrecht von Haller, the Swiss physiologist, defined the sensibility of the body in 1752 by dissecting and tormenting live animals, while claiming to feel for them the strongest compassion. Many puzzling instances of fellow-feeling in the period testify that the ethical foundations of sensibility were based on concepts and theories that were curiously Janus-faced. In the discourse of the benevolent, philanthropist ideology that sensibility builds upon, what makes it possible for such problems and dilemmas to emerge?

This chapter will explore how enlightenment concepts of sympathy evolved in a way that made it possible for such diverse and often-contradictory critiques to be voiced in the eighteenth century. The chapter deals with the two-sided, uncanny nature of sympathy by carrying out an investigation of concepts of sympathy in their creation and transformations in the period. My contention is that the ambivalence of other-regarding sentiment is related to the coexistence of disparate yet interconnected notions of sympathy in the eighteenth century, some mechanistic and some based on imaginary processes of identification. The origins of the distinction between an impulsive (and potentially excessive) versus a selective (and potentially self-interested) operation of sympathy, on which many eighteenth-century attacks on sensibility are based, can be traced back to the interconnections and the development of these concepts. The frequent dissatisfaction with sentimental morality is thus interrelated with the problematic conceptualisations of affect in the period.

The term sympathy was used widely in the literature of science, medicine and philosophy, and, in fact, surfaces in all areas of eighteenth-century life, including market reports, music, and even contemporary calculations of longitude. It denoted various instances of agreement, concord, harmony, consonance and correspondence. Apart from denoting an affinity between things by virtue of which they were similarly affected by the same influence, it also signified a harmony and correspondence of feelings, and a capacity for sharing or entering into the emotional states of others. In the medical and philosophical literature, it referred to various intra- and intersubjective processes of correspondence and harmony. Sympathy was responsible for the communication between bodily organs and distant body parts. It also provided a possible answer to the question of how bodily feelings were turned into ideas, or how thought and emotion were physically channelled into bodily expression or motion. This chapter will begin by following through the emergence of sympathy into a core concept of eighteenth-century moral philosophy, paying particular attention to the ways in which mainstream eighteenth-century moral theories accounted for the dysfunctions of other-regarding sentiment. For the majority of scholarship that deals with the moral philosophy of the Scottish Enlightenment, the dominant understanding of sympathy is a binding force or an emotional chain that brings communities together. Here I will bring into my discussion a frequently overlooked, magnetic-mechanistic notion of sympathy, whose history reaches back to earlier, seventeenth-century explanations of attraction, and explore its interrelationships with subsequent notions of moral sentiment as well as its importance for understanding the ambivalence of sensibility. The surfacing of magnetic and mechanistic notions of sentiment in the period, I will argue, conveyed anxieties related to the disruptive – and politically threatening – force of excessive feeling which would spread from person to person, like an infection. Passions in the crowd were communicated through the mechanisms of sympathy, resulting in panic, enthusiasm or violence, but the same force of sympathy was imagined by enlightenment thinkers to be a powerful means of social cohesion and a moral force that constituted the foundation of self and society.

The mechanism of sentiment that can both forge and disrupt the sympathetic bond will be further explored through Henry Mackenzie's 'The Story of La Roche', a narrative that voices the problem of excess by playing off against each other diverse, yet interconnected notions of sympathy. Here Mackenzie envisions a kind of religious sentiment that partially relies on mechanistic notions of affectivity, yet whose potentially disruptive force is channelled into a productive, healing capacity. The ambivalence underlying the notion of sympathetic identification will be addressed through the analysis of Adam Smith's *The Theory of Moral Sentiments*. This section will investigate how a concept of sympathy based on imaginary identification can remain fundamentally solipsistic and become the very source of the social differences it is meant to alleviate. For Smith, sympathy is part of an economy of pleasure, and a key – but unresolved – dilemma posed by the *Theory* concerns the reason why sympathy with unpleasurable situations is possible in the first instance. Looking beyond the spectatorial, theatrical structure of sympathy centralised by Smith scholarship, I will argue that the healing role of narrativity and storytelling inscribed into sympathy's construction is crucial for understanding its operation within an economy of pleasure. The final section of this chapter will explore the legacies of sympathy in therapeutic techniques and practices from the late eighteenth century to the present, tracing the conceptualisation of interpersonal affective relations from mesmerism to psychology, psychoanalysis, philosophy and the neurosciences. This section will seek continuities between enlightenment notions of sympathy and later concepts, including empathy, transference, and identification.

Sympathy and the debate on human nature

Sympathy became an important concept of eighteenth-century sensibility through the widespread influence of the moral sense school of philosophy in diverse cultural fields in the period. These thinkers, including the Third Earl of Shaftesbury, Francis Hutcheson, David Hume and Adam Smith, responded critically to the pessimistic views of human nature that were rife both in secular thought and in dogmatic

Calvinist doctrine in the seventeenth century, and their responses led to a debate that continued throughout the eighteenth century. One of the reasons for sympathy's ambivalence is that sympathy was repeatedly conceptualised and defined in eighteenth-century moral philosophy within the context of this debate.

Notions of other-regarding sentiment in the early eighteenth century were born in opposition to the materialist Thomas Hobbes's influential – and at its time, inflammatory – epicurean account of human nature. In his *Leviathan* (1651) Hobbes claims that human nature is ultimately self-interested, forever driven by appetites and desires. The centre of Hobbes's moral theory is a mechanically defined man, whose heart is 'but a Spring; and the Nerves, but so many Strings; and the Joynts, but so many Wheeles, giving motion to the whole Body, such as was intended by the Artificer'.[7] This mechanical man, however, is a dynamic machine, whose every activity and feeling is constituted by motion. Motion can be detected even in seemingly immobile activities like sensing and imagining, and it is the foundation of those desires and aversions which form the basis of human nature. And in turn, all further passions and emotions, including other-regarding sentiments like benevolence and pity, result from such, mechanically imagined, desires and aversions (*Leviathan* 119–26). For Hobbes, the state of desiring is continuous and never-ending, 'For as to have no desire is to be dead' (*Leviathan* 139). But human happiness does not simply consist in the satisfaction of desires and appetites. Felicity means a continuous shift of desire from one object to another, in order to secure a contented life. The reason for this is that man 'cannot assure the power and means to live well, which he hath at present, without the acquisition of more', which results in 'Contention, Enmity, and War: Because the way of one Competitor, to the attaining of his desire, is to kill, subdue, supplant, or repell the other' (*Leviathan* 161). Thus, Hobbes's mechanical man, because he is forever driven by his desires, is a competitive being naturally in a state of war and rivalry.[8]

In the eighteenth century, the Hobbesian view regarding human nature came to a renewal in the philosophy of Bernard Mandeville. Like Hobbes, Mandeville argued that man is naturally selfish and unsociable, and even other-regarding feelings like pity and compassion can be explained from the self-interest inherent in human nature.[9] Moreover, in *The Fable of the Bees* (1724) – a treatise whose central idea was conceived in 1705 – Mandeville also claimed that self-interest and private vice could actually contribute to the wealth of society. As far as other-regarding feelings are concerned, he contended that compassionate and charitable acts are motivated by the desire to avoid the pain caused by the suffering of another person. For instance, it is our interest, he claimed, to save an infant ready to drop into the fire: 'The Action is neither good nor bad, and what Benefit soever the Infant received, we only obliged our selves; for to have seen it fall, and not strove to hinder it, would have caused a Pain which Self-preservation compell'd us to prevent [...].'[10] Mandeville argued that individual acts of crime, greed, pride, luxury and other vices and self-interested actions have certain economic advantages. By fostering commerce and involuntarily supporting the growth of professions, self-interest contributes to the benefit of society.

During the seventeenth and eighteenth centuries the moral theory of Hobbes and his followers, together with other religious and secular views where human nature was disparaged, received ongoing criticism from a number of thinkers. The Cambridge Platonists and the Latitudinarian divines upheld the view that other-regarding feelings were inherent in human nature, emphasising the importance of benevolent, social passions.[11] These ideas found expression in the works of Anthony Ashley Cooper, the third earl of Shaftesbury, who, in his *Characteristics of Men, Manners, Opinions, Times* (1711), set out to challenge the view that interest governs the world. Shaftesbury claimed that a natural sense of right and wrong, a 'natural esteem of virtue and detestation of villainy' is 'a first principle in our constitution and make'.[12] According to Shaftesbury, we have 'natural affections' that promote the good of the public. These powerful, generous affections for our fellow creatures are pleasurable, and their lack is a definite source of misery. Thus, since our natural affections make us sociable, we receive most of our pleasures from others by communication, reflection or participation in the good of others. For Shaftesbury, sympathy is a crucial aid to practising – and enjoying – our social affections; it is the mechanism through which such social pleasures reach us. We sympathetically receive the feelings of others through various channels, 'from accounts and relations of such happinesses, from the very countenances, gestures, voices and sounds, even of creatures foreign to our kind, whose signs of joy and contentment we can anyway discern' (*Characteristics* 204).

While Shaftesbury advocated natural sociability and claimed that we have an inbuilt sense to distinguish virtue from vice, the concept of the 'moral sense' itself comes from the Scottish philosopher Francis Hutcheson, one of the most important disseminators of Shaftesbury's ideas.[13] Hutcheson calls moral sense the ability to approve of and be pleased with whatever is virtuous, that is, those actions and affections that promote the public good. In *An Inquiry into the Original of Our Ideas of Beauty and Virtue* (1725) Hutcheson argues that the 'true springs' of virtuous actions cannot lie in self-interest, self-love or the pleasure one may gain from acting kindly. If this were the case we would only practice those virtues that are pleasant to us and, consequently, would stay away from people who suffer in order to avoid the pain of compassion. Instead, 'we croud about such objects, and voluntarily run into pain, unless reason, and reflection upon our inability to relieve the miserable, countermand our inclination, or some selfish affection, as fear or danger, over ballances it'.[14] Hutcheson concludes that such disinterested acts can only be explained by innate benevolence, which is the universal foundation of moral sense. Human nature is ultimately benevolent and is 'scarce capable of malicious, disinterested hatred' (*Beauty and Virtue* 132). Sympathy is also a 'sense' in Hutcheson's philosophy. In addition to the moral sense, Hutcheson claims that we possess several other senses, and one of them is the public sense, also called 'sensus communis' or 'sympathy'. As he describes it in *An Essay on the Nature and Conduct of the Passions and Affections* (1728), the public sense is 'our Determination to be pleased with the happiness of others, and to be uneasy at their misery'.[15] This public sense is 'a most natural instinct', and 'not the effect of any confused ideas' (*Passions* 21). The operation of the public sense is not motivated by self-love or self-interest but by a disinterested desire for the happiness of others.

In the philosophy of David Hume, sympathy becomes the foundation of the moral sense. According to Hume, our disinterested appreciation of benevolence can be explained from an inbuilt and unquestionable sympathy. Sympathy, as Hume puts it in his *Enquiry Concerning the Principles of Morals* (1751), is 'a principle in human nature', or a point where 'it is needless to push our researches so far as to ask, why we have humanity or fellow-feeling with others'.[16] This inbuilt capacity for fellow-feeling enables us to appreciate the humanity and benevolence of others and to distinguish between moral and immoral actions. According to Hume, even the most selfish person has other-regarding sentiments. We are always inclined, from our natural philanthropy, to wish for the happiness and well-being of others. Hume agrees with Shaftesbury and Hutcheson that 'absolute, unprovoked, disinterested malice has never perhaps place in any human breast' (*Enquiry* 227). Sympathy is the final principle beyond which Hume's enquiry does not propose to go. 'There are', he writes, 'in every science, some general principles, beyond which we cannot hope to find any principle more general. No man is absolutely indifferent to the happiness and misery of others. The first has a natural tendency to give pleasure; the second, pain. This every one may find in himself' (*Enquiry* 220). This sympathy or fellow-feeling enables us to join in the happiness and sorrow of others, to feel compassion for those in deep distress, and even to find interest in a piece of news. It also makes it possible for us to enjoy what we would now call intellectual and aesthetic pleasures, which, according to Hume, are based on sympathetic emotional response. 'Every moment of the theatre', writes Hume, 'by a skilful poet, is communicated, as it were by magic, to the spectators, who weep, tremble, resent, rejoice, and are inflamed with all the variety of passions, which actuate the several personages of the drama.' Similarly, 'the perusal of history seems a calm entertainment; but would be no entertainment at all, did not our hearts beat with correspondent movements to those which are described by the historian' (*Enquiry* 222–3).

However, even in the works of those who depict humankind as intrinsically driven by kindly, social passions, other-regarding sentiments have their limits. None of the moral sense philosophers of the early eighteenth century deny the existence of self-love and self-interest in human nature, and for Shaftesbury, Hutcheson and Hume, their presence may even be beneficial for society at large. In addition to altruistic feelings, Shaftesbury points out the dominance of the self-affections in human nature. These self-affections, however, are not always in conflict with other-regarding affections, and their presence in the individual can even be beneficial for and their lack detrimental to the public good. 'A creature really wanting them', argues Shaftesbury, 'is in reality wanting in some degree of goodness and natural rectitude and may thus be esteemed vicious and defective' (*Characteristics* 196–7). In Hutcheson's view, self-love and benevolence 'may jointly excite a man to the same action' (*Beauty and Virtue* 29–30), while Hume emphasises that the great power of self-love has an important function for the operation of society. As Hume writes in the *Enquiry*, 'Self-love is a principle in human nature of such extensive energy, and the interest of each individual is, in general, so closely connected with that of the community, that those philosophers were excusable, who fancied that all our concern for the public might be resolved into a concern for our own happiness and preservation' (*Enquiry* 218). Ultimately, however, no matter how selfish a person is, 'he must unavoidably feel some propensity to the good of mankind' (*Enquiry* 226). While human nature is not altogether good and benevolent, there is always 'some particle of the dove kneaded into our frame, along with the elements of the wolf and serpent' (*Enquiry* 271).[17]

On the other hand, self-interest can limit the power and range of our other-regarding sentiments. While benevolence is a universal characteristic of human nature, Hutcheson does not deny that the degree of our benevolence can vary. As he writes in the *Inquiry*,

We have already endeavour'd to prove, 'That there is a universal determination to benevolence in mankind, even toward the most distant parts of the species': But we are not to imagine that this benevolence is equal, or in the same degree toward all; there are some nearer and stronger degrees of benevolence, when the objects stand in some nearer relations to our selves, which have obtain'd distinct names, such as natural affection and gratitude; or when benevolence is increas'd by greater love or esteem [...]. (*Beauty and Virtue* 195)

Here the weaknesses and limits in the construction of universal benevolence are signalled by the metaphor of Newtonian gravity, revealing the mechanical – and often-imperfect – operation of the moral sense: 'This universal benevolence toward all men, we may compare to that principle of gravitation, which perhaps extends to all bodies in the universe; but, like the love of benevolence, increases as the distance is diminish'd, and is strongest when the bodies come to touch each other' (*Beauty and Virtue* 198). Similarly for Hume, while sympathy is instant and 'unavoidable', it can never be perfect and it still has to operate within certain boundaries. We enter into sentiments more easily that resemble those we feel every day (*Enquiry* 222). And there are also inequalities in our affections, depending on whether the object is physically and emotionally closer to or more distant from us. While in Hutcheson benevolence varies in strength according to the dictates of gravity, Hume's sympathy follows the rules of perspective. In the same way as we perceive an object larger when it is close to us, our sympathy is more intense when it relates to a closer object: 'A statesman or a patriot, who serves our own country in our own time, has always a more passionate regard paid to him, than one whose beneficial influence operated on distant ages or remote nations.' Moreover, Hume admits that our own self and our own interests are always our number one priorities. The farther away we get from ourselves the weaker our emotion becomes. Sympathy 'is much fainter than our concern for ourselves, and sympathy with persons remote from us much fainter than that with persons near and contiguous' (*Enquiry* 229). The metaphors of gravitation and vision signal the imperfections that are built into the construction of other-regarding feeling due to the prevalence of self-interest in human nature; and when sympathy acts mechanically it can also fail to operate. Inbuilt moral feeling has its limits, and in cases like this, as Hume claims, the power of our judgement is necessary to correct the inequalities of our sympathy.

The impulsive nature of sympathy, as imagined by Hutcheson and Hume, carries another potential concern with regard to eighteenth-century forms of fellow-feeling: the possibility of excessive sentiment and the consequent threat to individual identity and social cohesion. The writings of the Scottish moralist Henry Mackenzie reflect critically on the possible problems inherent in previous philosophical accounts, suggesting that sympathy, when impulsive, can be all-inclusive and be used to manipulate the benevolent – but gullible – philanthropist. When Harley, the protagonist of *The Man of Feeling* (1771), meets a beggar on his way to London, he finds him an undeserving object of charity, because the beggar's art of fortune-telling admittedly implies making up the stories people want to hear about their future. Somewhat reluctantly though, Harley still drops a coin, performing the act of charity against his own sound judgement:

> Harley had drawn a shilling from his pocket; but virtue bade him consider on whom he was going to bestow it. – Virtue held back his arm: – but a milder form, a younger sister of virtue's, not so severe as virtue, not so serious as pity, smiled upon him: his fingers lost their compression; – nor did virtue offer to catch the money as it fell.[18]

While the scene is light and humorous, in the context of the novel's tragic outcome it voices an underlying anxiety about the operation of one's sentiments. Here the man of feeling acts like a puppet that is moved by the strings of his emotions. His charity is not a voluntary act but the work of an irresistible force: the mechanical operation of sympathy.

Earlier in the century Bernard Mandeville already drew attention to the problem that sympathy sometimes operates even when it should not. In *The Fable of the Bees* he gives a rather sharp critique of the rhetoric beggars use in order to persuade us to give alms even when we would not otherwise want to do so. The beggar, Mandeville writes, invites you to view 'the worst side of his Ailments and bodily infirmities', he gives you 'an Epitome of his Calamities real or fictitious', appeals to God and religion, and flatters your pride. 'People not used to great Cities', – like Mackenzie's Harley – 'being thus attack'd on all sides, are commonly forc'd to yield, and can't help giving something tho' they can hardly spare it themselves' (*Fable* 267). Thus, Mandeville warns us that our sympathy may be often manipulated by 'undeserving' objects, even when our self-interest would not allow for a sympathetic response to take place. As a result, 'pitiful People often give an Alms when they really feel that they would rather not' (*Fable* 267). But the desire to get away from the all-too-familiar sight of – often-faked – misery can also motivate these charitable acts. Thus, Mandeville objects, 'thousands give Money to Beggars from the same motive as they pay their Corn-cutter, to walk Easy. And many a Half-penny is given to impudent and designedly persecuting Rascals, whom, if it could be done handsomely, man would cane with much greater Satisfaction. Yet all this by the courtesy of the Country is call'd Charity' (*Fable* 268).

While this may sound cynical enough, one will find that Hutcheson and Hume also disapprove of practising benevolence toward 'undeserving' objects. As Hutcheson writes in the *Inquiry*, 'when our benevolence to the evil encourages them in their bad intentions, or makes them more capable of mischief; this diminishes or destroys the beauty of the action, or even makes it evil, as it betrays a neglect of the good of others more valuable [...]' (*Beauty and Virtue* 163).[19] Mandeville's remarks, as well as Mackenzie's beggar episode in *The Man of Feeling*, imply a critique of the idea of an innate, impulsive other-regarding feeling that is advocated by Shaftesbury, and, later, Hutcheson. The mechanical response to an impulse of charity highlights a possible conflict between the moral sense and Hutcheson's 'public sense' or sympathy: even when the moral sense would help us make the right ethical decision, the instinct of sympathy or the 'public sense' seems to be able to counteract this impulse. Sympathy, if it is indeed an instinct inherent in human nature, will transgress the boundaries of prudence and operate unselectively. And if sympathy operates impulsively and irrespective of who its object is, it can easily become excessive and endanger those who practise it, bringing poverty, isolation and even physical destruction to the man or woman of feeling. Mechanical notions of sympathy may thus signal an anxiety about a potentially disruptive excess built into the earliest conceptualisations of fellow-feeling in mainstream eighteenth-century theories of impulsive moral sentiment.

The mechanism of sympathy

By the mid-eighteenth century, sympathy had established its status as a feeling that is instrumental in the formation of communities and the social bond. The notion of moral feeling as a binding force is present in the writings of the Cambridge Platonists, the Latitudinarians, and Scottish moral sense philosophers who, in the wake of Shaftesbury, aimed to refute Hobbes's claim that man is naturally driven by selfish appetites. For Hutcheson, the moral sense is a 'secret chain' between each person and mankind that makes it possible for us to have positive or negative feelings for people even in distant ages and countries (*Beauty and Virtue* 110–11). In the philosophy of Francis Hutcheson, David Hume, Adam Smith, Henry Home (Lord Kames) and Hugh Blair, sympathy emerges as 'the great cement of human society', the creator of civilised social existence.[20]

But sympathy is not simply a form of sentiment that holds communities together. It is also a kind of sentiment that travels quickly from person to person – a concept that makes frequent appearance in a variety of discourses throughout the period. 'Dangerous' passions, such as enthusiasm, are described in these terms, but so are other-regarding sentiments, like sympathy. And this mechanically-imagined concept makes it possible that even in its earlier philosophical conceptualisations sympathy can convey a double meaning; it does not merely refer to an altruistic, benevolent, community-forming capacity. As John Mullan points out in *Sentiment and Sociability*, even a text as emphatic about the positive capacity of common feelings as Shaftesbury's *Characteristics* (1711) allows the same sympathy that operates as a form of pleasurable sharing of sentiments also to be a dangerous contagion and disruptive force. The positive, unifying principle hides in itself the potential of corrupting the very unity it is able to create. Sympathy can lead people to break down restraints, and has the ability to grow into enthusiasm and thus to conjoin people in an undesirable way. As Shaftesbury writes in 'A Letter Concerning Enthusiasm', every passion raised in a multitude and conveyed by sympathy can be called 'panic', which flies from face to face like an infectious disease. And 'the disease', writes Shaftesbury, 'is no sooner seen than caught' (*Characteristics* 10).[21] However, while sympathy is the mechanism by which 'bad' feelings can travel, it is exactly sympathy that can cure the disease of enthusiasm and panic. Shaftesbury encourages a sympathetic rather than a harsh and punitive attitude in officers responsible for justice and order. The magistrate 'should have a gentler hand and, instead of caustics, incisions and amputations, should be using the softest balms' and, 'with a kind sympathy', he should enter into the passion of the people and 'endeavour, by cheerful way, to divert and heal it' (*Characteristics* 10–11).

Similarly, Hume describes the mechanism of sympathy as an interpersonal transmission and communication of emotions. In Book 2

('Of the Passions') of the *Treatise of Human Nature* (1739–40), he writes that we can feel what another person feels, because we 'receive by communication their inclinations and sentiments, however different from, or even contrary to our own'.[22] This force is responsible for resemblances, and the difficulty, even in the case of men of greatest understanding, to follow one's own inclinations and reason and not to be diverted by someone else's. A person's emotions have an instant effect on the observer due to the mechanical operations of sympathetic transfusion: 'A cheerful countenance infuses a sensible complacency and serenity into my mind; as an angry or sorrowful one throws a sudden damp upon me.' One feels the passions 'more from communication' than from one's 'own natural temper and disposition' (*THN* 317). Similarly, in *An Enquiry Concerning the Principles of Morals* feelings are infused, diffused, transfused, communicated and excite a 'sympathetic movement' in our breast. Good humour is a 'flame' that 'spreads through the whole circle; and the most sullen and morose are often caught by it'.[23] When delightful sentiments are communicated, they 'melt' the spectators 'into the same fondness and delicacy. The tear naturally starts in our eye on the apprehension of a warm sentiment of this nature: our breast heaves, our heart is agitated, and every humane tender principle of our frame is set in motion, and gives us the purest and most satisfactory enjoyment' (257). On the other hand, we find 'wrangling, and scolding, and mutual reproaches' unpleasant: 'The roughness and harshness of these emotions disturb and displease us: we suffer by contagion and sympathy [...]' (257–8).

The feeling that binds people together and the 'contagious' feeling one can catch have common roots in earlier, magnetic and mechanistic explanations of sympathy. These explanations were widespread by the early eighteenth century, and they infiltrated all kinds of discourses irrespective of the writers' moral or religious views, including magnetism, occultism, medicine, mechanistic science, materialism, moral philosophy and literature. During the seventeenth century, sympathy was defined as an attraction that made similar material particles migrate towards each other. According to Patricia Fara, the operations of sympathy and magnetism were treated as analogous in the eighteenth century; the words 'sympathetic' and 'magnetic' were often used interchangeably at a popular level, which echoed earlier, Neoplatonic beliefs in a harmonising, synchronised universe.[24] Based on the notion of a natural attraction between similar particles, occult or difficult-to-explain phenomena were often attributed to the workings of sympathy. One famous example is Kenelm Digby's attempt to explain 'rationally' the workings of the powder of sympathy, a mysterious solution said to heal wounds from a distance – even from overseas – by the power of migrating particles that attracted one another. One simply dipped the bandage, imbrued in blood, into the solution, and the particles of blood were meant to migrate back to the wound, drawing with them the healing powder and thus bringing about a cure. As Digby pointed out, sympathy made it possible not only to heal, but also to torment from a distance. Boiling the milk of a pregnant woman was thought to cause agony in her as the fiery particles of milk tended back to their original place. Richard Browne explained how the pleasure of music and dance could cure both mood-related and physical illnesses through a mechanical operation of sympathy, turning the body into a vibrating and trembling feeling-machine. Perhaps the most extreme way of making use of sympathy for alternative ways of healing was put forward by H.M. Herwig, who suggested that performing operations on the bodily excretions and secretions of the patient had a sympathetic healing effect from a distance.[25]

As Fara argues, with the seventeenth and eighteenth centuries' fascination with magnetism, the language of sympathetic attraction penetrated into the descriptions of the physical, spiritual and human worlds. During the eighteenth century, the inherited connotations of magnetism enriched people's discussion. After the influential seventeenth-century theories of cosmic magnetism by Anastasius Kircher and William Gilbert, many educated eighteenth-century people continued to see the universe as permeated with a divine, magnetic power, whose workings, like those of God, were mysterious. Such natural sympathies and antipathies extended to almost all aspects of life. The sympathetic nature of magnetism came to be linked with phenomena that were perceived as forms of attraction; for instance, growing grapes were thought to facilitate sympathetically the fermentation of wine in the cellar, and the mother's desires and experiences during pregnancy could sympathetically shape the appearance of the unborn baby. Magnetic influences were used to draw out pains from the body and guard against miscarriage, and religious enthusiasm was also explained 'rationally' as a form of sympathy.[26] Such magnetic associations continued to appear in encyclopaedias throughout the eighteenth century, and even Newton's theory of gravity did not entirely displace Gilbertian, magnetic explanations of cosmic attraction. While the end of the century saw the growth of scepticism and intolerance towards sympathetic powders and magnetic healers, the imagery of magnetism and sympathetic attraction continued to proliferate in the writings of the period. At the end of the century writers still reiterated

Kircher's magnetic imagery; magnetic cures continued to be prescribed and Digby's sympathetic powders were still advertised a hundred years later.[27]

But sympathetic explanations to natural phenomena were also rife in dominant medical literature. The important question of how bodily feelings are turned into ideas, or how thought and emotion are physically channelled into bodily expression or motion was a great mystery in the period, and fascinated many philosophers and medical doctors in the seventeenth and eighteenth centuries. This intrasubjective transmission, as well as the possibility of transferring emotions intersubjectively from one person to another, was also frequently attributed to the operation of sympathy and explained by the attraction or migration of particles, or by a sympathetic harmony of the nerves.[28] According to the Edinburgh physiologist Robert Whytt – the first influential physiologist to introduce nerve theory into Scottish medicine – the connection between mind and body, as well as the harmony between distant organs and body parts, could be attributed to nervous sympathy. The vitalist Whytt explained sympathy from a 'sentient principle' rather than solely from mechanical rules and saw it as the basis of involuntary motion and non-rational mental phenomena. Moreover, this nervous sympathy extended to interpersonal connections too, opening up the possibility for sympathy to structure ethical and social relations:

> There is a remarkable sympathy, by means of the nerves, between the various parts of the body; and now it appears that there is still a more wonderful sympathy between the nervous systems of different persons, whence various motions and morbid symptoms are often transferred, from one to another, without any corporeal contact or infection.[29]

It was Whytt's influential idea of body–mind sympathy and the physiological concept of nervous sensibility as developed by enlightenment medicine that philosophical, moral theorists of sensibility and sympathy would build upon. For the Scottish literati, sensibility and feeling turned into a basis for morals, social life and the advancement of civilisation – and were sometimes seen as criteria to distinguish the rude, uncivilised and labouring poor from the refined, sophisticated and polite upper classes and civilised nations.[30]

Mechanistic and magnetic metaphors of affectivity and sympathy constantly cropped up alongside the notion of the sympathetic bond in the writings of many eighteenth-century thinkers who debated moral questions in the wake of Shaftesbury from diverse, and sometimes conflicting, moral and religious standpoints.[31] In one of his early contributions to the *Guardian*, Bishop George Berkeley, who later became a dedicated opponent of Shaftesbury, compared moral sympathy to the universal principle of attractive power which is 'the key to explain various phenomena of nature'.[32] As we have seen earlier, in Hutcheson's *Inquiry* universal benevolence was imagined in terms of Newtonian gravitation to highlight the weaknesses and imperfections in its mechanism (*Beauty and Virtue* 198). But eighteenth-century accounts of the sympathetic imagination also rely frequently on mechanistic and magnetic metaphors. In Alexander Gerard's *Essay on Taste* (1759), passions can be infused and caught, 'as if by infection', while the force of sympathy can enliven the ideas of the passions thus received from others, so they become our own passions. Gerard's sympathetic imagination works like a magnetic field, selectively drawing to itself certain ideas.[33] Similarly, in Adam Smith's moral theory as well as in the works of those thinkers who have been influenced by materialism (including Joseph Priestley and William Godwin), the sympathetic imagination operates according to mechanical principles.[34] Emotional transfusion, contagion, material migration and magnetic or gravitational attraction are among the forms in which the binding force of sympathy was conceptualised during the long eighteenth century. While these interrelated notions are different sides of the same phenomenon of attraction, the long survival of such mechanistic metaphors in the long eighteenth century made it possible for sympathy to acquire and retain connotations of a 'dangerous', contagious capacity besides the cohesive force whose operation this could disrupt. Moreover, it also provided a conceptual framework for imagining the dysfunctions of sympathy in terms of the inconstant operation of gravity or the selectivity of the magnet's attractive force. Therefore, mechanistic metaphors of sympathy would provide a discursive framework suggestive of the malfunctions and also of the disruptive energies inherent in other-regarding feeling in the period.

Healing sensibility and the sympathetic bond: 'The Story of La Roche'

Henry Mackenzie's 'The Story of La Roche', published in the *Mirror* in 1779, is a curious meeting point of eighteenth-century philosophy, religion and sensibility. Alongside the notion of sympathy as an affective chain, Mackenzie's story also features a mechanistic concept of sympathy – a sentiment that acts like an infection or a contagion – that could potentially undermine sympathy's community-forming capacity. Here, however, the disruptive power of contagious feeling is channelled into a productive, healing force. Read in the context of Mackenzie's novels and periodicals, the story's preoccupation with cohesive but contagious sentiment demonstrates the ways in which a narrative could register and negotiate contemporary anxieties about excessive sensibility.

In 'The Story of La Roche' a Scottish sceptical philosopher travels to France in search of a quiet place to write his philosophical treatise that later 'astonished the world'.[35] Here he learns that a Swiss clergyman, M. La Roche, had arrived in the same village the evening before. La Roche has been travelling around in Europe with his daughter, in order to ease the pain of loss caused by the death of his wife. Instead of getting better, however, La Roche falls seriously ill. The philosopher happens to be the only person in the neighbourhood with some medical knowledge. He runs to the assistance of the minister and helps him recover from the dangerous fever. The story sketches the ties of friendship that develop between the devoted Protestant La Roche and the sceptical but benevolent philosopher, who accompanies the minister and his daughter on their journey back to Switzerland. The philosopher spends some time in the beautiful Swiss village where La Roche and his daughter live, and he is invited back again three years later, for Mademoiselle La Roche's wedding. This time, however, a scene of tragedy and mourning awaits him: he has to learn that Mademoiselle La Roche died of a broken heart after her fiancé was killed in a duel. Our clergyman, however, is not devastated. Instead of breaking down under the weight of his calamities, he finds consolation in the belief that he will soon be reunited with his lost loved ones. On the pulpit his tears dry up, and his countenance assumes 'the glow of faith and hope'. The philosopher is moved by La Roche's faith. And later, whenever he remembered the powerful consolation given to his Swiss friend, 'he wished that he had never doubted' (*Works*, 4.207).

Religion in this story is a form of sensibility, and it borders on enthusiasm. As Mackenzie writes, 'La Roche's religion was that of sentiment, not theory. The ideas of his God, and his Saviour, were so congenial to his mind, that every emotion of it naturally awakened them. A philosopher might have called him an enthusiast; but, if he possessed the fervour of enthusiasts, he was guiltless of their bigotry' (*Works*, 4.192). But La Roche's religious warmth is far from being the dangerous and disruptive force many contemporaries describe enthusiasm to be. Rather, it is a source of pleasure and healing, which can be communicated and spread to induce similar pleasurable affections in others and bring others into a community. La Roche's religious sensibility is something like an added sense; La Roche compares it to the musical powers that he and his daughter possess. While the philosopher lacks this religious sense, due to his innate benevolence he is not immune to the power of feelings through which La Roche's faith is transmitted.

When the painful memory of her mother's death interrupts Mademoiselle La Roche's organ playing during a church service, the philosopher cannot resist the feelings that travel, like an infection, from person to person. And eventually the philosopher is also included in the community this feeling produces through the power of contagion:

> Something was said of the death of the just, of such as die in the Lord. – The organ was touched with a hand less firm; – it paused, it ceased; and the sobbing of Ma'moiselle La Roche was heard in its stead. Her father gave a sign for stopping the psalmody, and rose to pray... He addressed a Being whom he loved, and spoke for those he loved. His parishioners catched [sic] the ardour of the good old man; even the philosopher felt himself moved, and forgot, for a moment, to think why he should not. (*Works*, 4.191–2)

As we find out at the end of the story, not only does La Roche's sentiment connect those who possess an inbuilt sense for this feeling but it also links together the living and the dead. In this way, it can offer consolation and cure in the state of bereavement. After the death of Mademoiselle La Roche, our clergyman refuses to mourn, and instead, he is back in the church preaching. He encourages his parishioners, saying: 'Go then, mourn not for me; I have not lost my child: but a little while, and we shall meet again never to be separated' (*Works*, 4. 205). Thus, instead of letting go of his lost objects as one would do in the state of mourning, La Roche maintains the attachment by forging a link between the living and the dead. La Roche's sensibility offers an alternative to mourning – something that has healing effects without the pain that the mourner has to suffer. Here faith is a matter of feeling, and those who possess this feeling – living or dead – belong to the same select community. Sentiment is the bridge that links together separate worlds.

The idea of an affective bridge that forges a select community through immediate feeling is part of the sentimental aesthetic Mackenzie developed earlier in his career, in the course of his long-lasting correspondence with his cousin Elizabeth Rose of Kilravock. This intellectual exchange began in 1768, before the conception of Mackenzie's first novel, *The Man of Feeling*, and it led to the development of many of his ideas on literature and art. The correspondence was in itself a kind of affective glue – forging intimacy and creating an illusionary together-ness between the two loving but separated cousins. Elizabeth Rose was normally the first person to read and evaluate his manuscripts while still in their conception, and Mackenzie discussed with her not only his works, but his readings, ideas and opinions that occurred to him during the writing process. He acknowledged Elizabeth's influence on him, praising her talents and learning. He wrote to her in October 1770 that 'you are not only Mistress of my Thoughts but have them even in Embryo', and that 'I am more & more a Philosopher every time you write me'.[36] At this stage of his writing career, Mackenzie's works were written, as he claims, 'from the immediate Feeling', and they helped to fight distance and re-create a lost immediacy: 'I can be with you in your Walks & your Bower without taking up so much Room as to need your building a larger. Nay you will find that I have actually transported myself thither by the Lines at the Bottom of this Letter' (*ER* 17).

In his letters to Elizabeth Rose, Mackenzie categorises different forms of art on the basis of how they achieve their effect:

> Some Arts are immediately address'd to the Mind and have nothing mechanical at all about them such as Poetry, Eloquence, & so forth – others are conve'd thro' the Medium of Senses which in some Degree are Pieces of Mechanism. Sculpture & Painting for instance are the Property of Sight; but even in these the Difference of the Organs of Sight do not affect the Capacity of a Vertuoso: it is somewhat other-wise I imagine in Music; The Ear is so framed in some that, without any Connection with Tenderness of Feeling in general, it is not only capable of an accurate Distinction of Sounds, but communicates to the Mind a delicate Sense of Pleasure from their Effects. (*ER* 9)

A good musical ear directly brings about aesthetic appreciation for those who possess it. The listener has to have an excellent inbuilt sense that makes him particularly susceptible to musical enjoyment. In Mackenzie's description, sentimental writing is somewhat similar to music in that both depend on an intimate bond created by the recognition of a shared – musical or emotive – capacity. Sentimental writing mechani-cally affects a community whose members possess a sense for refined feeling. The language of sentiment works by a sudden recognition of some hidden power that has always been there in the reader, and which the story of sentiment brings to the surface. 'Believe me', he writes, 'where genuine Sentiment and Feeling are at bottom, [...] the Reader will be pleas'd in Proportion as these Qualities reside in himself' (*ER* 17). Sentimental writing works by depicting minor details which 'their Intimates' can recognise, and thus their passions are aroused (*ER* 37). Such subtleties make one feel 'that Pleasure which is alwise experience'd by him who unlocks the Springs of Tenderness and Simplicity', claims Mackenzie when discussing Goldsmith's *Deserted Village* (*ER* 49–50). The way the literature of sensibility speaks to the heart and creates a link between author and reader is 'like finding some Family Picture in a Stranger's House; we conclude ourselves acquainted, & are Friends at first Sight' (*ER* 51–2). Thus, affective details bring about a scene of recognition by revealing a hidden but already existent familiarity among the members of a community.

By Mackenzie's time the sentiment that connects person to person is something with which the eighteenth-century reader was quite familiar, from both religious and secular contexts. For Mackenzie, the philosophical tradition of Hutcheson, Hume, Smith, Kames and Blair was a direct source of influence, where feeling, as we have seen, is both a bond and a mechanism of transmission or attraction.[37] In 'The Story of La Roche' religion is sentimentalised according to common notions of affectivity – magnetic-mechanistic as well as moral-cohesive – that were predominant in diverse discourses throughout the eighteenth century. However, here it is transformed into a healing and practicable form of sentiment.[38] This sentimentalisation of religion, I would like to argue, is part of Mackenzie's larger project, voiced throughout his oeuvre, promoting a form of sensibility that responds to contemporary concerns about the ambivalence of moral feeling by offering a model for other-regarding sentiment that could also work in social practice.

One of the early anxieties that Mackenzie's writings undertook to address was the concern that sensibility and sympathy could be unworldly and harmful, and that they could disrupt and isolate, rather than forge communities. The sources of the widespread fear of excessive sensibility and social disruption in the period were multifaceted. As far as the Scottish context is concerned, John Mullan argues that the Scottish Enlightenment's focus on sociability was related to the loss of Scottish identity after the Act of Union. In Scotland, claims Mullan, politeness and intellectual cohesiveness functioned as a substitute for the political identity that the nation had lost.[39] Historians of the Scottish Enlightenment claim that the loss of national identity also brought about a threat of moral decline in the context of a transforming economic and social system. Mackenzie and the eighteenth-century moralists found it important to uphold urgent ethical values within the framework of a society that many of them saw as increasingly competitive, fragmented and individualistic. In Scotland, John Dwyer argues, moralists like Adam Smith, Hugh Blair and John Drysdale found the emerging bourgeoisie selfish and irresponsible, and some of them painted a threatening picture of the moral consequences of economic change. The Scottish literati condemned the spread of consumerism in Edinburgh, and their essays developed strategies for avoiding moral corruption and communal disintegration in the wake of the new commercial environment.[40] While the tone of enlightened discourse remained relatively optimistic before 1763, after the Seven Years' War previously latent concerns started to come to the fore. Various factors such as war on the Continent, discontent in America, and the French Revolution all contributed to a growing sense of disillusionment among the Scottish literati. By the late 1770s, the threat of disintegration became audible and the optimism that characterised the vision of Hutcheson and Hume started to fade.[41] In this social and cultural climate, Mackenzie himself seemed to lose faith in the intrinsic benevolence of human nature. As he wrote in his *Reminiscences*, 'At twenty, I read Rochefoucauld with indignation; at forty, with doubt; – and now at sixty, almost, tho' unwillingly, with conviction of the truth of his maxims.'[42]

But in a society riven by interest, sensibility could forge social cohesion and sympathetic bonds only in so far as it was compatible with prudence and politeness. Sentiment, taken to an extreme, carried yet another pervasive and politically sensitive concern. During the eighteenth century many worried that the excess of altruistic feeling had the power to disrupt gender and class boundaries and thus to threaten the balance of the social and political order. The ideal of the 'man of feeling' could potentially push men beyond reformed manners into the realm of the effeminate and unmanly, while women, pursuing the dictates of their feelings, could transgress the prescribed boundaries of domestic, patriarchal sexuality. Rousseau's novel, *Julie, or the New Heloise*, presented a case where sentimental values like pity, affection and sensibility functioned as bases for the revolutionary transgression of sexual and class boundaries. During the violent phase of the French Revolution, the period's fascination with the uncontrollable mechanism of impulsive or 'contagious' feeling was exploited in the works of many literary, medical and political writers, underlining the energy and power inherent in feelings that fuel group attitudes and behaviour.[43] Conversely, the ideology of sympathy and benevolence could also function as a form of social control that helped maintain the status quo and support existing power relationships. Hutcheson's and Hume's insistence on selective acts of charity pointed to the darker, ambivalent side of the charitable impulse, problematising the fine line between the 'deserving' and 'undeserving' objects of benevolence. Humanitarian acts could take place to reward the obedience of the socially inferior and to affirm hierarchy. John Dwyer draws attention to the element of elitism and condescension lurking behind Scottish Enlightenment concepts of sympathy, pointing out that even the most humane affects of sentimentalism formed part of a latent system of social layering, distancing and control. Exercises in benevolence could transform the objects of sympathy into victims of power when they refused to follow established social rules and expectations.[44]

While, as we shall see in Chapter 3 of this volume, Mackenzie's *The Man of Feeling* addresses the moral economy of power relations structured into tearful, sympathetic encounters, Mackenzie's concerns regarding the disruptive, excessive capacity inherent in benevolent, cohesive other-regarding sentiment are voiced in 'The Story of La Roche' as well as in further essays and stories published in the *Mirror* and the *Lounger* throughout the 1770s and 1780s. In a story called 'Effects of Sentiment and Sensibility on Happiness' (1780), Mackenzie claims that 'sentiment, like religion, had its superstitions, and its martyrdom' and that 'there are bounds beyond which virtuous feelings cease to be virtue' (*Works*, 5. 4). In his essay 'On novel writing' (1785), he warns against a 'sickly sort of refinement' as well as those moral and religious virtues that can never be put into practice (*Works*, 5. 185). Like the excesses of religion, the extremes of sentiment are also morally wrong. They make the achievements of everyday life seem unsatisfying; in this way, they make us unhappy, and should therefore be avoided.[45] In 'The Story of La Roche' sentiment is powerful and transgressive, yet it remains healthy and productive. Religion, like all other forms of sentiment, needs to stay within the boundaries of politeness in order to fit in with Mackenzie's model for practicable sensibility. Only in this form, carefully distanced from enthusiasm, can a potentially excessive form of sympathy be offered as a practicable model for the readers of the *Mirror* and the *Lounger* in the 1770s and 1780s.

Sympathetic identification: Adam Smith's *The Theory of Moral Sentiments*

Over the course of the eighteenth century sympathy comes to be seen increasingly as the work of reflection and imagination rather than a mechanical communication or contagion of sentiment. Even for

Hume, sympathy is not always a matter of mechanical transfusion. On the micro-level of individual emotional response, a subtle element of thinking and reflection is inscribed into the process of a mechanically communicated feeling:

> When any affection is infused by sympathy, it is at first known only by its effects, and by those external signs in the countenance and conversation, which convey an idea of it. This idea is presently converted into an impression, and acquires such a degree of force and vivacity, as to become the very passion itself, and produce an equal emotion as an original affection. (*THN* 317)

This seemingly direct transmission of affect, upon philosophical scrutiny, turns out to be a complex process that involves intellectual activity. The foreign affection enters the other person through external signs. The mind has to read the external signs that convey an idea of the other's affection, which idea is then converted into an impression.

The element of mental – reflective or imaginative – activity structured into sympathy will be the very spot that Adam Smith's theory opens up. The work of the imagination was often alluded to in previous conceptualisations of sympathy, but it becomes the focal point of Adam Smith's definition.[46] Smith's moral theory centres wholly on the concept of sympathy, which he imagines as a form of identification produced by the workings of the imagination. Smith makes sympathy the constructive core of human consciousness and subjectivity, considering it as the founding principle of all human morality and social existence. Hutcheson's separate ethical notions of moral sense, public sense and sense of honour all come together in Smith under this single moral faculty. Smith's theory makes moral sympathy and other-related affections the crux of the psychological processes that structure human subjectivity, anticipating in this sense Freudian ideas on psychic structure and ego formation as well as intersubjective psychoanalytic theories, and raising issues that Freudian psychoanalysis would later call metapsychological.[47]

In *The Theory of Moral Sentiments*, Smith undertakes to look behind the surface of a notion of sympathy that appears to be transfusion or contagion:

> Upon some occasions *sympathy may seem to arise merely from the view* of a certain emotion in another person. The passions, upon some occasions, *may seem to be transfused* from one man to another,

instantaneously, and antecedent to any knowledge of what excited them in the person principally concerned. Grief and joy, for example, strongly expressed in the look and gestures of any one, *at once affect the spectator* with some degree of a like painful or agreeable emotion. A smiling face is, to every body that sees it, a cheerful object; as a sorrowful countenance, on the other hand, is a melancholy one.[48]

What seems to take place here is an instantaneous wandering of emotions from one person to the other, the kind of mechanism which is prevalent also in Hume's *A Treatise of Human Nature*. Behind this apparent transfusion, however, Smith finds complex processes of identification:

> By the imagination we place ourselves in his situation, we conceive ourselves enduring the same torments, we enter as it were into his body, and become in some measure the same person with him, and thence form some idea of his sensations, and even feel something which, though weaker in degree, is not altogether unlike them. His agonies, when they are thus brought home to ourselves, when we have thus adopted and made them our own, begin at last to affect us, and we then tremble and shudder at the thought of what he feels. (*TMS* 12)

Thus, in *The Theory of Moral Sentiments*, sympathy is defined as our ability to be carried across the boundaries of our own persons through the workings of the imagination. As our senses cannot provide a guideline to deducing someone else's affections, identification is the only way we can make sense of the situation of the other. The result is an intersubjective identity created through a partial bodily and affective identification, which implies borrowing the feelings that belong to the other person – that is, placing parts of the other into the self. The feelings thus grafted into us start living their own life and have a physical impact on our body. The other, so to say, becomes part of an extended self.

There are several quite apparent contradictions within Smith's theory of sympathy. He considers various types of fellow-feeling, such as compassion and pity, as original passions of human nature; but at the same time he questions the universality of these feelings. He claims that other-regarding emotions are always present in the human mind and can be felt equally even by those who disregard laws and violate others, yet he builds his system on the assumption of an original selfishness and a general absence or 'dullness' of sensibility. While earlier British moralists insist on the innate nature of humane and benevolent behaviour, passions of self-centredness play a fundamental role in Smith's moral and economic theories. As John Dwyer argues, selfish behaviour is an important factor in *The Theory of Moral Sentiments*, and a degree of self-centredness is built into the sympathetic process. However, Smith's idea of self-interest, Dwyer claims, does not mean aggressive competitiveness and antagonism, but merely denotes preferring of one's own welfare to that of others, and a desire to better one's own condition. This natural preference, which everyone has for their own happiness above that of others, also allows for the existence of sociability.[49]

According to Eugene Heath, what is at stake in *The Theory of Moral Sentiments* is an investigation of whether a set of other-regarding principles can arise out of a situation in which individuals are not constrained by moral demands and are directed by self-interest and limited benevolence.[50] I would like to maintain that the self-regarding aspect in Smith's sympathy is important, because it implies a subjectivist epistemological position, whose appearance in the period will be the basis of some of the ethical dilemmas often associated with emerging discourses of sensibility. Smith's concept of self-centred sympathy figures a position of reading and interpretation that constitutes knowledge only within the emotional and cognitive framework of the subject, on whose internal world the knowledge of the other completely depends. Consequently, the issue in Smith's text is not simply, as Heath proposes, whether a set of other-related principles can grow out of an initial state of self-interest. Rather, the question arises whether Smith's other-regarding principle, even when it does emerge, can ever be more than self-regarding, and whether sympathy is not, as it were, an 'uncanny' concept, with a meaning riven by internal contradictions.

This section will trace the way in which self-centredness and the lack of sympathy come to be inscribed into the very definition and structure of sympathy, and will reflect on how such instances of dysfunction are linked to concerns about defining human consciousness and recognising otherness. According to *The Theory of Moral Sentiments*, sympathy operates somewhat selectively. While its structure allows us to feel for those who suffer, sympathy creates the very social hierarchies and tensions that it is meant to transgress and alleviate. Here I will examine how Smith's definition of sympathy as imaginary identification allows for such a controversial concept of sympathy to emerge. I will argue that this is made possible by Smith's employment of a concept of sympathy that is bound up with the aesthetic. While previous scholarship emphasised the element of spectatorship built into the structure of sympathy, I would like to draw attention to an often-overlooked aspect of the scene of viewing: the act of telling or imagining a story. This element not only accounts for the healing potential of sympathy, but also explains the ambivalence inherent in its operation. It allows for limit-cases of sympathy to emerge (including our sympathy with those whose story cannot be heard, such as the dead), which cases reveal the difficulties of recognising difference and understanding otherness. The operation of sympathy in terms of the aesthetic and the fictional makes helping behaviour possible in the first instance, and it also enables us to enjoy literature and art. But the same structure also allows for the flip side of sympathy to emerge during the workings of other-regarding sentiment.

Like Hutcheson and Hume, Smith often emphasises the mimetic nature of altruistic feeling, resorting to images of mechanism and automatism when describing its onset. The emotion 'springs up' in us at the sight and thought of another person's suffering or joy, demonstrating the seemingly instantaneous nature of these bodily and psychic affects. When a stroke is about to hit another person, 'we *naturally* shrink and draw back our own leg or our arm [...]'. When observing someone else's passion, 'an analogous emotion *springs up, at the thought* of his situation, in the breast of every attentive spectator'. Persons of delicate constitutions, when looking at the exposed sores of beggars, 'are apt to feel an itching or uneasy sensation in the correspondent part of their own bodies' (*TMS* 12–13, emphases added). While these sympathetic feelings are the products of the imagination, the onset of a reaction of identification seems as automatic and immediate as it was in the case of earlier conceptualisations of other-regarding affections.

Despite the metaphors of mechanism and immediacy, however, Adam Smith's sympathy does not work universally either. In fact, Smith's idea that sympathy is a subjective work of imagination is based on his many counter-examples and observations of the emotions we cannot easily sympathise with, because we find it impossible, inconvenient or even painful to imagine and enter into the other's situation and feelings. In order words, the imperfections of sympathy are due to the fact that sympathy operates through imaginary identification. Far from being natural and automatic, sympathy sometimes requires an endeavour – and often it simply does not come about. Eugene Heath draws attention to an instance where Smith's description reveals the effort that sympathetic identification requires of the spectator.[51] The spectator has to '*endeavour, as much as he can*', to place himself into the other's situation; he has to be attentive to the '*minutest incidents*' of the case, and '*strive to render as perfect as possible*' his identification (*TMS* 26, emphases added). Moreover, there are several passions with which we cannot sympathise, or when we do, our sympathy is not complete. These are feelings that originate in the body, such as violent pain, hunger or sexual passion. What we reproduce is not the exact passion of the other, but secondary feelings that arise from the original situation, such as fear or grief. In the case of bodily pain, we sympathise with the sufferer's fear – that is, with an affect of the imagination – but not with the bodily agony. In order for sympathy to take place, the affect has to be accessible through intellectual reflection (*TMS* 35).

While we easily enter into the other's feelings of joy, we are not naturally disposed to be sensible to and sympathise with their sorrows. When we sympathise with joy, 'our *heart swells* and *overflows* with real pleasure: joy and complacency *sparkle from our eyes*, and *animate every feature of our countenance, and every gesture of our body*' (*TMS* 57, emphases added). On the other hand, while someone narrates their suffering, 'bursts of passion' 'choke' them in the middle of the narration, and our emotions cannot 'keep time' with those of the narrator (*TMS* 57). We experience the discrepancy between our feelings and those of the sufferer as a want of our sensibility, and even work ourselves up into an artificial sympathy to re-create the equilibrium of feeling (*TMS* 58). The so-called 'unsocial passions' – such as hatred, anger and resentment – do not carry the benefit of any pleasurable bodily sensation, and affect the onlooker with feelings of dissonance, cacophony and disagreeable bodily sensations. Hatred has a 'hoarse, boisterous, and discordant voice' (*TMS* 45), which makes the observer 'tremble' and be overcome with fear, so that even the 'stouter hearts are disturbed' (*TMS* 45). As Smith writes: 'There is, in the very feeling of those passions, something *harsh, jarring, and convulsive*, something that *tears and distracts the breast*, and is altogether *destructive* of that composure and tranquillity of mind which is so necessary to happiness [...]' (*TMS* 46, emphases added). As sympathy with joy offers us agreeable physical sensations, hatred repels us through bodily reactions.

Most importantly, however, a feeling of sympathy that is based on imaginary identification fails to operate in social situations where it would be most required. In the chapter 'Of the origin of ambition and of the distinction of ranks' Smith argues that we are prone to sympathise with the rich and the great rather than the poor. We emulate and admire the rich, and feel compassion at the fall and suffering of a king, but we blindly and indifferently turn away from the sight of poverty. Paradoxically, while sympathy is meant to be the passion that alleviates the suffering caused by social inequality, in Smith's theory sympathy is precisely the source of such differences, which it even helps to maintain. For David Hume too, differences in social class bring about selective and often-ambivalent emotional responses. There is something 'extraordinary' and 'seemingly unaccountable' in our responses to the situation of the rich and poor. As Hume avers, we 'naturally respect the rich', and feel contempt for the poor. But he insists that our regard for the rich is without self-interest and is not based on any potential benefit we would enjoy as a result of their acquaintance. He attributes our immediate positive and negative reactions to the association of ideas that are produced at the site of riches and poverty. Accordingly, 'when we approach a man who is, as we say, at his ease, we are pleased with the pleasing ideas of plenty, satisfaction, cleanliness, warmth; [...] on the contrary, when a poor man appears, the disagreeable images of want, penury, hard labour, dirty furniture, coarse and ragged clothes, nauseous meat and distasteful liqueur, immediately strike our fancy' (*Enquiry* 247–8).[52]

Enlightenment moral philosophers tackle the conundrum caused by the selective operation of sympathy by understanding sympathy within an intricate network of pleasure and unpleasure. In the writings of Hutcheson and Hume sympathising with suffering causes pain for the spectator, yet, bearing the other's pain and reacting sympathetically is natural, and a proof of one's benevolence. Hume, who explains sympathy as an automatic 'catching' of emotions, insists that sympathy is pleasurable only when it concerns pleasurable emotions, or emotions of a person close to us. Smith, however, maintains that painful situations can induce sympathy on condition that there is a pleasurable gain for the spectator. The strongest sympathy is triggered either by riches and magnanimity or by the greatest calamity, while small vexations excite no sympathy at all (*TMS* 52). In other words, whatever the situation, the presence of sympathy in Smith's theory always indicates the presence of pleasure in the observer. As Hume puts it, pleasure is the hinge of Smith's system. But Hume finds Smith's argument related to the pleasure of sympathy rather unsatisfactory. If all sympathy was agreeable, he observes critically of Smith's *Treatise*, 'An Hospital would be a more entertaining Place than a Ball'.[53] And indeed, Smith's argument begs the following questions: If sympathy depends on pleasure, what motivates us to sympathise with suffering and to feel for the victims of tragedy and misfortune? In cases like that, what can possibly be the source of the pleasurable gain for the spectator? And, perhaps more importantly, what makes it possible for sympathy to operate in two seemingly opposite directions, namely, for the rich and the great on one hand, and for those in great misfortune on the other?

In *The Theory of Moral Sentiments*, the answer, I believe, lies in the nature of the pleasurable gain. Here the identification with the other is part of a broader aesthetic desire for order, system and the levelling of inequalities and differences of feeling. The key to the controversial operation of Smith's notion of sympathy lies not simply in its dependence on pleasure, but in the way pleasure is bound up with the aesthetic. Throughout his works Smith often argues that the production of systems and machines, and a pursuit of order as opposed to chaos and disorder are motivated by feelings of pleasure. In his *History of Astronomy* Smith contends that the mind takes pleasure in observing and discovering resemblances between objects. We find order more agreeable than chaos, hence our philosophical investigations into the connecting principles and invisible chains that bind together disjointed natural objects. In his *Essays on Philosophical Subjects* Smith writes that the creation of machines and systems in the history of science and philosophy is the product of noticing a defect in the system, which will urge scientists driven by a desire for perfection to improve it and discover new and better systems.[54] In Smith's view, we are fascinated by balance and structure, towards which humans strive constantly. Like the systems and machines in his *Essays on Philosophical Subjects*, sympathy, sensibility and morality in *The Theory of Moral Sentiments* are aesthetically motivated creations that satisfy our need for order and balance. As it is described in *The Theory of Moral Sentiments*, our admiration for the rich often derives from a similar desire for a perfect system: 'We are eager to assist them in completing a system of happiness that approaches so near to perfection; and we desire to serve them for their own sake, without any other recompense but the vanity or the honour of obliging them' (*TMS* 64). In this way, sympathy creates its own vicious circle: we are constantly trying to come up to the requirements of a system of sympathy, which, in this way, will emerge as the founder of social differences and inequalities which themselves call for the operation of sympathy to alleviate the suffering that arises from them.

The fact that sympathy is embedded in the realm of the aesthetic has important consequences for its operation. Scholarship, especially the work of David Marshall and John Bender, has emphasised the spectatorial element in Smith's sympathy. In *The Figure of Theater*, Marshall analyses the element of viewing, spectatorship and fictionality built into the structure of Smith's sympathy. He argues that Smith's concept of sympathy addresses the theatricality of the way people faced each other in the world. In *The Theory of Moral Sentiments*, every act of sympathy is also a scene of reading – no matter if the object is a real or a fictional scene.[55] In Smith's theory, understanding real life suffering is made possible by what Smith's mentor, Lord Kames, would call 'ideal presence' in his *Elements of Criticism* (1762). The term denotes a state that resembles a reverie, an unreflected 'waking dream', 'a fiction of the imagination' through which the reader is 'transported as by magic into the very place and time of the important action, and [is] converted, as it were, into a spectator, beholding every thing that passes'. It is the same state of mind – an imaginary, ideal presence – through which we are capable of sympathising with real-life suffering as well as enjoying a tragedy, a historical narrative or a work of fiction. Similarly in Smith, both aesthetic enjoyment and sympathetic response to everyday situations are based on processes of imaginary identification.[56]

But in order to understand the curious, Janus-faced operation of Smith's sympathy, one needs to focus on a somewhat neglected aspect of the scene of sympathy. The important point underlying the ambivalence of sympathy, I would like to argue, is not the spectatorial aspect as such, but the element of narrating or imagining a story within this framework of spectatorship. Smith claims that our sympathy is always imperfect until we are informed of the cause of misfortune. The expression of emotion (lamentations or the signs of joy) awakens our curiosity, and tempts us to initiate a conversation with the other and to ask them to tell their story. 'The first question we ask is, What has befallen you? Till this be answered, though we are uneasy both from the vague idea of his misfortune, and still more from torturing ourselves with conjectures about what it may be, yet our fellow-feeling is not very considerable' (*TMS* 14–15). It is through the knowledge of the story, that is, when the other's emotion becomes manifest in a told or imagined narrative – either in language or as a coherent sequence of mental images – that a sympathetic emotional response can come about. In other words, the act of imaginary identification presupposes the act of hearing, reading – or, in the absence of these, imagining – a story. This accounts for the therapeutic nature of sympathy, and, to some extent, for the sense of pleasure one gains from scenes of benevolence. The pleasurable aspect of Smithian sympathy, I believe, relies on bringing affect into the field of representation, which brings about not only the pleasure of the spectator, but also a healing consolation for the sufferer.

But the story of the other is not always accessible, and often it does not even exist. The creative act of imaginary storytelling can lead to certain limit-cases, where our fellow-feeling has indeed no legitimate source in the other, making sympathy operate even when it should not. In *The Theory of Moral Sentiments* these extreme cases of sympathy include feeling a passion for someone that the other cannot or does not feel. One can blush for the rudeness and imprudence of someone who has no sense of the impropriety of his behaviour, or one can also sympathise with the mad who are often insensible of their own misery. The compassion, in these cases, arises from an impossible situation created from the point of view of a split subject, who is at once spectator and object of viewing: it derives 'altogether from the consideration of what he [the spectator] himself would feel if he was reduced to the same unhappy situation, and, what perhaps is impossible, was at the same time able to regard it with his present reason and judgement' (*TMS* 15). These cases show that sympathy, where based on imaginary identification, can be wholly centred on the self, calling into question the possibility of recognising the other and distinguishing their feelings from ours in any scene of sympathy. The sympathy of the mother who is distressed at the illness of her baby gives voice and shape to an affect that the infant cannot verbalise. The mother joins to the baby's 'real helplessness' 'her own consciousness' of that helplessness and 'her own terrors for the consequences' of the disorder, 'and out of all these, forms [...] the most complete image of misery and distress' (*TMS* 15). Thus, through her sympathy, the mother will express in the conscious, symbolic realm the affect that in the other belongs to the field of the unsymbolisable and inexpressible. The mother constructs a story around the baby's suffering, and fills it with her own emotions. Her sympathy is a way of symbolising, imaging and giving consciousness to someone else's feelings. What constitutes the intensity of the mother's affect is this conscious symbolisation and imaging, which, in its turn, will bring about subsequent thoughts and feelings, such as fear and anxiety about the baby's future. Interestingly, however, Smith's own discourse repeats the imaginary act he describes, where the 'real' helplessness of the infant is treated as less significant, and almost completely emptied out. Smith trivialises the infant's feelings when he notes with a curious lack of sympathy that the infant 'feels only the uneasiness of the present instant, which can never be great' (*TMS* 15).

Yet another such limit-case is our sympathy with the dead, where all feeling attributed to the other is entirely the result of a fictional narrative woven around an affect. In Smith's view, the idea that death is a fearful, melancholy condition results from imaginary processes:

The idea of that dreary and endless melancholy, which the fancy naturally ascribes to their condition, arises altogether from our joining to the change which has been produced upon them, our own consciousness of that change, from our putting ourselves in their situation, and from our lodging, if I may be allowed to say so, our own living souls in their inanimated bodies, and thence conceiving what would be our emotions in this case. It is from this very illusion of the imagination, that the foresight of our own dissolution is so terrible to us, and that the idea of those circumstances, which undoubtedly can give us no pain when we are dead, makes us miserable while we are alive. (*TMS* 16)

In an act of identification we exchange roles with the dead: we become the dead who, paradoxically, mourn the loss of the living. Through our fellow-feeling we slip into the other's dead body and animate it: 'we put ourselves in his situation, as we enter, as it were, into his body, and in our imaginations, in some measure, animate anew the deformed and mangled carcass of the slain' (*TMS* 83). Our conception of death and all our negative emotions and thoughts related to it are due to this exchange of roles. It is not we who lost the dead person, but the dead who have lost our company. It is not we who feel resentment towards the murderer, but the corpse who claims revenge (*TMS* 83). Out of this relationship with the dead a fictional world of horrors is created where ghosts 'rise from their graves to demand vengeance upon those who brought them to an untimely end' (*TMS* 83). As with the infant and the mother, Smith distinguishes between what he calls the real experience of feeling that belongs to the object of sympathy, and the feelings of the spectator. The sympathetic spectator imagines that it is miserable to be deprived of the sun and the company of people, to be laid in the cold earth, and be obliterated from the affections and memory of friends and relations. Smith insists, however, that the spectator overlooks the 'real importance' in the situation of the dead, which is 'that awful futurity which awaits them', as well as 'the happiness of the dead' and the 'profound security of their repose' (*TMS* 16). While assuming that we as spectators create the dead as melancholy through lending them our feelings and consciousness in an act of identification, Smith claims to recognise the 'real' condition of the dead, which is not void of affect either, but charged with feelings of happiness and security. Like the reading that assumes the dead as melancholy, this interpretation also stays within the framework of sympathetic imagination.

Finally, if sympathy can be theorised in terms of imaginary identification, the most obvious limit to our fellow-feeling will turn out to be the intensity of our own feelings. According to Smith, our ability to sympathise with the other comes from measuring the other person's feelings against what we would feel or know in his or her case: 'I judge of your sight by my sight, of your ear by my ear, of your reason by my reason, of your resentment by my resentment, of your love by my love' (*TMS* 23). If we find that the other's emotions do not match what we would feel in the same situation, we consider the other person's feeling disproportionate, and experience the displeasure of not being able to sympathise with them. We are shocked at the other's excessive grief, and consider the manifestation of their emotion as a form of weakness or folly and their feelings unjust and improper (*TMS* 19–21). As Smith's sympathy has an originally solipsistic structure, it gives no opportunity for the true recognition of the difference and validity of another person's feelings. The other is acknowledged in so far as he or she matches up to the self. What governs our moral actions is not the regard for an external other, but that other drawn into the very core of the self – something Smith calls the 'man within the breast' or an 'impartial spectator'. Philanthropy, when other-directed, is always, from the beginning, self-centred: 'It is not the love of our neighbour, it is not the love of mankind, which upon many occasions prompts us to the practice of those divine virtues. It is a stronger love, a more powerful affection, which generally takes place upon such occasions; the love of what is honourable and noble, of the grandeur, and dignity, and superiority of our own characters' (*TMS* 158).

The limit-cases of Smith's theory of sympathy, and his attempt to separate the feelings of the spectator from those of the object of sympathy, point to the questions and contradictions sympathy and sensibility have to face later on in the period: How do we account for the failures of sympathy? Would the recognition of the other *as other* be the exact point where sympathy breaks down? Smith's moments of trivialising the baby's pain as well as imagining the dead as happy and secure draw attention to a curious lack of sympathy built into the very construction of sympathy. For Smith, it is the prerequisite for sympathy that we are not able to recognise and understand the affects of the other, and therefore we lend our own feelings, consciousness or soul to the objects of our fellow-feeling. Sympathy, as Smith imagines it, derives from a lack of immediate experience of what others feel, and an inability to form an idea of it (*TMS* 11). In order to sympathise, we empty out the other's emotions and fill the empty space with our own narratives and feelings. In fact, it is exactly because sympathy is constructed in the context of fiction, narrative and the aesthetic that selfishness, cruelty and the lack of sympathy can enter into its very foundations. However, it is not only the possibility of indifference, cruelty and misrepresentation of the other's feelings that such a construction of sympathy is responsible for. A similarly extreme case of sympathy allows us to step beyond the boundaries of everyday reality and enter into the emotions produced in works of fiction. Accordingly, we feel joy for the happiness of literary heroes, and feel grief for their distress. We enter into the gratitude of their friends, and feel resentment against their enemies (*TMS* 13). Thus sympathy makes the pleasure of reading possible in a way that transforms the reader or spectator into a participant in a fictional world. As we animate the dead, so we turn away from the pain of the other, adore the rich and the powerful, or make real – and identify with – the characters of fiction.

Sympathy's legacies: empathy, transference, psychoanalysis

But the history of sympathy does not end here. The interrelatedness of sympathy and the imagination became a growing philosophical tenet in the eighteenth century, and ideas of sympathetic identification circulated widely in British literature and thought well into the Romantic period.[57] However, the legacy of sympathy is manifold, leading our enquiry away from its early magical and philosophical conceptualisations on to psychoanalysis and contemporary social psychology, ethics and neuropsychology. The connections are particularly strong between eighteenth-century notions of sympathy and both traditional and less traditional forms of healing, especially in so far as the relationship between patient and therapist is concerned. From the nineteenth century to the present, occult, magnetic-mechanistic conceptualisations of affective transfer have lived on alongside notions of the emotional bond and identification. In this respect, the history of sympathy is closely interrelated with the history of psychiatry and psychoanalysis, creating a framework in which the age of sensibility and that of Freud and his successors are theoretically and historically linked.

Several historians of science, medicine and psychiatry have researched the relationship between psychoanalysis and eighteenth- and nineteenth-century magnetic and suggestive forms of treatment. Henri F. Ellenberger claims that there is an uninterrupted continuity between early forms of healing, magnetism, hypnotism, and the modern dynamic schools of psychoanalysis and psychiatry.[58] However, it has been argued that the affective aspects of the therapist–patient relationship were greatly underestimated throughout the nineteenth century and only came to the foreground with Freud's discovery of the transference around 1891–2. Before this time the patient–therapist relationship was understood in non-affective terms, mainly as magnetic, mechanical or suggestive.[59] Animal magnetism, as practised by Franz Anton Mesmer between 1778 and 1784, postulated the operation of a magnetic fluid between the magnetist and his patient. It was, as Mesmer claimed, an application of Newtonian philosophy to the purposes of healing. The therapist's aim was to restore the balance of this fluid in the patient, who allegedly experienced magnetic convulsions and 'crises', which were thought eventually to bring about a cure. According to Alison Winter, mesmerism and similar phenomena are part of the history of agreement and of the sympathetic bonding power that united a population. Winter shows that the history of mesmerism in Britain – like that of sympathy – is a social and political issue in that it is intertwined with questions of leadership, charisma, influence and authority. Mesmerism and its associated practices could become tools for modelling the nature of human interaction and social power, featuring striking instances of human automatism and manipulation.[60] Chertok and de Saussure, tracing continuities throughout the long nineteenth century regarding the relationship between therapist and patient, argue that more complex, innovative forms of magnetic treatment were practised by Mesmer's disciples until the mid-nineteenth century, after which the term 'animal magnetism' came to be abandoned in favour of 'hypnotism'. Hypnotism was instituted by some practitioners as a relationship of sympathy, but a purely mental one. James Braid, a British hypnotist-turned-surgeon, claimed that the phenomena previously attributed to magnetic forces took place entirely in the subject's brain. Hypnotism in his theory is the patient's strong sympathetic capacity. Patients, he claimed, have a remarkable tendency to sympathise and imitate, which leads them to observe and copy the therapist's gestures. Hippolyte Bernheim and the Nancy School understood hypnotism as a form of suggestion. Jean-Martin Charcot and his school, on the other hand – whose famous lectures Sigmund Freud also attended at the Salpêtrière in Paris – saw hypnotism as a form of somatic excitability induced by the application of metals and magnets. Metals and magnets were thought to be able to affect the nervous system, and even to transfer neuropathic states and symptoms from one patient onto another, thus – somewhat like the seventeenth-century powder of sympathy – bringing about their curative effect from a distance.[61]

Psychoanalytic theory and practice makes extensive use of all those notions of emotional, intersubjective transfer – including the idea of magnetic-mechanistic transfusion of feeling, the emotional bond, and affective identification – that came under the umbrella term 'sympathy' during the long eighteenth century. The psychoanalytic concepts of identification, transference and counter-transference developed by Freud and his successors are by no means identical with seventeenth- and eighteenth-century notions of sympathy, but they all denote various intersubjective processes that are arguably continuous with earlier conceptualisations of sympathy. Magical, mechanical ideas of emotional transfer are tackled mainly in Freud's essays regarding occultism and thought-transference. Freud speculates that potentially mechanistic processes may be found behind ostensibly magical ways of transferring emotions and thoughts from one person to another. In his lecture on 'Dreams and Occultism' (1933), he discusses spontaneous, non-verbal forms of communication such as telepathy and thought-transference. Telepathy is the process when 'an event which occurs at a particular time comes at about the same moment to the consciousness of someone distant in space, without the paths of communication that are familiar to us coming into question'. According to Freud, there is, primarily, an emotional connection, or some form of emotional investment, between those people between whom this form of communication can take place. The other example Freud brings up is thought-transference, where the 'mental processes of one person – ideas, emotional states, conative impulses – can be transferred to another person through empty space without employing the familiar methods of communication by means of words and signs'.[62] Freud suspects that there might be a scientific explanation to how this transfer happens, comparing the operation of these mechanisms to that of wireless telegraphy and the telephone receiver. What lies between two people's mental acts 'may easily be a physical process into which the mental one is transformed at one end and which is transformed back once more into the same mental one at the other end'.[63]

Freud proposes that – as we have seen with early notions of sympathy – the interpersonal transference of thought and emotion can allegedly be explained by mechanical processes. Moreover, he also speculates that such non-verbal forms of transmission are an original, archaic method of communication that, in the course of phylogenetic evolution, have been replaced by the better method of signals and signs that can be picked up by the sense organs. But the older method, Freud avers, 'might have persisted in the background and still be able to put itself into effect under certain conditions – for instance, in passionately excited mobs'.[64] But the idea of mechanical communication also surfaces in relation to the way psychoanalytic technique itself operates. When addressing the question of occult phenomena, Freud admits that 'analysts are at bottom incorrigible mechanists and materialists', who expect 'finally to exclude the wishes of mankind from material reality'.[65] Accordingly, in 'Recommendations to Physicians Practising Psycho-Analysis' (1912), the work of the analyst is seen as a technical process deprived even of sympathy and modelled on the mechanism of the telephone receiver. The analyst, writes Freud, should be like the surgeon, 'who puts aside all his feelings, even his human sympathy, and concentrates his mental forces on the single aim of performing the operation as skilfully as possible'. In the analytic process, the receptive unconscious of the analyst has to be turned towards the 'transmitting unconscious' of the patient. 'Just as the receiver converts back into sound waves the electric oscillations in the telephone line which were set up by sound waves, so the doctor's unconscious is able [...] to reconstruct that unconscious, which has determined the patient's free associations.'[66]

The idea of the social bond as developed by Scottish Enlightenment philosophy has its place in social psychology as well as in the theory and practice of psychoanalysis. The social psychologists Gustave Le Bon (*Psychologie des foules*, 1895) and William McDougall, who was heavily influenced by Le Bon (*The Group Mind*, 1920), aim to account for the processes that characterise group formation and group mentality. In Le Bon's and McDougall's accounts one will come across the same processes and feelings that Shaftesbury and Hume had also pointed out earlier in the eighteenth century. One important difference is the emphasis, in the modern accounts, on the way in which individual suggestibility and the quick transfusion of emotion in the crowd serve the purposes of an influential leader. In a group, they write, every sentiment and act is contagious; as a result of the magnetic influence of the group, a near-hypnotic state takes over the individual who thus becomes particularly suggestible. For Le Bon, the individual forming part of a group becomes an 'automaton' who impetuously acts upon his ideas and feelings and tends to be more easily overtaken by spontaneity, violence and enthusiasm.[67] In McDougall's account, like in Hume, emotions in the crowd are sympathetically reverberated and intensified. Individuals are carried away by the common impulse due to the operation of an instinctual, primitive sympathetic response. This is a form of contagion, where the perception of an affective state automatically arouses the same affect in the person who perceives it. The individual who thus loses his power of criticism increases the excitement in other people, and in this way, the affective charge becomes intensified by mutual interaction. In groups like this the mental activity of the individual is less free; the sense of moral responsibility and individual intelligence are lower, and, in consequence, the group as a whole becomes more fickle, emotional, impulsive and violent.[68] Thus, in the accounts of Le Bon and McDougall sympathy is a politically charged phenomenon, and it explains the violent tendencies brought to the surface by strong, contagious and ambivalent feelings that spread uncontrollably among group members.

Similarly to Adam Smith, however, Freud also finds processes of identification beyond cases of apparent mechanistic contagion. In *Group Psychology*, he argues that emotional ties, rather than magical processes, constitute the essence of the group mind. Freud identifies two kinds of emotional bonding: identification, which takes place between members of the group, and object-relation, which manifests itself in the love and admiration felt for the group leader. Identification is the earliest expression of an emotional tie with another person. It is the basis of the ethical aspect of psychic life – of our ability to feel sympathy or empathy – as in later life we limit our aggression towards those whom we can identify with. Identification is linked with the Oedipal phase of infantile development: before the Oedipus complex, the little boy takes a special interest in the father: he wants to be like him, and take his place. The father, so to say, becomes his ideal. Later, with the onset of the Oedipus complex and the development of the boy's erotic feelings towards his mother, his identification with the father becomes hostile. A desire to be the father will be exchanged for a desire to replace him. Thus, Freud claims, identification is ambivalent from the start: it can be an expression of tenderness, but also a wish for someone's removal. It behaves like a derivative of the oral phase, in which the object we long for is cannibalistically assimilated by eating and it is thus also annihilated at the same time. While working with hysterics, Freud discovered that deep, unconscious psychological processes of identification operate behind what looks like imitative forms of behaviour or an ostensible 'catching' of certain emotions and symptoms. He found, for instance, that a hysteric girl's developing the same tormenting cough as her mother signified her unconscious wish to replace her. He also observed that a group of girls 'caught' the same fit of hysteria as a repressed form of jealousy when one of them received a secret love letter.[69]

Thus, the inherent ambivalence of the mechanism of identification explains for Freud the darker side of group psychology, that is, the co-presence of contradictory emotions and the tendency for violence in groups held together by the bonds of love. Moreover, it is also emphasised by psychoanalysts that identification, as in the theory of Adam

Smith, can sometimes be based on egotistic, self-centred processes and motives. The psychoanalyst Sándor Ferenczi claims that the excessive love, hate and sympathy characteristic of neurotics are transferences by means of which long-forgotten psychic experiences and affects are reactivated. The impressionability and capacity of neurotics to feel intensely for others and their philanthropic and magnanimous deeds are only reactions to these unconscious instigations and are thus egotistic actions.[70] Ferenczi talks about a type of identification called introjection, which comprises our various ways of relating emotionally to other people. In the process of introjection – including all kinds of normal or pathological object love – we take into the self a large part of the outer world, thus widening and extending our ego to what is outside. 'In principle,' writes Ferenczi, 'man can love only himself; if he loves an object he takes it into his ego.'[71] As in Adam Smith's theory, entering into the other's emotions always means bringing parts of the other back into an extended, magnified self. But identification and the social bond also have an important ethical, civilising role. Freud argues that individuals show undisguised antipathies and aversions towards strangers, which intolerance vanishes, at least temporarily, within a group. Group formation is based on love, and love is capable of turning egoism into altruism.[72] Initially, writes Freud, the individual members of the group cherish feelings of love for the group leader, but they also harbour hostile, envious feelings towards the other members whose affectionate impulses are all directed to one and the same person. When each individual understands that they cannot be the chosen object of the leader, they demand that none of them should be. Following from this demand for equality, their hostile feelings are subsequently turned into a positive tie by means of identification that takes place among group members. Thus, social feeling is a result of turning around a hostile relationship into a positive one by means of identification. The identification that takes place between members of the group, together with love for the group leader (described by Freud as the taking of the figure of the leader into the self to replace the ego-ideal), constitute the dynamic that guarantees the formation and cohesion of groups.

As we shall see in Chapters 3 and 5 of this study, the ambivalence inherent in identification will have important implications not only for group mentality but also for the individual psyche in its intersubjective relations. Identification becomes a seminal factor during the process of mourning and the feeling of melancholia, which are also key affective processes within the discourse of sensibility. But it can also play an active role in the psychoanalytic setting, in the processes of transference and counter-transference. Transference and counter-transference arguably constitute a most important legacy within the field of psychoanalysis of the eighteenth-century interpersonal bonds theorised via the notion of sympathy. Transferences are displaced affects, thoughts and fantasies carried over into the analytic setting from the patient's previous relationships, including the relationship with the patient's earliest, parental objects. Often the transference manifests itself in feelings of intense emotion – such as love, hate, anger or anxiety – towards the analyst, which are mostly misplaced and undeserved. Transferences are thus a new edition of old feelings and other psychic experiences revived in new circumstances, which tend to re-awaken feelings originally directed to their first objects. They are not restricted to the analytic setting, however, but operate in our everyday lives, colouring all interpersonal relationships.[73]

The notion of counter-transference, on the other hand, refers to those feelings and impulses that arise in the analyst towards the patient during the analytic process. In a more restricted sense it denotes the analyst's unconscious responses to the patient's own transference. Hanna Segal emphasises that the counter-transference of the analyst is very different from the patient's transference in that the analyst, while opening his mind towards the patient, has to maintain a distance from his own feelings and impressions, and to observe his own reactions and use them for understanding the patient's experience but at no point be swayed by his own emotions.[74] Freud first identified transference as a form of resistance that stands in the way of analytic progress; however, he later found that transference can be put to positive use, as it actualises the past in symbolic form so it can be replayed and worked through to a different, more positive outcome. Similarly, counter-transference was originally considered to be a disturbance in analysis, preventing the analyst from getting an objective view of the patient, but now it is increasingly recognised as an important tool for understanding the analysand. In both transference and counter-transference, processes of identification play a crucial role; the mechanisms of projection, introjection and projective identification are important factors within the analytic setting.[75] According to Heinrich Racker, the analyst's counter-transference comprises a set of identifications, which determine the way in which the analyst is able to understand the patient's transference. This set of identifications that takes place between the analyst and the patient in the counter-transference is what Racker calls empathy.[76] For Hanna Segal, empathy in the counter-transference is a form of 'psychoanalytic intuition' or 'feeling in touch'. This implies a double relation to the patient. 'One is receptive, containing and understanding the patient's communication; the other active, producing or giving understanding, knowledge, or structure to the patient in the interpretation [...] In other words, we are deeply affected and involved but, paradoxically, uninvolved in a way unimaginable between an actual good parent and a child.'[77]

But empathy itself is not first and foremost a psychoanalytic concept. From the late nineteenth century to the present, sympathy and its closest cognate, empathy, have become important and controversial terms in diverse cultural fields. The term 'empathy' (from the Greek 'empatheia') was coined by Edward Titchener (*A Beginner's Psychology*, 1915). In Titchener's work, empathy meant 'feeling oneself into'. The term itself was as a translation of the German aesthetic concept, *Einfühlung*, which was used first by Theodor Vischer in 1846 and then by Violet Paget, and subsequently by Theodor Lipps (*Aesthetik*, 1903) to explain the process of grasping the meaning of a work of art by means of projection and identification. It was also Lipps who developed empathy extensively as a psychological concept, which has since become an object of study within the domains of philosophy, empirical psychology, sociology and psychoanalysis. In *Group Psychology* Freud touched upon the question of empathy during his discussion of identification, claiming that empathy 'plays the largest part in our understanding of what is inherently foreign to our ego in other people'.[78] In the field of psychoanalysis, empathy emerged as a matter of technique for the analyst – an alternative to gaining insight through evenly suspended attention or the interpretation of the patient's free associations. According to Ferenczi, the technique of empathetic listening could be useful, especially in the case of more severely disturbed patients. The importance of empathy was reconsidered in the latter half of the twentieth century within the field of psychoanalysis and by the proponents of Self Psychology, including the work of Heinz Kohut and his successors. For Kohut, empathy is a value-free stance adopted by the analyst towards the patient, which also engenders a powerful emotional bond within the therapeutic dyad. It is an affective in-tuneness as well as a cognitive information gathering and processing, which makes the core of the self more easily accessible than interpretative confrontation.[79] Thus, outside of aesthetics, empathy began to mean an inquiry into the consciousness and the psychic reality of another person, and, in the fields of sociology and anthropology, the process of gaining access to areas that are psychologically or culturally distant from the observer's standpoint.[80]

The affinities between sympathy and empathy have been subject to debate in twentieth-century psychology, and while some (Lauren

Wispé, Robert Katz) sought to establish the differences, others (Deutsch and Madle) emphasised the difficulty of distinguishing between the two. Perhaps what is more important for our purposes than a clear definition of these concepts is the way in which they raise problems that are continuous with sympathy's eighteenth-century conceptualisations and the way in which they have affinities with the eighteenth-century debate on the innate egotism or altruism of human nature. The twentieth-century debate in the field of psychology revisits many questions that are similar to the points raised in the eighteenth-century accounts, including the extent to which the self loses itself in its fusion with the other or preserves its autonomy; the question whether the focus in sympathy and empathy is on the self or on the other; whether sympathy and empathy are acts of communication or acts of understanding; and whether sympathy and empathy are predominantly emotional or intellectual responses. In his survey of this debate, Thomas J. McCarthy concludes that both sympathy and empathy are forms of psychic participation. 'For the time being', he writes, 'the basic distinction is that empathy is the comprehensive understanding of another's experience, and sympathy is the feelingful response to that achieved understanding. Yet this will be seen to be clearly inadequate, because empathy is also an emotional phenomenon, just as sympathy is also an intellectual one.'[81] McCarthy observes that in most psychological accounts of sympathy and empathy, the role of the self proved more focal than the role of the object. As the psychologist Martin Hoffman puts it, 'empathy may be uniquely suited for bridging the gap between egoism and altruism, since it has the property of transforming another person's misfortune into one's own feeling of distress. Empathy thus has elements of both egoism and altruism.'[82]

Recent work in social psychology and neuropsychology has offered new evidence that relates to the issues raised by the three-century-old debate on the sources of other-regarding impulses and behaviour. Today the questions of whether helping behaviour is selfish or not and whether it is a matter of feeling or thought receive much scientific attention. In *Empathy: A Social Psychological Approach* Mark H. Davis claims that the dominant view in psychology used to postulate that all helping behaviour is egotistic, that is, that all altruistic acts ultimately result from a desire to increase the welfare of the helper rather than the victim. Thus, altruistic acts were thought to be carried out to gain or to avoid internally administered rewards such as feelings of pride and sanctions such as feelings of guilt or shame. Davis also claims, however, that recent research by C. Daniel Batson has provided a strong foundation for the position that at least some forms of altruistic helping are the result of a genuinely non-selfish motive to aid another in need. This 'true altruism' is solely intended to benefit the target and is not egotistic in its motive; in this case, the helping act is not carried out in order to avoid feelings of guilt or in expectation of pleasurable feelings of reward. Batson's contention is that the emotional response of empathy is the source of a truly altruistic motivation.[83]

Empathy is a subject of interest today within the social neurosciences too. It has been shown that when we see someone else in pain this activates the same brain areas as when we experience pain ourselves. According to Chris Frith, what we can share in empathy is the mental experience of pain, not its physical aspect. When we see someone else in pain the areas of our brain that become active are those that are activated with the mental experience of pain – for instance, areas that work when we anticipate the pain that the touching of a hot object would give us. Moreover, it has been shown that people who are more empathic show greater brain activation when they see another in pain. Recent research in neuropsychology has also confirmed the existence of our desire for so-called 'altruistic punishment'. This means that our empathetic responses to other people are dependent on the ethical judgements we make regarding their behaviour. Singer et al. conducted an experiment in which they engaged volunteers in a game, in which two confederates sometimes played unfairly. When the game finished, the volunteers were made to observe the confederates receiving pain, during which time the brain activity of the same group of volunteers was measured with functional magnetic resonance imaging. The scientists found that the participants exhibited empathy-related activation in pain-related brain areas towards fair players. However, the empathetic responses were significantly reduced when observing an unfair person receiving pain; moreover, there was also an increased activation in brain areas that correlated with an expressed desire for revenge. Thus, Singer et al. conclude that empathic responses are influenced by other people's social behaviour: we tend to empathise with fair opponents while desiring the physical punishment of unfair players.[84]

In the light of psychoanalysis and psychology the question repeatedly arises of what exactly the flip side of sympathy is. In 1961, Stanley Milgram conducted a famous psychological experiment in order to understand the causes that can compel ordinary human beings to commit acts of cruelty as demonstrated by the Holocaust. During the experiment, the subjects are told that they are taking part in a study on the effect of punishment on learning and memory. The subjects take the role of teachers, and are made to believe that they are delivering electric shocks to a learner, who is actually a confederate of Milgram's. The subject is made to believe that the learner receives the shocks when he fails to memorise word pairs. The shocks are administered from a shock generator that runs from 15 to 450 volts. The higher levels are labelled as 'strong shock', 'very strong shock', 'intense shock', 'extremely intense shock', 'danger: severe shock' and 'XXX'. Each teacher gets a sample shock of 45 volts, in order to demonstrate that the pain he or she is to inflict on the learner is genuine. The learner is strapped into his chair, with electrodes attached to his wrist. The teacher can hear the learner grunt, scream, kick, cry to be let out, complain of chest pain (the teachers are told before the experiment that the learner has a 'weak heart'), and finally fall silent as the voltage increases. The teachers do not appear to enjoy the experiment either. They protest; some jump out of their chairs and threaten to walk out; most subjects, however, stay on and proceed with the experiment. In fact, over 62 per cent of the subjects continue switching the buttons all the way up to the maximum level of 450 volts.[85]

Milgram concludes that the experiment displays the human potential for slavish obedience. The subjects did not really want to continue with the experiment: yet they did go all the way. Their actions were the result of their vulnerability to social pressure and authority, which are thus able to undermine human empathy. But this conclusion has been questioned in recent philosophical accounts by C. Fred Alford and Arne Johan Vetlesen. In his 1997 book, *What Evil Means to Us*, Alford argues that Milgram's conclusion excludes one very important consideration: the possibility that the subjects actually enjoyed shocking the victim. Looking at the films of the experiment, Alford is struck by the 'grotesque nervous laughter', 'the giggling fits' of the teachers.[86] He posits:

> What if what the teachers really want, what they long for [...] is permission to hurt someone. Permission does not just mean someone's saying, 'Go ahead. It's okay.' The teachers have a conscience; they know it is not. They have to be virtually forced to do it, compelled by authority. But not really. The structure of the Milgram experiment protects them from knowledge of their own sadism, while allowing them to express it. That is what they want, that is what they do, and that is what they get pleasure from – embarrassed pleasure, guilty pleasure, but it is still pleasure [...]. The assumption that normal men might be evil is the hidden variable, the most straightforward and obvious explanation of all, the one that cannot be uttered.[87]

Thus, in Alford's discussion of evil, where evil is seen as the absolute lack of altruism and a deliberate attempt to cause harm to someone else, evil is divorced from its usual philosophical framework of self-interest in which it was often seen previously, and the focus appears to shift to the role of innate sadistic impulses. Alford's Melanie Klein-inspired theory also goes against the grain of mainstream twentieth-century theories, where evil is usually detached from individual agency and is seen as a symptom of social circumstances or as a by-product of the individual's obedience to authority. Instead, Alford directs attention to the social micro-level on which evil takes place most of the time, being a personal and emotionally charged affair. He maintains that there is an intention in human nature to inflict pain and suffering on someone else, relating evil to sadism. Building on Melanie Klein's ideas on envy and projective identification, Alford argues that evil and sadism are motivated by the relief sought in placing one's sense of vulnerability and dread onto another person, so as to be rid of it and be able to control it 'out there', in the other. Evil is tied into the effort of making external what originates inside, in the search of a psychological relief from an existential burden. Using – and simultaneously critiquing – Alford's theory, Vetlesen analyses the act of evildoing in various twentieth-century contexts, including the Holocaust and the war in the former Yugoslavia. According to Vetlesen, evil is often produced where the 'existential psycho-logic' and the 'organisational socio-logic' meet halfway, where individual and system mutually reinforce each other in the pursuit of a common target for persecution and destruction. Thus, his analysis shows that the question of other-regarding feeling and its lack remains, as it was in the eighteenth century, a sociopolitically charged question.[88]

The problem of empathy is especially urgent today when we are increasingly attentive to the ways in which different forms of media, literature and art affect and manipulate our feelings or when we aim to understand human motives that result in individual and collective evildoing, including mass murder and genocide.[89] Thus, when researching sympathy in a broad historical and theoretical framework one will find that the problem of sympathy is not solely an eighteenth-century problem and, throughout its long history, sympathy repeatedly reveals its darker side. Sympathy is, so to say, an 'uncanny' concept. It is, as Freud writes, 'like a buried spring or a dried-up pond. One cannot walk over it without always having the feeling that water might come up there again'.[90] Writings by philosophers, medics, psychologists and psychoanalysts across centuries tend to show that ambivalent emotions and attitudes, as well as certain ego-related and self-centred unconscious processes are ingrained in the operation of other-regarding feelings like sympathy, empathy and pity. They draw attention to the possible dangers that can arise when such concepts and feelings – carrying a repressed and often unacknowledged side – are used to fuel ideologies, movements, revolutions and wars. Approaching the history of these feelings with a critical eye and uncovering the deeper implications of their operation in the past and present will go a long way towards understanding the disillusionment such concepts and feelings as ideological apparatuses seem repeatedly to bring about. It may not be a groundless speculation to state that we are looking at a characteristic of human behaviour that always motivates and remains behind the upheavals of philanthropy and humanitarianism, and that the so-called 'Adam Smith problem' is not only an Adam Smith problem, but an ever-present consequence of the uncanny presence of what is other and what is repressed within the self.

2
The Feeling Machine

Without all doubt, the torments which we may be made
to suffer, are much greater in their effect on the body
and mind, than any pleasures which the most learned
voluptuary could suggest, or than the liveliest imagination, and the most sound and exquisitely sensible body
could enjoy. (Edmund Burke, *A Philosophical Enquiry*)

'King Chaunticlere', the guillotine and the politics of physiology

This chapter will continue to investigate the sympathy question and to
uncover further possible layers of the flip side of sensibility by looking at
affective response in its eighteenth-century medical context. First, let me
begin by a story from the French Revolutionary period, when medical
conceptualisations of the body's response to stimulus strongly shaped
the face of political ideas and aspirations. 'King Chaunticlere; or, The
Fate of Tyranny' appears in the radical publisher Daniel Isaac Eaton's
Politics for the People; or, Hog's Wash (1793) – a weekly journal created by
Eaton with the intention of bringing radical ideas closer to the masses.[1]
The story, according to Eaton, was part of a public speech given by John
Thelwall at the Chapel Court Society, aiming to refute the claim that the
love of life (regardless of the quality of that life) is stronger in us than the
love of liberty. In Eaton's account, Thelwall made his point by referring
to the emphasis placed by contemporary physicians on the importance
of separating involuntary motion from voluntary, willed actions, which
are primarily determined by thought, feeling, or judgement. In order to
demonstrate the strength of the 'love of life', a member of the debating
society cited an anecdote about a black slave, whose hands and feet had

been cut off as a punishment for trying to escape and who is then put into a large frying pan to make him revoke his 'impious love of liberty'. To this Thelwall responded with sad irony:

> In the midst of his torments, we are told, that one of his companions, more compassionate than the rest, rushed towards him, and, aiming a blow with his cudgel, would have dashed out his brains, had not the poor mutilated wretch conceived (such is the curious reasoning that is offered to us by the tame advocates of life without liberty) that the tortures of the frying pan were preferable to instant death, and therefore lifted his poor bleeding stumps, with sudden terror, and broke the force of the blow. Now, if this magnaminious [sic] advocate for the *frying pan of despotism*, had happened to have reflected a little on the physical laws of the animal frame, he would have known that this motion of the arms was merely involuntary, and that neither love, nor fear, nor liberty, nor any other preference of the judgment, had any thing at all to do with it – it being natural to all animals, after they had long been used to perform certain actions in consequence of any particular stimulus [...] to continue those actions, by mere mechanical impulse, whenever the usual objects are presented, without ever reflecting what it is they are doing: just as men of base and abject minds, who have been long used to cringe and tremble at the names of kings and lords, for fear that they should be clapped up in bastiles [sic], or turned out of their shops: continue to cringe and tremble, when neither shops nor bastiles happen to be present to their imaginations.[2]

To make his point clear, Eaton's Thelwall continued to demonstrate 'this difference between mental and muscular action' (103) by an anecdote about a domineering game cock, 'King Chaunticlere' (the figure of tyranny in the narrative), who terrorises the rest of the chickens in the farmyard. Not only did this bird 'drive his subjects' into 'foreign wars and domestic rebellions', but he also snatched at 'every little treasure, that the toil of more industrious birds, might scratch out of the bowels of the earth' (104). While strongly inclined to revere his game cock's decorative feathers and pompous appearance, Thelwall, out of an innate aversion to 'bare faced despotism', finally decided that the best way to protect the peace of his farmyard is to cut the bird's throat and 'rid the world of tyrants'. Wanting to show compassion even when bringing down his tyrannical bird, Thelwall claims that 'if guillotines had been in fashion, I should certainly have guillotined him, being desirous to be merciful even in the stroke of death, and knowing, that the instant the brain is separated from the heart (which, with this instrument is done in a moment,) pain and consciousness is at an end [...]' (105). Yet, after his execution the bird still continued 'the same hostile kind of action, bouncing, and flapping, and spurring, and scuffling about, till the muscular energy (as they call it) is quite exhausted' (105–6). This, argued Thelwall in the story, similarly does not mean that the bird proceeded to bounce and struggle from the conviction that life is worth preserving even after the loss of his head, but that his motions arose from the body's involuntary contractions – something that physiologists around the mid-eighteenth century called irritability.

Thelwall's speech in Eaton's *Hog's Wash* is an intriguing intersection of physiology and politics, which problematises sympathy and compassion while arguing that the pain of torture and execution erases class difference. The bodies of both king and subject, rich and poor, human and animal, are subject to the same mechanical rules of physiology – 'for anatomists can tell you, that arms are only wings without feathers, and wings are nothing but feathered arms' (105). Moreover, the fine bird, stripped of all his 'trappings', was found 'tough and oily' and 'no better than a common tame scratch-dunghill pullet' (105). The nuanced physiological allegory helps Thelwall (and Eaton) put forward the radical political point that freedom for the poor means the same as power and wealth for the rich: something that makes life worth living. Furthermore, the anecdote links muscular irritability directly to politics by claiming that the habitual respect of authority in the face of tyranny is similar to habitual muscular motion. Those who once have been taught to 'cringe and tremble' in front of their superiors continue to do so when no actual threat is 'present to their imaginations'.[3]

The fable, however, appears to be somewhat different in the biographical account given by Thelwall's widow, Boyle C. Thelwall, in *The Life of John Thelwall, by his Widow* (1837). Here the bird's post-mortem contractions are seen as purely mechanical motions rather than the continuation of aggressive, tyrannical habits: 'What was my astonishment and surprise, when I saw this headless King Chanticleer, for some seconds after, attempt to kick and spur in all directions, and even stretch up the stump of his neck, as if making an effort to crow!' Most importantly, however, no direct analogy is drawn between reflex movements and habitual social attitudes. Thelwall's widow claims that Eaton 'dressed up' the story 'in certainly very strong terms, which Thelwall would never have used'.[4] Eaton's rendition of Thelwall's speech fully highlights its possible radical, political implications. As John Barrell points out, Eaton's anecdote implies that the existence of political institutions turns out to depend on how to induce and how to break a conditioned muscular reflex.[5]

But Eaton's version of the fable refers to yet another contemporary scenario where humanitarian impulses and theories of enlightenment physiology intersected with the politics of the period: the guillotine and the mechanics of capital punishment. While originally invented in a philanthropic spirit, the guillotine during the Reign of Terror came to be seen as a controversial instrument of execution which put medical knowledge and compassionate sentimentalism to the service of radical, and violent, politics. The idea of introducing a machine for decapitation in Revolutionary France was born out of a predominantly humanitarian impulse: to replace previous, cruel forms of punishment such as breaking on the wheel or burning at the stake. The old regime in France allowed for class differentiation in its institutions of punishment (nobles were beheaded, whereas commoners were hanged). The guillotine, on the other hand, was designed by Dr Guillotine and Dr Louis as an egalitarian, torture- and relatively pain-free way of capital punishment after the new Penal Code of 1791. In the spirit of the new political system, public torture and the painful, humiliating punishment of hanging were proposed to be replaced by a form of execution that would operate quickly and indiscriminately. To this end, an apparatus was put forward which, according to Dr Louis, 'will not give rise to any feeling and will be hardly discerned at all'. As Philip Smith puts it, the guillotine 'provided a "revolutionary" mode of execution in which the moment of fate dramatized the brisk, rational, precise, clean and humanist spirit of the new France. The technology played a telling counterpoint to the baroque grotesqueries of torture and the primitive dangling corpse'.[6]

But the guillotine and its effects on sensation and feeling were an object of debate amongst physicians and politicians in the 1790s. No matter how philanthropic the intentions behind its adoption, many contemporaries harshly critiqued the actual effects of the machine on its human victims. In contrast to previous methods of execution that put the emphasis on the painful process of dying, the guillotine brought about an immediate transition from life to death, doing away with the victim's protracted ordeal. This, however, raised profound questions about life, consciousness and human subjectivity. Many disputed whether death under the guillotine was instantaneous, and whether one could still detect in the severed head signs of consciousness and feeling. Similarly to Thelwall's fascination with the headless game cock desperately flapping about in the farmyard, the popular imagination remained intrigued by apparent signs of movement and facial expression observable on the dead body. The most well-known stories are those of Charlotte Corday's head allegedly blushing, 'at the indignity' when the executioner's assistant slapped one of its cheeks, or the rumour – often cited by the guillotine's antagonists – that Mary Stuart's head spoke shortly after her execution. Such anecdotes, alongside experiments researching the vestiges of life in the severed head, survived well into the twentieth century – together with the use of the guillotine in France.[7] The crux of the eighteenth-century debate was the question of whether the signs observable in the decapitated head were indexes of sensibility (a capacity that ultimately belongs to the soul) or irritability (mere muscular contractions and the property of the body only). If life, feeling and consciousness were not altogether extinguished by the fatal stroke the humanitarian nature of the new device could rightly be questioned.

In the years after 1794, doctors Soemmering, Oelsner and Sue disputed the claim that the machine could bring about immediate, painless death, arguing for the survival of feeling and a sense of self, for a few seconds, in the guillotined person. Placing the seat of feeling and its apperception in the brain, they argued that 'in the head separated from the body by this form of execution, feeling, personality, and sense of self remain alive for some time, and feel the after-pain that affects the neck'.[8] Not only does this premise cast doubt on the relative humaneness of the machine, but it also presents it as a most horrific and paradoxical device that forces the victims to witness their own execution, when they are already dead. As the surgeon Sue writes, 'What could be more horrible than the perception of one's own execution, followed by the after-thought of one's having been executed?'[9] Those defending the guillotine (including Cabanis, Gastellier, Léveillé and Sédillot) attributed the visible motions and convulsion of the head to the body's mechanical responses to stimulus, which did not involve any awareness or sensibility. Sédillot averred that 'Soemmering [. . .] attributes to the faculty of sensation all that which is only the automatic irritability to which our bodily parts are susceptible, as we know, for a long time after death and while functioning has ceased.'[10] This argument, however, had to be supported by a new theory regarding the seat of consciousness and feeling. If the brain alone is responsible for our sense of self and our capacity to feel then life could indeed survive in the head for some time after decapitation. In this case, the 'head separated from its body hears the noise of the crowd' and 'the severed head feels itself dying in the basket'.[11] Unlike Thomas Willis,

Descartes and the anti-guillotine doctors, Cabanis and the guillotine's defenders did not localise the seat of life in the brain, but argued instead that the vital principle had no specific centre. Consciousness was explained in terms of the coordination of the totality of the parts of the body, connected by the spinal cord. Once this harmony was disrupted, especially by the separation of the brain from the spine, the sense of self was broken and life came to an end. At the moment of decapitation, argues Léveillé, the brain loses its vital energy, and sensation, personality and the sense of self go with it.[12]

The question of whether the mind can think and perceive in the absence of the body, as we shall see in this chapter, was a central area of investigation for many medical writers of the eighteenth century. Some, including the mid-century doctor and materialist philosopher Julien Offray de La Mettrie, were interested in the reverse: whether the materiality of the body needed anything like the mind to think, feel and perceive. During the French Revolution, and especially with the launch of the guillotine, however, the interaction between body and mind came to be seen as a socially and politically charged question. Reluctantly, however, in the anecdote of 'King Chaunticlere' John Thelwall chooses to stand on the pro-guillotine side when executing his allegorical bird. While not a medic by profession, the materialist Thelwall had a vivid interest in the study of physiology. Not only did he attend classes in Guy's Hospital in London, but he also became a member of the Physical Society, where in 1793 he gave a lecture on animal vitality. In this lecture, published in the same year under the title *An Essay Towards a Definition of Animal Vitality*, Thelwall challenged the dominant, vitalist ideas propagated by John Hunter, and claimed that life resulted from material causes and not from any kind of non-material substance superadded to matter. His conviction, according to Eaton's pamphlet, that the instant separation of the head from the body brings an end to consciousness and feeling is in harmony with Thelwall's materialist views. The flapping, bouncing and other convulsive motions observed in the beheaded game cock are mechanical contractions rather than manifestations of consciousness and sensibility.[13] Thus, as the example of the guillotine shows, the interpretation of bodily signs in a living creature's response to painful stimulus had become in the period the uncanny hinge where the humanitarian ideology of sensibility and the violence of the Terror could imperceptibly conflate. The potential humanity or inhumanity of the guillotine, as we have seen, turns on the concepts of sensibility and irritability – concepts which belong to a medical field of enquiry that encompasses the nature of stimulus response, the question of the seat of the soul, and the nature of body–mind connection. In what follows, these notions will be further mapped within the matrix of eighteenth-century British and Continental medical ideas.

This chapter explores contexts in which muscular and nervous responsiveness emerged into central questions for medical, physiological redefinitions of human subjectivity. The material will be a segment of the large-scale eighteenth-century European physiological controversy centred on basic ontological questions – in other words, the 'science of man'. The medical findings that emerged within this debate continued to be influential, and had a lasting impact on the literature and moral philosophy of sensibility in Britain in the latter half of the eighteenth century. It cannot be my ambition here to give an overall historical account of eighteenth-century medical standpoints on the question of body, mind and soul in the period; this has already been outlined by several historians and historians of science, including G.S. Rousseau, John P. Wright and John Yolton. Rather, this chapter will look at medical writing as a textual construct and an important locus for the production of feeling. I shall focus specifically on three participants of the European medical controversy that crystallised broadly around the mind and body question in the mid-eighteenth century. Julien Offray de La Mettrie's *L'Homme machine* (1747), Albrecht von Haller's *A Dissertation on the Sensible and Irritable Parts of Animals* (1752) and Robert Whytt's *Physiological Essays* (1755) will be read closely, with particular attention on the ways in which sympathy, affectivity and their lack surface in their discourse. The chapter will also reflect on how the lack of sympathetic emotional response emerges in medical experimentation as a component of scientific neutrality and empirical professionalism.

Eighteenth-century Europe saw the proliferation of medical experiments enquiring into the existence and substance of the soul and the vital forces of the human and animal body. The question of what makes animate beings live and move and what distinguishes humans from other living creatures intrigued many medical writers during the seventeenth and eighteenth centuries. Major thinkers of the seventeenth century, including William Harvey, Francis Glisson, Georgio Baglivi and Giovanni Borelli, explored the mechanics of animal motion and the workings of the living, muscular machine. Questions of motion and feeling remained central to the work of the most influential and internationally known physician of the first half of the eighteenth century, Herman Boerhaave, whose celebrated medical school at Leiden attracted thousands of students from abroad. On their return to their home countries, many of Boerhaave's disciples became founders of schools themselves. Boerhaave's iatromechanist (or, in other words, medical mechanist) system was founded on the Cartesian dualism of mind and body. The iatromechanist thinkers argued that life is no more than the movement of solid and liquid parts and that the human body, as far as its natural actions are concerned, is nothing more than a complex system of mechanical and chemical movements that obey mathematical rules. The iatromechanist Boerhaave imagined the human body as a complicated hydraulic machine and held that the body's physiological functions were separate from the operation of the soul and could be described and understood in mechanical terms. The soul, therefore, was not considered to be necessary for the fundamental physiological processes of the body, including the vital motions of the heart and blood.[14]

The French medical man and materialist philosopher Julien Offray de La Mettrie, the Swiss physiologist Albrecht von Haller and the Scottish anatomist Robert Whytt were all influenced by Boerhaavian medicine, but their works represent three distinct – yet, in many respects interconnected – physiological standpoints on the question of body, soul, motion and feeling. Both La Mettrie and Haller had studied with Boerhaave at Leiden, but they developed his doctrine in different directions. The materialist La Mettrie, perhaps the most notorious French *philosophe* of the time, questioned the existence of the immaterial, spiritual soul, arguing that matter in itself was capable of thought and feeling. In his 1747 polemic *L'Homme machine*, he famously claimed that 'man is a machine' in the sense that the soul, just like the body, is material. Albrecht von Haller, on the other hand, kept the body and soul strictly separate, identifying two distinct functions allegedly unique to them: irritability and sensibility. Irritability – an instantaneous, contractive reactivity to stimulus – was the property of the muscle tissue, while sensibility – the capacity to feel – was the quality inherent in the nerves and was thus the property of the soul.

Boerhaave's influence reached Britain directly with the foundation of the Edinburgh medical school in 1726, where the four appointed professors had all been the pupils of the influential Dutch physician. Theories of sensibility in enlightenment Scotland owe much to the influence of the Leiden school and its leading figure. But Edinburgh medicine, while based on the Dutch model, gradually moved away from Cartesian dualism in the course of the century, emphasising the importance of the nervous system and sensibility as the bridge between bodily and mental functioning. It was the Edinburgh physiologist

Robert Whytt – appointed as professor of medicine in 1747 – who imported Haller's concept of irritability into Scotland, but in a modified form. Whytt was a vitalist, meaning that he denied the independence of the body from the soul and claimed that the body's life and movements were subject to an immaterial force. He attacked both La Mettrie's materialism and Haller's mechanist standpoint, and claimed that both body and mind were under the influence of what he called the 'sentient principle'. In this respect, sensibility for Whytt had a superior power over the body's irritability.[15]

The idea of stimulation and nervous response remained fundamental principles of life and motion in the work of many prominent medical men during the latter half of the century. William Cullen, John Brown and Erasmus Darwin were all exposed to Whytt's ideas at Edinburgh, but they all departed from his conceptualisation of irritability and sensibility and developed further theories on the vital principle. As Maureen McNeil writes, Whytt's notion of the 'sentient principle' as a mediator between incoming stimuli and outgoing motions paralleled subsequent medical concepts such as Cullen's 'excitement', Brown's 'excitability' and Darwin's 'spirit of animation'.[16] Cullen was Whytt's successor as professor of physiology at Edinburgh, and his physiological ideas dominated the Edinburgh curriculum in the second half of the eighteenth century. Cullen was initially accepting of mechanistic views. Educated at Edinburgh in the 1730s in the doctrines of Boerhaave, he built his theories on a mixture of contemporary ideas, including those of Haller and Whytt. But he concluded that mechanistic laws in isolation could not provide a comprehensive explanation to corporeal operations. Especially in his later works, Cullen considered the nervous system to be the basic motor of life. He thought that there was a primary motive power, a so-called excitement, resident in the nervous system. A normal quantity of excitement within the nervous system was the ideal state, and disease, as well as death, were characterised by a deviation from this norm. Life, therefore, consisted in the excitement of the nerves which, together with the entire body, were intimately connected with the soul.[17]

John Brown, Cullen's student and later opponent, called the body's ability to receive and respond to stimuli 'excitability', which, in his *Elementa Medicinae* (1780), Brown described to be a fundamental and quantitatively measurable feature of the living matter. Brown did not believe in specific, localised treatments; instead, he advocated the use of substances (like alcohol and opium) that would act as stimulants or depressants, restoring the normal level of excitability within the living organism. His medical system – also known as Brunonianism – elicited hostile responses from establishment physicians, including Cullen, Brown's former mentor.[18] During the last decade of the eighteenth century, Brunonianism functioned as an important link between science and politics. On the one hand, through its clash with orthodox medicine, Brunonianism became a channel for a sense of intellectual freedom within the sciences. It provided the basis of a counter-culture by means of which scientists encouraged a public distrust towards established forms of knowledge. This, as Tim Fulford argues, was a potentially radical move because orthodox views were thus unmasked as contributing to an ideology that served the financial and political interests of an already powerful elite. Moreover, Brunonianism became directly associated with political radicalism through the work of Brown's adherents, who included a number of medics, philosophers, poets and political writers such as Thomas Beddoes, Erasmus Darwin, John Thelwall and Samuel Taylor Coleridge. Brown's medical followers espoused materialism and many (Beddoes, Thelwall and Darwin) were active participants of the 1790s radical political scene. In their work, nervous physiology and the body's responsiveness to stimulus had a prominent place. In this way, ideas of mechanism and materialism in medicine and science – including the scientific preoccupation with stimulus response – came to be closely associated with political radicalism in England at the end of the eighteenth century. As Fulford avers, 'the new science was thus radicalism's most important single intellectual expression, the guarantor of its ideals and proof of its effectiveness'.[19]

Thus, irritability, together with its late eighteenth-century cognates, contributes to the (for the period) more troubling aspects of a culture of feeling – troubling in a sense that pertains not only to politics but, as we shall see in Chapter 4, also to sexual politics and psychology. By 'troubling' I refer to those cultural, literary and psychological aspects of eighteenth-century life – from unconscious resistance to open radicalism – which directly or inadvertently challenged established dynamics of power and structures of authority. For this reason, while nerves were undoubtedly central to the culture of sensibility, this chapter will draw attention to those (by cultural historians) often-marginalised medical phenomena that were equally important for the emerging sciences and philosophies of the human subject in the eighteenth century: the materiality of the body and its physical reactivity. Here I will trace the persistence of these issues as they filter into more central medical preoccupations in the course of the eighteenth century. In his recent critique of G.S. Rousseau's views, Hubert Steinke claims that not all enlightenment physiology was nervous, as a great deal of physiological discussion had very little or nothing to do with sensibility. As he writes, mechanistic physiology between Descartes and the mid-eighteenth century was predominantly interested in animal motion. This would change fundamentally in the course of the eighteenth century, and especially in its second half the nerve came to be the prime object of scientific enquiry. While around 1700 life was equated with motion and centred in the heart and muscle as its organs, by the end of the century life was envisaged as sensibility, a quality associated with the nervous system.[20] This chapter will be set within the framework of this shift, which Sergio Moravia calls a change 'from homme machine to homme sensible',[21] and will address the mechanical aspects that, nevertheless, remain structured into the body and soul of the 'sensible' man. In continuity with Chapter 1, this chapter will reflect on how the lack of sympathy is inscribed into eighteenth-century definitions of sensibility based on muscular and emotional reactivity, and how such instances of dysfunction are linked to concerns about defining human consciousness and subjectivity in the period. I will read La Mettrie, Haller and Whytt as seminal and symptomatic figures in the history and transformation of ideas crystallising around concepts of sympathy and sensibility. Mechanical and moral notions of sympathy whose history was explored in the previous chapter will be shown here in interaction and closer operation.

The medical treatises examined in this chapter all problematise the question of bodily or affective response in the context of emerging physiological and philosophical re-definitions of man. For La Mettrie, sympathy, the principle of harmony and attraction, is part of the large-scale operation of a single material substance. As he argues in *L'Homme machine*, what distinguishes human subjectivity from the animal or the object world, or the body from the soul, is nothing but a different organisation of matter. Sympathy is the ever-present principle that connects the parts of the material world, the living and the dead, and the different organs of the body, as well as the body and the soul. To be a machine and to feel, according to La Mettrie, is not a contradiction. However, in an incidental remark, he mentions an instance in human life when sympathy does not operate: it is the daydream when the communication between soul and body ceases. La Mettrie's remark suggests that it is exactly the moment when sympathy breaks down that distinguishes humans from the rest of the animal world. This fissure in the texture of material unity and harmony is an altered state of consciousness, a moment of fantasy and unawareness. It is only at such moments of non-sympathy that we seem to be able to escape the structure of the mechanical universe. Paradoxically, however, the breaking points of La Mettrie's materialist system of sympathy will make his text participate in the moral economy characteristic of the literature and philosophy of sensibility.

Whereas in La Mettrie's work the lack of sympathy is an accidental slip in the machinery of his all-pervasive materialism (a moment when, so to say, his text lets down La Mettrie's own argument), in the case of Haller and Whytt it concerns the morality of medical experimentation. The dispute between the Swiss physiologist and his Edinburgh colleague stages the emergence of sensibility in the framework of the breakdown – or rather the silencing – of sympathy as a form of moral and emotional response. This context will show sensibility to emerge as the morally problematic flip side of enlightenment reason. Here sensibility is a product of violence, and it comes to be defined through torture – dressed as a humanitarian act and performed for the benefit of mankind. As a counterpoint to Haller's experiments, the chapter will also examine the production of the benevolent face of sensibility and its compassionate rhetoric. Focussing on the perspective of the victim, the final section deals with scenes of violence as recorded by a collection of familiar letters published in 1760, during the Seven Years' War. It will aim to open up the all-familiar tropes that, by the mid-century, were characteristic of discourses of sensibility, which tropes contain locked into them stories of suffering and pleas of the brutalised, silenced and objectified other. Here sensibility emerges as the discourse of compassionate emotional response that has the potential to put an end to violence. It is, I will argue, only by taking into account the story of the other that one can understand the possible structure of cruelty behind the ostensibly rational aims of enlightenment scientific definition and categorisation.

Minds, bodies and machines: La Mettrie's *Machine Man*

> ...we are laid asleep
> In body, and become a living soul
> (Wordsworth, 'Tintern Abbey')

La Mettrie's *L'Homme machine* (1747) is one of the many treatises written in the wake of Descartes's proposition that animals, as well as the human body, are machines – an idea that initiated a long series of debates on the body, soul, feeling and human subjectivity that continued in the course of the eighteenth century. The idea of the beast-machine, put forward by Descartes in his *Discourse on the Method* (1637) and later in his *Passions of the Soul* (1650), implies the – for its period – unsettling conclusion that animals, as they do not have souls, lack the capacity to feel pain. It also implies that it is merely the presence of the rational, thinking soul as a spiritual substance that distinguishes humans from animals.[22] The stake of Descartes's idea of animal automatism, as Aram Vartanian argues in *Diderot and Descartes*, is not so much to claim that animals are unfeeling robots deprived of the vital principle or of sensation, but rather to explain their manifestations of life, sensibility and intelligence from solely mechanical causes. What his investigation targets is matter as it is capable of automatism, life and sensibility.[23] The medical doctor and materialist philosopher La Mettrie builds on the seeds of materialism inherent in Descartes's biology when he puts forward his provocative theory in *L'Homme machine*, namely, that the human soul is not essentially different from the material of the body. In Kathleen Wellman's reading of La Mettrie's relation to Cartesianism, La Mettrie manipulates the philosophical tradition against itself, and redefines Cartesian positions in accord with his own refutation of Descartes.[24] It is true that Descartes clearly denies the similarity of the brute soul and the human soul. He claims that the rational soul could not in any way be derived from matter, and that it is totally independent of the body, and therefore unable to die with it. La Mettrie, on the other hand, argues that Descartes implied a possible analogy between beast-machine and man-machine – an idea that was too dangerous to be put explicitly into writing in his time.[25] La Mettrie aims to uncover the implications underlying the Cartesian doctrine relevant to the possible automatism of humans. The absence of this argument in Descartes, according to La Mettrie, is 'a cunning device to make the theologians swallow the poison hidden behind an analogy that strikes everyone and that they alone cannot see'.[26]

For La Mettrie, to address the implications of Descartes's argument in the most provocative way, other factors would also have to play a role. For the context of La Mettrie's materialism, it needs to be considered that major scientific developments and discoveries of the eighteenth century led to the constant formulation and re-definition of the notion of human subjectivity in the medicine and philosophy of the age. In the wake of Descartes's philosophy and in the light of new discoveries, questions of what it means to be human and how to distinguish between human and other forms of organisation remained persistent in contemporary thinking. As Aram Vartanian and Philip Ritterbush claim, one crucial factor pushing forward La Mettrie's materialism was the investigation carried out by Abraham Trembley related to the freshwater hydra – a major scientific discovery of the time that attracted the attention not only of scientists, but also of philosophers and theologians on the continent and across the Channel.[27]

In 1740, Trembley discovered that polyps share the characteristics of both plants and animals. While they move and eat like animals, they can regenerate from their cut-off parts. Apart from surviving being cut into two, they can also reproduce the missing part and turn into a whole animal again. The existence of an animal-plant that, as Vartanian puts it, possessed 'a type of sensibility peculiar to insects when it evidently lacked all the senses and most of the organs proper to animals' fascinated the scientific imagination of its time and seemed to suggest that the sensible animal soul was, after all, sheer matter, and that it was eventually matter itself that possessed sensibility. The idea that the recreation and regeneration of animals was possible without external factors and an omnipotent moving force was a major boost to materialist thinking. Vartanian argues that for contemporary scientists such as Charles Bonnet, as well as Martin Folkes, president of the Royal Society in England, the polyp represented a link between animal and vegetable forms, which seemed to confirm eighteenth-century evolutionist theories and the 'scale of nature' hypothesis advanced by John Locke. Needless to say, the existence of creatures that constituted a link between plants and animals contradicted traditional theological positions that were widely accepted in the period, namely, that the three realms of nature God has established could not encroach on one another, and that reproduction resulted from the coupling of the sexes. It also challenged accepted scientific theories of reproduction that were mainly centred on the role of the egg and sperm.[28]

In the opinion of a contemporary mathematician, Gabriel Cramer, the consequences of Trembley's discovery meant a severe blow to those who defended the animal soul against Descartes's idea of the beast-machine. The animal soul indeed turned out to be what Descartes claimed: material, and divisible together with the body, of which it was merely a function.[29] Thus, the soul could now be seen not simply as an integral part of matter, but as something that self-sufficiently and automatically regenerated itself. Such an idea of self-regeneration encouraged materialistic theories of physiology. If matter re-created, there was no need for a soul constituted of a substance different from matter, or for a prime mover (God) external to the animal body. Obviously, the further dangers of this idea lay in its unavoidably suggesting an analogy to the human soul – an analogy which, despite its scandalous and threatening consequences, was fully pursued and realised by La Mettrie's polemic *L'Homme machine* in 1747. The idea was taken to an even further extreme in his *L'Homme plante* (1748), which drew up a perfect analogy between the human and the vegetable organism and aimed to show the uniformity of all living beings.[30]

Not only did *L'Homme machine* gain La Mettrie the epithet of 'Monsieur Machine' all over Europe;[31] it also earned him a scandalous reputation; even contemporary materialists found its irreligiousness and uncompromising materialism extreme and disagreeable. However, even before the publication of his infamous polemic, the medical doctor La Mettrie was forced into exile for his satires of the medical profession. Trained in Leiden under the most famous teacher of the period, Herman Boerhaave, La Mettrie took his medical vocation seriously, and he was disappointed by the corruption and ignorance of his fellow-medics in Paris. Another factor also contributed to his exile, namely, the scandal caused by his treatise, *Histoire naturelle de l'âme* (1745). This work, published anonymously, expresses scepticism of an immaterial and immortal soul, and investigates its functioning through the workings of the body. Here he also asserts the fundamental point that matter is capable of feeling. This treatise was seized by the police shortly after its publication, and condemned by the *Parlement*, and its author was identified and persecuted. La Mettrie managed to escape and spent the rest of his life in exile. He fled to Holland, but in 1747 the scandal following the publication of *L'Homme machine* put even his life in danger, forcing him to leave the country. Finally he found refuge in the court of Frederick the Great in Potsdam, Prussia, where he stayed until his early death in 1751.

For a long time, La Mettrie was seen by scholarship as a marginal figure of enlightenment medicine and philosophy. Recently, however, his achievement has been reassessed in the field of the history of science, and his importance has also been acknowledged by the neurosciences and in the study of artificial intelligence.[32] According to Katherine Wellman, La Mettrie's legacy was problematic for several reasons. First of all, many enlightenment thinkers, including Condillac, Helvétius, d'Holbach, Diderot and d'Alembert, owed much to La Mettrie's ideas; yet his continuing influence remained unacknowledged. Contemporary *philosophes*, including Diderot, shared many of La Mettrie's radical ideas. Yet, in the interest of the philosophical movement and in the hopes of having their ideas accepted by the academic establishment, they were more cautious in expressing and publishing them. The *philosophes* found La Mettrie's overt radicalism and his attacks on orthodoxy incautious and considered his attempt to associate his ideas with theirs dangerous, making them eager to deny any scholarly debt. Political reasons also contributed to the contemporary detachment from La Mettrie's philosophy. After the attempted regicide by Damiens in 1757, attacks on religion and authority, including the expression of republican ideas associated with the *philosophes*, became punishable by death, thus making the *philosophes* even more wary about voicing directly materialist views. Later, at the end of the eighteenth century, the attack on materialism came to function as part of an anti-revolutionary rhetoric, and, even though many nineteenth-century philosophers assumed positions similar to La Mettrie – and despite the fact that his collected works were re-edited in 1796 – the reluctance to acknowledge him did not grow any weaker.[33]

L'Homme machine was first published in 1747 in Leiden, by Elie Luzac.[34] As with *Histoire naturelle de l'âme*, its author remains anonymous, but adopts a different position. In the latter treatise, written under the pseudonym of Mr Charp, La Mettrie refutes Descartes's doctrine of animal automatism, and maintains a distinction between the animal and vegetative soul. However, by the time of the publication of *L'Homme machine* two years later, La Mettrie had come conclusion that this distinction cannot hold and the existence of a spiritual substance could be questioned. The object of La Mettrie's investigation in *L'Homme machine* is the ontological distinctiveness of humans, the key to which is finding what the human soul is and how it differs from the rest of the material body:

> Man is a machine constructed in such a way that it is impossible first of all to have a clear idea of it and consequently to define it. This is why all the greatest philosophers' *a priori* research, in which they tried, as it were, to use the wings of the mind, have failed. Hence it is only *a posteriori*, or by trying as it were to disentangle the soul from the body's organs, that we can, not necessarily discover with certainty the true nature of man, but reach the greatest possible degree of probability on the subject.[35]

'To disentangle the soul from the body's organs', therefore, is the project of La Mettrie's treatise, which project, as the *philosophe* shows, is not at all as clearly solvable as the Cartesian doctrine would have it. As both Kathleen Wellman and Ann Thomson claim, La Mettrie's aim in the treatise is not really to identify man as a machine, as the title would suggest, but to establish the nature of man by a posteriori, rather than a priori, evidence – by the empirical means of observing visible, bodily manifestations. By identifying human beings as machines La Mettrie does not imply that we are insensitive, unthinking and unfeeling automata. Rather, he shows how all these functions are made possible by the workings and organisation of matter. What La Mettrie asserts very provocatively is that man is no exception to the uniformity of nature, and even the most complicated human functions can be explained physiologically.[36]

La Mettrie describes human parts and functions in terms of a clockwork mechanism. The body is 'a machine which winds itself up' (7), it is 'nothing but a clock whose clockmaker is new chyle' (31).[37] The soul is the main spring, that is, the principle of motion (30), while the brain works like the strings of a violin (14), and possesses muscles for thinking (28). However, the metaphor of the machine serves a larger philosophical aim: it is a tool in the materialist argument that finally establishes that 'man is a machine and that there is in the whole universe only one diversely modified substance' (39). Matter alone, claims La Mettrie, is sufficient to produce all human functions without the necessity of an immaterial, spiritual soul. The thinking and feeling soul does exist, but it is part of matter, and is not organised differently from the body or other material organisations including animals, plants or inanimate things. Therefore, the human body and soul are indistinguishable from the rest of the mechanically constructed universe, and the distinctive feature of humanness cannot lie in a spiritual soul. Consequently, the Cartesian separation of body and soul, feeling and thinking, animal and human, are all questioned.[38]

It is important that La Mettrie retains the concept of the soul, but retains it as the name of an element in the material constitution of the human being. For La Mettrie, our mental faculties can be attributed to the soul, but this soul is no longer the ephemeral, divine, immaterial substance of earlier thinkers. The soul becomes 'a principle of motion or a tangible material part of the brain that we can, without fear or error, consider as a mainspring of the whole machine, which exercises a visible influence on all the others and even seems to have been made first' (31). Behind this faculty there lies the principle of movement, which induces animate bodies to feel, think, to have emotions and a sense of morality, and to 'behave in the physical sphere and in the moral sphere which depends on it' (26).[39] The soul, an 'instigating and impetuous principle', is situated in the brain, at the origin of the nerves, by means of which it exerts its control over the whole body. According to La

Mettrie, this explains the way the body and soul are connected, and even the surprising influence of diseases on the imagination (28–9).[40]

Thinking, feeling, perception, judgement and creativity are all faculties of the same principle, and are all produced by a material soul (15). The difference in the faculties is a matter of degree, and is due to the organisation of the material. In the course of the development of matter from a less complicated into a more advanced state, the capacity of thinking is added to the capacity of feeling, which itself is a development based on the presence of motion in the organised matter: 'Movement and feeling therefore invariably arouse each other in turn, both in whole bodies and in the same bodies when their structure is destroyed, to say nothing of certain plants which seem to exhibit the same combination of feeling and movement.' Thought follows from feeling, and the thinking matter is just one step further from the feeling matter (33). In the world of *L'Homme machine*, man is a highly developed system of material differing from the rest of the universe only in its organisation. In this theory, 'to be a machine and to feel, to think and to be able to distinguish right from wrong, like blue from yellow – in a word to be born with intelligence and a sure instinct for morality and to be only an animal – are thus things which are no more contradictory than to be an ape or a parrot and to be able to give oneself pleasure' (35). La Mettrie believed thought and feeling to be compatible with organised matter to such an extent that they seemed for him to be one of its properties, just like motive power, impenetrability and extension. There is no feeling vs thinking divide, no sensitive vs cognitive principle, but instead, something that produces both: a soul that is, after all, the body, organised differently.

While Descartes argued for the independence of the soul from the body, La Mettrie, as he imagines the soul to be integrated into the system of the body, claims a complete, inseparable togetherness and harmony in the operation of the two. In La Mettrie's system mental and physical activities are linked together by the automatic operation of an ever-present sympathy. This sympathy explains various psychosomatic phenomena. The disease of an organ produces mental disorders and leads to hysteria or hypochondria. Sympathy accounts for the influence of the imagination on the body, as well as the somatic manifestations of heightened mental, emotional states. Sexual desire, maternal imagination and philosophical or poetic creativity all form part of the activities and organisation of matter. The phenomenon of penile erection at the sight of a woman is explained by the operation of the body's springs which excite one another, leading to a chain of physical excitations caused by the 'riot and tumult of the blood and spirits, which gallop with extraordinary rapidity and swell the hollowed-out organs'. The transmission of affective and mental content from one individual to the other also takes place via material processes. The desires of the mother can get 'imprinted' on the foetus: the child bears the marks of the mother's imagination like soft wax that 'receives all sorts of impressions' (29). The conception of creative writing and philosophical thought cannot be imagined without accompanying physiological signs either. Philosophical thought makes the author's blood 'heat up' and the fever of his mind is transmitted to his veins. Sympathy explains why poetic expression of feeling and aesthetic enjoyment can even have dangerous consequences, and why the intense mental activity of great poets can lead to illnesses induced by an overactive mind (29–30).[41]

But to turn to the crux of our discussion: even though La Mettrie proposes a harmonious materialist universe governed by sympathetic connections, there are certain points in his text where the perfectly functioning system of sympathy slips into dysfunction. Many examples that aim to prove the consonance of the activities of body and soul achieve the opposite effect, and uncover breakages in the machine. Such instances of dysfunction surface in connection with illness, non-conscious states and extreme emotionality. I will argue that despite La Mettrie's claims to the contrary, in these unintentional instances the soul can indeed be disentangled from the mechanism of the body, and thus the distinction of the human from the rest of the harmonious, materialistic universe might emerge.

Normally, La Mettrie argues, the body and the soul work together in a sympathetic harmony. When the body is lively, the soul quickens up too, and vice versa. However, in sickness, 'sometimes the soul disappears and gives no sign of life and sometimes it is so transported by fury that it appears to be doubled' (5). Thus, in illness the harmony is so perfect that it is imperfect; the soul follows the body in such an extreme way that it disappears entirely and lets the person be all body. In extreme fury, on the other hand, the soul appears to be present with a double force, making the person into more soul than body. In another instance, 'we see a paralytic asking if his leg is in the bed; there a soldier who thinks he still has his arm, which has been cut off. The memory of former sensations and of the place to which his soul attached them creates the illusion of this type of delirium. It is enough to speak to him of the missing part, for him to remember it and feel all its movements[...]' (5–6).[42] This case is meant to support La Mettrie's argument of a soul–body concord: the soul feels what the body feels, and the soul's memory of a feeling can induce the same feeling in the body. On the other hand, this example also testifies to the opposite of La Mettrie's claim, namely, the soul's independent capacity to feel and imagine sensations, and its unawareness of the real state of the body. The soul, detached from the realities of the body, is living its own emotional life and having its own prosthetic illusions.

As prescribed by the dictates of sympathy, the body and the soul fall asleep together. When the body's movements slow down, the soul also feels lazy, and relaxes: 'If the circulation is too rapid, the soul cannot sleep; if the soul is too agitated, the blood cannot calm down; it gallops through the veins with an audible sound' (6). A long line of examples support this harmonious togetherness. In an incidental remark, however, La Mettrie mentions an instance of disruption in this sympathy. It is a state of mind La Mettrie calls a 'little sleep of the soul' or 'day-dreams' – which, in the French original appears as 'rêve à la Suisse' ('dreaming/thinking in the Swiss way'). This disruption of sympathy is described as follows:

> Finally, as only the cessation of the soul's function brings sleep, there exists, even during waking (which is then only a half-waking), *a sort of very frequent little sleep of the soul, or day-dreams*, which prove that the soul does not always wait for the body in order to go to sleep. For if it is not completely asleep, how close it is! Since it is unable to pick out a single object which it has noticed at all, among the great mass of confused ideas which, like so many clouds, fill as it were the atmosphere of our brains. (6, emphasis added)

The explanation of this state is part of an argument that aims to prove that neither the body nor the soul can go to sleep unless the one entirely follows the other. But it ends up revealing a defect in the system. This failure of sympathy is structured within the concept of sympathetic harmony: it is sympathy taken to the extreme. In the state of daydreaming, the body is awake, and therefore the soul cannot be completely asleep either. Yet it becomes independent of the body, not waiting for it to go to sleep. In this condition, the brain is filled with a mass of confused, unconnected ideas compared to clouds that inhabit the atmosphere. The soul is 'unable to pick out a single object' from this chaos. Instead of actively grasping one of them, it passively exposes itself to all, and slips into a state of reverie, figured as the spontaneous wandering of the soul in a mass of clouds. This is an instance when the body and soul are not together, and where an escape from the universal sympathy of matter gives opportunity for the autonomy and difference of human beings, and, thus, for a definition of human subjectivity. In La Mettrie's theory, even feeling and thinking make human capacities part of a homogeneous material universe. Hence a momentary defect in the workings of sympathy that allows for the soul to gain independence from the body will turn out to be distinctive of what is human. Ultimately, man escapes the system of the machine precisely through the state of being a perfect part of it.

'Rêve à la Suisse' is an intriguing point of La Mettrie's text. In Ann Thomson's 1996 Cambridge edition the phrase is translated as 'daydream', and in the 1749 English translation it occurs as 'reverie' or 'slumbers of the soul, which are very frequent'.[43] While the expression no longer exists in the French language, eighteenth-century dictionaries record it as a colloquialism, and, according to the *Dictionnaire de Trévoux* (1771), a comic expression. Throughout the eighteenth century, various dictionaries describe it as a proverb that means: 'ne rêver à rien', or 'ne penser à rien' (not to think of anything, to think on nothing).[44] The *Dictionnaire de l'Académie* of 1798 claims the proverb to indicate a state of mind when one has a pensive air, appears to be thinking of something, yet thinks of nothing.[45] The verb 'rêver' means not only 'to dream', but also 'to think, to meditate, to muse' or 'to chew the cud upon' according to Boyer (1748) and Chambaud (1761). It can also indicate a deranged or disturbed state of mind, such as 'to talk idly, to rave, to dote' or 'to pass melancholy thoughts' according to Boyer (1748). Generally speaking, the phrase denotes a state of absence of mind, distraction and inattention, which manifests itself either in a free wandering of thoughts or a seeming thoughtfulness that masks a total absence of any kind of mental activity. While the body is present, the soul is absent and far away. All in all, this is a long way from the harmony of body and soul La Mettrie argues for.

It is difficult to know what this expression has to do with the Swiss. In France, from the Middle Ages to the Napoleonic Wars, the Swiss worked as mercenary soldiers and guards. In the seventeenth century, the word 'Swiss' also indicated the porter in a great man's house whose uniform resembled that of the characteristic striped uniform of the Swiss Guards – a definition still maintained in eighteenth-century dictionaries. One might speculate that 'rêve à la Suisse' can derive from the pensive, absent-minded and seemingly unthinking attitude guards and porters assumed while waiting in the same place for long periods of time. On the other hand, the comic idiom also possibly implies a xenophobic assumption, namely that Swiss mercenary soldiers did not enter into deep reflection on the connection of ideas, not thinking on anything and being inclined to spare all mental effort. This idea might be supported by another pejorative connotation related to the Swiss in the expression 'boire à la Suisse' (1660), which, according to the *Dictionnaire historique de la langue française* is defined as 'boire beaucoup', that is, 'to drink a lot, like a soldier'.[46]

It is interesting to note that the Swiss allusion also appears in another context in La Mettrie's treatise, where it is a subtle reference to the author's position in contemporary scientific debates. The treatise was initially published anonymously, and at a certain point in the text the author pretends to be Swiss. This implied reference to a Swiss identity occurs in the context of La Mettrie's questioning the possibility of distinguishing between animals and humans on the basis of innate kindness and virtue, which (claims the author) some animals possess, while many humans do not. The passage evokes the Swiss mercenary morals, and juxtaposes human inhumanity with animal benevolence:

> The lion which I, like so many other people, have mentioned does not remember having refused to take the life of the man thrown to it in a spectacle that was more inhuman than all the lions, tigers, and bears that exist, while our fellow-countrymen fight, *Swiss against Swiss*, brothers against brothers, spy on each other, chain each other up or kill each other without remorse because the prince is paying for these murders. (20, emphasis added)

The mercenary context of 'Swiss against Swiss' ('Suisses contre Suisses') is, at the same time, an allusion to La Mettrie's scientific battle with another Swiss. For La Mettrie, assuming a Swiss identity means pretending to be a countryman of the eminent physician Albrecht von Haller, to whom *L'Homme machine* was originally dedicated. The notoriously provocative dedication to Haller is a sign of a stormy relationship between the two scientists, which started with La Mettrie's translation of Haller's annotated edition of Boerhaave's *Praelectiones academicae in proprias institutiones rei medicae* (1739). In his French translation, called *Institutions de médicine de M. Hermann Boerhaave*, La Mettrie added his own annotations without mentioning Haller's name or distinguishing his notes from those of Haller, which left the reader with the impression that all the commentaries were La Mettrie's own. This started a long controversy between La Mettrie and Haller. Haller accused La Mettrie of plagiarism – an accusation he renewed in a review he wrote about La Mettrie's *Histoire naturelle de l'âme*.[47]

La Mettrie's dedication of *L'Homme machine* to Haller was a form of revenge for this accusation: he publicly acclaimed Haller as the source of inspiration for its scandalous ideas, and called himself his friend and disciple – something that could easily undermine Haller's reputation.[48] Haller failed to recognise the sarcastic nature of this praise, and responded in a review by trying to detach himself from the ideas expressed in La Mettrie's work. The discovery of the author of *L'Homme machine* caused Haller further worries for having been associated with La Mettrie and his doctrines, and in 1749 he publicly declared that he had never corresponded with the author and did not share his philosophical opinions. However, beyond the satiric intent, something else might also have motivated La Mettrie's dedication – something that, according to Vartanian, was probably working in La Mettrie's mind on a less conscious level. In fact, Haller was really the person to whom he was indebted for the doctrine of muscular irritability upon which his work relies. Thus, the work acknowledges the true source of an important idea, after all. Moreover, Haller himself came to see La Mettrie later in his *Memoires* as an 'adversary-disciple' – and La Mettrie, as Vartanian claims, relied on and developed in his own direction Haller's idea of irritability.[49]

Therefore, I would like to argue, the expression 'rêve à la Suisse' marks an ambiguous position: it is a point of identity that hides diversity, a misleading identification where the apparent sameness is exactly where the difference can be found. This is also the site of the evocation of Haller and a Hallerian scientific position that places the principle of motion in matter yet believes in an independent, sentient principle. La Mettrie takes on the position of the Swiss, but not quite: he pushes Haller's materialism to its logical conclusions. It is exactly the doctrine of the irritability of matter (where he actually agrees with Haller) that turns 'Swiss against Swiss'; the materialist point – that is, their common denominator – is exactly what leads the two opinions into difference.

The occurrence in La Mettrie's text of the 'Swiss dreaming' marks a point similar to what Freud, in his *Interpretation of Dreams*, considers to be the mental activity that characterises the mind before falling asleep, during the free association required of the psychoanalytic patient and also in poetic creation – a point which allows psychoanalytic technique, creative writing and dreaming to intersect.[50] In 'rêve à la Suisse' involuntary thoughts are similarly allowed to protrude without the operation of critical, conscious checking mechanisms. On the one hand, the meaning of the phrase reveals a disruption of the sympathetic harmony, where the soul slips into its non-rational, mindless activities from time to time, when the self-checking, reflective capacities do not function. As if this mental state was acted out in the textual structure of La Mettrie's work, an unconscious slip can also be observed in the construction of La Mettrie's harmonious system. Here the disruption of sympathy occurs exactly where the system is the most perfect. It also ties into the Swiss alias of La Mettrie, used to cover his controversial relationship to Haller, a relationship of enmity behind phrases of ardent admiration, or the opposite: an act of acknowledgement and an admission of discipleship behind the apparent hostility. The very appearance of the definition of a non-conscious mental state is itself a non-conscious textual moment, La Mettrie's own daydream.

This is an instance when the body and the soul are not together, and where an escape from the universal sympathy of matter gives an opportunity for the independence of the soul and for difference, and eventually, we can argue, for a definition of human subjectivity. Since in La Mettrie's theory even feeling and thinking turn humans into a part of a homogenous material universe, a moment of defect in the workings of sympathy constitutes, I contend, the distinctive site of humanness. In the state of mindless, soulless reverie, we can escape the universal mechanism of sympathy, and, in this moment of difference, define ourselves as human – despite the opposite intention of La Mettrie's argument. It is the unconscious moment when sympathy breaks down, when the soul is independent of the body, that distinguishes the human from the rest of the animal and vegetable world. La Mettrie's blind spot shows that it is only in such moments that we are – paradoxically – not machines. In the lack of sympathy, humanity as difference can be found.[51]

A somewhat similar textual slip occurs in La Mettrie's argument about the compatibility of materialism with happiness and ethical behaviour, inadvertently showing how a compassionate, sentimental morality can be the product of the dysfunction of universal sympathy. Firstly, La Mettrie claims that nature creates all organisms as equal: 'Her power shines out as clearly in the creation of the meanest insect as in that of the most splendid human; she does not expend greater effort on the animal than on the vegetable kingdom, or on the greatest genius than on an ear of corn' (37–8). The materialist's recognition that we are all made out of the same matter by mechanisms dictated by nature will be the source of all morality and fellow-feeling:

> Whosoever thinks in this way will be wise, just, untroubled about his fate and consequently happy. He will look forward to death without fearing it and without desiring it, cherishing life and scarcely

comprehending how disgust can corrupt the heart in this delightful place; his respect for nature, thankfulness, attachment and tenderness will be in proportion to the feelings and the kindness he has received from her; he will be happy to experience her and to attend the enchanting spectacle of the universe, and will certainly never destroy her in himself or in others. What am I saying! He will be full of humanity and will love its imprint even in his enemies [...] He will pity the wicked without hating them; he will consider them as no more than misshapen men. But while pardoning defects in the construction of their minds and bodies, he will still admire just as much what beauty and virtue they possess. Those whom nature has favoured will seem to him more worthy of respect than those whom she has treated like a wicked stepmother. Thus we have seen that natural gifts, which are the root of everything that is acquired, will elicit from a materialist's mouth and heart a homage that is refused by everyone else without due reason. The materialist, convinced, whatever his vanity may object, that he is only a machine or an animal, will not ill-treat his fellows [...] Following the law of nature given to all animals, he does not want to do to others what he would not like others to do to him. (39)

Yet there is a paradox here. The very presence of humanitarian feeling draws attention to a problem with La Mettrie's initial assumption of materialist equality and universal sympathy. Even though everything is made out of the same material, nature has more gifted and less perfect creatures 'whom she has treated like a wicked stepmother' (39) – leaving unexplained the possibility of the existence of both madmen and geniuses.

La Mettrie claims that the source of love, pity and humane behaviour is the belief in the universality of matter: that the substance which constitutes humans is the same as what constitutes the material and the animal world. Yet pity and admiration are the mark of inequality: they contain an element of difference, based on the accidental malfunctioning of a materialist system. While they are based exactly on our sameness with the material and animal kingdom, pity and admiration also reveal a defect or a fortunate additional gift. Humanity and morality emerge in an attempt to patch up the malfunctions of an allegedly harmoniously functioning universe. Other-regarding acts and affects, such as compassion, forgiveness and respect, are therefore signs of the difference inherent in sameness, revealing a problem with the operation of natural forces. As La Mettrie puts it in a paradoxical and self-undermining passage meant to challenge the fundamental differences between humans and animals: 'Man is not moulded from a more precious clay; nature has only used one and the same dough, merely changing the yeast' (20). Difference, humane feelings and moral sentiments signify not simply the assumption of this 'same dough' in La Mettrie's materialism, but also what unfixes his argument: the introduction of an additional, different matter into the sameness of all matter, nature's 'changing the yeast'. In this way, through its fissures and without its author's intention, La Mettrie's text writes itself into an eighteenth-century tradition that tries to address the ever-increasing rift between the rich and the poor, the fortunate and the unlucky, thus becoming an unacknowledged ally of the literature and morality of sensibility.

Albrecht von Haller: irritability, sensibility and the body in pain

In *A Dissertation on the Sensible and Irritable Parts of Animals* (1752), the Swiss physiologist Albrecht von Haller distinguishes between two vital faculties in animate bodies, namely, irritability and sensibility:

> I call that part of the human body irritable, which becomes shorter upon being touched; very irritable if it contracts upon a slight touch, and the contrary if a violent touch contracts it but little. I call that a sensible part of the human body, which being touched transmits the impression of it to the soul; and in brutes in whom the existence of a soul is not so clear, I call those parts sensible, the irritation of which occasions evident signs of pain and disquiet in the animal. On the contrary, I call that insensible, which being burnt, tore, pricked, or cut till it is quite destroyed, occasions no sign of pain nor convulsion, nor any sort of change in the situation of the body. For it is very well known that an animal, when it is in pain, endeavours to remove the part that suffers from the cause that hurts it; pulls back the leg if it is hurt, shakes the skin if it is pricked, and gives other evident signs by which we know it suffers.[52]

For his contemporaries, Haller was a well-known professor of anatomy and botany working in Göttingen and famous for the discovery of the phenomenon he called 'irritability'. This he imagined to be an immanent contractibility of the muscle tissue, which he distinguished from sensibility, the capacity of feeling produced by the feeling soul. Unlike the materialist La Mettrie, Haller believed in a Cartesian concept of the soul, and held the actions of the mind to be distinct from the processes of the brain and nervous system.[53] The soul, he thought, could not be responsible for certain bodily processes which, on the other hand, could be explained solely by the mechanisms of matter. Haller, a former student of the influential Leiden professor, Herman Boerhaave, opened up new directions for the study of medicine and, through his investigation of the feeling and moving body, made an impact on the production and transformation of the concept of sensibility and irritability in most areas of eighteenth-century culture.[54]

Haller aimed to develop reliable and replicable experimental techniques for the study of the body, which techniques he and a group of followers and disciples practiced by performing physiological experiments on animals. Haller's ambition was to give empirical basis to everything that could be known about sensation and motion in the body, and thereby to challenge false theoretical assumptions that had previously resulted in the failure of human medical treatment. His aim was to make the body, the mind and vital mechanisms a medical and physiological, rather than a philosophical or metaphysical issue, and to make possible the consistent, empirical study of these faculties. Irritability and sensibility, according to Haller's working hypothesis, were two distinct functions in a living system. He defined irritability as the property of the muscular tissue, underlying all motion and contractive reactions, while sensibility, at least in humans, denoted the feeling capacity of the soul, and was restricted to the nerve fibre. In animals, where the existence of the soul was doubted, sensibility could be made visible by means of causing pain and through 'evident signs' of suffering. Irritability was a property responsible for involuntary motion – that is, the unconscious, ongoing operations of the animal machine. Sensibility, on the other hand, was related to the willed activities of the soul, which employed the nerves as a channel for communication.[55]

Performing vivisections on 190 animals, Haller tried out the validity of his working hypothesis and searched for the existence or non-existence of sensibility and irritability in most body parts. The experiments practically implied dissecting live animals, and applying various stimuli to their bodies by burning, cutting or lacerating each body part and organ with different instruments. He describes his gruesome experiments as follows:

since the beginning of the year 1751, I have examined several different ways, a hundred and ninety animals, a species of cruelty for which I felt such a reluctance, as could only be overcome by the desire of contributing to the benefit of mankind, and excused by that motive which induces persons of the most humane temper, to eat every day the flesh of harmless animals without any scruple. As in making these experiments I was obliged to try several which were useless, and to repeat others of them several times, to communicate to the whole of them would only be spinning out this treatise needlessly; wherefore I shall confine myself to relate those only which are of real use, and are found constantly true. (2)

Haller's example raises the concern that eighteenth-century sensibility, with its highly valued notions of compassion, virtue, benevolence and transparency of the body, may be based on acts incompatible with accepted definitions of sensibility. Pain, induced by the violence of medical experimentation, seems to be necessary for sensibility to manifest itself and to be defined.

Haller's dissertation on sensibility and irritability begins with the gesture of rendering his experiments significant from a humanitarian perspective, since they will serve the benefit of mankind, while displaying the conventions of sensibility on the scientist's part by claiming compassion for the victims. In his *Memoirs of Albert de Haller, M. D.* (1783), Haller's biographer Thomas Henry praises Haller's humanity and talent, and presents him as a man of feeling whose every step is directed by the advancement of humanity. Even his cruelty to animals is justified:

> The compassion he felt for the victim of his researches, is often apparent in the narrative of his experiments. We behold him, impressed with a kind of remorse; and omitting no occasion of expatiating on the utility which may be derived from them to mankind. He even seems desirous to believe that these animals suffer no pain, and unwilling to renounce the opinion of Descartes. He was convinced that an idle inquisitiveness, or a passion for reputation, could not justify our killing sensible beings in torments: and that whatever reason we may have to regard them as formed for our use, it is absurd and cruel to imagine, that they are designed also to be sport of our curiosity or vanity.[56]

Thomas Henry is so eager to depict Haller as the archetypal man of sensibility that he interprets Haller's bibliographic activity as a philanthropic effort to prevent others from suffering the useless trouble of reading through all the books they need for their research.

Despite paying tribute to philanthropy and admitting at the beginning of the *Dissertation* that the method of research implies cruelty,

Haller, however, never shows any moral reluctance to go on with the experiments. When an experiment has to be stopped, it is not because of the physician's emotional or ethical involvement, but because the experiment simply does not work: 'The reason why I have not discovered [the sensibility of the heart] myself is, that an animal whose *thorax* is opened is in such violent torture, that it is hard to distinguish the effect of an additional slight irritation' (28). Nevertheless, while Haller fails to recognise scenes of suffering as stimuli that elicit emotional and moral response, his text still seems to show awareness of the enormity of the sufferer's situation thus attacked at the very heart. By employing tropes of torture, the text redefines the participants in the experiment in terms of another discourse, turning the medic and his animal into torturer and victim. Haller uses the word 'torture' in phrases like 'cruel torture' (18) or 'violent torture' (28) with reference to the painful states the dissected animal might be experiencing. Unacknowledged affect thus reorganises signification.[57]

Torturing the other is used by Haller as a technique for healing the self. Animal suffering, implemented for medical purposes, serves a humanitarian aim. However, identification with the animal on the part of the physician is necessary to make animal suffering indicative of human suffering, so that it can be used for purposes of human medicine. The body is curable and capable of suffering – therefore capable of sensibility – if it is an animal body. The animal and the human, from this point of view, must possess the same capability for sensibility (or feeling pain). Haller's account of human sensibility is therefore dependent on the otherness from which humanity normally distinguishes itself. Paradoxically, the point of identification of the human with the animal in pain – the moment when the channel for sympathy and compassion is created – is a moment of cruelty: it is only by tormenting the other that the experimenter can experience and define human pain, suffering and fear.[58] Thus medicine becomes an instrument of torture in order to be able to function as medicine.

In *The Body in Pain*, Elaine Scarry claims that during the act of torture the institutions of civilisation (such as medicine, law and domestic objects) are alluded to, but in a deconstructed form. The healing function of medicine is unmade by turning doctors into actual agents of pain. Similarly, torture inverses the mechanism of the judicial trial by using punishment to generate evidence; or it makes the protective domestic scenery into a torture chamber where every object is a weapon that hurts the prisoner. Achievements of civilisation change their meaning in that they themselves turn into weapons and agents of the torturer, thus demonstrating that civilisation is being annihilated during the cruel act.[59] In the process of animal torture by dissection, however, the very nature of medicine proves to be inherently deconstructive: it can be an agent of civilisation only if it is cruel to civilisation's other. Practically speaking, it is not that torture deconstructs medicine as an achievement of civilisation, but that this achievement, by definition an agent for serving the benefit of human beings, is already on the side of violence.

The target of the discourse of torture is similar to Haller's aim in his experiments: to bring something preconceived and imperceptible, like sensibility, to the field of perception. This, in both cases, happens by means of building up systems of signification that are supposed to reveal something of the undecipherable internal phenomenon. Haller's experiments, by dividing the body into sensible and irritable parts that do not always overlap, turn the body into a signifying system. Sensibility, the signified, can never be manifest in itself. The nature of the experimental research reveals the assumption that it is considered as an immanent, hidden quality, both physiological and psychological. In Haller's system sensibility is signified by pain, another oblique phenomenon that makes itself manifest through the animal's body, for instance, through the animal's cries, the pulling back of the sore limb, or the shaking of the skin. What is *not* sensibility then, namely pain – a type of affect that is representable through motion and cries – signifies the sensibility of the body. Pain, the signifier of sensibility, is present in the organ if, on its violent irritation, the animal shows its signs, usually by bodily motion: 'For it is very well known that an animal, when it is in pain, endeavours to remove the part that suffers from the cause that hurts it; pulls back the leg if it is hurt, shakes the skin if it is pricked, and gives other evident signs by which we know that it suffers' (4–5). Accordingly, if there are no bodily manifestations, Haller denies pain and sensibility to the organ. On this basis he concludes that the lung, liver, tendons and kidneys are without sensation: 'I have irritated them, thrust a knife into them, and cut them to pieces, without the animal's seeming to feel any pain' (28). Besides denying feeling to the respective organs of the tormented animal, Haller's own lack of affect in conducting and describing such experiments amounts to a powerful negation of the reader's – if not his own – affective response.

Making pain signify is a problematic enterprise. For Scarry, a crucial feature of pain is its unsharability, which is guaranteed by pain's resistance to language. For the person in pain, claims Scarry, having pain means having certainty, while for the person not in pain the other's pain is the model of what it is to have doubt. Physical pain resists and destroys language, bringing one back to a state anterior to language. It is different from other interior states of consciousness, since these other states are usually accompanied by objects in the external world: having feelings for somebody or something moves the individual beyond the boundaries of his or her body. Physical pain, however, has no referential content, and therefore resists objectification in language. Thus, inventing linguistic structures for it involves an attempt to reverse the de-objectifying work of pain. Scarry calls the language of pain a 'language of agency'. This language communicates and categorises pain by associating it with the instruments that can cause it, which, because they have qualities like length or shape, can help make pain sharable by the one not in pain. Hence the expressions 'cutting pain' or 'burning pain', for instance. However, such a language of agency can never be the language of pain itself, since, as Scarry points out, it spatially separates what is conceived as pain from the body. The act of signification 'permits a break in the identification of the referent' and entails a 'misidentification of the thing to which the attributes belong', thus shifting the viewer's sense of reality from pain to instrument, and creating doubt concerning the other's pain. Thus, the other's pain, as pain, can never be expressed and understood. And it is the sadistic potential underlying this break that the structure of torture employs by making it possible to confer the reality of pain onto something else, such as the torturer's power.[60]

In his search for a concept of sensibility inside the living organism, Haller's text makes pain referential. He builds up a signifying chain, which interprets bodily reactions to stimuli as signifiers of pain, which in itself is a signifier of an internal quality, namely, sensibility. The biased nature of his enterprise is also made visible by the fact that pleasurable or other sensations are excluded from his definition of sensibility, since they cannot be made manifest by the signifying system he builds up. The body functions as a means of understanding something beyond it, as a medium that stands between the interpreter and the phenomenon; a readable, verbal construct that, though it eludes language, is forced back into signification, often by violence and cruelty.

Francis Barker, in his analysis of Rembrandt's *The Anatomy Lesson of Dr. Nicolaas Tulp*, argues that in the seventeenth century, the body of scientific examination was represented as multilayered. The dissection in Rembrandt's picture, performed on the body in a scene of instruction in front of an audience, contains allusions to the scene of torture as public performance. This body – as the object of a scientific gaze that does not see the body itself – is banished from discourse, denied as a body, yet remains present as a structured, organised object. The painting, he argues, is a palimpsest, making the modern body of scientific scrutiny contain the tortured, penalised body of an old regime. The spectacle of dissection, he claims, is not carried out only in the name of detached scientific curiosity but belongs also to a theatre of cruelty. The layers of the palimpsest become visible in the fissures of signification, where representation becomes problematic.[61]

Like Rembrandt's painting, Haller's eighteenth-century text is also a palimpsest. His readable system breaks up where he turns the body into a text and makes pain into a signifier. Besides a reference to torture, Haller describes his scientific disagreement with another contemporary, Schlichting, as a war fought by the two physicians, who gain information about the state of the brain by torturing their animal captives. Haller writes: '[...] I did not think of refuting him by authorities or reasons *a priori*, but judged it the best to *fight him with his own weapons, that is by experiments*. Wherefore I opened the skulls of several dogs with a *hammer and chissel*, which is a more commodious way than with a *trepan*, and exposed to view a large part of the brain [...]' (21, emphases added). The tools used in the experiment are described as weapons in a war, in which the captured victims are tortured for the sake of gaining scientific information. In Haller's text, different narratives collapse into each other. The tropes describing medical disagreement turn the scene of experiment into a battlefield, where physicians fight over the hidden secrets of the body. The wounding and cutting can only be repeated on 190 bodies if emotional response is silenced, and if the bodies and their feelings can be seen as mere signifiers. The result, however, is a traumatic text that acts out the suppressed affect in the form of its symptomatic wounds, and the metaphors that emerge from the breaches of signification.

Robert Whytt and the aesthetics of pain

In *Physiological Essays* (1755), Robert Whytt, the Edinburgh physiologist, responded to Haller's propositions. Like Haller, he too refuted the doctrines of materialism put forward by La Mettrie – in fact, he even found the Cartesian idea of the beast-machine unacceptable. As he claimed in a previous treatise, the *Essay on the Vital and Other Involuntary Motions of Animals* (1751), to which Haller's *Dissertation* was a response, no sensation or motion is possible without an immaterial principle.[62] Whytt traced the origin of all muscular motion and feeling, all conscious and unconscious actions, to the operation of what he called the 'sentient principle', which he associated with a unified, immaterial soul.[63] While Haller attributed the motions performed by amputated, dead body parts to muscular irritability, Whytt thought that this could be explained by the feeling that still remained in the nerves, on grounds that the sentient principle extended to all parts of the body. Whytt claimed that if we unquestionably attribute to the mind certain unconscious actions, such as penile erection, we cannot reject the idea that unconscious involuntary motions, such as the movement of the heart or the peristaltic motion of the intestines, are also the result of the same faculty.[64]

In *Physiological Essays*, Whytt reads the blind spots of Haller's *Dissertation* and finds some of the points where the signifying system built up by his opponent can be undermined. One of these blind spots is Haller's denial of pain (or any sensation) where there are no manifest and easily interpretable signifiers. According to Whytt, the ostensible lack of sensibility in various body parts is explainable by the fact that the greater pain caused by the anatomist's incision destroys the sensation of a lesser pain. The body can temporarily lose sensibility and irritability because of its immediate reaction to an intense feeling.[65] While in Haller the bodily symptom is structured as a metaphor (the symptom is the vehicle for sensation), in Whytt's text one can observe a metonymic chain in the way the relationship between motion and feeling is imagined. Haller creates a sharp distinction between sensibility and irritability, and he claims that irritability is the characteristic of the bodily substance, and its contractive force operates regardless of feeling, even after death. However, feeling as pain can be proved to be present, according to Haller, when motion as its sign is observable. Whytt does not deny sensation and the presence of the nerves to any part of the body, and claims the interrelatedness of sensibility and irritability. Irritability of any part depends on its sensibility. Motion, therefore, is not due to an innate quality within the matter – it cannot proceed from 'some unknown property of their insensible glue' as Haller claims – but it is a consequence of an uneasy feeling in the irritated part produced in order to lessen the unpleasant sensation. As motion is dependent on feeling, the cause of motion is the omnipresent sensation (214–15). The result is a signifying system of the body where motion is always a sign of pain (sensation), but pain does not always produce motion; the capacity for feeling is present everywhere, without necessarily having manifest signs. Whytt's text, instead of pinning down the meaning of sensibility and irritability as fixed and univocal entities, sees them as manifested in diverse and heterogeneous forms. In the case of motion a whole set of variations is presented, the set being logically organised into a structure of syntax, making motion into an elaborate language in which feeling might express itself.

What is this syntax made of? Whytt claims that sensibility and irritability can have different degrees and types (106–7). Young children, or people with delicate nerves and quick feelings, are 'subject to spasms and convulsive motions of their stomach, intestines, etc. and to palpitations of their heart, from such slight causes as would scarce sensibly affect men of firmer constitutions and less moveable nerves' (187). Whytt distinguishes between three types of irritability on the basis of its location and stimulus. In different types of irritability motion appears in the form of alternate or uniform contractions. The first is peculiar to muscles, where *inflammation* is due to 'the irritated vessels themselves, which are *agitated* with strong alternate *vibratory contractions*; by means of which the *moment* [sic] of the blood in them is greatly increased, and red globules are *pushed* into those vessels which, in a sound state, only receive serum or lymph' (137–8, emphases mine). Uniform contraction, on the other hand, is performed in the pores of the skin. In this case, muscles 'contract uniformly and equably during the time the stimulus operates, without any intermissions or alternate relaxations' (213). In the third type of irritability, redness and inflammation are '*excited* in every part of the body that is sensible, as often as acrid things are applied to it' (153). Motion presents itself in various forms, such as contraction, inflammation, convulsion, vibration, agitation, pushing and excitation. The meaning of the word is itself constantly in motion, displacing, surpassing itself, and acting out its own connotations and derivatives. 'To move' (which has 'emotion' among its derivatives) originates from words connoting 'to stir', 'to push', 'to set oneself going', 'to become displaced', 'to pass beyond' as well as 'to keep off, ward off, defend'. Motion constantly has to 'push' itself further, to 'pass beyond' every desire for stoppage, completion and closure. When it reaches its overall goal, motion extinguishes itself, leading to termination – something that motion has to 'ward off', 'keep off', in order to exist. Motion has to surpass or 'pass beyond' its own desire for closure, which would mean the end of motion; yet it must also be driven by such desire at the same time.[66]

In Whytt's text, the force that can put an end to motion by stopping and interrupting it is feeling: a sudden fear, joy, surprise or grief. 'Again', says Whytt, 'if the motions of muscles from stimuli were not owing to a feeling, How could the convulsive motions of the diaphragm in the hiccup be often immediately *stopped by sudden fear, joy, or grief*? [...] And why should the convulsive motions of the stomach and diaphragm in vomiting, be frequently *interrupted by extraordinary fear, or any great and sudden surprise?'* (215, emphases added). Here feeling presents itself in different forms; sensibility is not Haller's univocal 'sensibility as pain' any more, but its meaning is fragmented and dispersed into various types of affect. Yet sensibility, even if it is constantly in motion, remains the controlling force over motion. The interconnectedness of sensibility and irritability sets the whole body into a sympathetic movement that is coordinated by feeling:

> It is observable, that an irritation of the nerves, which are the most sensible parts, produces the most violent motions in the muscles; and when they are, by being stretched, rendered more susceptible of pain, still greater convulsions are occasioned by pricking them [...]. [T]hose motions, which are occasioned by stimuli, acting, not on the organs moved, but on distant parts [...], proceed from that sympathy, which prevails in the nervous system; and must be ascribed to an uneasy sensation in the part irritated, since all consent supposes feeling, and is inexplicable upon any other principle. (255–6)

Upon the irritation of various parts the body performs a harmonious motion, where distant parts of the body communicate. Due to the workings of sympathy, one part sets another into motion, until the whole body becomes a moving organism where each movement has an effect on the other, which effect, moreover, has meaning.

In *Laocoon's Body and the Aesthetics of Pain*, Simon Richter mentions that sensibility and irritability were influential concepts for philosophies of the aesthetic. 'Sensibility' is one of the first meanings of the concept of 'aesthesia', that is, the capacity for sensation, and 'irritability' is motion produced by a painful or pleasurable stimulus (*Reiz*). *Reiz* is a term present both in the discourse of German aesthetics, with the meaning of 'grace', and in eighteenth-century medicine, with the meaning of painful stimulus. As Richter points out, the use of *Reiz* and *reizbarkeit* in Herder's aesthetics and psychology was shaped by the influence of Haller's *Dissertation on the Sensible and Irritable Parts of Animals*.[67] However, what Robert Whytt's text so interestingly demonstrates is that the scientific conceptualisation of painful stimulus already happens in the field of the aesthetic, showing how an aesthetics of pain surfaces in the rhetoric of eighteenth-century physiology. As the tropes of his text show, the dissecting anatomist is no longer the viewer of suffering, but that of a performance, a work of art. Movement is regulated, coordinated and meaningful, like in a dance. The irritated, tortured, painful body becomes a dancing body, and the scientist's intellectual gaze turns into the gaze of the viewer seeking aesthetic pleasure in the discourse of torture. Motion that terminates in death is kept on by constant irritation in order to surpass its termination and thus to be able to heal the human.

Eventually, the heart – the blind spot of Haller's experiments – also opens up in the torture of dissection, and speaks 'the language of the heart' before the animal expires:

> The heart [of the dog], which was thus brought into view, appeared quite turgid, and continued in motion about five minutes: during which time it performed only between 60 and 65 weak vibrations; for they were not compleat contractions. While the heart was thus moving, warm spittle was first applied to it, then cold water, and, last of all, oil of vitriol, which shrivelled the parts it touched, almost in the same manner as a hot iron would have done; but none of them accelerated the heart's vibrations, which became gradually slower, till they ceased altogether. (206–7)[68]

In torture, the heart is made to speak the language of motion. Like a woman of sensibility, who faints, kneels and cries under the pressure of the inexpressible feelings of her heart, in dissection even the animal's heart – the symbolic organ of affect – can claim its own feelings by acting them out in vibrations and contractions that weaken in the act of forced signification. Whytt's text, by bringing its concepts (among them sensibility and feeling) into motion, acts out what he claims, that is, that sensibility and motion are interrelated. As the eternal motion of the body eventually becomes a symptom of sensibility, so the scientific text aiming to define sensibility will stage the motion inherent in the meaning of the concept. However, Whytt does indeed put an end to the motion of signification after all. The metonymic chain shifting from motion to sensibility cannot help moving further onto a final referent, the sentient principle: 'as *gravity* must finally be resolved into the power of that BEING who upholds universal nature; so it is highly probable, that the irritability of the muscles of animals is owing to that living sentient principle, which animates and enlivens their whole frame' (184).

The coordinated movement of the animals – a chain of signifiers in which sensibility is expressed and produced – is a texture woven somewhere between physician and animal. Sensibility is motion regulated by the stimulus of pain, a perverted puppet-dance mocking voluntary motion. As dictated by the force of the sentient principle and ultimately by the anatomist, the half-living, tortured animals and their separated, dead body parts in Whytt's text will perform this dance. The dance is somewhat similar to the mechanical yet graceful puppet-dance in Henrich von Kleist's story, 'Über das Marionettentheater'. In Paul de Man's interpretation of the text, the dancing puppets do not express by their motion any internal passion or emotion; the aesthetic effect is determined by the formality of the tropes that make up the dance. The dance of the puppets is truly aesthetic, writes de Man, precisely because of the lack of expressivity, because it is a motion that is not determined by desire. In the puppet-dance, 'the aesthetic power is located neither in the puppet nor in the puppeteer but in the text that spins itself between them. This text is the transformational system, the anamorphosis of the line as it twists and turns into the tropes of ellipses, parabola, and hyperbole. Tropes are quantified systems of motion.'[69] Whether motion, as Haller claims of irritability, is an innate, ever-present characteristic of the dead matter or, as in Whytt's opinion, is due to the sentient principle, the texture woven by motion and created in order to explain and make manifest an affect will paradoxically not be explainable as a signifying system referring to, or expressive of, affects.

Affect and sensibility – imagined as something hidden deep inside the living organism – are not possible to grasp by signification, yet they keep surfacing in the texts written about the quest for them. A possible field of the aesthetic and the literary emerges between scientist and animal, puppeteer and puppet, and in the interpretation that is constantly being created between reader and text. It is when these textures are made into representation, the process in which the experiments are written into a narrative, that the concept of sensibility itself is produced. The text woven by the experiments consists of a system of signifiers that lost its reference to sensibility as its original signified and starts living its own life producing sensibility in the process of its own coming into being. Even though the space for the emotional response allowed for scientist and reader is foreclosed from this discourse, affect announces its presence in the process of the creation of its (inadequate) representation, in the efforts this process implies. It surfaces at the points where signification breaks down and other discourses make themselves visible. It is in this way, from the emotions silenced by the physician (in processes that imply closing one's eye to violence, suffering, the aesthetic, and pleasure), that the concept of sensibility comes into existence.

Coda: the crying tropes of sensibility

What story would be told by the victims of Haller's experiments? What kind of text is produced when sufferers can verbalise their pain and intense feelings? Those who survive the plundering of the Cossacks in Prussia during the Seven Years' War admit the difficulty or impossibility of narrating their experience. In testimonies written by victims, the emergence of the familiar tropes of sensibility is just as inseparable from violence, torture and pain as it was in the medical setting. The accounts from which I will quote were published anonymously in 1760 as a volume of letters, written by clergymen robbed, attacked and viciously tortured during the war. The atrocities committed by the soldiers are 'Inhumanities exceeding all Expression', of which 'it is easier to say, Come and see! Than to describe it.'[70] Relating the events is itself a 'grievous Labour to my Heart' (12), and what is related is rarely one's suffering but often the suffering of others as a substitute for one's own pain. The writer of Letter 3 (1759) undertakes to describe how the soldiers torture him to make him give up his money, which he, having fallen victim to previous plunders and a bad harvest year, does not possess. While the priest sets out to narrate his own experience as exactly as possible, he has to admit that the report of his pain cannot be complete: 'As to my Sufferings, I confess, I am not able to give an Account of all of them. For what those Barbarians, the Cossacks, attempted upon me, when I was deprived of my Senses, I know not. I shall only relate, without any Aggravation, what I have seen and felt' (17). One reason for the difficulties of narrating the experience is that the experience is being interrupted by the frequent losses of consciousness – a state the author calls insensibility – caused by the extremities of pain and torture:

> My bare Head was covered with Blood and Swellings by one Stroke of a Pistol, and more with the Kantshuh; as was my whole Back miserably beaten and dyed with bloody Stripes, by the same Means, and by their naked Swords, by which they every Moment threatened to split my Head. With the Rope I was choaked one Time after another, so as to be deprived of Breath and Senses.
> [...] One gave me a Push on my Breast with his Feet; and another tore me, with my Back on the Ground, to the Door of the Chamber, fastened the Rope so as to choke me again, that I lost Breath and Feeling. In this Posture my Boots were pulled off with such a Force as to tear the Strings off the Knees, without being unloosed. I was left for

dead, and I don't know how I came to myself again. But when I did, I saw what was done, as the Strings of my Boots fell of my Knees.

[...] I begged on my Knees for Mercy and Compassion, pointing at the same time to my sore Body. But there was no Mercy to be found. Now they cried, Fire! In my own house was no Fire: wherefore they led me by the Rope into another House. One of them so benumbed me by a Stroke on my Head, that I fell to the Ground. In this Insensibility, my Cloaths, except the Breeches, were pulled off, and the Shirt drawn over my Head, and a fourfold Torture of Fire began. [...] As this, notwithstanding my lamentable Cries, was judged not hard enough, they lighted more Straw, and threw me down upon it half naked, keeping me fast on the Rope; and all that while that my Back lay on the lighted Straw, my bare Breast and Belly were whipped. (18–20)

Pain is experienced in a constant oscillation of consciousness and loss of consciousness, in a repeated survival of death, which the sufferer fears every time a new series of attacks starts, as he more than once 'recommended [his] Soul to the paternal Hands of God' (20). When the victim is not in the state of insensibility then he is in the state of pain, which is the only meaning of feeling during this scene of torture. Just as in Haller's text, it is in pain that the victim's sensibility can be grasped.

The most intense pain leads to 'insensibility', that is, a loss of consciousness and sensation. Sensation and insensibility are made interchangeable by the extremities of torture, where insensibility will paradoxically come to mean the most intense state of feeling. This state disrupts self and consciousness, and is too overwhelming to be fully graspable for the human mind. Like the flashbacks and nightmares of the victims of trauma, the narrative will necessarily become an attempt to get hold of the experience, where consciousness repeatedly fails to grasp the impossible encounter. While the letter sets out to account for the sufferer's feelings, what eventually gets textualised is the violation of the body – an experience partly unknown to the narrator due to his frequent losses of consciousness. The language of pain is thus realised as a language of agency, to use Scarry's phrase. The nature of pain can be perceived only through the victim's pleas for the torturer's mercy: he points at his sore body to elicit compassion, and evaluates his cries as lamentable. However, the soldiers are not moved; the victim's and the torturer's insensibility mutually reflect and enhance each other.

At a later point in the text there is a noticeable change in the discourse. First we hear the father (narrator of the previous paragraph) lamenting the misfortunes of the women and children, including his own family, attacked by the soldiers who break into the church building:

> But there my Heart bled, when, after a vain Attempt to break open the Doors, they climbed into [the Church] through the Window, when heart-breaking Shrieks of the Women and Children were heard; which increased when four of the *Cossacks*, which had jumped in, raged among the poor People, by beating and pulling off their Cloathes. [...] But what a mournful Sight, when the Beating and Plundering now began in the Church-Yard! O what an affecting Sight was it to me, when I observed my dear Wife under the Hands of these Savages; and what Grief pierced my Soul, when she was thrust to the Ground and robbed of the greatest Part of her Cloaths. The *Cossack*, which kept me by the Rope, led me to her, in my dismal Condition, which, at first, made me unknown to her; but, when she came to know me, she was most sorely grieved. Yet my Intersession to save her, because she was sick, through the Divine Interposition, had such an Influence upon the Hearts of these Savages, that they let her go half cloathed, without using any other Violence. (20–1)

When the tortured priest faces the suffering of others, including his own family, metaphoric expressions carrying connotations of bodily wounding or psychic suffering – 'my Heart bled', 'heart-breaking Shrieks', 'Grief pierced my Soul' – appear, together with the frequent use of exclamations, interjections and parallel structures. The victim's distorted, mutilated body, bearing the marks of torture, becomes another attempted representation of pain – a texture produced between torturer and victim. This marked body, now in the state of consciousness, brings about affective response in the wife who becomes 'sorely grieved'. While the soldiers have not been moved by the victim's own suffering, they are affected by viewing a scene of someone else's emotional response to the same suffering to which they had formerly been indifferent. At this point, as the victim writes, 'Some of these Barbarians, indeed, were moved to Compassion, and, upon their Desire, the most cruel *Cossack* of them all, in green Dress, was at last obliged to take the Rope from about my Neck' (21). In the state of consciousness, when the most intense affective experiences are lost and are present for the victim only in the form of memories, word-presentations carrying affective content appear. It is the language produced in the presence of emotional response – amidst the constant efforts to verbalise affect – that allows for the emergence of tropes familiar from discourses of sensibility.

The following letter, in a direct plea for compassion and pity, also testifies to the difficulties of writing the affective experience. Here a lamentation over present misery substitutes for the narration of past misfortunes which the author tries to, but cannot, relate:

My dear Friend!

You have often desired me to give you an Account of my Loss, and the Calamity caused by it: But though I know that I would find Compassion, and, if possible, even actual Relief from you, yet I could not prevail with my bleeding Heart to describe it. Now, I shall not any longer delay to comply with your Request; But don't expect Particulars; the Grief of my Heart will not suffer me to specify them, even to my Brother. Pray for me, that my God may be pleased to support me, that I may not perish under the Weight of my Calamity.

I endeavour, every Day, to forget my Misfortunes; but the encreasing Want is a heart-breaking Memorandum of my encreasing Distress. [...] My Tears find no Compassion. To supply all these Necessities, I have nothing in Store, and I live here only on the Mercy of God, which is the only Relief that is left me, and of which I do not despair.

[...] In the two first-mentioned Places, I was pillaged; and in the third, I was deprived of the part by the Flames. Thus cometh my Poverty and want as an armed Man, upon me. My Wife and Children, which before, I could embrace with Joy, I cannot now cast my Eyes upon, without being grievously touched. [...] The Calamity is universal, the dearness great; and I cannot prevail upon my Heart to apply to any Body for Relief. My Calamity renders me dumb and silent. – More Tears than Bread. [...] For, my dear Friend! be it made known unto God, my nearest Relations desert me. – I must desist writing any further; my Heart breaks, and my Sores are ripped up again. God be with you. Pity one in great Distress. Your Comforts will refresh our Hearts. (22–4)

The traumatic event remains an unknown calamity, an unnameable point that silences the narrator. His lamentations substitute for the particulars of the events that had taken place. The details are not specified, and their narration remains blocked by the sufferer's grief. He cannot relate what he intends to, because of the flowing of an expressionless stream of language impossible to withhold – a language deprived of signification or expressivity. This stream of language cancels itself out before it can communicate the narrator's story. Finding it physically impossible to continue, he stops writing. This blockage of communication is due to an overflow of affect which disorganises structures of signification, and cancels out communication.[71] The result is a text that claims to be the voice of silence, uttered by someone who is rendered dumb by calamities, whose grief and 'bleeding Heart' prevent the additional suffering of narration. The text stands there in place of sheer dumbness, as the language of silence. It is an inadequate representation of the traumatic event, since that event is the very point remaining absent from the text. The result is a language – 'between the cry and the silence' – deprived both of its communicative function and its expressiveness.[72]

In contrast to Haller's torturing and torturous text, here, through a structure of address and a direct appeal to the listener's emotions, a space is opened up for emotional response. The reader is called upon to bear witness to what he cannot relieve: the inexpressible suffering of the other. Responding with compassion and pity to the other's plea remains the only way out of the repetition of cruelty. Sigmund Freud refers to an episode in Tasso's *Jerusalem Liberated* in which Tancred, after having accidentally killed his beloved Clorinda, enters a magic forest and strikes at a tree, only to see the tree bleeding and hear the voice of the dead Clorinda – whose soul is imprisoned in the tree – complaining that he has wounded her once again. In Cathy Caruth's re-reading of Freud's text, the crux of the experience of trauma is not simply the unconscious and unwished-for repetition, but the moving and sorrowful human voice crying out from the wound, a voice that bears witness to the experience Tancred cannot know fully. The wound that speaks conveys the plea of another who is asking to be seen and heard, and thus, as Caruth writes, commands us to awaken. This poses an ethical imperative. In the repetition of trauma, it is not exactly Tancred's own wound that speaks, but the wound, the trauma, of the other.[73]

In this letter, the narrator attempts to forget, but the forgotten events keep reappearing in the tropes of the text. The tropes serve as instruments of memory, preserving and reproducing the fragments of the past, making it possible for the traumatic event to haunt the text by inhabiting its tropes. In this way, the text presents a constant struggle between memory and forgetting, narrating and suppressing. Every attempt to narrate the events turns into an overflow of tropes signifying silence. Yet the text of silence and forgetting reintroduces the event through tropes of wounding and physical injury. The silenced events are recalled by the tropes of 'breaking Heart', sores 'ripped up', or the images of poverty and want imagined as soldiers attacking the victim. Every trope turns into a wound that speaks and retains the memory of the past. The affect involved in a narration that tries to relate pain is present in the efforts of narration, representation, and the suffering included in giving meaning to the experience. It surfaces in the attempts to forget as well as in the verbal repetition of the traumatic event.

The experience of the overwhelmingly violent event cannot be grasped by the consciousness; the most direct experience occurs as an inability to know and to take part in the event consciously. As a result, the event keeps reappearing, using tropes as a means of its uncanny repetition. In this process, a discourse emerges that transmits one's suffering to others in dead and frozen metaphors and rhetorical devices that are passed on from one text to the other. These tropes are the means of awakening to consciousness, an awakening that can be handed on to other cultural contexts where the tropes of sensibility are used and produced. They urge for a realisation of the reader's ethical task, similar to the one suggested by Caruth, to recognise and uncover suffering – a request that is here inscribed into the tropes that repeat the burnt and tortured victim's cries and pleas. Following on Caruth's theory, I believe that discourses of sensibility – and discourses beyond sensibility – by carrying such tropes, will also carry the cry, and thus the ethical imperative for emotional response. Such tropes and textual devices are pleas to the reader; they migrate from one text to the other, and from one century to the next even, in order to compel us to listen and feel, and to stop the repetition of violence. They are pleas to acknowledge, as Joyce McDougal would suggest, the psychic component of affect and thus put an end to a Hallerian acting out. Every act of close reading the tropes and devices should at once be an act of reopening a speaking wound and a way of listening and reacting to the story of violence. Opening up the tropes of sensibility through reading can make the story of suffering – and the story of the pain and anxiety inscribed in the creation of these tropes – cry out.[74]

It might occur to us that, ironically, when writing about pain and human suffering for the sake of the scholarly re-examination of the concept of sensibility, one's reading cannot help re-enacting Haller's cruelty, and even his gesture of humanitarian apology. Are we traumatically repeating Albrecht von Haller's dissections? We too are ripping open (past) sores, one might say. How can a re-reading of traumatic texts and a textual exposure of cruelty and suffering be a form of wounding that teaches us to avoid the further generation of violence? To return to the questions at the beginning of this section, what do we have to face if we dare to listen and respond to the victim's cries? A close analysis of eighteenth-century physiological texts might draw our attention to the darker side of the achievement of enlightenment reason: the problem arises of how and where to draw the line where the rhetoric of humanitarian sensibility can unnoticeably slip into the pathology of paranoia and the justification for mass murder and genocide. What is the point where an ideology can emerge which claims that exterminating tens of thousands of those *other* people, those *other* children – who may be seen as no more than Haller's vermin – is necessary and beneficial for 'our' people and 'our' children to live and grow up in peace? Perhaps it is only by facing affects, awakening one's emotional responses and letting past tropes, past wounds – and ourselves – speak and cry that one might avoid the reoccurrence of cruelty. The traumatic repetition may only be stopped if the cries and groans of the victim and the manifestations of the other's pain are not treated as part of a readable signifying system and investigated with the detachment of enlightenment reason, but rather, are heard as the pleas of the other requiring recognition and response, opening a space for pity and compassion. It is indeed by opening such a space and listening to the other's voice that the chain of violence can be stopped. Therefore, negotiating the ethics of definition and analysis (whether it is experimental, textual or psychological) must precede the task Derrida sets for the psychoanalytic community; it must precede the task of analysing and questioning cruelty.[75] The very mode of questioning, even when the object of questioning is cruelty itself, can too easily assume the weapons of the torture chamber, the executioner's guillotine or the lethal injection.

Part II
The Literature of Sensibility

3
'I Will Not Weep': Tears of Sympathy in Henry Mackenzie's *The Man of Feeling*

The limits of tears

Tears are the crux of both the success and the failure of Henry Mackenzie's first novel, *The Man of Feeling* (1771). Fragmented, short, episodic, and over-abounding with scenes of weeping, *The Man of Feeling* was immensely popular in its day. Its success in the 1770s was due to its capacity to move and affect deeply, drawing the reader into a culture of tears. As contemporary opinions testify, crying over *The Man of Feeling* was the test of the sensibility of its early readers. By the time of the novel's publication, tears were more or less compulsory attributes and signifiers of a feeling heart and unquestionable morality. The anonymous critic of the *Monthly Review* insists that anyone 'who weeps not over some of the scenes it describes, has no sensibility of mind'.[1]

Tears, however, did not always come easily for everyone. In 1826, Lady Louisa Stewart recalls a childhood memory about the time when the novel was first published. As she writes to Sir Walter Scott: 'I remember so well its first publication, my mother and sisters crying over it, dwelling upon it with rapture! And when I read it, as I was a girl of fourteen not yet versed in sentiment, I had a secret dread I should not cry enough to gain the credit of proper sensibility.'[2] Those young and innocent minds on whom the culture of sensibility models itself paradoxically have to become versed in the feelings they are naturally expected to possess. As Harley, the hero of Mackenzie's novel, reflects: 'Our delicacies [...] are fantastic; they are not in nature!'[3] Harley himself, always identified as the overly sentimental character of Mackenzie's novel, is surprisingly tearless at many critical moments in the story. For instance, on the morning of Harley's departure for his London journey, his aunt bids him farewell 'with a tear on her cheek' (58). Peter, Harley's faithful servant is 'choked with the thought, and his benediction could not be heard' (59). The only person who can resist tears is Harley himself. He 'shook [Peter] by the hand as he passed, smiling, as if he said, "I will not weep"' (59). Harley's smile is turned into a cover for repressed tears only by the narrator's speculation. The narrator, through the lens of his sentimental expectations, trains the reader to read emotionally, to read through his tears.

This chapter will investigate the ways in which tears become central signifiers of sympathetic emotional exchange in Mackenzie's novel. John Dwyer avers that the role and complexity of tearful scenes in *The Man of Feeling* have been underestimated by most modern critics of Mackenzie's novel, who take the abundance of tears in the novel to be the sign of melodramatic and self-indulgent emotionalism. There is a tendency, Dwyer claims, to caricature the novel's tearfulness and overlook its pioneering psychological methods as well as their moral purpose and enormous ideological power.[4] Taking up Dwyer's point, this chapter will focus on one important aspect of the novel's intricate web of tearful responses, namely, the way in which the tears of sympathy form part of a sentimental reading practice.

Recent scholarship tends to be more concerned with the widening gap between sentimental morality and eighteenth-century social conduct than with the interactions between the two. The novel's melancholy tone, the inability of its hero, Harley, to achieve his goals in the competitive context of his society, as well as his isolation and death are frequently interpreted as an allegory of the failure of the morals of sensibility to function within the social practice of the period. According to John Mullan, the publication of *The Man of Feeling* in 1771 marks a turning point in the history of the genre, when 'sentimental morality cannot reflect at all on the practise of any existing society'.[5] The culture of self-interest, he claims, builds up a sentimental fantasy, victimising and isolating those who blindly and naively try to live up to its values. Susan Manning sees Mackenzie's life work as a sceptical inquiry into the effects of sentiment on human behaviour, while Stephen Bending and Stephen Bygrave claim that the sentimental novel has limited answers to the political problems of its time.[6] Maureen Harkin reads Mackenzie's novel as a self-conscious dramatisation of the powerlessness of novels to intervene in the social sphere. Rather than exposing the failure of sentiment to produce a viable ethical practice, she claims, *The Man of Feeling* tackles the limits of the novel's potential for changing the social sphere and for producing community. Through its tropes of mutilation, destruction and vulnerability of texts and objects, the novel negotiates conflicting positions about the possibility of literature as a form of social critique. While providing images of distress and sympathy, it spells out no effective means of opposition to the ills it depicts.[7]

What is not given sufficient emphasis in today's scholarship, however, is that – despite the recognised doubt concerning the practicability of sentimental values in the period – Mackenzie's novel is successful in realising a very important, affective, agenda, precisely through its tears. The novel demonstrates a belief in the ability of sentimental fiction intensively to form and reform the reading public, self-consciously acting out how such an education in feeling is brought about. As the responses of its first readers demonstrate, tears, while they could indeed be signs of truthful emotional reaction, were, at the same time, effective means by which a culture established its ideologies through the individual's affective responses.[8] Mackenzie's novel shows how an institutionalised culture of sensibility is produced, while demonstrating its own involvement in such cultural production. The novel enacts the process through which society becomes 'versed in sentiment', as it happens through individual processes of reading and a text's appeal to the individual on an emotional level. While it is true that *The Man of Feeling* does not directly draw up any agenda for the reformation of social ills, it shows how literature can realise its social and political agenda on the level of the individual's emotions. In this way, Mackenzie reveals the way in which the sentimental reader – a highly political product – is constructed by the means of reading itself. Far from representing a failure to actively participate in the social, both *The Man of Feeling* and its contemporary success demonstrate how a process of interpretation through affective response has the potential to connect fiction and life, and thus instantiates how reading that is performed in the private sphere also has public, social and political stakes. This reading practice, however, is problematic: where reading is expected to be a scene of sympathy it will be burdened with the moral ambivalence and discontent inherent in the concept of sympathy itself.

Through an analysis of Mackenzie's novel in the context of the literature and philosophy of sensibility, this chapter will trace the way in which the text self-consciously enacts the reader's education via the culture of tears. *The Man of Feeling* is said to be the most tearful novel of the eighteenth century, yet, I argue, its affectivity should not be taken for granted. Harley's sentimentality is created in front of our eyes by those who read and narrate him, drawing the reader of the novel into a similar, mimetic mode of interpretation. The mind of Harley is constructed like a mirror – alluding to the philosophical constructions of the feeling subject as imagined by David Hume and Adam Smith – which reveals more about those who read him than about Harley himself. Harley's mind not only reflects, but also improves the complexions of those who look into it. In this way, he is never the subject in question, but instead brings about a shift of focus, turning both narrator and reader into men of feeling. The chapter will argue that the 'man of feeling' consists in an always shifting perspective; it is a technique of reading rather than a clearly defined character type. The sentimental feeling subject is inseparable from a reading practice that operates through emotional response. The tears of the man of feeling always mark ambivalent moments of sympathy, which are also staged in other novels of the period, including Sarah Fielding's *The Adventures of David Simple* (1744), Oliver Goldsmith's *The Vicar of Wakefield* (1766), Laurence Sterne's *Sentimental Journey* (1768) and Mary Wollstonecraft's *Maria; or, the Wrongs of Woman* (1798). Novels of sentiment reflect critically on enlightenment theories of sympathy, where fellow-feeling unsettles the boundaries of the self and blurs the distinction between self and other. They warn us that moments of sympathy can cast doubt on true altruistic motive and can help maintain existing power structures. The ambivalent tears of sympathy, as we shall see, are the common concerns of eighteenth-century sensibility and intersubjective psychoanalytic theory.

Mackenzie's introductory chapter well illustrates how the novel of sensibility finds – and even produces – its own sympathetic readers. It positions the novel as a fragmented, damaged manuscript found by two unsuccessful hunters. The narrator and the curate, after the disappointment of missing their prey, look around to contemplate the melancholy locale, and talk about a man called Harley who had once lived there. Here the curate presents his company with a bundle of papers used by him as wadding – papers that contain the history of Harley in whom the narrator has taken an interest:

'I should be glad to see this medley', said I. 'You shall see it now', answered the curate, 'for I always take it along with me a-shooting'. 'How came it so torn?' ''Tis excellent wadding', said the curate. – This was a plea of expediency I was not in condition to answer; for I had actually in my pocket great part of an edition of one of the German Illustrissimi, for the very same purpose. We exchanged books; and by that means (for the curate was a strenuous logician) we probably saved both. (48–9)

While the narrator saves the manuscript that has been abused by the curate, it turns out that he himself treated his German Illustrissimi unkindly. Every text, the novel seems to say, has its own reader – and the novel of sensibility can be salvaged only by those kind-hearted creatures who are 'a good deal affected with some very trifling passages in it' (49). The survival of the text is due to its capacity to affect its reader almost to the point of tears. Its powers cannot extend to all readers, only to those select few who possess enough sensibility to be able to enjoy its 'medley'.

In Mackenzie's theory, formulated at the time of the novel's composition, sensibility mechanically operates among the members of a community who possess the capacity for refined feeling. He explains to his cousin, Elizabeth Rose of Kilravock, that the language of sentiment works by a sudden recognition of some hidden capacity that has always been there in the reader, and which the story of sentiment brings to the surface. On 31 July 1769 he writes, 'believe me, where genuine Sentiment and Feeling are at bottom, we cannot write with too much Freedom; and the Reader will be pleas'd in Proportion as these Qualities reside in himself'.[9] Sentimental writing works by depicting minor details which 'their Intimates' can recognise, and thus their passions are aroused (*ER* 37). The effect poetry has on its reader is 'like finding some Family Picture in a Stranger's House; we conclude ourselves acquainted, & are Friends at the first Sight' (*ER* 51–2). It needs a scene of recognition, brought about by literature, for an already existent familiarity and community to come to light. The function of the literature Mackenzie undertakes to write is to bring about such scenes of recognition. Thus, the introduction of *The Man of Feeling* offers two models with which the reader can identify, grouping the readers into those who would and those who would not save the novel from complete destruction. 'Which reader are you', the novel seems to ask, 'the curate or his friend?' The reader can testify to his or her true sensibility by reading on, and proving to be a better 'man of feeling' than the curate.

One of the novel's first readers, the educationalist James Elphinston, falls into the trap and immediately accepts the novel's invitation into the community of sentimental readers. Soon after the publication of *The Man of Feeling*, he expressed to Mackenzie his dissatisfaction with the fragmentary nature of the novel in a friendly correspondence. 'His truly sentimental friends', he writes, would like to see Harley's story 'in a more consistent dress; to see him begun, continued (though diversified) and ended, perhaps, with a prospect of similar prosperity.' In its present fragmented condition the introduction can please only those 'who cannot taste *the man of feeling*; and whose praise, if they should bestow any, would but make him blush'. Joining the group of the sentimental readers, he is happy that 'every reader of feeling' received Harley as a brother, but he finds the behaviour of the curate coarse and insensible.[10] No doubt, it should hurt the sensibility of true men of feeling that a novel of genuine emotion has an introduction where even the one who saved the manuscript from destruction refuses to weep over it, claiming that 'one is ashamed to be pleased with the works of one knows not whom'.[11] Elphinston probably never notices that the 'insensible' curate saved another text, the German Illustrissimi, which his sensible friend had destined for the same kind of destruction. Elphinston knew without thinking which party to join. Thus, the scenery of ruin and disappointment and the damage to the manuscript show a melancholy prospect not in order to express resignation and pessimism, but in order to call out for a community of men of feeling to salvage the fragments and turn back the process of destruction. The reader is invited – and even pressed – not only to read about, but also to *be* the true man of feeling, buying into an institutionalised culture of tears and compassion. Even if its fictional narrator did not weep, Mackenzie's contemporaries could not – or sometimes did not dare to – resist their tears.

Mirroring minds in eighteenth-century thought

Like the novel's manuscript, its protagonist is also an instrument devised to find – and produce – sentimental readers. Harley is a character who, like a mirror, deflects the reader's gaze, shifting it away from Harley onto all those who narrate, see and read him. To explain Harley's naïvely trustful way of reading the personality of others, the narrator of *The Man of Feeling* describes his protagonist's mind as follows:

> Though I am not of opinion with some wise men, that the existence of objects depends on idea; yet, I am convinced, that their appearance is not a little influenced by it. The optics of some minds are in so unlucky a perspective, as to throw a certain shade on every picture that is presented to them; while those of others (of which number was Harley) like the mirrors of the ladies, have a wonderful effect in bettering their complexions. Through such a medium perhaps was he looking on his present companion. (63)

The narrator places Harley's subjectivity within a framework of influential ideas circulating in eighteenth-century culture. The description of Harley's mind, however, simultaneously reveals the speaker's own narrative and epistemological standpoint. When describing Harley, the narrator interprets Harley's way of reading the world. While Harley reads the character of 'gentleman' into the sycophant who aspires to be one (66), the narrator admits that his own reading of Harley is also determined by subjective factors. The exposure of Harley's distorting vision is at the same time the narrator's self-exposure, and a confession of his own epistemological scepticism. His framework of thought is embedded in its context of contemporary philosophical ideas on subjectivity and perception – a Humean stance on the relations between the world, reason and the human subject, and a Berkeleyan perspective on vision.[12] It is the position of 'scepticism with regard to the senses' from which the narrator of *The Man of Feeling* admits to be speaking, and which also characterises Harley's way of reading the world through the influence of his own state of mind. The tentative 'perhaps' in the last line further unsettles our confidence in the narrator's actual knowledge. Claiming from a perspective of distorted vision and questionable knowledge that Harley's vision is distorted shifts the reader's attention from character to narrator. The immersion of the narrative voice in the philosophies of epistemological scepticism and uncertainty draws the reader into a narratological puzzle. We might wonder who the narrator's utterance actually relates to when he is speaking about the main character. Whose story are we reading here? And who, or what, is the man of feeling?

The metaphor of mind as looking-glass appears in a number of philosophical texts that helped to shape the ideas that were influential for the cultural production of sensibility. In writings by John Locke, David Hume and Adam Smith, this metaphor marks an instability or even crisis related to the concept of a coherent, self-sufficient, knowing and feeling subject.[13] Hume's *A Treatise of Human Nature* (1739–40) depicts human minds as mirrors that reflect passions, sentiments and opinions. In a self-inducing sympathy, a person's emotions and opinions are reflected by other minds in a multiplicity of reverberations, until original and mirror image become indistinguishable, and the dividing lines of subjectivities become blurred. In the chapter that investigates the source of our esteem for the rich and powerful, Hume writes:

> In general we may remark, that the minds of men are mirrors to one another, not only because they reflect each other's emotions, but also because those rays of passions, sentiments, and opinions, may be often reverberated, and may decay away by insensible degrees. Thus the pleasure which a rich man receives from his possessions, being thrown upon the beholder, causes a pleasure and esteem; which sentiments again being perceived and sympathised with, increase the

> pleasure of the possessor, and, being once more reflected, become a
> new foundation for pleasure and esteem in the beholder. [...] Here
> then is a third rebound of the original pleasure, after which it is dif-
> ficult to distinguish the images and reflections, by reason of their
> faintness and confusion. (365)

The consequence of such a multiple, sympathetic refraction is that it
becomes increasingly difficult to distinguish to whom one's feelings
actually belong. Feelings, mixed and intensified in their passage from
self to self, allow distinct subjectivities to slip into one another. The rich
man not only has material means, but he also possesses feelings borrowed from others who admire the pleasure of his riches. His emotions
are dependent on and constructed by someone else's feelings.[14]

In Adam Smith's *The Theory of Moral Sentiments* (1759) the figure of
the mirror refers to society, which provides the individual with feedback
on his or her behaviour and passions. It is through the internalisation
of this mirror that the individual's emotional development is brought
about. If one grows up in complete isolation, Smith argues, one will not
be able to think of one's sentiments and conduct, nor of the beauty or
deformity of one's face. Brought into society, the individual is instantly
provided with a mirror, which is placed in 'the countenance and behaviour of those he lives with, which always mark when they enter into,
and when they disapprove of his sentiments; and it is here that he first
views the propriety and impropriety of his own passions, the beauty
and deformity of his own mind.'[15] Smith uses the trope of the mirror
to argue that the moral and emotional self is not self-sufficient and
cannot develop without the reflection provided by our internal looking-
glass, representing the judgement of other moral, emotional and social
beings. Following the positive or negative responses of society to the
individual's actions and feelings, the person's 'desires and actions, his
joys and sorrows, will now often become the causes of new desires and
new aversions, new joys and new sorrows' (129). Morals and emotions
are born out of the judgements of the other within the self, which Smith
calls the 'impartial spectator' or 'man within the breast'. This impartial
spectator is the internalised mirror that – like Harley's mind – turns us
into a better person when we look into it. Thus, the mirror of society is
formative of the affective, moral self that it simultaneously inhabits.

The looking-glass metaphor in Mackenzie's novel brings into play
a similar disruption of coherence, subversion of self-sufficiency and
displacement of the centre of human subjectivity. Harley's mind, as we
learn from the novel, is a distorting mirror, which not only reflects, but

also improves the complexion of those who look into it. On the one hand, the trope of the looking-glass is used by the narrator to expose Harley's technique of reading – one that projects the reader's own goodness and benevolence onto the rest of the world. This explains Harley's social awkwardness and serves as the reason for his frequent exploitation and victimisation by fraudsters during his journey. For Harley, the world is benevolent and good, because he sees only himself in every countenance. On the other hand, as the metaphor of the mirror in its philosophical context suggests, Harley, even though he is presented as the central character, never becomes the subject in question. Every act of attention directed at him brings about the deflection of the viewer, and a shift of focus. Like the fawning crowd feeding the vanity and producing the passions of the rich in Hume's *Treatise*, Harley is no subject himself, but an object used for the production of someone else's subjectivity and passions – a subjectivity incomplete without the other. Like the manuscript found by the curate and his friend, Harley is searching for, and produces men of feeling. Where he turns up, the world shows a different face. In this way, the story of the man of feeling is always the story of someone else: of the one who sees, reads and narrates.

The man of feeling and the poor

Sentimental novels of the period often warn about the dangers inherent in moments of sympathy, as theorised by Hume and Smith, where the boundaries of the self are thrown into crisis and where the other's emotions can be mistaken for one's own. Scenes of charity can reveal the pitfalls of benevolence and highlight the darker side of the sympathetic impulse advocated by the philosophers of the eighteenth-century moral sense school. Encounters with the poor are a recurring motif in sentimental novels. Beggars, the poor, and the needy crowds surrounding a wealthy benefactor are the 'other' in whose presence the virtues of sensibility manifest themselves, and who hold up a mirror to the values, vanities and vices of sensible men and women of means. Most of the time, however, the scene of charity reveals more of the one who gives than the one who begs.[16] The beggar's way to earn his payment is often to assume the role of the double with whom the potential benefactor can easily identify. In Sarah Fielding's *The Adventures of David Simple* (1744), for example, David (the protagonist) is betrayed by his greedy younger brother, Daniel, who secretly forges the will of their deceased father, leaving David practically destitute. Daniel, who formerly pretended to love the benevolent and talented David, now abuses his impoverished brother and tries to make him his dependant. When the outraged David leaves his brother's house in despair, he gives away one of his last shillings to a beggar who appears to be his mirror image. As the beggar tells him, he too was 'turned out of doors by an unnatural brother'.[17]

Oliver Goldsmith's *The Vicar of Wakefield* (1766) calls attention to the possible discontent behind the narcissistic satisfaction of mutual mirroring. As is shown by both Goldsmith's and Fielding's novels, the danger for the sentimental benefactor lies in giving away much more than one's fortune; it can possibly lie in losing the centre of one's self and placing it in the other. Disappointed by the hypocritical flattery and mock-friendship of dependants, Sir William Thornhill, the wealthy aristocrat of Goldsmith's novel, walks around disguised as an honest but poor man, Mr Burchell, in order to find true friendship and virtue. When Sir William was younger, he enjoyed the adulation of dependants to such an extent that most of his pleasures were derived from flattery. The figure of Sir William takes to the farthest limits the outlook voiced in the moral philosophy of Anthony Ashley Cooper, Third Earl of Shaftesbury, and Francis Hutcheson. According to Shaftesbury, to possess 'natural affections' that promote the good and benefit of the public also involves having affections that make our own selves happy. A considerable part of our pleasure, he claims, derives from sharing the delight and contentment of others, and receiving positive affections in sympathy with them. Our acts are naturally performed with reference to another person, in expectation of the admiration, esteem, kindness or even flattery we receive in return. Francis Hutcheson – the most important disseminator of Shaftesbury's ideas in Scotland – explains altruism by the presence of a so-called 'moral sense' in human nature. This, Hutcheson claims, is an ability that makes us impulsively approve of and be pleased with whatever is virtuous, that is, those actions and affections that promote the good and well-being of others. Hutcheson also argues that our disinterested acts can only be explained by the innate benevolence of human nature, which is the universal foundation of moral sense.[18]

Goldsmith, however, shows how the idea of natural goodness and the belief in a love that both gives pleasure to the individual and creates the bonds of society can potentially turn against themselves, becoming the very tools of social isolation and the disintegration of the self. Sir William Thornhill 'began to lose private interest in universal sympathy' by a pathological form of sensibility:

Physicians tell us of a disorder in which the whole body is so exquisitely sensible that the slightest touch gives pain. What some have thus suffered in their persons, this gentleman felt in his mind: the slightest distress, whether real or fictitious, touched him to the quick, and his soul laboured under a sickly sensibility of the miseries of others.[19]

Making one's feelings entirely dependent on those of others not only brings about poverty, but impoverishes and empties out the very core of the self, threatening it with destruction. While his overgenerosity leads Sir William to give away his fortune, he gradually loses the adoration and flattery of those who used to need his support. The more he fits into the sentimental ideal, the less opportunity he has for practising this ideal. As his example shows, living exclusively for the social affections paradoxically quenches both the social feelings and the pleasures of the self that derive from such feelings: 'But in proportion as he became contemptible to others, he became despicable to himself. His mind had leaned upon their adulation, and that support taken away, he could find no pleasure in the applause of his heart, which he had never learned to reverence' (28). The self of the sentimental man of feeling is centred in the other, and is therefore not self-sufficient. Acting supportively and charitably towards the other is a personal need, motivated by easing one's own mental pain – comparable to the agonies of the sensible body – caused by the other's slightest distress. Besides, it is done in expectation of a reward, a positive feedback on which one's entire consciousness depends.

In *The Vicar of Wakefield*, Sir William Thornhill recognises a trap: dominance intermingled with too great reliance on the feelings of the other actually jeopardises the very mastery the self claims as its own. On the surface the charitable man of sensibility only lives for the good of the other. But the guise of the good man hides a structure that cannot be thought outside hierarchies. The bonds of love that create the social ties in Shaftesbury turn out to have the same root as the bond that ties together master and slave, as outlined later by Hegel. Extreme sensibility is not simply an intense reactive state of both mind and body, but a form of pathological dependence. Growing out of a mutual need, it is a form of dominance where even the person of higher social status ultimately becomes dependent for recognition and for his very existence on the people he supports. The 'natural affections' of the man of feeling, when put into social practice, remain narcissistic and do not make mutual recognition possible.

Jessica Benjamin addresses a similar problem in relation to classical (mainly Freudian) discourses of psychoanalysis, where interpersonal interactions are seen in terms of a subject–object relationship, which dynamic endangers the recognition of the other person as inherently independent from the perceptions of the self. As Jessica Benjamin argues, the other is 'not merely the object of the ego's need/drive or cognition/perception but has a separate and equivalent center of self. Intersubjective theory postulates that the other must be recognised as another subject in order for the self to fully experience his or her subjectivity in the other's presence.'[20] Benjamin claims that domination is not something to be readily assumed; it is not a psychological inevitability, but something that develops culturally out of the breakdown of an initial intersubjective state, a collapse of mutual recognition. For Hegel, she claims, as well as for classical psychoanalysis, the breakdown of this mutuality is inevitable. In Hegel's theory, the omnipotent ego, no matter how strongly it strives for independence, must still face a fundamental paradox: the independence and power of the master is interrelated with its being acknowledged by the subordinate party. The absoluteness of the self is inevitably undermined by the recognition of the other on which it necessarily depends.[21]

Thus, discourses of sensibility and psychoanalysis often struggle with similar questions regarding the vicissitudes of the self in its interpersonal relationships. Sentimental novels show how hard it is to grasp the psychological reality of such an intersubjective state and the recognition of the other as subject rather than object. What love, these novels seem to ask, could fulfil our wish for an intersubjective recognition when even the love of the good man, the love of benevolence that creates the social bond is like a hall of mirrors? The figure of the man of feeling, I would like to suggest, is a textual locus for the attempt to realise this mutuality which for most western societies has always remained a difficult task, if not an impossible one. The sentimental novel, if it cannot offer a solution, at least conveys the awareness of the necessity of such an ideal state. It achieves its goal by rendering reading problematic, showing why and how reading matters as an individual and affective task that also has social and political consequences. It is, after all, a process of reading in which the other person as similar or different, as object or subject, is understood. As sentimental novels show, the bonds of society are dependent on the transferential bond of the reading process and are shaped by the mutual emotional investment of the participants. The otherness of the other, however, remains difficult to access since it can only be found beyond the transferences on which the literature of sensibility depends, beyond the bonds of Shaftesbury's 'natural affections'.[22]

Playing with the literary tradition that centres on the figure of the benefactor, Mackenzie's Harley does not want to let the beggar hold up the usual mirror. Instead, he tries to allow space for the recognition of otherness. While the beggar offers Harley to tell his future – something all passers-by want to hear – Harley asks for the beggar's own story instead, giving him an opportunity to explain how he became a fortune-teller. Thus Harley wants to listen to the story of suffering that had always been silenced or disbelieved by others; as the beggar complains:

> I told all my misfortunes truly, but they were seldom believed; and the few who gave me a half-penny as they passed, did it with a shake of the head, and an injunction, not to trouble them with a long story. [...] I changed my plan, and, instead of telling my own misfortunes, began to prophesy happiness to others. This I found by much the better way: *folks will always listen when the tale is their own*; and of many who say they do not believe in fortune-telling, I have known few on whom it had not a very sensible effect. (61, emphasis added)

The beggar explains how 'every one is anxious to hear what they wish to believe' (61). If he wants to survive, the story he tells must be the fulfilled wish of the listener offered in the guise of the future.

The encounter between Harley and the beggar soon turns into a Humean meeting of mirrors, where wishes and stories are reflected and mingled in a multiplicity of reverberations. Harley urges the beggar to 'let me know something of your profession; I have often thought of turning fortune-teller for a week or two myself' (60). Understanding that Harley appreciates frankness, the professional liar confesses that he makes a living by telling lies. He endeavours to satisfy Harley with the true and 'entertaining' story he wishes to hear (60). Facing the man of feeling, he is compelled to show himself in a better light if he wants to profit from the encounter, so he boasts of having 'had the humour of plain-dealing in me from a child', and claims that 'I was in some sort forced to the trade, for I dealt once in telling the truth' (60). Harley gets what he wanted to hear; the story of the beggar's life remains Harley's wish fulfilment, presented as the truth behind the profession of lying, but still from within the economic conventions of that profession. The beggar ends up narrating the story of the interesting business Harley himself wanted to try out for a short time, in other words, exactly what the man of feeling 'wishes to believe' about begging. His story had to reveal the secrets of fortune-telling, be entertaining and worth Harley's money. While Harley's mind, so to say, betters the complexion of the beggar's narrative, the beggar's story, in its turn, reflects the wish of his benefactor.

The act of charity shows a similarly controversial face: 'Harley had drawn a shilling from his pocket; but virtue bade him consider on whom he was going to bestow it. – Virtue held back his arm: – but a milder form, a younger sister of virtue's, not so severe as virtue, not so serious as pity, smiled upon him: his fingers lost their compression; – nor did virtue offer to catch the money as it fell' (61). The man of feeling is an instrument, rather than the subject of his own emotions. His act of charity is not a voluntary, self-conscious decision of a sensible mind, but rather the work of an involuntary moment caused by the mechanical operation of sympathy. The sympathy between poor and rich is brought about by the cunning tale of the beggar, making the fantasy of the rich materialise in the story of the poor. It is on the basis of the illusion of similarity that an encounter can take place. Rather than being a scene of recognition and giving, Harley's act of charity remains an economic exchange that sustains social hierarchies.

It takes a feeling reader to identify every charitable act with a corresponding sensible heart – a reader for whom Harley's mind can function like a looking-glass that makes the complexion of the world better. Mary Wollstonecraft's novel, *Maria; or, the Wrongs of Woman* (1798), draws attention to the important political stakes of being educated into such a way of reading. Wollstonecraft shows how serious the problem becomes when the looking-glass that improves one's appearance is really a lady's mental mirror. Maria's reading, governed by the fantasy-image of a man of feeling who makes the world's face better, has tragic consequences. George Venables, her future husband, abuser and persecutor, gains Maria's love by performing a charitable act which, for Maria, is the emblem of a feeling heart. The guinea which Venables gives to Maria in support of the distressed Peggy, as Maria recalls, 'invested my hero with more than mortal beauty. My fancy [...] quickly went to work, with all the happy credulity of youth, to consider that heart devoted to virtue, which had only obeyed a virtuous impulse.'[23] As Maria has to learn from her own bitter experience, the ideal of the man of feeling can easily remain an empty pose, an apparatus through which the power imbalance of patriarchy reasserts itself. Obeying a virtuous impulse, as Harley did, does not necessarily imply a virtuous heart, hiding as it does the potential bonds that tie together master and slave: the unyielding dynamics of dominance.

Madness and the man of feeling

Harley's sympathetic lens even makes it possible for the horrors of the eighteenth-century madhouse to acquire a more pleasant complexion. Harley's friends are shown around in Bedlam by a cruel keeper, who introduces the mad 'in the phrase of those that keep wild beasts for shew' (67) and presents a terrifying scene of clanking chains, and horrid, wild cries. Harley himself, however, is approached by a 'decent-looking man' who offers to give him 'a more satisfactory account of the unfortunate people you see here' (67). The stranger goes up to him when Harley falls behind his companions and lingers within the world of Bedlam for a short time instead of following the rhythm of the sane. As it turns out at the end of the episode, this man is one of the inhabitants, and thinks himself to be 'the Chan of Tartary'. It is only the man of feeling among the visitors who is singled out and taken on a private tour of the madhouse. The world of the mad does not open up for the regular visitor – it can open up only for the man of feeling.

The mad guide's story of Bedlam is indeed different from the one the cruel keeper has to offer. The inmates are no longer wild beasts, madmen or maniacs but 'unfortunate people'. The mad Newtonian scientist whose cosmological calculations did not work according to plan is 'a gentleman who had once been a celebrated mathematician', who 'fell a sacrifice' to science (67). Harley is introduced to talented people, many of whom had once been renowned for their achievements. The mad guide characterises them through what they used to be rather than by naming them as anything in the present; their identity and humanity lie in the story of their past. As he points out to Harley, apropos of the businessman whom bankruptcy reduced to madness: '*this* [...] *was* a gentleman well known in Change-alley' (68, emphases added). The man who constantly recites poetry is introduced as a 'figure' who 'was a schoolmaster of some reputation', and interrupts their conversation as a 'voice' (68). From the guide's perspective he did not lose his wits by trying to solve a difficult problem but he 'came hither' – as if by his own will – 'to be resolved of some doubts he entertained concerning the genuine pronunciation of the Greek vowels' (68). The scholar of poetry is himself a figure. He is only a trope in the story Harley's guide tells about him – a trope of his luckier and more glorious past.

For the mad guide, Bedlam is a place inhabited by gentlemen, unfortunate people, voices, figures, ghosts and indefinable creatures whose identity can be caught only in the grammatical past tense. This scene of Bedlam is a text whose figures stand for stories of interesting and once successful human beings now turned into mere signifiers – a text completely different from what the cruel keeper offered the visitors, who, as a result, fled in horror. The different perspectives of the two guides construct Bedlam as a text dependent on its narrator, which text makes it impossible both for visitors and inmates to assume and construct stable identities. The inhabitants are confined by verbal signs that can mean anything depending on the reader: a prison-house of language. In the figure of the guide Harley finds his double, another man of feeling, and it is only between the two men of feeling – or two madmen – that a conversation can take place. Through the language of history and poetry, Harley and the guide enter into a mental domain which assumes the universality of madness and its underlying presence in all human actions. The guide proposes that madness is a condition that overflows the walls of Bedlam: 'the world, in the eye of a philosopher, may be said to be a large madhouse' (69). Harley agrees, and only after this agreement has been established does the guide reveal his 'true' identity as the Chan of Tartary, and therefore his delusion. Like the other inhabitants of Bedlam, he turns out to be a half-fictional character from a story of the past, a figure lacking existence in the present.

Sigmund Freud, in his reading of Wilhelm Jensen's *Gradiva*, gives account of an encounter where delusion and sanity have to speak the same language in order for a cure to take place.[24] The hero of Jensen's novel, the archaeologist Norbert Hanold, is driven by a delusion to find the reality behind an ancient bas-relief representing a girl with a distinctive gait. When tracing the reality of the gait in his present environment does not bring the desired results, he undertakes a trip to Pompeii, where he indeed finds a woman with the Gradiva-gait who matches his fantasy. The girl, Zoe Bertgang, Hanold's once-intimate childhood friend (whom the scholar had simply foreclosed from his consciousness), enters into a conversation with the obsessed archaeologist. By assuming the role of the revenant the man takes her to be, Zoe can uncover the nature of the other's madness. As Freud writes, she accepts the young man's delusion only in order to set him free from it. Curing his delusion is only possible by 'taking up the same ground as the delusional structure and then investigating it as completely as possible' (22). This encounter is not simply an encounter between sanity and madness as Freud presents it, but also a story about the politics of reading. It is an allegory of reading and recognising difference – an encounter between woman and man where woman, in order to be noticed, has to step into the male fantasy created around her existence.[25]

The Bedlam episode in Mackenzie's novel presents a similar scenario. Here the mad guide has to assume the fantasy of Harley in order that he may be heard. Becoming the reflection of the man of feeling, the mad guide presents a better, more humane, more sympathetic story of the horrors of Bedlam. The only way for madness to raise a voice against the dehumanisation and the forgetting imposed on it by society is to assume the identity of sanity. But when the guide reveals his identity, Harley for the first time notices – and shies away from – their difference. The moment otherness is revealed, it is instantly rejected by the man of feeling, whose fantasy it has been to see a world of feeling. When he discovers what world he has been in the process of entering, he is 'struck by this discovery', and abandons it: 'he had prudence enough, however, to conceal his amazement, and bowing as low to the monarch as his dignity required, left him immediately, and joined his companions' (69). The world of the mad needs to speak the language of sensibility in order to claim recognition – a recognition that is eventually denied even by the man of feeling himself.

In the women's ward, Harley listens to the story of the melancholy girl who lost her lover, Billy, and became a means of financial exchange in an unhappy marriage arranged by her father. The girl's madness lies in not being able to feel emotions or shed tears any more: 'I would weep too, but my brain is dry; and it burns, burns, burns!' (70) Harley's resemblance to the dead Billy activates a scene of mutual transferences: 'I would not have you weep: you are like my Billy; you are, believe me; just so he looked when he gave me this ring; poor Billy!' (70–1). While the girl identifies Harley with her lost lover, the melancholy Harley can similarly identify with, and sense his future in the fate of the dead Billy, who also left his lover in the hope of bettering his fortune. The mad girl, like Jensen's deluded Norbert, touches her companion, holds his hand and presses it to her bosom, and finally puts Billy's ring on Harley's finger. Harley's tears make the girl – previously thoughtful and silent – speak and feel again. The scene of sensibility also affects the other visitors: 'except the keeper's, there was not an unmoistened eye around her' (70). In contrast to Freud's reading of *Gradiva*, touching the other is not a test of the reality of the other; it does not provide a possible way out of the delusion, but remains within the bounds of the transference. It is by touching the body of Harley that the mad girl turns him into Billy and forces him back into the fantasy. The production of emotional responses characteristic of sensibility is made possible only by fastening tight the web of transferences by which both self and other are helplessly bound. The man of feeling needs to be (in) the other in order for sensibility to be produced.

The 'man of feeling', therefore, is not Harley; it is an emotional lens, a technique of reading (through feeling) rather than a pre-existent character or personality type. The construction of the 'man of feeling' implies an always shifting perspective. Harley, for those who read him, is a hollowed-out figure eternally mobilised by – and mobilising – someone else's emotions. This process is well illustrated by the scene of Harley's death. The narrator, a friend of Harley's, attempts to reanimate Harley's lifeless body, 'stretched without sense or feeling' in front of him:

> I took his hand in mine; I repeated his name voluntarily: – I felt a pulse in every vein at the sound. I looked earnestly in his face; his eye was closed, his lip pale and motionless. There is an enthusiasm in sorrow that forgets impossibility. I wondered that it was so. The sight drew a prayer from my heart; it was the voice of frailty, and of man! the confusion of my mind began to subside into thought; I had time to weep! (138)

Tears are the marks of an illusion experienced by the narrator. The illusion is that of *prosopopeia*, a trope through which the inanimate becomes animate. The pulse of the corpse is the narrator's own pulse, wished into the other's body. His illusory reanimation is an 'enthusiasm of sorrow' (97), in which the other's feelings are, in reality, one's own. In Adam Smith's *The Theory of Moral Sentiments* (1759), our horrific and melancholy picture of the dead is the result of a similar reanimation, which Smith theorises as an act of sympathetic identification. Our grief results 'from our putting ourselves in their situation, and from our lodging, if I may be allowed to say so, our own living souls in their inanimated bodies, and thence conceiving what would be our emotions in this case. It is from this very illusion of the imagination, that the foresight of our own dissolution is so terrible to us'.[26] By the end of the novel the narrator has become a Harley-figure. Sitting inside Harley's favourite place, the hollow tree, he turns into a container for noble feelings: Harley's lens of sympathy has softened his hatred of the world into pity. Similarly, when we mourn Harley we wish to revive the man of feeling by recovering our own humanity lodged in the other. The death of the man of feeling repeats the gesture of the novel's introduction, inviting us to mobilise our sympathy and reconstruct the community of genuine sentiment.

Like the curate's friend in the novel's introduction, readers did save this novel. It went through a large number of editions from 1771 until the end of the century, and has been constantly re-edited since.[27] But despite its textual survival, it is, like most sentimental novels, often deemed 'unreadable' by today's reading public. Its late-nineteenth-century editions even include an 'Index to Tears', where the taxonomy of tearfulness is clearly presented as a curiosity, with the possible intention to elicit a mirthful response in the audience.[28] While the novel has recently gained an increasing amount of critical attention from those specialising in the literature and history of sensibility, it remains on the margins of the literary canon, even in the light of the academic curriculum of major universities. The critical discourse through which the novel is salvaged today tends to turn away from the complexity of emotional response altogether or distances tearfulness into a historical past, which can only be understood by means of scholarly contextualisation. Mackenzie's novel is retained by foreclosing the issue of the tears it used to be able to trigger. We do not cry over sentimental novels any more. Instead, we produce scholarly analyses from a safely detached perspective in the present.

The novel's marginalisation, however, can raise important questions. Have our reading practices changed so much that we consider the eighteenth century's indulgence of the reader's emotions distasteful or difficult to comprehend? Or do we simply shed different tears now? Has the university itself become a means for institutionalising the foreclosure of emotional response? And how long can we safely live in what Maureen Harkin calls a 'distinctly post-sentimental age'?[29] Through its tears, Mackenzie's novel teaches us something about reading. Like Freud's interpretation of *Gradiva*, it exposes the way in which one is deluded or seduced into a shared fantasy, while showing the risks and difficulties that arise in any encounter with the other. In our age, as in Mackenzie's, texts exist that – as sentimental novels once did – compel us to absorb the values and ideologies of a culture by directly appealing to our tears or our feelings. A detachment from our own feelings (whether conscious of involuntary) does not help us to evaluate critically the cultural and political messages that surround us, but nor does an unreflected, purely sentimental response prove helpful.[30] Making us conscious that our emotional responses *do* exist is a task that must be addressed by future practices of critical reading, which need to negotiate a space for the experience of affectivity within the framework of its theory. This does not mean returning to a purely affective reading practice, but the acknowledgment of our emotional responses and a simultaneous preservation of our critical and historical insight. Reading the sentimental novel with an attention to the history *and* the experience of feeling may help us to evaluate the ways in which the seductions and fantasies of our own contemporary culture foreclose the issue of tears, which thereby escape being analysed and understood by the very practices on which we rely for understanding.

4
Women and the Negative: The Sentimental Swoon in Eighteenth-Century Fiction

> Oh write it not, my hand – the name appears
> Already written – wash it out, my tears!
> In vain lost Eloïsa weeps and prays,
> Her heart still dictates, and her hand obeys.
> (Alexander Pope, 'Eloisa to Abelard')

> Thus the content of a repressed image or idea can make its way into consciousness, on condition that it is negated. Negation is a way of taking cognizance of what is repressed; indeed it is already a lifting of the repression, though not, of course, an acceptance of what is repressed. (Sigmund Freud, 'Negation')

Introduction: medicine, psychoanalysis, and the swoon

Lord Dorchester, the male protagonist of Sarah Fielding's *The History of Ophelia* (1760), sets off to fight a duel in order to settle a misunderstanding caused by the naive Ophelia at her first ball. When Ophelia finds that Lord Dorchester left a will she understands the seriousness of the situation and falls into fits of fainting from which she barely recovers. A strikingly similar episode takes place in Elizabeth Inchbald's *A Simple Story* (1791). When Miss Milner hears the news that Dorriforth, her guardian, is about to fight a duel with Sir Frederick Lawnly, she 'sunk speechless on the floor'.[1] In both novels, the heroine's fainting is occasioned by a threat to the life of the man she loves – knowingly or unknowingly; yet social restrictions do not allow her to admit and express this feeling. While fainting reveals their deepest emotion, it is also a disadvantage for both heroines: it prevents them stopping the life-threatening event and assisting where they would be most needed.

By losing consciousness, they are forced into an inactivity that hinders the fulfilment of the very desire uncovered by their fainting. But what do novels of the period achieve by staging cases of female indisposition? And why do sentimental heroines faint, after all?

While in the mid-eighteenth century the sentimental symptom-language of tears, blushes and swoons was a fashionable indicator of genuine feeling, such expressions of sentiment were often surrounded by mistrust, suspicion and even ridicule in the period.[2] There are countless examples of critical attitudes targeted specifically at sentimental transparency. Henry Fielding's *Shamela* (1741) famously challenges the disinterestedness of authentic female emotion, while Hannah More's critique in 'Sensibility: A Poem' (1782) targets the potentially false and equivocal body language that is generally assumed to express genuine feeling. As she complains,

> [...]
> So exclamations, tender tones, fond tears,
> And all the graceful drapery Pity wears;
> These are not Pity's self, they but express
> Her inward sufferings by their pictured dress;
> *And these fair marks, reluctant I relate,*
> *These lovely symbols may be counterfeit.*[3]

But what makes these 'lovely symbols' so ambivalent throughout the eighteenth century? The female sentimental psychosomatic repertoire (fainting, silences, sighs, palpitations and states of mental distraction) is often taken for granted as an obvious sign of female sensibility, and the subtleties of its meaning are rarely explored in detail.[4] However, many eighteenth-century novels of sensibility respond in different, but self-conscious and politically challenging ways to crises of the female mind and body staged in sentimental writing as early as Richardson's *Clarissa* (1747–8). At a time when openly expressing emotions that related to sexuality was one of the greatest prohibitions affecting women, the discourse of sensibility came to function as a socially acceptable form of expression, a legitimate channel into which forbidden, repressed affects could be diverted. It is hard to find a sentimental novel without a swooning, dangerously ill or seriously distracted heroine, and fictional representations of the fainting, indisposed woman remain frequent throughout the long eighteenth century. Richardson's Pamela faints in order to avoid sexual intercourse, while Clarissa is unconscious while being raped by Lovelace, thus escaping mentally from an unwanted experience; Rousseau's Julie falls into a swoon during her forbidden kiss with Saint Preux.

This chapter intends to account for the controversial nature of sentimental symptoms by investigating such disruptions to female consciousness – disruptions that are traditionally interpreted as signs of female sensibility. Here I shall focus mainly on three literary texts born in the wake of Richardson's sentimental fiction: Sarah Fielding's *The History of Ophelia* (1760), Jean-Jacques Rousseau's *Julie, or the New Heloise* (1761) and Elizabeth Inchbald's *A Simple Story* (1791). I will read fictional instances where fainting, as well as altered bodily and mental states, seem to relate to what, at least for women in the long eighteenth century, may not be communicated openly: emotions, thoughts and desires that women, as social subjects, were not supposed to have. Tears, sighs and swoons are sometimes referred to as the 'vocabulary of sensibility' in literary criticism. I shall argue that these bodily signs are symptomatic of the limitations to feminine self-expression and reflect the discontents of eighteenth-century female psychosexual existence. The typical symptoms of sensibility form part of a complex psychopathology that often reaches beyond the concerns of contemporary medicine, staging affects, symptoms and conditions that cannot be understood merely from the 'nerves, spirits and fibres' of the eighteenth-century mind and body.[5]

This chapter will put particular emphasis on exploring the significance of fits of feminine fainting and swooning. There is a lack of satisfactory explanation of this phenomenon in eighteenth-century medicine, where it is seen as a somatic component of so-called 'nervous' illnesses and is mostly associated with the heart and its failures. Thus, fainting was seen by medicine as a problem ultimately pertaining to what comes to be known during the eighteenth century as muscular irritability. Irritability, as we have seen in Chapter 2, meant the contracting force inherent to the muscle tissue; it was responsible for bodily motions and convulsions, including the unconscious motions of the heart and the intestines. Novels of the period, however, contest the medical understanding of fainting: they radicalise physical reactivity by making it into a site of emotional and sexual assertion and resistance. In this way, they give an early language to emotions, unconscious elements and repressed forces long before Freud developed his terminology. Many novels of sensibility already stage cases of hysteria critically, conveying 'an individual's act of protest and rebellion directed against social conditions'.[6] Not only do they anticipate the insights, but they also critique the blind spots of Freud's interpretations.

Therefore, I will approach such psychologically induced states of consciousness and unconsciousness, using a methodological framework that connects their eighteenth-century medical explanations with psychoanalytic ideas, more specifically, ideas of negativity. While eighteenth-century medical writings relate fainting mostly to constitutional causes, opening up towards a larger history and theory of feeling will help us understand fainting as a psychosomatic phenomenon rooted in an intricate network of eighteenth-century affective, sexual and social factors. I will read states of indisposition in relation to what the psychoanalyst André Green calls 'the work of the negative'. Green's work is famous for his revision of the psychoanalytic theory of affect, and for developing a theoretical framework for the treatment of negative transferences and negative therapeutic reactions. In *The Work of the Negative* he explores the operation of the negative on a broad spectrum of cases ranging from normality to the extremely ill. The 'negative' refers, firstly, to the 'consistent rejection of what is intolerable to the ego, exemplified by the mechanism of repression'. Secondly, it includes the 'destructiveness of the death drive, that operates as a radical refusal of satisfaction and pleasure'. According to Green, the operation of the work of the negative includes a wide range of what he calls, in an umbrella term, 'negativising' tendencies: repression, negation, disavowal and the foreclosure and hallucination of psychosis.[7] My analyses of the novels will explore sensibility as the site of the negative, as it comes to function as a code system for transgressive – and often sexual – affectivity, the expression of which, coming up against social and linguistic conventions and inhibitions, becomes dominated by repression, loss of consciousness, blanks, and silences.

Eighteenth-century medical treatises deal only cursorily with fainting, and their explanation often remains elusive. In treatises on so-called 'nervous diseases', fainting is usually regarded as an accompanying symptom of other conditions such as hysteria or epilepsy.[8] In the medical terminology of the period, fainting, swooning and various states that involve the loss of sensation or consciousness are referred to by the technical terms 'syncope' and 'lipothymy' (or 'lypothymia'). These terms are still used in today's medical vocabulary. Even though syncope and lipothymy are listed in most medical dictionaries, they are often dealt with by means of short and insufficient explanations. For instance, the curious reader of John Quincy's dictionary from the early eighteenth century has to be satisfied with the following description: syncope 'comes from various Causes, but mostly hysterical, and is therefore to be treated as such, unless when manifestly from somewhere else, and then it is to be managed accordingly'.[9]

Perhaps the most elaborate discussion of these conditions is given in Robert James's *Medicinal Dictionary*. Here, syncope (from the Greek 'to cut' or 'strike') and lipothymy (from the Greek 'to leave' and 'mind') are seen as manifestations of a weak constitution, and represent two degrees of a sudden decay or failure of the natural forces.[10] Lipothymy, a lower degree of weakness, is characterised by a general depravity of motion and speech, and a failure of the sense organs termed 'insensibility'.[11] Syncope is a more serious condition than lipothymy. In addition to the loss of motion and sensation, it also includes loss of consciousness. While lipothymy looks like an overall paralysis of the body and the senses, syncope seems to mimic death:

> the Patient is deprived of all Manner and Strength, both of Body and Mind, and seems to be dead; for he [sic] falls to the Ground quite speechless, as if oppressed with a profound Sleep, and lies immoveable, without the appearance of Convulsions or Tremblings; the Pulse and Respiration are intercepted, the Limbs are refrigerated, and collapsed, he has the *Facies Hippocratica*, and a copious Eruption of cold Sweat about his Temples. (James, '*syncope*')

Syncope looks like a short, temporary death, from which the patient slowly comes back to life as the circulation is restored and 'all the suppressed Functions by little and little resume their Office' (James, '*syncope*').

Even in its eighteenth-century definitions, syncope links a psychosomatic state with the realm of the verbal, the poetic and the musical. In the field of poetics, for instance, syncope means the cutting short of a word by ellipsis ('o'er' instead of 'over', or 'e'en' for 'even'). Syncope, in the sense of contraction or elision, is also the name of a poetic device used for securing the cadence of a line, or making the line fit into the syllable pattern of the stanza. A syllable, so to say, needs to be sacrificed and cut for the sake of metrical regularity.[12] For musicians, syncope is a rhythmic form that subverts the order of stress in the bar and puts stress on what is regularly unstressed. In the medical condition of syncope, sensation and life are suspended or repressed by a stronger, debilitating force. Like a syncopated word, life is cut short and abbreviated by a sudden suspension of consciousness. As in music, a subversive shift of stress takes place: a state beyond consciousness suddenly comes to the fore and becomes more emphatic than consciousness. The regular rhythm of life is disturbed, and the patient, even when recovered from the fit, 'still complains of an extraordinary Lassitude and Imbecility of the Limbs, and of the whole Body' (James, '*syncope*'). In fact, such states could easily slip into more extreme states of dysfunction. The condition could degenerate from lipothymy to syncope, and, according to one later eighteenth-century source, from syncope to the even more serious 'asphixy'. In the latter, the pulse and breathing are totally extinguished, the body is cold, and the condition can be followed by death (Motherby, *'lipothymia'*).[13]

In eighteenth-century medicine, such losses of bodily and mental presence were regularly attributed to the heart and its failures, and were thought of as occurring in people of weak constitution. Even in cases where fainting originated in the mind, the condition was still linked to constitutional weakness and was therefore interpreted – and treated – as somatic. Syncope, according to Robert James, is 'a sudden Check or Stop put to the Motion of the Heart'. This suspension of the heartbeat, resulting from a disorderly circulation, could be caused by the passions and affections of the mind, as well as by other factors, such as bad diet, the temperature of the air, unusual smells, or indulging in 'the immoderate Use of venereal Pleasures' (James, *'syncope'*).[14] A constitution was weak if it was 'easily excited to disorderly Motions from some Slight external Cause' (James, *'syncope'*). Women, children and elderly people, owing to their weaker constitutions, were thought to be more prone to having fits of syncope and lipothymy – and, following from this, they were also considered to be more predisposed to becoming subject to violent emotions (fits of anger, fear and confused imagination). The pejorative connotations originally associated with 'faint' and 'fainting' are also reflected in Eric Partridge's etymological dictionary: from the entry on 'faint' the reader is redirected to the entry on 'feign', which is explained as 'feigned, hence cowardly', 'lacking in spirit, hence lacking consciousness'.[15]

According to the testimony of several medical dictionaries and treatises, fainting and various forms of female indisposition occurring in novels of sensibility were also typical symptoms of hysteria. In Robert Hooper's dictionary, hysteric fits were sometimes preceded by 'dejection of spirits, anxiety of mind, effusion of tears, difficulty of breathing, sickness at the stomach, and palpitations at the heart' – symptoms that were also indicative of one's sensibility. Fainting often accompanied the hysteric fit, where 'the person lies seemingly in a state of profound sleep, without either sense or motion' (Hooper, *Medical Dictionary*, *'hysteria'*). Not only did sensibility and hysteria share many common symptoms, but sensibility was also, so to say, a borderline condition – a possible cause as well as a common symptom of hysteria and other nervous (or mental) disorders. Extreme sensibility often appears in treatises on madness as a state on its borderline that can easily slip into insanity. Imagining madness as a somatic disease, several treatises eventually turn out to be about something other than madness: they end up describing those conditions that cause it or follow from it – that is, the emotional and mental states on its borderline. These include sensibility and the passions, which always surface from the blind spots of contemporary medical explanations.[16]

'Pronouncing the Word No': silenced negations in Sarah Fielding's *The History of Ophelia*

The eighteenth-century novel of sensibility presents an intriguing and complex picture about the female sentimental swoon. These novels are in dialogue with contemporary medical theories related to the female body, and they also anticipate some of the answers Freud and his successors offered when treating disorders traditionally associated with women. While staging such 'weaknesses of constitution', Fielding's *The History of Ophelia* reflects subversively on the image of women in the medical imagination of its time. Unlike Inchbald's fashionable and sociable Miss Milner, Ophelia comes from entirely outside polite social circles. While she falls into fits in the same situation as Miss Milner, Ophelia's story shows how a young woman comes to acquire, by her entrance into society, the delicacy and 'constitutional' weakness necessary for appropriately sentimental reactions. Fielding's novel, published in 1760, before Rousseau's *Julie, or the New Heloise* (1761) or *Émile* (1762), stages the theme – also prevalent in Rousseau – of the woman educated in innocence and isolation, promoting the values of natural, self-sufficient life opposed to the corruption of society. Ophelia is an orphan girl who grows up under the guidance of her aunt in a forest cottage on the Welsh border, protected from experience, relationships and unsettling emotions, until one day she is abducted by the rakish Lord Dorchester. He does not attack her virtue directly but takes her under his morally dubious protection, living with her on his country estate and in London, and surrounding her with an affluence of riches, while isolating her from sources of knowledge that could warn her of her danger. His secret intention is to make her his mistress, and convince her of the validity of his anti-marriage principles.

While *The History of Ophelia* is generally considered to be Sarah Fielding's most conventional novel, some of her critics have emphasised its subversive, feminist intentions masked in a linear, seemingly not very experimental form.[17] Linda Bree points out that an important dimension of the novel's subversiveness lies in its treatment of female behaviour that traditionally characterises sentimentalism. Bree notes the balance between Ophelia's sentimental capacities for tears and illnesses, combined with an unusual toughness. She draws attention to Ophelia's strength of character in the face of a series of abductions and dangers that prove to be debilitating for most sentimental heroines.[18] Here I would like to explore the more painful side of this psychological balance and maintain that while Ophelia comes out of these situations composed (and sometimes even entertained), she responds with weakness, fainting and illness to immediate stress, forcing her into passive inaction. This, however, is not in itself inconsistent with the novel's feminist undertones and is only seemingly in conformity with a disempowering feminine ideal. I would like to argue that, paradoxically, beyond the affirmative plotline of Ophelia's triumphs, strengths, and happy marriage in the end, the subversive intentions of the novel are consistently traceable through an economy of negation that is subtly woven into a story of Ophelia's emotional *Bildung*. This alternative, death-driven plotline questions the values and conventions of the sentimental narrative that *The History of Ophelia* seems ostensibly to adopt.

Fielding's novel stages the process in which the woman of sensibility, with all her attributes of female delicacy, comes into existence. Ophelia's Welshness is set in opposition to the corruption of English society as seen through the eyes of the innocent abroad.[19] While happy and healthy in her forest cottage, and boasting of a naturally strong constitution, Ophelia repeatedly falls seriously ill, becomes melancholy and 'half distracted', wishes to die, and during her adventures in the world frequently loses the power of speech, feeling or consciousness.[20] After her abduction, her swoons, fits, illnesses and nearly mortal fevers rapidly follow one another, even at times when she is afraid only of the threatening mental projections induced by 'fearing every Thing, yet fixing upon Nothing' (155). Violent and distressing emotions follow the heroine's forced initiation into a world of physical coercion, masks and passions. Illness, as Ophelia emphasises, is a condition characteristic of her changed circumstances, and comes with her removal from her original environment. As she writes: 'The natural Strength of my Spirits and Nerves, which had then never felt any of the Disorders, that, in a Degree, afflict almost every Constitution in this Country, and by which, even mine has suffered since, returning, I bid adieu to my native Simplicity of Life' (55). Fever, physical breakdown and death-wish, as Peter Sabor observes, accompany her traumatic transition into adulthood, which takes place through her transportation from her natural, healthy cottage life in Wales to the sickly state of urban English society.[21]

In Ophelia's England, illness seems to be a general social condition. When our heroine visits Tunbridge, a popular eighteenth-century bathing resort, she is surprised by the number of people she encounters, mostly cheerful and engaged in noisy forms of entertainment that 'seemed too loud for the trembling Frame of an Invalid' (211). Unfamiliar with the social function of the spa, she had anticipated seeing a group of suffering individuals, but instead she encounters the whole psychosomatic landscape of English society, where the ill sit together with the healthy, and where symptoms of all possible disorders abound in a cacophonous mixture of conversation and music. The general humming of human voices consists of the names of hundreds of diseases: 'all in such a Confusion of Tongues, that it was impossible to appropriate to each their respective Complaints, but served to convince me that all Distempers were there assembled' (211). It is in such a Babel-like confusion of tongues that Ophelia has to find her way and acquire the psychosomatic language of illness and disorder. The culture of female sensibility she is in the process of entering is produced from the entangled signifiers of health and disease.

Fainting, so typical and frequent in descriptions of women in the period, was often associated with stays and corsetry. Beyond the assumptions of its being a serious health risk and a torture to the female body, the historical symbolism of lacing is multifaceted. As Valerie Steele writes in her historical study on the corset, while stays were often experienced as an assault on the body, they also had significance beyond their role as instruments of female oppression and sexual exploitation. Hiding, shaping and exposing the female body at the same time, they simultaneously represented respectability and sexual allure, discipline and erotic display. Women's bodies were restricted and made socially acceptable by being fitted into the underwear (initially made by men) – conveying the symbolism of sexual penetration via the penetration of the holes of the stays, an activity often assisted by men themselves. Stays and corsets undoubtedly contributed to producing many of the sentimental feminine attributes of the age, suggesting fragility combined with eroticism. By the very fact that it offered necessary support, the ideology behind the corset presupposed physical weakness. As far as medical consequences are concerned, Steele claims, even a moderately tight corset restricts the respiration and makes one rely on upper-diaphragmatic breathing, which creates palpitations of the breast. As has been confirmed by modern medical experiments using tight-laced, Victorian corsets, fainting is likely to have occurred during physical activity, such as dancing – something that further reinforced the idea of the constitutional weakness and disability of the female body.[22]

But Fielding's Ophelia refuses to wear stays. Accustomed to an unusual simplicity of dress, a natural hairstyle and a thin waistcoat as an undergarment, she soon becomes the object of public observation. In Lord Dorchester's country house, she is led into an apartment that abounds in rich dresses and ornaments. She cannot wait to try on her new clothes and jewels, but 'immediately threw away the stiff Stays, which seemed to [her] invented in perverse Opposition to Nature, and one of the Proofs with which this Country abounded, that Man in his Folly had declared open War with her, and by pretending to improve, had so spoiled her Work, that scarcely any Traces of the Divine Artificer remained' (61–2). Her losses of sense and consciousness, then, are not due to corsetry. Rather, I would suggest, they represent an available and socially acceptable form of emotional expression. In Ophelia's case, illness and fainting is a language – often a language of protest by which she says 'no' to the social pattern she is forced into by her violent abduction. Physical indisposition permits her to resort to the figure of the syncope. She censors and cuts short her conscious, healthy state, so as to be able to fit into her new plot and meet new emotional requirements – just as a word is cut short to fit the rhythm of the line in which it features. Syncope is a means of protest, but it also serves as a survival strategy, representing the only (cut and broken) form in which Ophelia can become the protagonist of the narrative that is imposed on her by the expectations of a culture in which she always remains a foreigner.

Syncopated sense and consciousness accompany Ophelia's initiation into experiencing, expressing and reading many of the passions with which she had been unfamiliar in her state of innocent isolation. Far away from social influences, the eighteenth-century woman – often accused of emotional excess – starts out naturally void of overwhelming passions. As an epitome of female blankness, Fielding's Ophelia is a predecessor of Rousseau's Sophie, Saint-Pierre's Virginie, or Edgeworth's Virginia, brought up in isolation entirely for her future husband's benefit.[23] Ophelia's cottage life is an idyllic state of contentment and joy; her first violent and distressful passions arise with her abduction. Unlike her aunt, who uses all her powers of persuasion to entreat the disguised man to let go of her niece, Ophelia is so paralysed by the first overwhelming emotions of her life – terror, fear and grief – that she 'had not Power to speak' and became 'almost senseless' (51). As in the state of lipothymy described by contemporary medicine, she loses sensation and speech – exactly those faculties that would have helped her to escape.

When Lord Dorchester unmasks his face following Ophelia's abduction, the discovery of a hypocrisy that she never previously experienced arouses the emotions of hatred and anger. She gives vent to her powerful feelings, but their expression is so forceful that it silences her:

> [...] although this was, I believe, the first Passion I had been in, it had none of the Weakness of a new Emotion. A Person bred up in the continual Exercise of her Rage could not have expressed herself more strongly than I did to his Lordship, who endeavoured to soothe and pacify me, and he so far succeeded, that I lost all Utterance, from the Violence of my Tears: He seemed to feel my Sorrow and wept with me. (52)

Unfamiliar with a culture of violence and emotion, Ophelia's expression of rage is silenced by the very means of its expression. Encouraged by Dorchester's tears (which she takes to be the tears of sympathy), Ophelia recovers the power of expression, asking her abductor to take her back to her aunt: 'the Excess of my Sorrow and Despair, made me eloquent' (52). But speech driven by overwhelming emotion once more brings about the impossibility of verbal expression. Appealing to the compassion of Lord Dorchester, she makes her pleas as forceful and tragic as possible, rendering herself all the more miserable: 'I painted my Wretchedness in such strong Colours, that I at last became dumb with Horror at the melancholy Prospect [...]' (53). This process culminates in a more serious silencing: illness and fever, which she expects to be fatal. Finally, she looks forward to a death caused by fear and the grief she feels for what she has lost. Overwhelmed with the novelty of new emotions, not having yet learnt to balance the affective and the symbolic, Ophelia is paralysed – literally immobilised by her illness, which thus constitutes both the means and the limit of her protest.

Lord Dorchester, like Hamlet (who condemns all female innocence as pretence), regularly and unjustly doubts and misunderstands Ophelia's naivety. Unfamiliar with the passion of jealousy, Fielding's Ophelia cannot comprehend Lord Dorchester, when – wrongly suspecting that she is in love with someone else – he abandons her, leaving behind only a farewell letter and a settlement of an annual sum. Once more overwhelmed with emotions at Lord Dorchester's behaviour, Ophelia's mind becomes as disordered as that of her Shakespearean namesake. Soon a set of serious illness follows, making her look forward to a desired death.

She feels 'deprived of [her] Senses', gives vent to her 'Distractions', and runs out of the room 'with an Air so frantic' that it terrifies her maid (123). Mentally distracted, losing her senses, and falling into a high fever, she is literally out of her mind. Playing with the reader's expectations based on the distracted heroine of *Hamlet*, Fielding's novel invokes the act of suicide, the evident outcome of this trajectory, which nevertheless remains unpronounceable in the novel.

During her visit to Bedlam, Ophelia finds that the mad escape into a pleasurable fantasy world. In Bedlam, the ambitious man can be a king, the woman disfigured by smallpox can find an admirer in everyone, and the zealous author can finally reconcile wit and riches (205–8). These are instances that Freud, in 'The Neuro-Psychoses of Defence' (1894), calls hallucinatory psychoses – a flight into illness from incompatible claims of reality. Freud's example in this paper could well have been one of the Bedlamites encountered by Ophelia or the mad girl encountered by Harley in *The Man of Feeling*: a young woman abandoned by her lover and living in a happy dream, where her lover is ever-present. Freud explains the mechanism of such psychoses through the operation of a form of the negative: the total rejection of an impulse coming from reality. Freud considers hallucinatory psychosis as an energetic form of defence, whereby the ego rejects an unpleasurable idea, together with its accompanying affect, and behaves as if it has never occurred at all. In this way, psychosis constructs an imaginary alternative to a hated reality.[24] For Ophelia, on the other hand, the example of Bedlam teaches mankind 'to bring their Passions under the direction of Reason' and 'to fix their inconstant Minds, and expel every fantastic Whim, lest they should gain Strength' till they arrive at the excess of which Bedlam is the example (207). Instead of lifting the repressions that force people to contain and deny socially unacceptable emotions and desires, Ophelia's story educates her to live in a world debilitated by constraints. Falling victim to the symptom-language of sensibility is the price she has to pay for retaining her sanity. She cannot be the subject who utters, so – like Freud's hysteric patients – she turns her entire body and mind into a means of signifying. Her symptoms are often as complex as hysteric symptoms which, as Freud found during his analysis of Dora, can have several layers of meaning and constitute an intricate system of tropes that resist interpretation.[25]

Ophelia is not the only victim of a code that restricts women's access to utterance. When she is later abducted by the Marchioness of Trente, Ophelia is entrusted to the care of the Marchioness's cousin, Mrs Herner. But her jailer is a slave herself. Impoverished by her own imprudence and finding no other means of subsistence, she is entirely dependent on her wealthier cousin, who cruelly takes advantage of her subordinate situation. In this servitude, she loses all liberty of thought and verbal expression, and becomes a yea-sayer. As Ophelia describes her:

> She entirely forgot the Method of pronouncing the Word No; her Language was composed of Nothing but Expressions of Assent and Affirmatives; and she would contradict her own Senses, as often as her violent and capricious Cousin, happened to err. So accustomed to obey, she scarcely could find out Terms that would express her Refusal of the Liberty she dared not grant me. I sometimes mistook her Negatives for Consent, and should not have discovered my Error, had she not checked me, when I was going to act in Consequence of it. (164)

Not being able to say 'no' becomes a sign of servitude. Even though Ophelia despises Herner for 'Pride that licks the Dust' (164), she too is forced into a social situation where the grammatical negative is ineffective. Denied the chance to say 'no' to the will of their superiors and expected to be obedient, the female characters of the novel end up with a set of affirmatives they have to manipulate covertly in order to express their intention. Twisting meanings, however, only makes women more vulnerable to misreading. The female 'no', since it is silenced, is easily interpreted as 'yes'.

Disguised by bodily symptoms, Ophelia's desire remains unreadable – and frustrated. It oscillates between the constant longing for her innocent, native state and the emergence of her love for Dorchester. Like Freud's Dora, she is disbelieved and misunderstood; her wish to return home is constantly counteracted, and later she has to learn that the person she loves is motivated by dishonest intentions. Even though Fielding's novel ends with the happy marriage of the two protagonists, Ophelia's frequent losses of consciousness testify to the operation of an alternative, death-driven line of plot, which is fuelled by the wish to escape from the sentimental narrative itself. Time and again, Ophelia longs to go back to her aunt, or desires death as an alternative. Not knowing the exact place of her origins, and unable to escape, she repeatedly becomes indisposed and falls into swoons, 'passing out' of her own story. Her passions are induced by violence, her adventures take place against her will, and most of the time her greatest desire is to be through with it all. The work of the negative operates in Fielding's construction of the character of Ophelia, who sometimes seems to wish not to be a heroine of a sentimental novel, not to have strong feelings, and not to be the woman of feeling – a desire that can only be expressed through the feminine repertoire of sensibility, fainting, illness, and delicacy of constitution. It is only through such sentimental attributes that the fictional woman of feeling – a figure for unconscious female protest – can say 'no' to the plot forced on women in the eighteenth-century novel of sensibility.

Missed encounters in Rousseau's *Julie, or the New Heloise*

In her discussion of the political significance of Rousseau's *Julie, or the New Heloise*, Nicola Watson claims that in the second half of the eighteenth century, Julie's transgressive love story, cast as a novel of sensibility, came to be a figure for revolutionary politics and for the anxieties surrounding female sexuality and national identity, as well as class mobility.[26] This section will explore how this novel could convey the radical energies of sensibility by tying the discontents of gender, class and national identity into the matrix of sentimental psychosomatics. The crux of the novel's potential to convey allegorically social resistance, I argue, lies in the construction of the feeling woman – a construction determined by absence and negativity.

In the introduction to the 1997 English edition of Rousseau's *Julie, or the New Heloise* (1761), Philip Stewart and Jean Vaché draw attention to an interesting shift of emphasis in the history of the novel's title. As they point out, from the eighteenth century onwards, Rousseau's novel comes to be simplified to *La Nouvelle Heloise* in its various editions and in works of literary scholarship.[27] However, Rousseau paid a great deal of attention to the choice of his novel's title. He himself usually referred to it as *Julie*, and carefully designed the layout of the full title to the first edition, which translates as *Julie or the New Heloise; Letters of Two Lovers Who Live in a Small Town at the Foot of the Alps*. Nevertheless, as Stewart and Vaché emphasise, the book soon became *La Nouvelle Heloise* for its readers, translators and critics, while the main title, *Julie*, came to be regarded as a subtitle, and was gradually pushed to the background – or even dropped.[28] In a 1764 edition, the title was changed to *La Nouvelle Heloise* without Rousseau's permission. William Kenrick's English translation of 1761 contained the most significant changes and emendations in the period. Kenrick renamed the main character, and he re-titled the book *Eloisa: Or, a Series of Original Letters Collected and Published by J. J. Rousseau*. His four-volume translation circulated widely in eighteenth-century England, and was re-edited several times between 1761 and

1810. To round off the process, from the late nineteenth century onwards many leading literary historians and Rousseau scholars took *La Nouvelle Heloise* for the title of Rousseau's novel.[29] Thus Julie's name, removed from its original position on the first title page, was repressed or even blanked out – pushed into the unconscious of literary history.

But Julie is not only suppressed on the title page of the novel's many editions. The erasure also repeats itself on the level of the narrative, in the context of the passionate dynamic that evolves between the two lovers, Julie and Saint Preux. While for literary history it is the story of Heloise that covers the void created by the absence of Julie's name, for Saint Preux it is the fantasy of the woman of sensibility – Saint Preux's imaginary sexual object. What Saint Preux falls in love with is not Julie's personal charms, but a 'touching combination of such lively sensibility and unfailing gentleness', 'the tender pity for all the sufferings of others', a 'sound judgement and exquisite taste'. These can be summed up as 'the attractions of the sentiments far more than those of the person' (I, letter 1, 26). In the letter that Saint Preux writes to Julie from the mountains of Valais, he confesses his favourite obsession, watching her house from a solitary cleft. He admits that to 'penetrate right into your room' and relive the pleasures that they experienced in the bower is only a 'vain phantom of a troubled soul' (I, letter 26, 74); even Julie's innocent daily activities are the productions of his imagination. The Julie of his daydreams helps her mother in her domestic duties, intervenes for an imprudent servant, consults the pastor about the suffering of others, and consoles a widow and an orphan. She also scans one of Saint Preux's letters with tearful eyes (I, letter 26, 74–5). Thus, Saint Preux's fantasy-creature is a woman emotionally attuned to the suffering of the world, and one who responds to her absent lover's letters with tears of melancholy. For the Saint Preux of the first part of the novel, producing the imaginary figure of the woman of feeling is a creative act of sublimation which functions as a possible outlet for desires that cannot be fulfilled at the time.[30]

It is through Saint Preux's fantasy of the woman of feeling that the lovers' sexual desire is eventually fulfilled. When viewing Julie from the mountains of Valais, Saint Preux dreams of a woman who acts with pity and compassion towards others. Julie appropriates exactly this fantasy-figure to fulfil her own desire:

> I dared observe too long this dangerous spectacle. I felt myself troubled by his transports, his sighs oppressed my heart; I shared his torments, thinking I was merely compassionate. I saw him in

convulsive agitation, about to faint at my feet. Love might have spared me; O my Cousin, *it was pity that undid me*. It was as if in order to seduce me my fatal passion had covered itself with the mask of every virtue. (I, letter 29, 78–9, my emphasis)

Julie feels cheated by her own virtuous emotions which, she thinks, are only a disguise in which forbidden passions can become manifest. Prohibition of desire channels it in a different direction; thus sublimated, it is transformed into another, socially acceptable and even desirable emotion, pity. Sexual feeling *as* sexuality is blanked out; it becomes a moment of non-experience that takes place in a state beyond consciousness: 'Without knowing what I was doing I chose my own demise. I forgot everything and remembered only love. So it is that a moment's distraction has undone me forever' (I, letter 29, 79). The affects of sensibility thus function as a legitimate channel through which forbidden feelings can manifest themselves, allowing Julie to satisfy the passion that is under prohibition.

For Julie the sexual act is a moment of absence; for Saint Preux, on the other hand, it is Julie's absence that increases sexual desire, almost to the level of ecstasy. He turns up to their secret tryst unarmed, but he brings a pen (called a 'guilty pen', *'plume criminelle'*, in Julie's first letter of confession), which he uses to kill time by writing until his lover's arrival.[31] He reconstructs the absent Julie piece by piece from her scattered clothes in an intense and erotically charged scene of writing:

All the scattered pieces of your raiment present to my ardent imagination those of your person which they secret. This light bonnet which is graced by long blond hair it affects to cover: this happy neckerchief of which at least once I shall not have to complain; this elegant and simple dishabille which so well states the taste of her who wears it; these dainty slippers which fit easily on your lithe feet; this slender corset which touches and enfolds... what an enchanting shape... two slight curves in front... oh voluptuous spectacle... the whalebone has yielded to the form that pressed into it... delightful imprints, let me kiss you a thousand times!... Ye Gods! ye Gods! What will it be when... ah, I think I already feel that tender heart beating under a happy hand! Julie! My charming Julie! I see you, I feel you everywhere, I breathe you with the air you have breathed; [...] How fortunate to have found ink and paper! I express what I feel to temper its excess, I hold my transports in abeyance by describing them. (I, letter 54, 120)

Tony Tanner interprets Saint Preux's behaviour as that of the fetishist, raised to the height of masturbatory excitation by rummaging through and kissing a woman's clothes, and finding relief from his overwhelming passion in writing.[32] But I would argue that Saint Preux's fetishism is a peculiar one. His fetish is not really Julie's clothes, as Tanner claims. It is not lifeless objects that arouse Saint Preux's passion, but the fantasy-creature, the 'delightful imprints' of which Saint Preux writes. His fetish is the woman constructed from the negative imprint of Julie's absence; and it is this 'article of clothing' that (whoever wears it) inflames Saint Preux's imagination.[33]

The fantasy-Julie consists in a negative image: the head that is not in the bonnet, the empty, foot-shaped holes in her slippers, and the marks and indentations Julie's breasts made in her corset. Saint Preux worships the idealised, socially approved corset-shape into which Julie's body is made to fit. He gets excited by the marks of shaping, where the constricted curves of the female body responded to the pressure given to them by the tight undergarment. The objects of his admiration are the imaginary breasts rebelliously pressing against – yet remaining within – the corset, which Julie's actual breasts have already escaped. His idol is the dressed-up body longing to be undressed, struggling with, yet staying inside its socially enforced constraints. The indentations in the fabric were produced by Julie's body before undressing for the sexual act, when still virtuous yet already desiring. Saint Preux's object is this transgressive body, pressed into the decent but erotic costume of the woman of feeling. His fetish is a subversive, revolutionary fantasy; it is the negative image of the woman – an image out of which the reality of woman can be constructed but simultaneously negated. His Julie is not a unified person, but a bundle of body-parts scattered like her clothes, cut into pieces, and captured by Saint Preux's writing, which, in turn, is fractured by dots and exclamation marks.

Julie as a tangible object is similarly absent for Saint Preux in moments of erotic contact; instead of revealing herself in her otherness, she shows Saint Preux the depths of his own mind. When the lovers' hands touch against their will, Saint Preux feels a 'tremour', a 'fever or rather delirium', Touching Julie blocks out the experience; instead of the other's body, it makes Saint Preux encounter his altered state of mind, one that verges on illness and madness: 'I cease to see or feel anything, and in that moment of alienation, what can I say, what can I do, where can I hide, how can I answer for myself?' (I, letter 1, 27) The encounter that stages Julie's absence most powerfully is the lovers' first kiss, as described by Saint Preux. While Saint Preux feels engulfed by 'heaven's fire', and is about to reach the heights of ecstasy, Julie falls into a swoon: 'Thus, alarm extinguished pleasure, and my happiness was no more than a flash' (I, Letter 14, 52). In this moment, it is not Saint Preux who threatens the innocence of Julie. It is Julie, falling unconscious, who possesses destructive phallic force. As he complains about the intensity of her kisses, which are 'too acrid, too penetrating, they pierce, they burn to the marrow... they would drive me raving mad'; they make Saint Preux wish to expire at Julie's feet or in her arms (I, letter 14, 52).

Julie's absences, I would like to argue, form part of a larger affective dynamic in the novel, which constitutes the narrative's major structural force. The most decisive factor in the progression of *Julie*'s plot is the dynamics of the negation and affirmation of subversive affect. David Marshall interprets both Julie's and Clarissa's absences from their encounters with their respective lovers as acts of resistance and escape. As Clarissa flees from Lovelace's intrusions into unconsciousness and death, so Julie takes flight from Wolmar by dying.[34] I would like to suggest, however, that another important element of Julie's 'absences' is provided not by her attempts to escape from Wolmar, but rather by her reassertion of her transgressive desire for Saint Preux in her last letter – a desire that is at the core of her subjectivity. Julie's fainting from the kiss foreshadows further similar intense encounters, including the episode of Julie's deathbed scene.[35] During the last couple of days preceding her death, Julie is radiant and lively, and she even seems to take pleasure in dying. Death, as her last letter explains, is an opportunity for her to reawaken the passion that brought her alive, and which she had long been trying to stifle (VI, letter 12, 608). She dies with Saint Preux's name on her lips, slipping out of life before Wolmar, the master-reader of her mind, could enter her room. The scene of the first kiss is part of the same dynamic of negation and reassertion of intense emotion, in which death and the *petite mort* of the kiss are linked together. Here Julie's sexual desire is not allowed to reach the surface of her consciousness. While sexuality has to be negated – note Julie's constant claim that she desires only platonic, chaste love – Julie's 'yes' is available only in her unconscious.[36] In an act of swooning she makes her unconscious available for the encounter. In this way, however, experiencing sexuality becomes impossible: the affirmation of subversive desire takes place through what the psychoanalyst André Green calls the work of the negative. At this moment, Julie becomes a blank, reflective surface for Saint Preux. Her kiss pierces, burns and penetrates, because Saint Preux encounters his own phallic desire at its deepest root.[37]

The first kiss – which took place in the presence of Julie's cousin, Claire – is repeated years later, when the married Julie is ordered by her husband, Monsieur de Wolmar, to re-enact the kiss in the dreaded bower, where, as Julie writes to Claire, 'all the misfortunes of my life began' (IV, letter 12, 402).[38] This time, it is Julie, not Saint Preux, who describes the experience:

> Rising, he embraced us, and would have us to embrace also, in this place... in this very place where once... Claire, oh good Claire, how dearly you have always loved me! I made no objection. Alas! how wrong I would have been to object! That kiss was nothing like the one that had made me so dread the bower. For this I sadly congratulated myself, and recognized that my heart was more changed than I had heretofore dared believe.
>
> As we were about to head back to the house, my husband stopped me by the hand, and pointing to the bower we were leaving, he said to me with a laugh: Julie, fear this sanctuary no more; it has just been profaned. You don't want to believe me, Cousin, but I swear to you that he has some supernatural gift for reading what is in hearts: May Heaven let him ever keep it! (IV, letter 12, 407)

Wolmar's intention is to annihilate the former emotional experience by 'profaning' it, that is, to deprive it of the sacred significance with which the event and the place are invested. His aim is to cover the past with the present and thus to release Saint Preux from the grip of his memories.[39] For Julie, however, it is doubtful that such a cure from her passion can ever take place. While she is convinced that she no longer has her dangerous passion, her description of the kiss still bears the textual traces of the negative. The kiss itself remains an indescribable, empty spot, silenced, eluding linguistic representation. She refers to the first kiss by dots, and indicates the second by a blank and by the negative formula of what it was *not* like. Repetition – through the negative – remains the sign of the repressed.

Henry Mackenzie's *Julia de Roubigné* (1777), one of the novels conceived in Britain in the wake of Rousseau's *Julie*, explores the potential extremes underlying the situation where the woman's 'no' and 'yes' are forcefully subverted by the logic of patriarchy. Mackenzie's novel openly problematises the heroine's inability to eradicate an affect that needs to be forgotten after she is married against her heart's desire. While at her wedding, Julie feels happiness, rebirth and that a hand 'lifts the veil of error from my eyes and restores me to myself in spite of me' (III, letter 12, 292).

The same cannot be said of Julia de Roubigné. Mackenzie's Julia, though in love with her tutor and childhood friend, Savillon, remains chaste before her marriage to the wealthy Spanish aristocrat, Montauban. As Peter Mortensen sees the relationship between this work and its French predecessor, Mackenzie radicalises Rousseau's novel. Where Julie to all appearances convinces herself that she has renounced her love for Saint Preux, Mackenzie's Julia 'frets and resists from the outset'.[40] Unlike Rousseau's Julie, Julia visibly carries the burden of her secret 'no', shedding 'silent tears' at the altar when she has to say 'yes': 'Had you seen her eyes how they spoke, when her father gave me her hand! There was still reluctance in them – a reluctance more winning than all the flush of consent could have made her.'[41] Julia, like Julie, is not allowed to say 'no' to marriage – but she maintains her resistance throughout her marriage, keeping Savillon's portrait locked up in a drawer, and uttering his name only in her sleep (II, Letter 35, 123–4). However, Julia's husband, Montauban, finds the portrait covered in tears. Getting a glimpse of what in Rousseau's novel remained hidden, the jealous husband murders Julia and commits suicide in an act of mad rage.

During the time of her marriage, Rousseau's Julie has to behave as if always in the presence of an omniscient spectator. Her mind becomes similar to the person of great firmness and constancy described by Adam Smith in *The Theory of Moral Sentiments* (1759). Smith's men of constancy, becoming their own conscience, create their internal equilibrium by turning into that part of the self which is observing the part affected by feeling: 'He *almost* identifies himself with, he *almost* becomes himself that impartial spectator, and scarce even feels but as that great arbiter of his conduct directs him to feel.'[42] But as the word 'almost' indicates, even in Smith's example this identification cannot be complete, though it is nearly perfect. In Rousseau's novel, the banished part of Julie's split self keeps resurfacing in critical moments of her story. Such moments include her last letter reinstating her passion, her hidden tears during the dangerous boating adventure, and her inability to stay with Saint Preux at the solitary cleft where her lover many years ago wrote the letter that caused the loss of Julie's innocence. Her marriage is an attempted reintegration of her self, not by accepting the unconscious content, but by trying to turn herself into one readable consciousness and to identify with her conflicting desire for filial obedience and virtue.

Manifestations of the negative, including scenes of female fainting, indisposition and death, signify moments of absence from which Saint Preux's object of desire – the woman of feeling – is constructed. In

Rousseau's novel, the woman of sensibility is a cultural fantasy through which the feeling woman is both seen and negated. *Julie, or the New Heloise* is a novel of resistance and revolution, and it stages a woman's struggle within the bounds of this cultural fantasy. Julie's sensibility originates in her responses to the non-recognition and attempted erasure of her affects – in the struggle between the negativisation of affect and the affect's survival, reinstatement and forceful reappearance. The radical potential of sentimental psychosomatics lies in its interconnectedness with such psychic struggle. Julie's absences convey transgressive desire, crossing the boundaries and prohibitions of contemporary patriarchal society. A historically available image for women's emotional expression is thus able to function as a negative means for expressing what would otherwise be unsayable. Through the veil of negativity, Julie can become an empty space not only for the imagination of Saint Preux, but also for that of the eighteenth-century reader. Her absences will become a sign of sensibility, creating an allegorical space for the potential containment of contemporary revolutionary fantasies.

Negative affirmation in Elizabeth Inchbald's *A Simple Story*

While states that reach beyond the conscious experience in *The History of Ophelia* express silent (and often-unconscious) protest against rape, abduction or participation in the sentimental narrative, the nonverbal symptom-language of sensibility in novels written in the wake of Rousseau's *Julie, or the New Heloise* functions as a way of asserting subversive and repressed desire. Inchbald's *A Simple Story* is one of these works. Staging the vicissitudes of female desire following Rousseau's *Julie*, Inchbald's novel is as much a novel of repression as of sensibility. In a letter to Inchbald, Maria Edgeworth aims to discover 'the secret of [the novel's] peculiar pathos'. She finds that

> it is by leaving more than most other writers to the imagination, that you succeed so eminently in affecting it. By the force that is necessary to repress feeling, we judge of the intensity of the feeling; and you always contrive to give us by intelligible but simple signs the measure of this force. Writers of inferior genius waste their words in *describing* feeling; in making those who pretend to be agitated by passion describe the effects of that passion, and talk of the *rending of their hearts*, &c. A gross blunder! as gross as any Irish blunder; for the heart cannot feel, and describe its own feelings, at the same moment.[43]

Thus, according to Edgeworth, the novel's effect lies in representing powerful feeling by representing its repression. The gaps and silences make us imagine the force of the emotion, the measure of which lies not in its expression but in what is manifest in the wake of its repression. At the level of both story and storytelling, *A Simple Story* is, so to say, syncopated: structured around gaps, absences and silences, making the novel's discourse convey what can be said in lieu of blocked, forbidden and thus unutterable affective elements.

In *The English Jacobin Novel*, Gary Kelly notes that 'Mrs. Inchbald reveals an astonishing *penetration into deep psychological disturbance and its symptoms* which had to wait over a century for fully scientific exposition.' Inchbald, he avers, is 'at her best in depicting the struggle to suppress deep feeling'.[44] The penetration of the depths of the human psyche seems indeed to be a critical issue in *A Simple Story*. The same term, 'penetration', is used in Inchbald's novel to describe the sharp and quasi-omniscient method by means of which human character can be deciphered beneath its confusing and mysterious surface. In the first half of the novel, this technique of penetrative reading is practised by the male protagonist's former tutor, Sandford, who claims to have the ability to see through surfaces and thus to work upon the passions of others. Sandford 'knew the hearts of women, as well as those of men' and 'saw Miss Milner's heart at the first view of her person'. What he sees is folly – but never her true emotions.[45]

In the case of Dorriforth, his former pupil, such penetrative reading can easily be performed with success. Dorriforth's readability appears unproblematic and unquestionable. His face is entirely lucid; his sensibility is defined in terms of this perfect transparency, that is, as a harmony of verbal, facial, and emotional expression:

> On his countenance you beheld the feelings of his heart – saw all its inmost workings – the quick pulses that beat with hope and fear, or the placid ones that were stationary with patient resignation. On this countenance his thoughts were pictured, and as his mind was enriched with every virtue that could make it valuable, so was his honest face adorned with every emblem of those virtues – and they not only gave a lustre to his aspect, but added a harmonious sound to all he uttered; it was persuasive, it was perfect eloquence, whilst in his looks you beheld his thoughts moving with his lips, and ever coinciding with what he said. (8–9)

As his face reflects his mind and character, so his speech reflects his thought, which can even be seen in his looks. Language is not only a pure expression of the inside, it is almost entirely unnecessary, since his thoughts make their way directly to the outside without need of verbal communication. The only function of the linguistic expression seems to be decorative and rhetorical: to add persuasion and eloquence to thoughts and feelings which hardly require the efforts of expression and interpretation. As there is no need for language, there is no need for penetration either; the surface can reveal the depths of the psyche.

From the very beginning, however, the novel presents both a more intense need for and failure of this technique of penetrative reading when it comes to the female protagonist, Miss Milner. This failure goes hand in hand with a crisis of feminine linguistic expression, which surfaces in connection with the Protestant Miss Milner's scandalous, transgressive desire for Dorriforth, her Catholic priest guardian.[46] Dorriforth is not simply a father substitute to her, or a priest of a different religion. He is also tied by a vow of celibacy, similar to 'that barrier which divides a sister from a brother' (74). Miss Milner is seen by other characters as coquettish, fickle and unintelligible. Unlike Dorriforth, she does not possess the transparency that makes possible the kind of reading her guardian and Sandford are trained to produce. Even though Sandford 'fixed his penetrating eyes as if he would look through her soul' (58), all his reading skills are inadequate to understand Miss Milner. In the end, he has to admit 'That the mind of a woman was far above, or rather beneath, his comprehension' (88).[47] Miss Milner's behaviour starts to become increasingly confusing when Dorriforth requests her to give account of her affections and her marriage intentions. She is put under pressure to decide upon a marriage partner and shows a lively interest in one of her suitors, Sir Frederick Lawnly, yet answers with a definite 'no' when Dorriforth asks her whether he is the man she would approve for a husband:

> Upon this close interrogation she discovered an embarrassment, and a confusion beyond any she had ever before given proofs of; and in this situation she faintly replied,
>   'No, he is not.'
>   'Your words tell me one thing,' answered Dorriforth, 'while your looks declare another – which am I to trust?' (51)

More than a century later, Sigmund Freud was similarly intrigued by the complexities of negation that he observed during his work with hysteric patients. He found that negation always contains an element of affirmation; it implies taking cognisance of an unconscious content.

Even though negation does not mean the acceptance of repressed material, it already involves a lifting of the repression, making it possible for the repressed material to surface into consciousness.[48] The psychoanalyst André Green further explored the operation of the negative. In 'Negation and Contradiction', he mentions a female analytic patient, whose passionate rejection of the analyst's interpretation was always followed by prominent, characteristic gestures of negation. Green discovers that these exaggerated gestures repeat the situation of a childhood experience, when the patient's refusal to eat a dish of tomato rice offered to her by her mother was accompanied by the same violent negating gestures. As a child, the patient did not attend school until a later age, because of her mother's ambiguity and her own phobia about not performing well, which, as it later became clear, only served as a rationalisation of the fear of leaving her mother. Enraged by the child's refusal to eat, her mother dragged her to school as a punishment, where, as it turned out, the child was doing surprisingly well. As Green finds, the child achieved her unconscious desire to be sent to school by not wanting to go there, then by misbehaving at home and by saying 'no' to her mother. The negative thus functioned as the actual means by which an unconscious, positive desire could achieve its goal. In the analytic setting, the patient introjected or said 'yes' to the analyst's interpretation by means of a similar act of negation. Green calls this 'negative affirmation', in which case 'the apparent expulsion really carried with it, in the opening necessary for the utterance of this "no," a "yes" which slipped surreptitiously into her'.[49]

Miss Milner also has recourse to the negative in order to preserve or fulfil a secret desire: her forbidden passion for her guardian. Her resistance to 'penetration' is closely tied into the context of marriage and sexuality. It is only as regards her sexual object-choice that Miss Milner is impenetrable by the phallic reading techniques practiced in Dorriforth's household. The affirmation of her desire for her guardian appears in the guise of the negation of marriage intentions in general. In order to prevent a duel between Dorriforth and Sir Frederick, she agrees to marry the latter, only to protest against this again when the immediate danger – that of losing Dorriforth – subsides. The function of this 'no', apart from her rejection of Sir Frederick as a marriage partner, is a hidden 'yes' to her secret desire for Dorriforth. Even when her love becomes conscious to her, it needs to be hidden and disguised. Practically speaking, Miss Milner never says yes to Dorriforth, not even at the moment of their marriage. At the wedding scene, in response to Sandford's question as to whether she loves him, her only answer is: 'Oh heavens!' (191).

Their mutual confession of love also gets lost in the gaps of narration; all the reader learns is that 'Within a few days, in the house of Lord Elmwood, every thing, and every person wore a new face. – His lordship was the profest lover of Miss Milner' (136). In addition to negation, gaps and silences, Miss Milner also uses the symptom-language of the body to communicate within the constraints of Dorriforth's patriarchal household. Her unreadability thus can be seen as one of the many ways in which Miss Milner's body expresses what she is not allowed to feel. When Dorriforth is planning to marry the emotionless Miss Fenton and goes out in the evening, Miss Milner cannot touch her dinner. When she learns that he did not dine at Miss Fenton's, she puts a piece of food into her mouth. Like Green's patient who was unwilling to swallow the tomato-rice, eating and not eating have meanings related to her secret. Thus, for Miss Milner, the non-verbal sign-system of sensibility, instead of conveying an authentic expression of emotion, reveals itself as the pathological symptom-language of repressed desire.[50]

The second part of the novel continues the story after a 17-year break.[51] Dorriforth inherits an aristocratic title and now, as Lord Elmwood, he is granted a dispensation from his vow of celibacy and marries Miss Milner. We learn that during Lord Elmwood's three-year absence in the West Indies, Miss Milner, now Lady Elmwood, has renewed her relationship with Sir Frederick. At her husband's return, she runs away in shame, leaving behind her daughter, Matilda. Lord Elmwood cannot be reconciled, and decides to banish his wife and daughter, promising never to see them again. In this part of the novel, Dorriforth's earlier, transparent sensibility shows its dark side in rigidity, cruelty, and lack of forgiveness, proceeding from Dorriforth/Lord Elmwood's 'resentment [rather] than his tenderness' (202). When he learns about his wife's infidelity, it is his sensibility which prevents him from forgetting his lost happiness and which 'urged him to fly from its more keen recollection as much as possible'. He banishes their child Matilda and decides 'never to see, hear of, or take one concern whatever in her fate and fortune', forbidding her and her mother's name to be pronounced in his presence (202). Even when he permits Matilda to enter his house, she has to remain forgotten and ostracised, making everyone realise that the most prudent behaviour toward her is to 'take no notice whatever that she lived among them' (221). As a result of his prohibition on the name of Lady Elmwood and Matilda, and the denial of his own emotions, the once transparent Lord Elmwood now becomes unreadable to the penetrating eyes of Sandford.

The figure of Matilda comes to embody what Lord Elmwood intends to block out of his and others' consciousness: the memories of a lost felicity as well as Lady Elmwood's infidelity – curiously missing from the narrative and buried in the 17-year gap between the two parts. By her father's cruelty, Matilda is turned into an absence, a sign, a reminder, always standing for something else. Her external appearance reminds everyone of her mother, 'risen from the grave in her former youth, health, and exquisite beauty', while her temper is rather that of her father – an emblem of their happy union that must now be forgotten (221).[52] Even Rushbrook, Lord Elmwood's nephew, falls in love with her phantom (as Sandford calls it) before even meeting her (317). Objects and persons become 'infected' with the daughter's presence, serving as carriers of her and – by association – her mother's memory. After Matilda moves into Elmwood Castle, the repressed content manifests itself in a contagious reorganisation of signification. For Lord Elmwood himself, the house comes to mean Matilda, and therefore, Miss Milner. His mood visibly improves after she moves into the house (224–5), and he does not depart for his business until an unusually late time of the year, feeling himself, he says, 'more attached to this house at present, than ever I did in my life' (243).

Since Matilda is never allowed to see her father, it is his everlasting absence that becomes invested with emotional significance, making the negative of her father more real for her than his actual presence, which consists only of a distant childhood memory. Matilda's relationship with her father's absence develops into an organised object-relationship to such an extent that the presence of the real object, and the affects such an encounter might arouse, are seen as destructive: 'I am now convinced [...] that to see my father, would cause a sensation, a feeling, I could not survive' (220).[53] The object has gone beyond the boundaries where life and consciousness could reach, and thus can only be encountered if the subject is transported into the realm of absence.

Matilda's desires are transferred to the representations she can find of her father. The closest of these is the full-length portrait in front of which she sighs and weeps, and from which she shrinks back with fear (220). As Terry Castle observes, Matilda tests her father's command in subtle, obsessive ways: she haunts his library, gazes at his portrait with fear and admiration, listens to the sounds of his carriage, and watches him through her window.[54] When her father leaves the house and she is at large, she reconstructs her father from his traces:

In the breakfast and dining rooms she leaned over those seats with a kind of filial piety, on which she was told he had been accustomed to sit. And in the library she took up with filial delight, the pen with which he had been writing; and looked with the most curious attention into those books that were laid upon his reading desk. – But a hat, lying on one of the tables, gave her a sensation beyond any other she experienced on this occasion – in that trifling article of his dress, she thought she saw himself, and held it in her hand with pious reverence. (246)

Matilda's behaviour mirrors that of Rousseau's Saint Preux passionately rummaging through Julie's clothes. However, while Saint Preux desires a fantasy-reconstruction, Matilda is obsessed with her father's absence. As the ghost and scapegoat of patriarchy, punished for the failure of domestic felicity, she is forced into a world of the negative. It is not the father who is invested with her emotions of 'piety', 'delight', 'curious attention' and 'pious reverence', but rather all those objects that signify his not being there.

The second part of Inchbald's *A Simple Story* features a passionate fainting scene in the episode where Lady Matilda and her father meet for the first time. For Matilda, fainting in the presence of her father means something similar to the absences of Rousseau's Julie from her physical encounters with Saint Preux. The long-awaited contact between a desiring woman and the object of her desire fails to become a conscious experience:

> her *fears* confirmed her it was him. – She gave a scream of terror – put out her trembling hands to catch the balustrades on the stairs for support – missed them – and fell motionless into her father's arms.
>
> He caught her, as by that impulse he would have caught any other person falling for want of aid. – Yet when he found her in his arms he still held her there – gazed on her attentively – and once pressed her to his bosom.
>
> At length, trying to escape the snare into which he had been led, he was going to leave her on the spot where she fell, when her eyes opened and she uttered, 'Save me.' – Her voice unmanned him. – His long-restrained tears now burst forth – and seeing her relapsing into the swoon again, he cried out eagerly to recall her. – Her name did not however come to his recollection – nor any name but this – 'Miss Milner – Dear Miss Milner.' (273–4)

Like Green's patient in the tomato-rice episode, Matilda has to have recourse to the work of the negative to express affirmation. For Lord Elmwood, Matilda is the living emblem of the repressed, and her appearance marks its return. Here the act of negation creates an opening where the repressed content can come to light, and a 'yes' can surreptitiously slip in through the utterance of 'no'. While Matilda remains nameless and negated, through her negation Lord Elmwood recognises her banished mother. When Lord Elmwood is about to repeat the abandonment of his lost object by leaving her lifeless body on the floor – just as he turned his back on the dead body of his wife – Matilda starts to speak. This time he turns, however, and instead of abandoning the body along with his emotions, he sheds his long-repressed tears, and thus, at last, mourns his lost wife. Matilda's body, falling back into the swoon and repeating the threat of loss, finally makes him acknowledge and name the object of his love: Miss Milner. When catching his fainting daughter, Lord Elmwood cries out for and calls back to life his dying wife – reliving the deathbed scene in which his unforgiving rejection prevented him from taking part. The encounter also brings back to him repressed emotions and makes his face readable again, agitated 'with shame, with pity, with anger, with paternal tenderness' (274).

Inchbald's novel, by staging the erasure of its female figures, brings into consciousness the silencing and negation of woman (even to the point of death) lurking behind the revolutionary ideal represented by Rousseau's *Julie*. Read as a late-eighteenth-century response to Rousseau, *A Simple Story* presents the troubling scenario where a potential Saint Preux-figure, gaining power, recreates the oppressive structure of domestic terror he formerly assisted in overturning. The woman of feeling, even in 1791, is not allowed to be present as a feeling woman. Her feelings are tolerated only so long as they can be used for the re-establishment of patriarchal power. The novel exposes sensibility as part of the psychopathology of the patriarchal household and offers an insight into the shaping effects of social repression on pathological forms in the eighteenth century. These forms include – besides the figure of the domestic tyrant – the woman of feeling, of which both Miss Milner and Lady Matilda are manifestations.

In 1791, when the novel was published, a reviewer of Inchbald's novel – whom scholarship identifies as Mary Wollstonecraft – criticised the weakness of Matilda's character, and was disappointed that the author was not able to provide a more empowering model for eighteenth-century women readers:

> Why do [all female writers] poison the minds of their own sex, by strengthening a male prejudice that makes women systematically weak? We alluded to the absurd fashion that prevails of making the

heroine of a novel boast of a delicate constitution; and the still more ridiculous and deleterious custom of spinning the most picturesque scenes out of fevers, swoons, and tears.[55]

It is true that fainting, as eighteenth-century medical theories often assume, is a sign of 'weakness' in so far as swoons and illnesses stand in for verbal expression or cancel out satisfying encounters. While the fictional representation of the sentimental swoon – as a display of feminine weakness – was a frequent object of criticism in the period, reading the literature of sentiment in the context of a broader history of feeling provides a more complex picture. Many eighteenth-century and Romantic novels explore female concerns hidden behind a so-called 'language of feeling' that reach well beyond contemporary explanations of female indisposition. Like hysteria, the sentimental novel becomes a mode of thinking about sexuality and the sexual object.[56] These novels are, to some extent, already in Freud's league; and by their sensitivity to gender they provide a form of social critique which not only predates Freud's achievement but also points towards more recent psychoanalytic – and feminist – insights. Novels of sensibility exploit the possibilities offered by the work of the negative, and by their presentation of the negated, oppressed, banished woman, they perform an act of affirmation, taking cognisance of the discontents behind woman's fevers, swoons, and tears. They thus give a covert – and often-unintended – critique of the pathology of social repression by exposing sensibility itself, in the form of the 'woman of feeling', as its symptom.

5
Godwin's Case: Melancholy Mourning in the 'Empire of Feeling'

'There are moments, when any creature that lives, has power to drive one into madness. I seemed to know the absurdity of this reply; but that was of no consequence. It added to the measure of my distraction.' In his *Memoirs of the Author of a Vindication of the Rights of Woman* (1798), this is William Godwin's description of his feelings shortly after questioning the nurse just coming out of the room where his wife, Mary Wollstonecraft, lies dying. To Godwin's question, what she thought of her mistress, the nurse responded that 'in her judgment, she was going as fast as possible'.[1] Godwin's distracted condition during Wollstonecraft's fatal illness continued well beyond her death. It is from the state that verges on the borderline of madness that he started to mourn her. After Wollstonecraft's death from septicaemia following the birth of the future Mary Godwin Shelley, Godwin, symbolically taking his dead wife's place, moved into her room at the Polygon, where she used to live and work separately from Godwin during the day. Here he immediately immersed himself in work, re-reading all her books and letters. As a reaction to his pain at her loss he started writing the *Memoirs*, and also began to edit and then publish her posthumous works in 1798, among them her last, unfinished novel, *Maria; or, the Wrongs of Woman*, and her letters to Gilbert Imlay.

Much scholarly attention has been paid to the unfortunate consequences of the publication of Godwin's *Memoirs of the Author of a Vindication of the Rights of Woman*. Despite Godwin's respect and good intentions, the book – with an honest account of his wife's sexual affairs, suicide attempts and unorthodox religious ideas – scandalised contemporaries, and was an inevitable blow to the feminist views associated with Wollstonecraft's life and work. After the publication of the *Memoirs*, Wollstonecraft's work, now considered inseparable from the life and death her ideas were seen as leading to, was largely ignored and her name was only invoked as a warning until the end of the following century.[2] Her reputation suffered intensely from what the public saw as tasteless exposure. Even friends like Southey were disappointed and accused Godwin of a 'want of feeling in stripping his dead wife naked'. Roscoe condemned him for mourning her 'with a heart of stone'.[3] Cruel jokes written by Tory journalists proliferated, while the Reverend Richard Polwhele saw the hand of Providence operating in Wollstonecraft's life, death and the *Memoirs*: 'she died a death that strongly marked the distinction of the sexes'. The *Anti-Jacobin*, in one of its volumes anonymously edited by Polwhele, cross-referenced 'Wollstonecraft' and 'Prostitution' in its index.[4]

While in our time successful critical attempts have greatly restored Wollstonecraft's reputation and significance, and incorporated her works into the study of literary and cultural history, Godwin's mourning has not yet been fully understood. There seems to be some resistance on the part of scholarship equally to do justice to both sides – perhaps shying away from a critical position that risks not being feminist enough when recovering a feminist icon. What does it mean to mourn 'with a heart of stone' a person one deeply loved – a mourning that, besides 'stripping his dead wife naked', threatened to damage Godwin's own reputation in the eyes of his – and even our – contemporaries?[5] How is it possible to demonstrate a paradoxical 'want of feeling' under the influence of the most powerful emotions? This chapter reads Godwin's writings produced at the time of Mary Wollstonecraft's death (his *Memoirs*, letters, notes and diary) as they were created in the vortex of overwhelming emotions induced by loss. As I will argue, the growth of affectivity and sensibility that has often been observed in Godwin's writing during this period is the result of a complex and emotionally ambivalent psychological process: melancholy mourning. Godwin's case reaches beyond the boundaries of the eighteenth-century understanding of melancholia, raising questions that point towards the ideas of Freud and his successors. Also, as this chapter will hope to show, Godwin's mourning – as registered in his writings – offers an alternative case study, which in many respects differs from, and poses new questions to, existing psychoanalytic views.

Freud discusses the two processes in his 1917 essay 'Mourning and Melancholia', and later in *The Ego and the Id* (1923). In his terminology, the work of mourning implies a gradual withdrawal of the libido from the lost loved object during a long and painful process. The attachment is given up bit by bit, through the testing of external reality, until the ego becomes free and uninhibited again. For Freud, the key to understanding melancholia lies in identification. Melancholia develops when the free libido is not placed onto another object after the loss, but is withdrawn into the ego. The ego identifies with the abandoned object and draws it into itself, thus the object loss is transformed into an ego loss, splitting the ego. Melancholia has certain unique symptoms, such as a strong diminution of self-esteem, harsh self-reproaches, as well as ambivalent feelings towards the object. According to Freud, the self-reproaches are in reality accusations against the internalised object, who is also the real target of the ego's simultaneous feelings of love and hatred.[6]

As Freud emphasises in his earlier essay, mourning and melancholia share similar structures. Both are reactions to a loss and imply a painful mood, inhibition or loss of interest in pleasurable activities. Both aim to prolong the existence of the object, and involve the long and gradual withdrawal of libido – even though in the state of melancholia this withdrawal is unconscious. As is pointed out by many readers of Freud, including Judith Butler, David L. Eng and David Kazanjian, the two are bound together more closely in Freud's later work. In *The Ego and the Id*, melancholic identification is a prerequisite for letting the object go, as well as for the constitution of the ego. As parting with the object is never entirely possible, the ego contains a history of its lost objects.[7]

Godwin's case probes the meeting points of mourning and melancholia as they take place in writing and find expression in language. His literary activity sets in motion the processes that define the interface of mourning and melancholia: the taking in and simultaneous giving up of the lost loved object; in other words, the process of losing as it creates the object as internal, while allowing one to part with it at the same time. First I will discuss Godwin's letters written to his friends and relations after Wollstonecraft's death, together with Wollstonecraft's tormenting, suicidal letters to Gilbert Imlay, and examine processes of identification between Godwin and his melancholy love object. I shall trace how the internalised other transforms the self from within and argue that the growth of affectivity in Godwin's writing is the result of such intersubjective transformation. Then I will read Godwin's hurtful letters and ostensibly emotionless diary entries as the language of melancholia fuelled by the conflicting emotions of love, hate, triumph and aggression. My contention is that Godwin's *Memoirs*, and also the image of Wollstonecraft they present, are a further product of this ambivalent language. As a case of melancholy mourning, Godwin's case instantiates how sensibility, together with a controversial image of Wollstonecraft, is produced through an inherently ambivalent process: the vicissitudes of identification burdened with the simultaneous love and hatred of the survivor.

Godwin and Wollstonecraft: destructive correspondences

In September 1797, in a strange boost of creativity at a moment of debilitating grief, Godwin sat down with Wollstonecraft's papers to prepare them for publication and to salvage and preserve as much as he could of the literary remains of his beloved wife. He devotedly undertook to pay her a literary tribute, as 'the world is entitled to some information respecting persons that have enlightened and improved it'.[8] Simultaneously, he kept up his correspondences with his friends and relations, informing them of the sad news and receiving their condolences. Written by a man overwhelmed with feeling, some of these letters end up discussing the difficulty – or impossibility – of their own production. In the end, Godwin often confers the task of writing on his friends. The letters that he did write convey inordinate passions polarised between intense anger and overflowing gratitude, targeted at a world split into 'good' and 'bad' objects. On the day of his wife's death, he wrote to his friend, William Nicholson, that 'expressions of attachment and kindness from a man I have known so long, and value so highly, are consolatory and soothing beyond imagination'.[9] The letters he sent to Elizabeth Inchbald, however, are full of accusations written in a particularly aggressive tone, and, as Inchbald puts it, more resembled 'distracted lines than anything rational'.[10] Even the letter in which he informs Inchbald of the death of his wife is loaded with reproaches: 'My wife died at eight this morning. I always thought you used her ill, but I forgive you. You told me you did not know her. You have a thousand good and great qualities. She had a very deep-rooted admiration for you.'[11]

Godwin's angry letters to Inchbald refer back to an incident that happened shortly after his marriage to Wollstonecraft had been made public. The marriage meant an open confession that Wollstonecraft had not been married to Gilbert Imlay previously. Inchbald – like Amelia Alderson Opie and Sarah Siddons – was one of those friends who did not react to the marriage favourably and who turned away from Wollstonecraft out of social prejudice – or possibly even jealousy. When she found out about the marriage, Inchbald withdrew her invitation to a theatre party that she had previously made to Godwin. We do not know exactly what happened at the theatre, but when the couple turned up for the play, Inchbald made a comment that both Wollstonecraft and Godwin found insulting.[12] The friendship between Godwin and Inchbald started in the early 1790s and continued after the incident; after Wollstonecraft's death, however, Godwin's silenced resentment escalated into aggression and eventually undermined their relationship.

Even the short report of death quoted above is used as a declaration of war. Inchbald tries to pacify and console Godwin, takes an understanding attitude and urges him to express his emotions: 'Write to me again. Say what you please at such a time as this; I will excuse and pity you.'[13] Each new letter Godwin writes, however, carries a new and harsher attack, until the theatre incident returns with its full force. In Godwin's re-reading of the past event, it grows into an unpardonable offence against an idealised and revered object, who can only be recovered in writing:

I must endeavour to be understood as to the unworthy behaviour with which I charge you towards my wife. I think your shuffling behaviour about the taking places to the comedy of the *Will* dishonourable to you. I think your conversation to her that night at the play base, cruel and insulting. There were persons in the box who heard it, and they thought as I do. I think you know more of my wife than you are willing to acknowledge to yourself, and that you have an understanding capable of doing some small degree of justice to her merits. I think you should have had magnanimity and self-respect enough to have shewed this. I think that while the Twisses and others were sacrificing to what they were silly enough to think a proper etiquette, a person so out of all comparison their superior, as you are, should have placed her pride in acting upon better principles, and in courting and distinguishing insulted greatness and worth; I think that you chose a mean and pitiful conduct, when you might have chosen a conduct that would have done you immortal honour.[14]

Inchbald, in her repeated attempts at consolation, attributes Godwin's accusations to his feelings and sees in his letters the language of a man under the influence of strong, uncontrollable emotions. As she writes in one of her replies: 'I could refute every charge you allege against me in your letter; but I revere a man, either in deep love or in deep grief: and as it is impossible to convince, I would at least say nothing to irritate him.'[15] However, Godwin does not stop the flood of insult and Inchbald finally ends their friendship.

Inchbald's attribution of Godwin's attacks to his grief invites the critical reader of their correspondence to see his writings produced during that period as expressions of mourning and melancholia. The stake of these writings – the outcome of which is the publication of the *Posthumous Works of Mary Wollstonecraft* in 1798 – is that they had an important role in the formation of the image and reputation of Wollstonecraft in Godwin's time, and even in subsequent centuries. The *Memoirs* and Wollstonecraft's letters, as presented by Godwin, have functioned as targets of critique as well as crucial sources of available information about her life and relationships.[16] Godwin composed and compiled these writings from details that he asked for in letters to friends and relations shortly after Wollstonecraft's death. There is, however, something peculiar in the tone of his letters, which strikes us when we read them together with Mary Wollstonecraft's letters to Gilbert Imlay – letters of a deserted lover that Godwin read and edited after her death. These are letters written in a passionate tone during her previous, stormy relationship with the American Imlay, a relationship which began in Revolutionary France and culminated in disappointment. After the birth of their illegitimate child, Fanny, Imlay's commitment to the affair evidently started to wither. His neglect and betrayal of Wollstonecraft, who was striving to maintain the relationship at all costs, contributed to her two consecutive unsuccessful suicide attempts in 1795. The relationship ended, and Wollstonecraft had to come to terms with the reality of her loss.[17]

After Wollstonecraft's death, Godwin, dearly in love with his wife, was left behind, just as Wollstonecraft had been abandoned earlier by the unfaithful Imlay. In his yearning for a lost loved object, Godwin steps into a role similar to Mary Wollstonecraft yearning for her always absent lover, Gilbert Imlay – a yearning that, as Claire Tomalin observes of Wollstonecraft, transformed a clever and strong-willed person into 'a creature eager, dependent and trembling'.[18] Wollstonecraft's letters to Imlay around the time of her two suicide attempts in 1795 are full of reproaches for his absence and neglect, and they speak of deep dejection and despair. These letters are composed from within a similarly distracted mental state as had led to Godwin's letters to Inchbald. Due to Imlay's absences, and in the midst of weaning her child, Wollstonecraft's thoughts are constantly preoccupied with ideas of death, destruction and suicide. Waiting for Imlay's answers, which rarely arrive, she complains that her life is 'a living death' tormented by uncertainty.[19]

While many of Wollstonecraft's suicide threats and farewell letters promise to be the final one, there are always subsequent letters. Even after her second suicide attempt at Putney Bridge in November 1795, her revived voice cannot stop attacking the unfaithful, insensible lover. This voice of aggression and despair, twice recovered from the brink of the grave, unceasingly and repetitively tortures Imlay with reproaches for treating her badly, neglecting her and not responding to her letters. Her inability to remain silent only aggravates the vicious cycle of neglect, aggressive response, and the further alienation such a response entails. She tortures him precisely by promising not to torture, and by the very act of narrating how she tries to hide her sorrows in order not to trouble him with them: 'You tell me that my letters torture you; I will not describe the effect yours have on me. [...] I mean not to give vent to the emotions they produced.' However, the rest of the letter is nothing more than an elaboration of these emotions. 'Forget that I exist: I will never remind you', Wollstonecraft writes in one letter, 'Be free – I will not torment, when I cannot please.' The letter itself is a means of reminder and torment. Far from sparing him the troubling circumstances, in the very same letter she cannot help giving a detailed, physiological description of the bodily condition induced by her suffering: 'I am agitated, my whole frame is convulsed, my lips tremble, as if shook by cold, though fire seems to be circulating in my veins.'[20] After Wollstonecraft's unsuccessful attempt at drowning, her accusing voice cries out in the very act of promising silence: 'If I have any criterion to judge of right and wrong, I have been most ungenerously treated: but, wishing now only to hide myself, I shall be *silent as the grave* in which I long to forget myself.'[21] The grave from where she speaks, however, never proves to be silent. The next letter speaks out again with the sadistic desire to torment Imlay with her pain and to see him suffer. The voice is that of the accusing and revengeful ghost, someone defying death only for the sake of taking pleasure in punishment. She complains that 'my heart thirsts for justice from you', and, as she adds, 'Even at Paris, my image will haunt you. You will see my pale face, and sometimes the tears of anguish will drop on your heart, which you have forced from mine.'[22]

In these letters a peculiar, ghostly narrative voice is created, which speaks from the position of someone surviving and desiring death at the same time – swaying between extremes in the borderline territory of life and death, sorrow and distraction. Often the discourse differs little from Godwin's own description of his mental state bordering on distraction after the death of his wife. Wollstonecraft's letters repeatedly act out and literalise the trope of the oxymoron, producing a voice of silence and a discourse of 'living death'. Embarking on her trip to Scandinavia, Wollstonecraft writes to Imlay from Hull 'in a sort of a tomb-like house'.[23] In one of her last letters written to Imlay, dated November 1795, after her second suicide attempt, she writes: 'In fact, 'the decided conduct which appeared to me so unfeeling,' has almost overturned my reason; my mind is injured, I scarcely know where

I am or what I do. [...] My life therefore is but an exercise of fortitude, continually on the stretch, and hope never gleams in this tomb, where I am buried alive.'[24] The voice of the *almost* dead calls out from beyond the tomb – a tomb that is life itself, burying reason that is *almost* over-turned. Here Wollstonecraft the survivor cries out from the realm of the 'almost', where sadness slides into insanity and the life that entombs her is already beyond death. Her head is *'disturbed'*,[25] and in her letters 'the agonies of a *distracted* mind were but too faithfully pourtrayed'.[26] The anger and impatience felt at Imlay's persistent, cruel silence finally chokes one of her letters: 'What have I to do here? I have repeatedly written to you fully. Do you do the same, and quickly. Do not leave me in suspense. I have not deserved this of you. *I cannot write*, my mind is so distressed. Adieu!'[27] The expression accelerates through a short, passionate question, a request, an order and a reproach, until suddenly the writing is cancelled out by the intensity of emotion, as if repeating the author's act of self-destruction. If not overtly threatening suicide, Wollstonecraft's letter acts it out by its rhetorical construction. Even when the author is not decidedly suicidal, her letter is.

The bodily symptoms of shaking and trembling often surface in Wollstonecraft's letters in relation to her uncertainties and the emo-tional ambivalence of the Imlay relationship. These concerns become closely entwined with Wollstonecraft's attempt to formulate an atti-tude to sensibility. The oscillating dynamic of shaking and trembling implies uncertainty and signifies swings of mood between hope and despair. 'Trembling' is a metaphor Wollstonecraft uses in a letter to Imlay, subsequently published in her *Letters from Scandinavia* (1796), which aptly expresses her ambivalent feelings towards sensibility as a component of female education. She spends much time 'musing almost to madness' and philosophising over sensibility from the state of mel-ancholy induced by parting from her daughter for the first time. In 'Letter Six', she feels 'affected' by the sympathy the Norwegians express towards her, a woman travelling alone. Responding sympathetically to their sympathy and hospitality, she comments that the kindness of the simple people 'increased my sensibility to a painful degree' (*Short Residence* 97). It is from this state of increased sensibility and suffering in the absence of her lover and her child that she expresses anxiety about the future of her daughter:

> I dread lest she should be forced to sacrifice her heart to her principles, or principles to her heart. *With trembling hand I shall cul-tivate sensibility*, and cherish delicacy of sentiment, lest, whilst I lend

fresh blushes to the rose, I sharpen the thorns that will wound the breast I would fain guard – I dread to unfold her mind, lest it should render her unfit for the world she is to inhabit – Hapless woman! what a fate is thine! (*Short Residence* 97, emphasis added)

Again, these reflections and ambiguities are spelt out from within melancholy that is *almost* madness. This melancholy is caused by a loss within the loss, occasioned by Wollstonecraft's temporary parting with her daughter in a state of absence and foreignness.[28]

Writing in a fragile state of sensibility, this Wollstonecraft is different from, if not too distant from, the harsh critic of sensibility in *A Vindication of the Rights of Woman*. Sensibility in the *Rights of Woman* contributes to the emergence of female softness. Far from being constitutional, this softness is argued by Wollstonecraft to be a social product. By being educated in sensibility, she claims, women are made slaves to their senses, neglecting the development of skills that could be more empowering for their social existence. In the *Rights on Woman* sensibility is criticised as an institutionalised culture of weakness, made fashionable in order to appeal to women, but the cultivation of which brings about their own social enslavement. Wollstonecraft directly links sensibility with materiality. She describes it as a realm that women are encouraged to inhabit, having been denied access to the culture of rationality:

And what is sensibility? 'Quickness of sensation, quickness of perception, delicacy.' Thus is it defined by Dr Johnson; and the definition gives me no other idea than of the *most exquisitely polished instinct.* I discern not a trace of the image of God in either sensation or matter. Refined seventy times seven they are still *material*; intellect dwells not there; nor will fire ever make lead gold![29]

Sensibility is instinct, even though – paradoxically – 'exquisitely polished'. Being related to materiality, it is directly opposed to the faculties of the intellect and the needs of an immortal soul. This binary fades away by the time of the *Letters from Scandinavia*. Here the state of sensibility – as a materially determined condition – can fuel philosophical reflection and even bring about a critique of sensibility itself.

While the *Rights of Woman* considers miserable those 'whose cultivation of mind has only tended to inflame its passions',[30] her *Letters from Scandinavia* assume a position in the midst of inflamed passions – heightened almost to madness – to express concern about such an overwhelming sensibility, yet simultaneously to testify to the legacy of feeling. The letters are the product of a hopeless pining and a desire to attract the attention of an indifferent lover. As Godwin puts it in his *Memoirs*, it is a book that was 'calculated to make a man in love with its author', producing a language of feeling that is at the same time a discourse of creative ideas. While the philosophical and critical language of sensibility did not manage to revive Imlay's love, Godwin, the philosopher, proved to be its ideal reader. He fell in love with an author who shed the 'occasional harshness and ruggedness of character' that characterised the *Rights of Woman*, and who was softened by the suffering of unrequited love, thus falling victim to 'the romance of unbounded attachment' (*Memoirs* 249).

As Daniel O'Quinn observes in the context of Wollstonecraft's second novel, *Maria; or, the Wrongs of Woman* (1798), trembling occurs when a woman's idealising fantasy projected on a man is successfully fitted to that man's seduction strategy. The protagonist, Maria, trembles with emotion when George Venables, her future husband, gives away a guinea in a false act of charity, calculated to make Maria – a woman of fortune and sensibility – fall in love with him. Maria's miserable fate is thus, to a great extent, due to her falling for her mental projections. She falsely identifies Venables as a man of feeling, and her future lover, Darnford, as the Saint Preux of fantasies induced by novel-reading.[31] In the *Letters to Imlay*, I would argue, moments of trembling come about when the narrator, in love with her fantasy projection, is held in suspense as to the man's willingness to step into the image of such a projection. Trembling signifies anxious moments of expectation and uncertainty. It occurs in moments of hope, and is caused by a woman's refusal to come to terms with the reality of loss and rejection. As Wollstonecraft writes to Imlay from Le Havre, full of expectation, 'Still I cannot indulge the very affectionate tenderness which glows in my bosom, without trembling, till I see, by your eyes, that it is mutual.'[32] Like those women – educated in feeling – whom she attacks in the *Rights of Woman*, or like the sentimental heroine whose unhappy fate was brought about by her emotional fragility, Wollstonecraft is at the mercy of tormenting and destructive feelings. In her letters to Imlay, her sensibility is presented as a deep-rooted propensity that she has no power to master, and which threatens her independent subjecthood.

Thus conceived, trembling inevitably has a dark side. With the potential to escalate into the more forceful movement of shaking, it becomes symbolic of death and destruction in Wollstonecraft's letters, as when Wollstonecraft writes: 'I have been treated ungenerously – if I understand what is generosity. You seem to me only to have been anxious to shake me off – regardless whether you dashed me to atoms by the fall. In truth, I have been rudely handled.'[33] 'Shaking off' is the metaphor Wollstonecraft uses to figure Imlay's indifference to the clinging affections by which she tries to remain attached to him despite his cruelty. To be shaken off and dashed to atoms by the other is a mortal threat to her subjectivity. After finding out about Imlay's infidelity for the first time, she feels that her 'soul has been shook' and a suicide attempt follows.[34] Trembling and shivering reappear as signals of death in Godwin's description of Wollstonecraft's last days of septicaemia. A few days after Wollstonecraft's delivery, Godwin sent for a male practitioner, Dr Poignard, who immediately resorted to surgery to extract the unejected placenta. The operation was not only painful, but also fatal; Wollstonecraft lost a lot of blood, and on 3 September 1797 the onset of the infection was marked by uncontrollable fits of shivering. As Godwin describes it: 'Every muscle of the body *trembled*, the teeth *chattered*, and the bed *shook* under her. [...] She told me, after it was over, that it had been a struggle between life and death, and that she had been more than once, in the course of it, at the point of expiring' (*Memoirs* 267, emphases added).[35]

In Godwin's account of his wife's last days in his *Memoirs*, Wollstonecraft's condition oscillated between distressful fits and promising improvement, making it difficult for Godwin and his friends to give up hope until the last minute. While Wollstonecraft – in the manner of Rousseau's Julie – kept her patience and affectionate nature, it is now Godwin who 'dwelt with *trembling* fondness on every favourable circumstance' (*Memoirs* 268, emphasis added).[36] During the last two days, the shivering fits ceased entirely, on which Carlisle observed that her continuance struck him as miraculous, encouraging him to look out for favourable appearances. These, however, never arrived. By the morning of 10 September, Wollstonecraft was dead, just like Julie at the end of Rousseau's novel.

In many respects, Godwin's mourning repeats the behaviour of the melancholy and suicidal Wollstonecraft of her letters to Imlay. In Godwin's letters to Inchbald, Godwin acts as if he was trying to do justice to Wollstonecraft, and seems to identify with the role of the revengeful tormentor. It is the same voice Wollstonecraft had assumed in her despairing letters to Imlay. It almost seems as if Godwin had internalised the role of a Wollstonecraft driven by a desire for vengeance and had stepped into the character of a haunting ghost-Mary who posthumously punishes her offenders. He adopts the impossible subject position assumed by the writer of the suicide note, a dead subjectivity imagined to be still alive and capable of serving justice. Thus, Godwin's case displays the process of mourning *in statu nascendi*, in the process of its being structured like melancholia. It shows that the role of the mourner and the deserted lover are similarly constructed through processes of identification which, in turn, are burdened with ambivalent feeling.[37]

In 'Mourning and Its Relation to Manic-Depressive States', the psychoanalyst Melanie Klein mentions the case of Mrs A – a 'normal', non-pathological mourner – who, a few days after the death of her young son, started sorting out letters in the house, keeping her son's letters and throwing others away. In Klein's interpretation, this was an attempt to restore and keep the dead person safely inside, while separating the 'good' objects that belong to him from the indifferent or harmful 'bad' objects. Such obsessive behaviour patterns, claims Klein, often accompany normal mourning.[38] As in Godwin's case, they are the mourner's way of reconstructing from the mingled fragments of good and bad the lost other as a good object, inside oneself. Godwin's polarisation of voice between extreme kindness and hostility, and his sharp distinction between good and helpful friends and bad and harmful ones could be signs of a similar shattering and rearrangement of the inner object-world. However, Godwin's writing and editing takes place at the early stages of loss, when mourning is still an illness, and where the other is being taken into the self and separation has not yet fully begun. His mourning is burdened with ambivalence – something that, for Freud, is a distinctive characteristic of melancholia. Moreover, Godwin internalises a melancholy object, a Wollstonecraft who is full of her own losses. The love object she is constantly in the process of losing in her letters to Imlay is only a replica of earlier lost objects. By the time of the Imlay relationship, Wollstonecraft had struggled through the end of an unrequited love affair with the painter Fuseli, as well as the deaths of her mother and her close friend, Fanny Blood. For Godwin, it is this object – containing multiple, never-healing wounds – that starts living its own life when taken inside, transforming both self and writing. Moving into his wife's study, surrounding himself with her objects, undertaking the care of her children, and immersing himself in her writings, Godwin internalises the melancholy object he lost, partly turning into and acting like – identifying with – Wollstonecraft. In his creative mourning, the object is never entirely lost, but, together with the subject, gets caught up in the process of losing and taking in. What emerges is a cluster of subjectivity-fragments, a subject-in-process between a dead and a living self, a Godwin turning into Mary – but a somewhat softened and emotional Mary of sensibility, more like the Mary of the *Letters to Imlay* than the radical and feminist Mary of the *Rights of Woman*.[39]

'Genuine sentiments' and Godwin's diary

In 1796, in the first surviving letter of their correspondence, Wollstonecraft writes of sending Godwin 'the last volume of Heloise'. She encourages Godwin, the well-known philosopher of reason, to express more of his feelings, and warns him not to make her into an object of his writing: 'I want besides to remind you, when you write to me in *verse*, not to choose the easiest task, my perfections, but to dwell on your own feelings – that is to say, give me a bird's-eye view of your heart. Do not make me a desk "to write upon," I humbly pray' [...].[40] The period between 1796 and 1798, with the emotional intensity of the Wollstonecraft relationship and her subsequent death, was a time when the question of feeling forced itself to the forefront of Godwin's philosophy. As Gary Kelly points out, after Wollstonecraft's death, Godwin, giving himself completely to the memory and works of his wife, re-educated himself in sensibility.[41] Could this new, emerging sensibility have, at least to some extent, been the product of his melancholy mourning?

In his miscellaneous notes of 1798, Godwin drew up a project of the literary works he intended to complete. Dissatisfied with his *Political Justice* for its 'not yielding a proper attention to the empire of feeling', he planned the correction of 'certain errors' in this work. In his notes he emphasised the power that feeling, as opposed to reason, possesses over the course of human action:

> The voluntary actions of men are under the direction of their feelings: nothing can have a tendency to produce this species of action, except so far as it is connected with ideas of future pleasure or pain to ourselves or others. Reason, accurately speaking, has not the smallest degree of power to put any one limb or articulation of our bodies into motion.[42]

In the preface of his 1799 novel, *St. Leon*, he mentions his eagerness to see affections and judgement as reconcilable faculties, and to revise *Political Justice* according to this view. Here he refers to his *Memoirs* of Wollstonecraft as a work in which he already stated a similar opinion about the value of feelings.[43]

In his ruthless self-analysis of 1798, Godwin was far from considering himself as the cold, unimpassioned philosopher of reason he had often been held to be. While he saw himself as 'too sceptical, too rational', he attributed his coldness to social anxiety and a fear of others' opinions. He pointed out that the 'two leading features of my character are sensibility and insensibility'. His mind, 'though fraught with sensibility, and occasionally ardent and enthusiastic, is perhaps in its genuine habits too languid and unimpassioned for successful composition, and stands greatly in need of stimulus and excitement'. He represented himself as a 'nervous' character, who loses self-possession in scenes that require action, and is overwhelmed with a debilitating frightfulness or strong passions: 'my heart palpitates, and my fibres tremble; the spring of mental action is suspended'.[44] His increasing preoccupation with the 'empire of feeling' is expressed in the following letter written after Wollstonecraft's death, where he harshly and indignantly responds to a friend who doubts the sincerity of a compliment Godwin had paid him earlier:

> I am sure that I wrote nothing more in my last letter to you than my genuine sentiments, and I gave you credit for the discernment to distinguish between real feeling and unmeaning panegyric. It is, I believe, a part of the English character, to feel that sort of *mauvaise honte*, which prevents men from giving utterance to their sentiments of each other; and two friends\here/ will sometimes hold commerce for years, always talking upon general subjects, and neither assured of the rank he holds with the other. I conceive this is to be very vicious. I regard it to be my duty, and I find it fraught with secret pleasure, to tell every man what I think of him, more especially when I find cause for approbation. We all of us, I believe, stand in need of this encouragement. I love these overflowings of the heart, and cannot endure to be always heating, and being heated by my friends, as if they were so many books.[45]

Here Godwin treats genuine emotional expression as something inevitable and habitual in his behaviour – an assumption that obviously surprised his correspondent.

While the appreciation of genuine feeling becomes increasingly integral to his personality, many of Godwin's letters echo the struggles in Wollstonecraft's writing between affectivity and expression. Yet, as I hope to show by the analysis of these letters, a language of sensibility grows out of the conflict Godwin experiences between writing and blocked expression. Apart from his correspondence with Inchbald, written in the aggressive, distracted language of loss, he repeatedly has to confess – in writing – his inability to write. He asks his friends to send the sad news to other friends and relatives, being unable to do it himself. In one of his letters he complains about the dangers of writing his emotions, which, though tempting, can lead to a frightening mental state:

> I wrote several letters on the day succeeding this dreadful, incurable calamity, till I felt myself called upon by every principle of justice and reason to lay down my pen and write no more. The effects that employment produced in me alarmed me. Since that time I have carefully abstained from writing on the subject. I could not however refrain from putting down these few lines to you: but I dare not trust myself to express or dwell upon my feelings.[46]

Another letter to Mrs. Cotton, a friend of Wollstonecraft's, begins as follows: 'Dear Madam, – I cannot write. I have half destroyed myself by writing. It does more mischief than anything else. I must preserve myself, if for no other reason, for the two children.'[47]

While writing is destructive, dangerous or even impossible, Godwin mentions a more soothing, even healing form of literary activity: reading, compiling and editing the papers Wollstonecraft left behind. Her papers, personal objects, their common friends and the children all function as traces of Wollstonecraft, and arouse pleasurable feelings of melancholy:

> I have a melancholy pleasure in living in the midst of objects, which have been rendered interesting to me by her presence. I choose to indulge this melancholy. I think I understand something as to the management of my own mind, and know how to cultivate a virtuous melancholy, without indulging it to a dangerous extreme. I am at present employed with the papers she left behind, and compiling some materials for an account of her life. This employment soothes without agitating me.[48]

For Godwin, everything related to his lover leads to the cultivation of the language of loss and melancholy in which he takes pleasure. Feeling inconsolable, and finding his loss 'irreparable',[49] preserving the other in himself and writing as if he were the other – these are the only activities that alleviate the pain. Perhaps this is the point where

Godwin experiences and understands the pleasure that comes from the emotionally charged perception and recollection of objects that Wollstonecraft talks about in her *Letters from Scandinavia*. The act of reading and compiling her papers is a melancholy occupation, yet it is a way of preserving the lost object and not letting it go. The pleasure of melancholy comes from defying the call of reality and counteracting the work of mourning.

It is also significant that such an immersion in melancholy should be intertwined with a painful, yet pleasurable sensibility. Nine days after Wollstonecraft's death Godwin admits again that there is a pleasurable aspect to his suffering and grief: 'I find a pleasure, difficult to be described, in the cultivation of melancholy. It weakens indeed the stoicism in the ordinary awareness of life, but it refines and raises my sensibility.'[50] Even on the day of Wollstonecraft's death he writes to his friend Holcroft that he does not want to be consoled. And a month later, in October 1797, he writes:

> I am still here, in the same situation in which you saw me, surrounded by the children, and all the well-known objects, which, though they talk to me of melancholy, are still dear to me. I love to cherish melancholy. I love to tread *the edge of intellectual danger, and just to keep within the line which every moral and intellectual consideration forbids me to overstep*, and in this indulgence and this vigilance place my present luxury.[51]

This is the language of the borderline condition of melancholy in mourning, which for Godwin results in an increase of sensibility. He produces the impossible, yet possible, language of the inability to mourn: the language of intense grief sliding into extreme pleasure. Everything that the loved one left behind gains new significance relevant to the mourner's loss; they all point to a lack – in the survivor.

There is one document, however, that does not seem to fit within the painful, passionate discourse of his writings from this period. Godwin's diary, a rigorous written testimony of its time, systematically records all the events surrounding Wollstonecraft's childbearing, illness and death. The diary consists of a series of small booklets, in which each page is divided by horizontal red lines into seven narrow parts to be filled in with the events of the day. The historical events of his time are also noted in red ink. All the entries are written in a characteristic business-like, note-taking style, full of abbreviations in order to fit everything into the small space he provided for each entry. Quoted in full, the following diary entries cover the period

from three days before the birth of Mary Godwin Shelley to the burial of
Mary Wollstonecraft on 15 September 1797:

Aug. 27. Su.   Gould calls: call on Ritson: Mart. [?] dines; adv. M Hays &
 Stoddart.

28. M.   Call on Fuseli & Inchbald; adv. Tattersal: theatre, Merchant of
 Venice; –.

29. Tu.   Barnes calls: walk to Booth's, w. Wt: read, en famille,
 Werter, p.127.

30. W.   Mary, p. 116, R Fell & Dyson call: dine at Reveley's: Fenwicks &
 M. sup: Blenkinsop.
 Birth of Mary, 20 minutes after 11 at night.
 From 7 to 10 Evesham Buildings.

31. Th.   Fetch Dr. Poignard: Fordyce calls: in the evening, Miss G, EJ, M
 Reveley & Tuthill: JG calls.

Sept. 1. F.   Call on Robinson, Nicholson, Carlisle & M Hays: Johnson
 calls.
 Favourable appearances.

2. Sa.   Carlisle, Montagu, Tuthill, Dyson & M Reveley call: worse in the
 evening. Nurse

3. Su.   Montagu breakfasts: call with him on Wolcot n, Opie n, Lawrence n &
 Dr Thompson n. Shivering fits: Fordyce twice. Poignard, Blenkinsop
 & nurse.[52]

4. M.   Blenkinsop: puppies. Johnson & Nicholsons call: Masters calls. E
 Fenwick & M sleep. M Hays calls.
 Pichegru arrested

5. Tu.   Fordyce twice: Clarke in the afternoon. M Hays calls.

6. W.   Carlisle calls: wine diet: Carlisle from Brixton: Miss Jones sleeps.

7. Th.   Barry, Reveley & Lowry call: dying in the evening.

8. F.   Opie & Tuthill call. Idea of Death: solemn communication. Barry:
 Miss G sleeps.

9. Sa.   Talk to her of Fanny & Mary: Barry.

10. Su.   20 minutes before 8 _____

_____

Montagu, M, Miss G and Fanny dine.

11. M.   Carlisle calls: Montagu at tea.

12. Tu.   Johnson and Ht n call: Montagu and Miss G at tea.

13. W.   Ht n, Opie n & Dyson n call: Miss G removes: Fenwicks sup from
           Fordyce: write to Inchbald, Tuthill & Parr.

14. Th.   Write to Mrs Cotton. Barbauld on Devotion, p. 22. Fenwicks and
           PV sup.

15. F.   Funeral: M's lodgings. Write to Carlisle. Purley, p. 50. Fawcet
          dines; adv. Fenwicks.[53]

These entries were written at the time of emotional intensity and personal tragedy, and, yet the language can hardly be called a language of
feeling. The entries record the steps through which a scene of childbirth
gradually turns into a scene of illness, dying and death.

When discussing Godwin's diary and Wollstonecraft's death, scholars
tend to point out the curious three lines indicating Wollstonecraft's death
on 10 September. This diary entry, however, is often misquoted, and is
never followed beyond the telling horizontal lines. Charles Kegan Paul,
for instance, fully cites the diary entry from the childbirth on 30 August
up to the three lines. As he observes, 'the hand-writing never falters,
the same precise abbreviations and stops are used, till the last, when
occur the only lines and dashes which break the exceeding neatness of
the book'.[54] Importantly, however, in the original manuscript the entry
for 10 September does not stop at the three lines, but is followed after
Wollstonecraft's death in the morning by the mention of a dinner with
Montagu, M, Miss G and little Fanny in the evening. The entries related to
his wife, except for the one death entry, are in no way different from other
entries on sundry subjects, such as visits, meetings or dinners, which continue after her death like before. The diary does not seem to suggest that
Wollstonecraft's childbirth, illness and dying would have been Godwin's
sole preoccupation. It is only her death, blanked out of verbal representation, that can momentarily disrupt the almost compulsively strict pattern.
The diary-machine – as a techné – soon recovers its usual mode of record-
ing Godwin's daily regime. On the night of her death, a dinner entry is
already squeezed into the same rubric, and the following day, on the other
side of the red dividing line, visits of friends are recorded. Although they
are visits of condolence, their representation is not any different from that
of social events and friendly outings.

Despite the fact that most of these entries do not differ from those written at other times of his life, the slip into the non-verbal makes us read

them as a representation of what Godwin calls in the *Memoirs* a state of anxiety and grief, verging on madness. The entries themselves do not contain any verbal expression of emotion. 'Favourable appearances', Wollstonecraft's getting worse, and the phase of her dying are conveyed in a detached language, which, written while the events and feelings took place, is still the immediate verbalisation of feeling. Only the quick phrases and abbreviated words stand there as the channel for happiness, hope, fear, love, anxiety and grief. At the change from uncertainty to certainty, from hope to grief, from parental happiness to Wollstonecraft's illness and death, Godwin's writing does not undergo any transformation but, on the day of her death, it simply slips from the verbal into the non-verbal. Like Wollstonecraft in her *Letters to Imlay* – so overwhelmed with strong feeling at her lover's absences that she cannot write – Godwin's words are silenced too. A reader well-versed in sentimental writing will know instantly what this could mean. As words fail to convey uncontrollable feelings, they need to be channelled into graphic expression. Intense feeling is marked only by the graphic slip into aposiopesis, a favourite trope of the novel of sensibility. Thus, with the appearance of Godwin's three lines, the meaning of the seemingly affectless presentation becomes entirely dependent on the act of reading; only knowledge of the context and of Godwin's account in the *Memoirs* allows us to interpret it as the language of powerful emotion. It is the act of reading that turns this form of writing – unstoppable and insensible – into a writing of sensibility. This act of reading – dependent on context, intentions, but in any case on the reader's projections – considers it as the production of a 'heart of stone' or a heart of feeling.

At the meeting point of mourning and melancholia, it is surprising to have symbolisation at all, especially the often detached, affect-denying, documentary-like tone of the diary. Thus, Godwin's mode of writing calls attention to the conceptualisation of mourning and melancholia in relation to language and signification. In *Black Sun*, Julia Kristeva offers an interpretation of depression different from the explanations given by classic psychoanalytic theory (as represented by Freud, Abraham and Klein). Her reinterpretation starts out from the problematic explanation of the affect of sadness in psychoanalysis. Traditionally, she argues, psychoanalytic theory accounts for the ambivalence and heightened superego-functioning in melancholia by the operation of the mechanism of identification. Thus, in melancholia the reproaches against oneself are always implied attacks against the object turned back to the ego, and this is what sadness is an expression of in Freud.[55]

However, as Kristeva points out, these theories do not always hold. In the case of narcissistically depressed individuals, sadness is not a disguised attack against the frustrating and absent other, and sorrow does not conceal the guilt of secretly plotting against the loved and hated object. These people do not consider themselves as wronged, but as afflicted with a fundamental deficiency. The mourning of such melancholic patients does not find a clearly identifiable referent; instead it fixes on an unsymbolisable 'Thing' – a point that does not lend itself to signification. Their sadness, she writes, is 'the most archaic expression of an unsymbolisable, unnameable narcissistic wound, so precocious that no outside agent (subject or agent) can be used as referent'. The question arises for Kristeva: 'Is mood a language?' Sadness becomes an expression of that it is something impossible to put into a symbolic form. The mood itself stands for the representation, like a language. Sadness, and all affect, writes Kristeva, is 'the psychic representation of energy displacements caused by external or internal traumas'. It is pre-sign and pre-language, a form of representation preceding linguistic forms. Affects stand 'on the frontier between animality and symbol formation.' Grief becomes an early language-substitute, appearing exactly because representation is not possible, and thus acquiring the function of representation.[56]

In Kleinian psychoanalysis, melancholia is typically seen as a problem involving symbolisation. The impossibility of symbolising a loss causes illness by hindering the work of mourning. Adult mourning, argues Melanie Klein, repeats the processes that take place during the infantile 'depressive position' – a crucial developmental stage in the baby's early life. During the time of weaning the infant goes through a state that is comparable to mourning, experiencing feelings such as pining for the mother, as well as hatred, triumph, idealisation and a desire for reparation. According to Klein, these feelings are reactivated in every experience of mourning and depression in later life. Julia Kristeva writes that during early infantile development, affect arises because there are no available means for symbolic expression yet. Only by learning language, that is, by creating a symbolic referent to what is lacking, is it possible to overcome the sadness of the depressive position. In cases of adult depression, symbolisation (in the form of literary representation) can also function as a therapeutic device. Thus, both for the infant and the adult it is through symbols that the work of mourning and the separation from the lost object can successfully take place.[57]

Godwin's case, however, appears to stage a conflict between producing language and separating from the object in the process of mourning. For

Godwin, it is precisely the act of writing that functions as the means by which the incorporation of melancholia is performed. The turning of the self into the object takes place through writing – a writing that insists on keeping the object alive and not letting it go. It is the act of writing that brings about the blockage to mourning and becomes the very medium of melancholia. The verbal products composed by Godwin under the immediate influence of grief (his letters, diary entries and the *Memoirs*) threaten their writer by their destructiveness, producing a vehicle for the ambivalence characteristic of melancholia and becoming a channel for feelings of love, hate, triumph and aggression. These writings turn the symbolic into the realm where the problem and the impossibility of symbolisation are paradoxically expressed. Godwin's writing will thus be the very realisation of the structures and affects of melancholia that simultaneously tie into and hinder the work of mourning.

Memoirs: the crypt of writing

Godwin's development of a language of affectivity and sensibility is the result of his attempt to come to terms with and define what he had lost with the death of Wollstonecraft. Through his writings, Godwin aims to salvage and integrate into his work the affective and intellectual qualities he attributed to his wife. In the *Memoirs*, he claims that the loss is personal and private; it is the loss of something related to him, within him. As he defines its most important aspect at the end of the *Memoirs*: it is 'the improvement that I have for ever lost' (*Memoirs* 272). This is the influence of a certain intellectual-affective capacity Godwin himself did not have, and which was granted to him by her presence. As Godwin sees it, their creative minds were incomplete without each other, lacking qualities that were made available only by the other's presence. While Godwin had powers to reflect on topics from all perspectives and a capacity for constant re-evaluation and re-examination, he did not have an 'intuitive perception of intellectual beauty' (*Memoirs* 272). This is precisely where Godwin sees Wollstonecraft's strength and importance. Godwin's Wollstonecraft could form right judgements by speculation only, and she accepted and rejected opinions spontaneously, without much reasoning, yet with soundness. Her strong impulsiveness and intuitiveness were capable of influencing other minds by bringing about an unmediated communication between them. Her intellect differed from Godwin's in that it perceived instantaneously by forming quick impressions, while the other learned by degree. As Godwin describes it:

> In a robust and unwavering judgment of this sort, there is a kind of witchcraft; when it decides justly, it produces a responsive vibration in every ingenuous mind. In this sense, my oscillation and scepticism were fixed by her boldness. When a true opinion emanated in this way from another mind, the conviction produced in my own assumed a similar character, instantaneous and firm. [...] This light was lent to me for a very short period, and is now extinguished for ever! (*Memoirs* 273)

The powers of her intellect and her spontaneity of judgement, as well as her religion and philosophy, were 'the pure result of feeling and taste' (*Memoirs* 272). What is lost with her is this 'light' with its capacity to create a sympathetic contact between minds. It is an affective potential that also relates to the intellect – an affect with direct access to the mind and a power to exceed boundaries between subjectivities. This affect could function as a form of communication, replacing – and thus becoming – language.[58]

One will find similar conceptualisations of feeling in Wollstonecraft's writing. In her letters to Godwin she described affection as a kind of feeling that reaches the intellect, lending it the capacity to function like language. Emotion in her discourse often mingles intellectual appreciation with sexual desire: 'I should have liked to have dined with you to day, after finishing your essays – *that my eyes, and lips, I do not exactly mean my voice, might have told you that they had raised you in my esteem.* What a cold word! I would say love, if you will promise not to dispute about its propriety, *when I want to express an increasing affection, founded on a more intimate acquaintance with your heart and understanding.'*[59] This affection is communicated by the sexual body, without words. Masked as esteem, it is love based on intellectual, as well as emotional, knowledge of the other. In another letter, sexual feeling is inseparable from the act of thinking, and is aroused by means of an internalised Godwin: 'let me assure you that you are not only in my heart, but my veins, this morning. I turn from you half abashed – yet you haunt me, and some look, word or touch thrills through my whole frame – yes, at the very moment when I am labouring to think of something, if not somebody, else. Get ye gone Intruder!'[60] Here the image of the other connects thought and feeling, mind and body. This image haunts and inhabits the self almost parasitically, and, attached to its affects, behaves as its constitutive part.

Godwin may well have learnt from Wollstonecraft the importance of incorporating within one's self an emotionally invested object. In *Letters from Scandinavia* Wollstonecraft outlines the way in which memories are inscribed into the mind by way of emotionally charged sensations and impressions:

> When a warm heart has received strong impressions, they are not to be effaced, Emotions become sentiments; and the imagination renders even transient sensations permanent, by fondly retracting them. I cannot, without a thrill of delight, recollect views I have seen, which are not to be forgotten, – nor looks I have felt in every nerve which I shall never more meet. The grave has closed over a dear friend, the friend of my youth; still she is present with me, and I hear her soft voice warbling as I stray over the heath. Fate has separated me from another, the fire of whose eyes, tempered by infantile tenderness, still warms my breast; even when gazing on these tremendous cliffs, sublime emotions absorb my soul. (*Short Residence* 99–100)

Sentiments are produced in a quick and sympathetic response to what is sublime and beautiful in nature. 'Nature', writes Wollstonecraft, 'is the nurse of sentiment' and 'the harmonised soul sinks into melancholy, or rises to extasy, just as the chords are touched [...]' (*Short Residence* 99). Nature inspires the process of recollection, and remembering a past experience, person or object will once again induce the emotion through which it was first inscribed into the imagination. Such sentiments and impressions are so strong that they can be perfectly reactivated through the work of memory, even after the death of those objects who left these impressions in the soul. Thus, by carefully retracting and internalising every experience the soul can contain in the form of recoverable marks all its losses and their affective components. Feeling and sentiment are therefore important means of retaining and preserving in the self one's dead, lost and otherwise irrecoverable objects – a process one might want to resort to when trying to counteract the pain of loss.

The image of Wollstonecraft created in Godwin's *Memoirs of the Author of A Vindication of the Rights of Woman* is indeed an image inscribed and produced through emotion. As I have been arguing in this chapter, this image emerges from the salvaging of a loved object through the process of identification. During this process, however, the object has gone through an interesting transformation. In the *Memoirs*, Wollstonecraft is presented as a self-sacrificing woman of feeling. As Godwin portrays her: 'the sensibility of her heart would not suffer her to rest in solitary gratifications' (*Memoirs* 214). Here even Wollstonecraft's radical and feminist *Rights of Woman* is seen as integral to a special form of sensibility.

While the book, according to Godwin, sometimes testifies to a 'rigid, and somewhat amazonian temper', it also possesses a 'trembling delicacy of sentiment, which would have done honour to a poet (*Memoirs* 231–2). The sensibility Godwin attributes to her is the pathological and often dangerous excess of feeling that contributes to the misery and death of so many sentimental heroes, from Fielding's David Simple to Mackenzie's man of feeling and Goethe's Werther. In Godwin's melancholy salvaging, Wollstonecraft is seen as a 'female Werter' whose mind seems 'almost of too fine a texture to encounter the vicissitudes of human affairs, to whom pleasure is transport, and disappointment is agony indescribable' (*Memoirs* 242). In other words, her pleasure and pain are the products of her intense emotional susceptibility.

However, the actual outcome of the publication of Godwin's *Memoirs* was very different from the intended preservation and affective inscription of a loved and valued person. Thus, while Godwin's writings were meant to function as a memorial, they contributed instead to Wollstonecraft's 'burial' and erasure – acting more like a tomb. His portrayal of Wollstonecraft as a sentimental heroine who possessed an emotionality that Godwin claimed to lack thus fills for him a narcissistic gap, where the desired qualities lodged exclusively in the other are carefully distilled. Godwin's writings from this period do not dwell on his feelings, as Wollstonecraft urged him to do, and they do not make her 'a desk "to write upon"', either. These are writings that stand for and behave as feelings, repeating the operation and production of feelings that are seen in Wollstonecraft's writing as a form of reinscription. Recovering her sensibility is also a process of losing – losing her as something else, while retaining what Godwin fell in love with. At the end of the *Memoirs*, even the inscription engraved on her tombstone is reproduced:

Mary Wollstonecraft Godwin,
Author of
A Vindication
Of the Rights of Woman:
Born 27 April, 1759:
Died 10 September, 1797.

By repeating the engraving, the *Memoirs* function as an epitaph, memorialising Wollstonecraft as the dead author of the *Rights of Woman*. Therefore, the *Memoirs* themselves are a form of engraving, burying her in the tomb of sensibility, yet marking this with the inscription of feminist authorship. Her identity and her feminism are thus carved into the tombstone of Godwin's affectivity, his written memorial.

In *The Shell and the Kernel*, the psychoanalysts Nicolas Abraham and Maria Torok present cases of pathological mourning, in which the work of mourning is blocked or otherwise made impossible. When an object loss cannot be acknowledged as such, an incorporation of the lost object takes place, forming what they call a 'psychic crypt' or tomb inside the ego. The loss is 'buried alive in the crypt as a full-fledged person', creating a 'whole world of unconscious fantasy [...] that leads to its own separate and concealed existence'. The 'ghost of the crypt comes back to haunt the cemetery guard, giving him strange and incomprehensible signals, making him perform bizarre acts, or subjecting him to unexpected sensations'. Thus, such patients often act out the desires and motivations of the object they carry inside them, aiming to satisfy the unmourned objects they have identified with. Abraham and Torok call this pathological form of mourning 'melancholy mourning'. This involves a paradoxically reverse scenario, where it seems as though it is the lost object who is grieving the loss of the mourner. It is this suffering, loving, dejected phantom object – who is 'simply "crazy" about the melancholic' – that the mourner identifies with.[61] In Godwin's case, however, something different takes place. While the loved object is over-invested at the time of its sudden and premature loss and the ego is dependent on it, the loss does get acknowledged and acted out – in writing, which writing is transformed by the presence of the object. Unlike the illness of mourning described by Abraham and Torok, Godwin's case is marked by the presence of symbolisation, but only to act out the process of melancholic incorporation. Symbolisation paradoxically becomes the medium for the inability to mourn. Thus, we might say, it is not the psyche, but the writing that becomes the crypt.

Mary Wollstonecraft's loss provided Godwin with an ever-recurring motif that would surface in his writing for the rest of his life. In his later fiction, however, the 'crypt', so to say, is opened up, and Godwin becomes rather critical of his earlier sentimentalisation of Wollstonecraft. *Fleetwood; or, the New Man of Feeling* (1805) and *Mandeville: A Tale of the Seventeenth Century* (1817) are both stories about the psychology of misreading or misrepresenting woman. *Fleetwood* is a guilt-ridden exposure of the self-centredness underlying the eponymous protagonist's jealousy, ambivalence and cruelty towards his devoted but melancholy wife, Mary. *Mandeville* exposes a pathological mind trapped in its own self-enclosed world and tormented by bad feelings. Mandeville sentimentalises his sister, Henrietta, into an epitome of sympathetic philanthropy, but his pathology is revealed in the huge discrepancy between his own interpretation of the events of his life and the perspective of other characters. The figure of the melancholy mourner surfaces in the character of Mandeville's uncle, Audley Mandeville, whose extreme sensibility is caused by the loss of his lover – a blow he never quite recovers from. Godwin's literary working-through continues even as late as *Deloraine* (1833) – a novel that reflects on the process of idealising and burying woman.[62]

On the basis of Godwin's case I have been arguing that symbolisation, instead of bringing about the work of mourning, can, in some cases, turn into its obstacle and become a means of maintaining the pathological state of melancholia. What is the importance of such a psychoanalytic argument for the study of literature – or any form of writing? What does it mean that a script can be a crypt: an agent of melancholia that entombs another into the writer's self and text? Godwin's case is part of a modern history of melancholia. It shows continuities with the ways in which psychoanalytic writers think about melancholia and mourning, linking Godwin's experience with the ideas of Freud, Klein, Kristeva and their successors and suggesting a framework for a long history of feeling. As Godwin's example of 1797 shows, even in contexts as distant from psychoanalysis as the eighteenth century, emotions hide complex processes of identification, disturbing the boundaries of the self and re-structuring, transforming and dividing subjectivity. Such a crisis of subjectivity can have far-reaching consequences regarding the ethical implications of reading and authorship. Who will claim responsibility and a right to authorship where a text, as Inchbald pointed out, uses the language of grief? If the troubling emotions of melancholy mourning transform subjectivity into a subject-in-process – into a self turning into the other – who is writing Godwin's angry and revengeful letters, his affectless, 'stonehearted' diary or the *Memoirs* that ruined Wollstonecraft's reputation? Is there really an author, a responsible self behind the long period of resistance to Wollstonecraft's work and feminist ideas?

Even if one leaves these questions open, it is enough to say that a discourse of sensibility, emerging out of feelings that disrupt and divide the self, necessarily raises an ethical concern. The pleasurable pain of Godwin's cherished melancholia might have to do with unconsciously entering a problematic subjecthood in which the responsibilities and burdens of an authorial self are lifted. Out of the experience of strong emotions emerges a form of writing in which authorship is blurred and responsibility suspended. Sympathy, a cornerstone of eighteenth-century sensibility, is a feeling with similarly problematic consequences, due in part to its being based on processes burdened with ambivalence. I believe that it is here, in the disrupting identificatory and sympathetic processes built into its discourse, that we can find the seductive – and for the period, dangerous – potential of reading the behaviour, ideology and novels of sensibility. The 'heart of stone' and the heart of feeling can speak the same language, after all.

Notes

Introduction: Sensibility from the Margins

1. The expression 'age of sensibility' was first used by Northrop Frye in 'Towards Defining an Age of Sensibility', *ELH* 23.2 (1956): 144–52. The phrase 'culture of sensibility' is used by Barker-Benfield in *The Culture of Sensibility: Sex and Society in Eighteenth-Century Britain* (Chicago: University of Chicago Press, 1992).
2. Hannah More, *Sacred Dramas [. . .] To which it is added, Sensibility: A Poem.* 5th edn (1782; London: T. Cadell, 1787) 284.
3. Mary Wollstonecraft, *A Vindication of the Rights of Woman*, ed. Miriam Brody (London: Penguin, 1992) 153–6.
4. Anne C. Vila, 'Beyond Sympathy: Vapors, Melancholia, and the Pathologies of Sensibility in Tissot and Rousseau', *Yale French Studies* 92 (1997): 88–90. For critical attitudes to sensibility in the period see also John Mullan, 'Sensibility and Literary Criticism', *The Cambridge History of Literary Criticism*, eds. H.B. Nisbet and Claude Rawson, vol. 4 (Cambridge: Cambridge University Press, 1997) 419–33; R.F. Brissenden, *Virtue in Distress: Studies in the Novel of Sentiment from Richardson to Sade* (London: Macmillan, 1974) 56–64; Chris Jones, *Radical Sensibility: Literature and Ideas in the 1790s* (London and New York: Routledge, 1993) 1–19.
5. Thomas Dixon claims that the word 'emotion' is currently used too liberally and often anachronistically to refer to theories that were in fact about passions, affections or sentiments. Dixon explores the development and use of specific concepts, including the passions and the emotions in *From Passions to Emotions: The Creation of a Secular Psychological Category* (Cambridge: Cambridge University Press, 2003) 11. While 'emotion' in the eighteenth century mainly denoted agitation and disturbance, Dixon argues that 'by around 1850 the category of "emotions" had subsumed "passions", "affections" and "sentiments" in the vocabularies of the majority of English-language psychological theorists'. Thus, by the mid-nineteenth century, 'emotion' had become the most popular term for phenomena such as hope, fear, love, anger, jealousy, and so on (98).
6. Samuel Johnson, *Dictionary of the English Language*, 2 vols (London: W. Strahan, 1755).
7. For literary-critical discussions of the notion and definitions of sensibility see, for example, Barker-Benfield, *Culture of Sensibility*, xvii–xxxiv; Markman Ellis, 'Sensibility, History and the Novel', *The Politics of Sensibility: Race, Gender, and Commerce in the Sentimental Novel* (Cambridge: Cambridge University Press, 1996) 5–48. For the belief in natural goodness and the relationship between sensibility and the moral philosophy of the period see Stephen D. Cox, *'The Stranger Within Thee': Concepts of Self in Late-Eighteenth-Century Literature* (Pittsburgh: University of Pittsburgh Press, 1980) 25; John Mullan, 'Sympathy and the Production of Society', *Sentiment*

and Sociability: The Language of Feeling in the Eighteenth Century (Oxford: Clarendon Press, 1988) 18–56; Ellis, *Politics of Sensibility*, 10–14; Janet Todd, *Sensibility: An Introduction* (London: Methuen, 1986) 23–8.

8. According to Markman Ellis, sensibility operates within a variety of fields of knowledge, including the history of ideas, aesthetics, religion, political economy, science, sexuality and popular culture. Ellis sees the novel of sensibility as an amalgamation of these discourses: 'In the novel, in other words, sensibility comes together' (Ellis, *Politics of Sensibility*, 8). According to Janet Todd, the presence of sensibility in all fields of life can be accounted for in its pervasiveness and contagious nature. The close interrelatedness between literature and life operates 'not through any notion of a mimetic depiction of reality but through the belief that the literary experience can intimately affect the living one. So literary conventions become a way of life' (Todd, *Sensibility*, 4, 75).

9. For a 'vocabulary' of sensibility see Todd, *Sensibility*, esp. 77, 65–128. Brissenden discusses the term 'sensibility' with its meanings, connotations and origins within what he calls an 'identifiably "sentimental" vocabulary', among the terms 'sentiment', 'sentimentality', 'sense' in *Virtue in Distress*, see esp. the chapter '"Sentimentalism": An Attempt at Definition', 11–55.

10. G.S. Rousseau, 'Nerves, Spirits, and Fibres: Towards Defining the Origins of Sensibility' (1975), *Nervous Acts: Essays on Literature, Culture and Sensibility* (Basingstoke and New York: Palgrave Macmillan, 2004) 166.

11. Barker-Benfield, *Culture of Sensibility*, 6. Medical men in the first half of the century were particularly influential agents in the circulation of the theory and the vocabulary of the nerves. Their treatises were not written for a specialised audience; rather, they were intended for all those members of the general public who found themselves suffering from such ailments. See G.S. Rousseau, 'Science Books and Their Readers in the Eighteenth Century', *Books and Their Readers in Eighteenth-Century England*, ed. Isabel Rivers (Leicester: Leicester University Press; New York: St Martin's Press, 1982) 217.

12. Barker-Benfield, *Culture of Sensibility*, 23–36.

13. Ibid., 7.

14. Mullan, *Sentiment and Sociability*, 200–40; Ann Jessie Van Sant, *Eighteenth-Century Sensibility and the Novel: The Senses in Social Context* (Cambridge: Cambridge University Press, 1993); Anne C. Vila, *Enlightenment and Pathology: Sensibility in the Literature and Medicine of Eighteenth-Century France* (Baltimore and London: The Johns Hopkins University Press, 1998).

15. Christopher Lawrence, 'The Nervous System and Society in the Scottish Enlightenment', *Natural Order: Historical Studies of Scientific Culture*, eds. Barry Barnes and Steven Shapin (Beverley Hills and London: Sage, 1979) 24–5.

16. Hubert Steinke, *Irritating Experiments: Haller's Concept and the European Controversy on Irritability and Sensibility, 1750–90* (Amsterdam and New York: Rodopi, 2005) 234.

17. In the *Essay Concerning Human Understanding*, Locke suggested that God could add to matter the capacity of thought. David Hume, like Descartes, talks about the human body as 'a mighty complicated machine' and mentions 'instinct or mechanical power'. For Locke's materialist statement and a history of materialist thought in Britain see John W. Yolton, *Thinking*

Matter: Materialism in Eighteenth-Century Britain (Minneapolis: University of Minnesota Press, 1983) 14, 30, 32.

18. In his *Observations on Man* (1749) he held that the body functioned as an independent mechanism. Importantly, however, he also postulated the existence of the immaterial soul.

19. For Beddoes and his materialist adherents see Neil Vickers, 'Coleridge, Thomas Beddoes and Brunonian Medicine', *European Romantic Review* 8.1 (1997): 47–94. For materialist ideas in the Romantic period see also Alan Richardson, *British Romanticism and the Science of the Mind* (Cambridge: Cambridge University Press, 2001), esp. 1–38.

20. For the various meanings of sympathy see Ephraim Chambers, *Cyclopaedia; or, an Universal Dictionary of Arts and Sciences*, 2 vols (London: D. Midwinter, 1741–3), Chambers, *A Supplement to Chambers's Cyclopaedia, or, Universal Dictionary of Arts and Sciences*, 2 vols (London: W. Innys, 1753) and Chambers, *Cyclopaedia; or, an Universal Dictionary of Arts and Sciences* (London: J. F. and C. Rivington, 1786).

21. While in the eighteenth century the concept of sympathy was used to denote all these processes, it is important to note that Max Scheler's twentieth-century phenomenological account strives to divorce fellow-feeling from other kinds of attachments such as an immediate community of feeling, emotional infection and identification. 'Fellow-feeling proper' presupposes an initial apprehension of another person's feelings and a subsequent reproduction of these feelings. In this case, the other person's suffering and the spectator's commiseration are two phenomenologically different acts. Scheler's project thus removes the question of fellow-feeling from the realm of enlightenment ethics and challenges the idea that an ethics can wholly be based on sympathy. See Max Scheler, *The Nature of Sympathy*, trans. Peter Heath (London: Routledge and Kegan Paul, 1954), esp. 5–36.

22. In *The Theory of Moral Sentiments* (1759) Adam Smith argues that sympathy is based on our ability to imagine what we would be feeling in another person's situation. Much influential scholarly work builds on Smith's concept. John Bender, David Marshall and John Dwyer focus on the element of spectatorship and theatricality built into Adam Smith's concept of sympathetic imagination. See John Bender, *Imagining the Penitentiary: Fiction and the Architecture of Mind in Eighteenth-Century England* (Chicago and London: University of Chicago Press, 1987); David Marshall, *The Figure of Theater: Shaftesbury, Defoe, Adam Smith and George Eliot* (New York: Columbia University Press, 1986); John Dwyer, 'Enlightened Spectators and Classical Moralists: Sympathetic Relations in Eighteenth-Century Scotland', *Sociability and Society in Eighteenth-Century Scotland*, ed. John Dwyer and Richard B. Sher (Edinburgh: Mercat, 1993) 96–118. Robert Mitchell's *Sympathy and the State in the Romantic Era* (New York and London: Routledge, 2007) also understands sympathy in terms of identification based on the workings of the imagination. Adela Pinch, on the other hand, explores the literary history of a Humean notion of emotion, which is based on the communication and contagion of sentiment (*Strange Fits of Passion: Epistemologies of Emotion, Hume to Austen* [Stanford, CA: Stanford University Press, 1996]). Patricia Fara's *Sympathetic Attractions: Magnetic Practices, Beliefs, and Symbolism in Eighteenth-Century England* (Princeton,

NJ: Princeton University Press, 1996) is the first monograph devoted entirely to the mechanistic notions of the concept; here the history of sympathy is presented as part of the history of magnetism.

23. Dixon, *From Passions to Emotions*, 70. Dixon explores the nuances of these concepts in *From Passions to Emotions* 62–97.

24. Susan James, *Passion and Action: The Emotions in Seventeenth-Century Philosophy* (Oxford: Clarendon Press, 1997), esp. 65, 81, 86. Descartes, James argues, distinguished between actions and passions of the soul. While actions proceeded directly from the soul and were initiated by it, passions were received by the soul and had to be caused in the soul by something else. For Descartes, the passions of the soul were 'for the most part passive perceptions of bodily motions' (James, *Passion and Action*, 91, 94). For the materialist Hobbes, on the other hand, passions were physical endeavours towards an object (appetites) or away from an object (aversions). While they were thoughts, they consisted of interacting sets of motions, and they were manifestations of our underlying pursuit of power (James, *Passion and Action*, 131–4).

25. Albert O. Hirschman, *The Passions and the Interests: Political Arguments for Capitalism before Its Triumph* (Princeton, NJ: Princeton University Press, 1977) 41.

26. Ibid., 42–66.

27. Annette C. Baier, *Death and Character: Further Reflections on Hume* (Cambridge, MA: Harvard University Press, 2008) 3–5. The interrelations of passions and personhood in the eighteenth century are complex. As Adela Pinch observes, for Hume passions can produce an individual person, rather than the other way around (Pinch 22–3). For a discussion of persons and passions see also Annette C. Baier, *A Progress of Sentiments: Reflections on Hume's Treatise* (Cambridge, MA: Harvard University Press, 1991).

28. William M. Reddy, *The Navigation of Feeling: A Framework for the History of Emotions* (Cambridge: Cambridge University Press, 2001) 122–4, 325.

29. Brycchan Carey, *British Abolitionism and the Rhetoric of Sensibility* (Basingstoke: Palgrave Macmillan, 2005) 11 and chapters 4 and 6. See also Candace Ward, 'Sensibility, Tropical Disease, and the Eighteenth-Century Sentimental Novel', *Discourses of Slavery and Abolition: Britain and Its Colonies, 1760–1838*, eds. Brycchan Carey, Markman Ellis and Sarah Salih (Basingstoke: Palgrave Macmillan, 2004) 63–77. Ward shows how tropical disease theorists used the language of sensibility to justify the slave trade.

30. Amit S. Rai, *Rule of Sympathy: Sentiment, Race, and Power 1750–1850* (New York and Basingstoke: Palgrave, 2002).

31. I agree with Ellis's argument that the demise of sensibility is not a consequence or a symptom of political change and of the revolutionary controversy, as the politicisation of sensibility had largely occurred by the end of the 1780s (Ellis, *Politics of Sensibility*, 191). 'The issues under discussion recur in the literary and cultural crisis of the 1790s Revolution controversy. That is to say, the sensibility controversy is constitutive of the Revolution controversy (causal, influential) and not just a symptom of it' (198). Victoria Kahn outlines how a politics of sympathy emerged in the seventeenth century, before the core values of sensibility became more widespread, in *Wayward Contracts: The Crisis of Political Obligation in England, 1640–1674* (Princeton and Oxford: Princeton University Press, 2004) 223–51. The 'politics of pity' is

discussed by Luc Boltanski, following Hannah Arendt's theory outlined in *On Revolution*. See Boltanski, *Distant Suffering: Morality, Media and Politics*, trans. Graham Burchell (Cambridge: Cambridge University Press, 1999) 3, 102–3. Arendt draws a clear distinction between pity and compassion. As she writes, 'for compassion, to be stricken with the suffering of someone else as though it were contagious, and pity, to be sorry without being touched in the flesh, are not only not the same, they may not even be related'. See *On Revolution* (Harmondsworth: Penguin, 1973) 85. Max Scheler also argues for a difference between emotional infection and what he calls 'fellow-feeling proper' and sees the two as phenomenologically distinct. See Scheler 12–15.

32. Bransby Blake Cooper, *The Life of Sir Astley Cooper, Bart.*, vol. 1 (London: John W. Parker, 1843) 241–2.

33. Michael Bell, *Sentimentalism, Ethics and the Culture of Feeling* (Basingstoke: Palgrave, 2000). See also Andrew Gibson, '*Sense and Sensibility* and Postmodern Ethics', *Passionate Encounters in a Time of Sensibility*, ed. Maximilian E. Novak and Anne Mellor (Newark: University of Delaware Press; London: Associated University Presses, 2000) 247–64. Gibson explores the significance Austen's notion of sensibility has for postmodern ethics.

34. Boltanski, *Distant Suffering*, 151.

35. Daniel Heller-Roazen, *The Inner Touch: Archaeology of a Sensation* (New York: Zone Books, 2007) 289. While Heller-Roazen observes a fading of feeling in our modern life, in *Cato's Tears and the Making of Anglo-American Emotion* (Chicago and London: The University of Chicago Press, 1999) Julie Ellison puts sensibility within a larger frame and argues its continuity with 1990s liberal guilt. While I agree that forms of sentimentality do occur in modern culture, I maintain that, unlike in the eighteenth century, sentimentality is no longer a dominant and widely accepted part of political and cultural interaction. Daniel Gross's *The Secret History of Emotion: From Aristotle's Rhetoric to Modern Brain Science* (Chicago: University of Chicago Press, 2006) is also worth mentioning here. Gross explores a hidden tradition, in which emotions are seen as socially constructed and distributed unequally. Rather than being biologically determined and available for all, emotions are defined by their scarcity – not their excess. Gross argues that this notion of emotion is different from the one offered by the Scottish Enlightenment and stands out as an alternative to sensibility's excess.

36. Some amongst the modern approaches to literature, however, do attend to the role of emotion. The work of I. A. Richards shows an interest in the reader's response and the psychology of reading. A theoretical approach that makes affective response focal is reader-response criticism. For the problematics of reading, reader-orientated critical approaches and readers' response see Andrew Bennett (ed.), *Readers and Reading* (Harlow: Longman, 1995) and *Reading Reading: Essays on the Theory and Practice of Reading* (Tampere: University of Tampere, 1993). For a recent exploration of post-structuralist theory's engagement with feeling (though not necessarily with emotional response) see Rei Terada's *Feeling in Theory: Emotion after the 'Death of the Subject'* (Cambridge, MA and London: Harvard University Press, 2001). A detailed account of the place of emotional response in the history of literary theory and criticism would be a valuable subject for future research.

37. W. K. Wimsatt and Monroe Beardsley, 'The Affective Fallacy', *Twentieth Century Literary Criticism: A Reader*, ed. David Lodge (1949; London: Longman, 1972) 345, rpt. of *Sewanee Review* 57 (1949): 31–55.

38. Ibid., 356.

39. Emma Mason and Isobel Armstrong, 'Introduction: Feeling: "An Indefinite Dull Region of the Spirit"?', *Textual Practice* 22.1 (2008): 14. James Elkins raises similar questions within the field of art criticism. He claims that our critical methods do not allow sufficient space for emotional intensity. See *Pictures and Tears: A History of People Who Have Cried in Front of Paintings* (New York and London: Routledge, 2001) 13, qtd. by Mason and Armstrong, 'Introduction', 14. A similar critique is voiced by Emma Mason in 'Feeling Dickensian Feeling', *19: Interdisciplinary Studies in the Long Nineteenth Century* 4 (2007): 1–19, 31 October 2008, http://www.19.bbk.ac.uk.

40. G. W. F. Hegel, *Aesthetics: Lectures on Fine Art* (Berlin Lectures, 1823–29), trans. T. M. Knox, *German Aesthetic and Literary Criticism*, ed. David Simpson (Cambridge: Cambridge University Press, 1984) 208–9, qtd. by Mason and Armstrong, 'Introduction', 1. William Hazlitt, 'On Poetry in General' (1818), *Romantic Criticism 1800–1850*, ed. R. A. Foakes (London: Edward Arnold, 1968) 109–10, qtd. by Mason, 'Dickensian Feeling', 15.

41. George Santayana, *The Life of Reason; or, the Phases of Human Progress* (London: Constable, 1905) 284.

42. See Mark H. Davis, *Empathy: A Social Psychological Approach* (Madison, WI: WCB Brown and Benchmark, 1994); C. Daniel Batson, *The Altruism Question: Toward a Social-Psychological Answer* (Hillsdale, NJ: Lawrence Erlbaum, 1991); Chris D. Frith, *Making Up the Mind* (Malden, MA: Blackwell, 2007); Tania Singer et al., 'Empathic Neural Responses are Modulated by the Perceived Fairness of Others', *Nature* 439 (26 January 2006): 466–9; C. Fred Alford, *What Evil Means to Us* (Ithaca and London: Cornell University Press, 1997); Arne Johan Vetlesen, *Evil and Human Agency* (Cambridge: Cambridge University Press, 2005); and Keith Tester, *Compassion, Morality and the Media* (Buckingham, PA: Open University Press, 2001). These connections shall be further explored in Chapter 1 of this monograph.

43. R. F. Brissenden, *Virtue in Distress: Studies in the Novel of Sentiment from Richardson to Sade* (London: Macmillan, 1974) 58 and 140–1.

44. I am referring to Rousseau's eponymous article, which set the ground for subsequent work on the medical context of sensibility. Following Rousseau, Barker-Benfield also understands the physiology of sensibility as a discourse of nerves, spirits and fibres (*Culture of Sensibility*, 15–23).

45. The problem with the 'application' of psychoanalysis as a 'body of knowledge' by means of which literature, as a 'body of language', can be explained is pointed out in Shoshana Felman, 'To Open the Question'. *Yale French Studies* 55–6 (1977): 5–10.

46. To some extent, historicism is immanent to psychoanalysis. As Paul Hamilton writes of Freud's technique, the method of psychoanalysis 'lets us reinterpret the past in new ways which then necessitate a reappraisal of the present. Freud's essentially historicist procedures return us to a present now rendered uncanny in its mixture of sameness and difference, familiarity and strangeness'. See *Historicism* (London: Routledge, 1996) 126.

1 Philosophies of Sympathy

1. Markman Ellis, *The Politics of Sensibility* (Cambridge: Cambridge University Press, 1996) 2, 49.
2. R.F. Brissenden, *Virtue in Distress* (London: Macmillan, 1974) 56–64.
3. *Anti-Jacobin* 36 (1798): 284. Canning's poem and Gillray's caricature appear next to each other in this issue.
4. For an analysis of Gillray's caricature see Ellis, *Politics of Sensibility*, 190–200.
5. For the concept and connotations of 'interest' and its longer history see Albert O. Hirschman, *The Passions and the Interests: Political Arguments for Capitalism before Its Triumph* (Princeton, NJ: Princeton University Press, 1977).
6. Pierre Carlet de Chamblain de Marivaux, *Le Paysan Parvenu; or, The Fortunate Peasant*, trans. Anon. (1735; New York and London: Garland, 1979) 50–2, 271–2.
7. Thomas Hobbes, *Leviathan*, ed. C.B. Macpherson (London: Penguin, 1985) 81, hereafter *Leviathan*.
8. For Hobbes's materialism and his influence see Samuel I. Mintz, *The Hunting of Leviathan: Seventeenth-Century Reactions to the Materialism and Moral Philosophy of Thomas Hobbes* (Cambridge: Cambridge University Press, 1962).
9. Mandeville's ideas developed in response to the doctrines of Christian neo-stoicism as well as the benevolent ideas voiced later by the Third Earl of Shaftesbury in his *Characteristics*.
10. Bernard Mandeville, *The Fable of the Bees*, ed. Phillip Harth (Harmondsworth: Penguin, 1970) 92, 264, hereafter *Fable*.
11. Norman S. Fiering, 'Irresistible Compassion: An Aspect of Eighteenth-Century Sympathy and Humanitarianism', *Journal of the History of Ideas*, 37. 2 (1976): 198–202.
12. Anthony Ashley Cooper, Third Earl of Shaftesbury, *Characteristics of Men, Manners, Opinions, and Times*, ed. Lawrence Klein (Cambridge: Cambridge University Press, 1999) 187 and 178, hereafter *Characteristics*.
13. The important seventeenth-century forerunners of the idea of the moral sense are discussed by Peter Kivy in *The Seventh Sense: Francis Hutcheson and Eighteenth-Century British Aesthetics* (Oxford: Clarendon, 2003) 3–24.
14. Francis Hutcheson, *An Inquiry into the Original of Our Ideas of Beauty and Virtue; in Two Treatises.* (London: J. Darby, 1725) 141, hereafter *Beauty and Virtue*.
15. Francis Hutcheson, *On the Nature and Conduct of the Passions with Illustrations on the Moral Sense*, ed. Andrew Ward (Manchester: Clinamen, 1999) 13, hereafter *Passions*.
16. David Hume, *An Enquiry Concerning the Principles of Morals*, ed. L.A. Selby-Bigge (Oxford: Clarendon Press, 1975) 219, hereafter *Enquiry*.
17. For ideas of self-interest in eighteenth-century philosophy see Milton L. Myers, *The Soul of the Modern Economic Man: Ideas of Self-Interest, Thomas Hobbes to Adam Smith* (Chicago and London: University of Chicago Press, 1983).

18. Henry Mackenzie, *The Man of Feeling*, ed. Maureen Harkin (Plymouth: Broadview, 2005) 61.
19. See also Hume, *Enquiry*, 180.
20. The idea of a sentimental polity held together by small-scale sympathetic exchanges that linked the individual to a larger national unit was common in Scottish Enlightenment writing. See Dwyer, *The Age of the Passions: An Interpretation of Adam Smith and Scottish Enlightenment Culture* (East Linton: Tuckwell, 1998) 9 and Christopher Lawrence, 'The Nervous System and Society in the Scottish Enlightenment', *Natural Order: Historical Studies of Scientific Culture*, eds. Barry Barnes and Steven Shapin (Beverley Hills and London: Sage, 1979) 31–3.
21. John Mullan, *Sentiment and Sociability: The Language of Feeling in the Eighteenth Century* (Oxford: Clarendon Press, 1988) 26. One must note, however, that Shaftesbury shifted the meaning of enthusiasm to form the basis of a range of creative human activities rather than only connoting religious extremism. See Lawrence Klein, introduction, *Characteristics*, by Anthony Ashley Cooper, Third Earl of Shaftesbury (Cambridge: Cambridge University Press, 1999) xxix–xxx.
22. David Hume, *A Treatise of Human Nature*, ed. L.A. Selby-Bigge (Oxford: Clarendon, 1978) 316, hereafter *THN*.
23. See pages 221, 254, 178, 257 and 250.
24. Patricia Fara, *Sympathetic Attractions: Magnetic Practices, Beliefs, and Symbolism in Eighteenth-Century England* (Princeton, NJ: Princeton University Press, 1996) 149.
25. Kenelm Digby, *Of the Sympathetic Powder: A Discourse in Solemn Assembly at Montpellier* (London: John Williams, 1669); Richard Browne, *Medicina Musica: or, a Mechanical Essay on the Effects of Singing, Musick, and Dancing on Human Bodies* (London: John Cooke, 1729); H.M. Herwig, *The Art of Curing Sympathetically or Magnetically [...] With a Discourse Concerning the Cure of Madness, and An Appendix to Prove the Reality of Sympathy* (London: Tho. Newborough, 1700).
26. See John Trenchard's explanation of religious enthusiasm in *The Natural History of Superstition* (London: A. Baldwin, 1709).
27. Fara, *Sympathetic Attractions*, 6–9 and 147–94.
28. The boundary between the body and the soul, matter and thought, and how exactly the transmission operates remains a mystery for the psychosomatic medicine of the period. See George Cheyne, *The Natural Method of Cureing the Diseases of the Body, and the Disorders of the Mind Depending on the Body* (London, 1742) 94–5, William Smith, *A Dissertation Upon the Nerves* (London: W. Owen, 1768) 42, and Robert Whytt, *Observations on the Nature, Causes and Cure of Those Disorders that have Commonly Been Called Nervous* (Edinburgh: T. Becket, 1765); see also David Fairer, 'Sentimental Translation in Mackenzie and Sterne', *Essays in Criticism* 49.2 (1999): 132–51.
29. Whytt, *Observations*, 219–20.
30. Lawrence, 'The Nervous System', 19–40, see also Fara, *Sympathetic Attractions*, 199. For a history of the physiological notions of sympathy see James Rodgers, 'Sensibility, Sympathy, Benevolence: Physiology and Moral Philosophy in *Tristram Shandy*', *Languages of Nature: Critical Essays on Science and Literature*, ed. Ludmilla Jordanova (London: Free Association, 1986) 116–58.

31. As Thomas Dixon points out, the writings of Shaftesbury and Joseph Butler are amongst the works that feature mechanistic ideas and vocabulary. Shaftesbury endorsed the view of the animal machine, according to which animals were solely motivated by their passions and affections, lacking rational or moral agency. Joseph Butler argued that human beings were virtue-making machines regulated by conscience and self-love. Given Butler's highly influential role throughout the eighteenth and nineteenth centuries, argues Dixon, Butler's adoption of the machine model for the human being marked a shift of the Christian tradition towards a more mechanistic anthropology (Dixon, *From Passions to Emotions*, 89–91).

32. *Guardian* 49 (7 May 1713), and 126 (5 Aug. 1713), qtd. in Fiering, 'Irresistible Compassion', 204.

33. Alexander Gerard, *Essay on Taste* (London: A. Millar, 1759) 75, 86, 169–70, 173–4, qtd. in Walter Jackson Bate, 'The Sympathetic Imagination in Eighteenth-Century English Criticism', *ELH* 12.2 (1945): 153. Cf. Akenside's earlier use of the same simile in *The Pleasures of the Imagination* (1744), 3.312–47.

34. It is important to emphasise that mechanistic notions of sympathy are not due to a materialist influence, but these notions also surface in the writings of materialist thinkers such as the medical doctor Julien Offray de La Mettrie's *L'Homme machine* (1747). For the mechanical operation of the sympathetic imagination in Priestley see *Lectures on Oratory and Criticism* (London: J. Johnson, 1777) 136–7, qtd. by Bate, 'The Sympathetic Imagination', 152. Adam Smith's notion of sympathy will be further discussed later on in this chapter.

35. Henry Mackenzie, 'The Effects of Religion on Minds of Sensibility: The Story of La Roche', *Works of Henry Mackenzie*, vol. 4 (London: Routledge-Thoemmes, 1996) 178, hereafter *Works*. Mackenzie's contemporaries identify the philosopher in this story as David Hume, who sought the seclusion of a small French town, La Flèche, when composing his *Treatise of Human Nature* in the 1730s. Mackenzie depicts his fictional philosopher as a man who is often criticised for the lack of warmth and feeling, but who is ultimately benevolent and tolerant towards his friend's religious devotion. As far as we know, the real-life Hume met no M. La Roche, and no direct religious influence softened his heart or his principles while working on the *Treatise*. In fact, according to Ernest Campbell Mossner, Hume's biographer, the young Hume at the time was a lot less tolerant regarding matters of faith than Mackenzie depicts him in this story. See *The Life of David Hume* (Oxford: Clarendon Press, 1980) 103.

36. Henry Mackenzie, *Letters to Elizabeth Rose of Kilravock: On Literature, Events and People 1768–1815*, ed. Horst Drescher (Edinburgh and London: Oliver and Boyd, 1967) 57, 36, hereafter *ER*.

37. These philosophers – except Hutcheson who died in 1746, a year after Mackenzie was born – were members of the Edinburgh Select Society, founded by Hume and Smith in 1754. As a lawyer of aristocratic descent, Mackenzie knew well and socialised with these literati, who all contributed to the intellectual scene of Edinburgh, promoting polite learning and sensibility.

38. La Roche's religious sensibility in Mackenzie's story owes more to prevalent eighteenth-century ideas of sympathy and moral sense than to any

immediate religious influence. As far as Mackenzie's religion is concerned, it is most likely that he was a religious Moderate in the Hutchesonian vein. Hutcheson himself was tutor of a dissenting academy in Dublin before becoming professor of moral philosophy at Glasgow. His education coincided with a period of significant change in the Church of Scotland, where orthodox Calvinist ideas of the original sin were challenged by a new emphasis on the altruistic powers of human nature. Hutcheson died in 1746, a year after Mackenzie was born, but his optimistic views on human nature remained influential in the Church and among the Edinburgh literati. Mackenzie was influenced by Moderate religious ideas and philosophical sentimentalism when he attended Edinburgh University. See Harold William Thompson, *A Scottish Man of Feeling. Some Account of Henry Mackenzie, Esq. of Edinburgh and of the Golden Age of Burns and Scott* (London and New York: Oxford University Press, 1931) 22. On the dissemination of the ideas of Shaftesbury and Hutcheson see Isabel Rivers, *Reason, Grace and Sentiment: A Study of the Language of Religion and Ethics in England, 1660–1780,* vol. 2, Shaftesbury to Hume (Cambridge: Cambridge University Press, 2000) 155, 157.

39. John Mullan, 'The Language of Sentiment: Hume, Smith, and Henry Mackenzie', *The History of Scottish Literature,* ed. Andrew Hook, vol. 2 (Aberdeen: Aberdeen University Press, 1987) 275.

40. John Dwyer, *Virtuous Discourse: Sensibility and Community in Late Eighteenth-Century Scotland* (Edinburgh: John Doland, 1987) 4.

41. John Dwyer, 'Introduction – "A Peculiar Blessing": Social Converse in Scotland from Hutcheson to Burns', *Sociability and Society in Eighteenth-Century Scotland,* eds. John Dwyer and Richard B. Sher (Edinburgh: Mercat, 1993) 13–14.

42. Henry Mackenzie, 'Reminiscences. Literary – Critical – Anecdotal', *Literature and Literati,* ed. Horst Drescher, vol. 2, Notebooks 1763–1824 (Frankfurt am Main: Peter Lang, 1999) 208.

43. The politics of sympathy surface in a variety of works, including Helen Maria Williams's *Letters from France* and William Godwin's *Caleb Williams.* Helen Maria Williams gives an account of the immense power sympathy and humanitarian feeling had during the Reign of Terror. The Jacobins in France dreaded sympathy. They were afraid that the royal family and the aristocrats whom they sentenced to the guillotine would save themselves by appealing to the sympathy of the people. 'Had the king been able to excite the pity of any part of that armed multitude which filled the vast Place de la Revolution, a profusion of blood might have been spilt – A civil war might have spread desolation through the city of Paris [...]. Had the king been conducted to the Convention, it is easy to imagine the effect which would have been produced on the minds of the people, by the sight of their former monarch led through the streets of Paris, with his hands bound, his neck bare, his hair already cut off at the foot of the scaffold in preparation for the fatal stroke – with no other covering than his shirt. At that sight the enraged populace would have melted into tenderness, and the Parisian women [...] would have attempted his rescue, even with the risk of life.' See H.M. Williams, *Letters Written in France,* eds. Neil Fraistat and Susan Lanser (Peterborough, ON: Broadview, 2001) 164–5. The group psychology of sympathy surfaces persistently during

the wars following the French Revolution; see, for instance, William Frend's 'The Effect of War on the Poor' (1793), John Thelwall's *The Tribune*, vol. 2 (1796) and Thomas De Quincey's 'The English Mail-Coach' (1848). The medical and political implications of feeling as stimulus response will be explored in the next chapter, in the context of the guillotine.

44. Dwyer, 'Enlightened Spectators and Classical Moralists: Sympathetic Relations in Eighteenth-Century Scotland', *Sociability and Society* 114–15.

45. As Jon Mee argues, Mackenzie allows religion into the public sphere only in the form of feeling, and not in the context of religious dispute. Periodicals were the guardians of politeness and civility, and the discourse of sensibility, Mee claims, served to regulate enthusiasm. La Roche's religion as a form of regulated, healing sensibility should also be understood in this framework. See Jon Mee, *Romanticism, Enthusiasm, and Religion* (Oxford: Oxford University Press, 2003) 49–51.

46. References to the sympathetic imagination before Smith can be found, for instance, in the work of George Butler, David Hume and Edmund Burke. For the role of imagination in the operation of sympathy see Walter Jackson Bate, 'The Sympathetic Imagination in Eighteenth-Century English Criticism', *ELH* 12.2 (1945): 144–64 and Robert Mitchell, *Sympathy and the State in the Romantic Era* (New York and London: Routledge, 2007). The necessity of the imagination for the operation of sympathy is also part of Mandeville's sceptical argument, which questions both the impulsive nature of sympathy and our natural ability to sympathise with distant objects (*Fable* 266). While sympathy for Smith is the foundation of human morality and social cohesion, his concept of sympathy implies a similar kind of scepticism.

47. What Smith's theory provides, from today's psychoanalytic perspective, is a detailed psychology often reaching beyond the experiences of the conscious mind. Note that the title of the French translation of Smith's book is *Métaphysique de l'âme* (1764).

48. Adam Smith, *The Theory of Moral Sentiments*, ed. Knud Haakonssen (Cambridge: Cambridge University Press, 2002) 13, emphases added, hereafter *TMS*. This and subsequent quotes by permission of Cambridge University Press.

49. John Dwyer, *Age of the Passions*, 14, 4, 15. On the importance of selfishness and the natural emergence of a class system and social hierarchy in Smith see also John D. Morillo, 'Emergence of Class Between Benevolent Sympathy and Passionate Ambition in Adam Smith's *Theory of Moral Sentiments*', *Uneasy Feelings: Literature, the Passions, and Class from Neoclassicism to Romanticism* (New York: AMS, 2001) 178–222.

50. Eugene Heath, 'The Commerce of Sympathy: Adam Smith on the Emergence of Morals', *Journal of the History of Philosophy* 33.3 (1995): 448.

51. Ibid., 454.

52. In a footnote, however, Hume admits that our responses in situations like this are often more complex. Another's good fortune frequently induces envy, which 'has a strong mixture of hatred', but often this feeling is simultaneous to feelings of respect, that is, 'a species of affection or good-will, with a mixture of humility' (*Enquiry* 248). On the other hand, the misfortunes of others

often cause pity. Pity, Hume writes, is 'a strong mixture of good-will', but it is also 'nearly allied to contempt, "which is a species of dislike, with a mixture of pride"' (*Enquiry* 248). Thus, while our reactions to the poor and the rich are complex and seemingly disparate, they share the common element of good-will. The source of these ambivalent emotions, however, remains unexplained in the *Enquiry*.

53. Letter dated 28 July 1759. J.Y.T. Greig, ed. *The Letters of David Hume*, vol. 1 (Oxford: Clarendon Press, 1932): 311–14, qtd. in Heath, 'The Commerce of Sympathy', 453. For Hume's objection to Smith's inconsistent argument on the pleasure of sympathy see Ian Simpson Ross, *The Life of Adam Smith* (Oxford: Clarendon press, 1995) 182–3.

54. Adam Smith, 'The Principles which Lead and Direct Philosophical Enquiries; Illustrated by the History of Astronomy', *Essays on Philosophical Subjects* (Dublin: printed for Messrs. Wogan et al., 1795), esp. 12–27, 43–79. According to Smith, the systems we create to describe the universe resemble machines: 'A system is an imaginary machine invented to connect together in the fancy those different movements and effects which are already in reality performed' (60). For the desire to attain the perfection of the system and the machine, and the pleasure arising from this accomplishment, see also *TMS* 211. According to Smith, even power and riches are 'enormous and operose machines contrived to produce a few trifling conveniences of the body' (*TMS* 213).

55. David Marshall, 'Adam Smith and the Theatricality of Moral Sentiments', *The Figure of Theater: Shaftesbury, Defoe, Adam Smith and George Eliot* (New York: Columbia University Press, 1986) 169. Marshall argues that sympathetic response and theatricality are closely interrelated in the period: 'to talk about how people responded to the sentiments of others was to talk about representation and theatrical distance, while to talk about how people reacted to the characters in a tragedy was to talk about the structure and experience of sympathy' (169). For a full discussion of the philosophical precedents of Smith's spectatorial idea see Marshall 168 and John Dwyer, 'Enlightened Spectators', 96–118. John Bender's *Imagining the Penitentiary: Fiction and the Architecture of Mind in Eighteenth-Century England* (Chicago and London: University of Chicago Press, 1987) discusses the social uses of this spectatorial idea. See also Boltanski's reading of Smith in *Distant Suffering*, 35–54, which also understands Smith in the framework of spectatorship. Boltanski emphasises the distance between spectator and sufferer, which, according to Smith, can only be bridged by the imagination.

56. Henry Home, Lord Kames, *Elements of Criticism*, 2 vols (1785; Routledge: Thoemmes, 1993) vol. 1, 90–5. See also Marshall, 'Adam Smith', 171.

57. While *The Theory of Moral Sentiments* was very popular in Britain and France, the wide circulation of the idea is not necessarily due to the direct influence of Smith's treatise. Ideas of the sympathetic imagination entered into cultural circulation via multiple channels; however, Smith's work directly influenced the literature and ideas of Scottish literati like Henry Mackenzie. Smith's *Theory* was also popular in France among the generation of *philosophes* that launched the *Encyclopédie*. For Smith's influence see Bate, 'The Sympathetic Imagination', esp. 145–58; Mitchell, *Sympathy and the State*, 88; Deidre Dawson, 'Is Sympathy so Surprising? Adam Smith and French Fictions of Sympathy'. *Eighteenth-Century Life* 15 (1991): 147–9. The work of William Godwin actively

engages with the most important eighteenth-century concerns regarding moral feeling. His 1805 novel *Fleetwood; or, The New Man of Feeling* (London: Richard Philips, 1805) emphasises the dysfunction and solipsism of sympathy inherent in Adam Smith's theory of imaginary identification. The protagonist Fleetwood claims that 'No man can completely put himself in the place of another [...]' (11).

58. Henri F. Ellenberger, *The Discovery of the Unconscious: The History and Evolution of Dynamic Psychiatry* (London: Fontana, 1970) 48. For the way in which the legacy of hypnosis lives on in psychoanalysis through the transference see Mikkel Borch-Jacobsen, *The Emotional Tie: Psychoanalysis, Mimesis and Affect*, trans. Douglas Brick et al. (Stanford, CA: Stanford University Press, 1992) 39–61.

59. Leon Chertok and Raymond De Saussure, *The Therapeutic Revolution: From Mesmer to Freud*, trans. R.H. Ahrenfeldt (New York: Brunner-Mazel Publishers, 1979) 61 and 114.

60. On Mesmer and animal magnetism see Alison Winter, *Mesmerised* (Chicago and London: University of Chicago Press, 1998) 1–13 and 306–43. Winter takes an approach that is different from histories that construct a linear trajectory from magnetic practices to Freud. She presents mesmerism as a diverse, fragile set of practices in the Victorian period, the history of which is a history of discord (11 and 306). For a linear trajectory see Chertok and de Saussure, *The Therapeutic Revolution*, 4–6. On animal magnetism in Britain and its connections with earlier notions of sympathy see Fara, who writes that in the language related to animal magnetism earlier, Neoplatonic connotations were revived – something that can also be observed in the 'magnetical sympathy' affecting Godwin's Caleb Williams (Fara, *Sympathetic Attractions*, 194–207).

61. For a history of hypnotism see Chertok and De Saussure, *The Therapeutic Revolution*, 36–60, esp. 39–40 and 50–2.

62. Sigmund Freud, 'Dreams and Occultism' (1933), *The Standard Edition of the Complete Psychological Works of Sigmund Freud*, ed. James Strachey et al., vol. 22 (London: Vintage, 2001) 36 and 39, hereafter *SE*. See also 'Psycho-Analysis and Telepathy' (1941) [1921], *SE*, vol. 18, 184.

63. *SE*, vol. 22, 55.

64. *SE*, vol. 22, 55.

65. Freud, 'Psycho-Analysis and Telepathy' (1941) [1921], *SE*, vol. 18, 179.

66. Freud, 'Recommendations to Physicians Practising Psycho-Analysis' (1912), *SE*, vol. 12, 115–16. For Freud's ideas on telepathy and occultism see Pamela Thurschwell, *Literature, Technology and Magical Thinking, 1880–1920* (Cambridge: Cambridge University Press, 2001) 115–50.

67. Gustave Le Bon, *The Crowd*, int. Robert K. Merton (Harmondsworth: Penguin, 1977) 32, 117–18. See also Sigmund Freud, *Group Psychology*, *SE*, vol. 18, 75–7.

68. William McDougall, *The Group Mind* (Cambridge: Cambridge University Press, 1927) 26–7, 45. See Also *SE*, vol. 18, 84–5.

69. *SE*, vol. 18, 106–7.

70. As Ferenczi continues: 'The fact that every sort of humanitarian reform movement, the propaganda of abstinence (vegetarianism, anti-alcoholism, abolitionism), revolutionary organisations and sects, conspiracies for or against the religious, political, or moral order, teem with neuropaths is similarly to be explained by the transference of interest from

censored egotistic (erotic or violent) tendencies of the unconscious on to fields where they can work themselves out without any self-reproach.' Sándor Ferenczi, 'Introjection and Transference', *First Contributions to Psycho-Analysis*, trans. Ernest Jones (London: Karnac, 2002) 36–8.

71. Sándor Ferenczi, 'On the Definition of Introjection', *Final Contributions to the Problems and Methods of Psycho-Analysis*, ed. Michael Balint, trans. Eric Mosbacher (London: Karnac, 2002) 316. See also Ferenczi, 'Introjection and Transference', 48.

72. *SE*, vol. 18, 102–3.

73. Freud, 'The Dynamics of Transference', *SE*, vol. 12, 99–108; 'Observations on Transference Love', *SE*, vol. 12, 159–71; 'Transference', *Introductory Lectures on Psycho-analysis*, *SE*, vol. 16, 431–47. Mikkel Borch-Jacobsen argues that the transference is the inheritance, so to say, in psychoanalysis of hypnotic suggestibility. In Borch-Jacobsen's reading of Freud's theory, transference, hypnosis and identification are closely linked. The type of rapport established through transference in the analytic relationship is of a hypnotic type; it resembles a trance where the subject speaks and thinks like another. What is repeated in the transference, as Freud imagines it, is an earlier emotional tie, which, at its core, hits on a more archaic emotional tie, identification. See Borch-Jacobsen, *Emotional Tie*, 54, 60.

74. J. Laplanche and J.B. Pontalis, *The Language of Psychoanalysis* (London: Karnac, 1988) 458 and 92–3 and Hanna Segal, 'Countertransference', *The Work of Hanna Segal: A Kleinian Approach to Clinical Practice* (New York and London: Jason Aronson-Rowman & Littlefield, 1981) 83, 81–7. For countertransference see also Donald Winnicott, 'Hate in the Countertransference', *International Journal of Psycho-Analysis* 30 (1949): 69–74; Paula Heimann, 'On Countertransference', *International Journal of Psycho-Analysis* 31 (1950): 81–4; R.E. Money-Kyrle, "Normal Counter-Transference and Some of its Deviations", *International Journal of Psycho-Analysis* 37 (1956): 360–6; Leon Grinberg, 'On a Specific Aspect of Countertransference Due to the Patient's Projective Identification', *International Journal of Psycho-Analysis* 43 (1962): 436–40.

75. For processes of projection and identification in the transference see Herman Nunberg, 'Transference and Reality', *International Journal of Psycho-Analysis* 32 (1951): 1–9. Projective identification is a concept used by Melanie Klein and subsequent British object-relations psychoanalysts for an early defence mechanism in which the subject projects parts of himself into the object in phantasy, and then identifies the object with these projected parts. See Laplanche and Pontalis 356–7 and Hanna Segal, 'Notes of Symbol-Formation', *The Work of Hanna Segal*, 53.

76. Heinrich Racker, *Transference and Counter-transference* (London: Hogarth, 1968) 134–6.

77. Segal, 'Countertransference', *The Work of Hanna Segal*, 86. See also Renuka Sharma's extensive survey of the role of empathy in psychoanalysis, *Understanding the Concept of Empathy and Its Foundations in Psychoanalysis* (Lewinston, NY: Edwin Mellen, 1993). Sharma assumes a possible genetic link between the nineteenth-century concept of empathy and the ideas of Vico and Hume on beauty and sympathy (2).

78. *SE*, vol. 18, 108.

79. Sharma, *Understanding the Concept of Empathy*, 34.

80. For the origins of the term empathy see Sharma, *Understanding the Concept of Empathy*, 1–7 and Thomas J. McCarthy, *Relationships of Sympathy: The Writer and the Reader in British Romanticism* (Aldershot: Scholar, 1997) 7.

81. McCarthy, *Relationships of Sympathy*, 7–8. For a detailed discussion of the sympathy–empathy debate in twentieth-century psychology see McCarthy, *Relationships of Sympathy*, 1–22.

82. M.L. Hoffmann , 'Is Altruism Part of Human Nature?', *Journal of Personality and Social Psychology* 40 (1981): 133, qtd. in McCarthy, *Relationships of Sympathy*, 16.

83. Mark H. Davis, *Empathy: A Social Psychological Approach* (Madison, WI: WCB Brown and Benchmark, 1994) 128, 133–41. See also C. Daniel Batson, *The Altruism Question: Toward a Social-Psychological Answer* (Hillsdale, NJ: Lawrence Erlbaum, 1991).

84. Chris D. Frith, *Making Up the Mind* (Malden, MA: Blackwell, 2007) 150–1; Tania Singer et al., 'Empathic Neural Responses are Modulated by the Perceived Fairness of Others', *Nature* 439 (26 January 2006): 466–9.

85. Stanley Milgram, *Obedience to Authority: An Experimental View* (1974; London: Pinter& Martin, 2005).

86. See the subject in experiment 2, whose speech 'is increasingly broken up by wheezing laughter', who is 'rubbing face to hide laughter' and 'cannot control his laughter at this point no matter what he does' (Milgram, *Obedience to Authority*, 54).

87. C. Fred Alford, *What Evil Means to Us* (Ithaca and London: Cornell University Press, 1997) 26. Milgram repeatedly attempts to rule out this possibility, arguing that 'although aggressive tendencies are part and parcel of human nature, they have hardly anything to do with the behaviour observed in the experiment. Nor do they have much to do with the destructive obedience of soldiers in war, of bombardiers killing thousands on a single mission [...]. The typical soldier kills because he is told to kill and he regards it as his duty to obey orders. The act of shocking the victim does not stem from destructive urges but from the fact that subjects have become integrated into a social structure and are unable to get out of it' (Milgram 167).

88. Arne Johan Vetlesen, *Evil and Human Agency* (Cambridge: Cambridge University Press, 2005) 130, 104–34.

89. For a cultural sociologist's approach to our emotional responses to the media see Keith Tester, *Compassion, Morality and the Media* (Buckingham, PA: Open University Press, 2001).

90. '"Heimlich"? ... What do you understand by "Heimlich"?' 'Well, ... they are like a buried spring or a dried-up pond. One cannot walk over it without always having the feeling that water might come up there again.' 'Oh, we call it "unheimlich"; you call it "heimlich."' Gutzkow qtd. by Sigmund Freud, 'The Uncanny', *SE*, vol. 17, 223.

2 The Feeling Machine

1. The original title, *Hog's Wash; or, a Salmagundy for Swine*, alludes to Burke's famous reference to 'a swinish multitude' mentioned in his *Reflections on the Revolution in France*. Eaton's intention was to challenge Burke's assumptions

about the ignorance of the masses. See Marilyn Butler, ed., *Burke, Paine, Godwin, and the Revolution Controversy* (Cambridge: Cambridge University Press, 1984) 185.

2. Daniel Isaac Eaton, 'King Chauntilere; or, The Fate of Tyranny', *Politics for the People; or, Hog's Wash* 8 (1793): 103. Further references will be given in parentheses in the text.

3. The publication of 'King Chauntilere' resulted in Eaton's imprisonment for seditious libel. The prosecution found obvious parallels between Eaton's representation of tyranny by the figure of the game cock and King George III. The equivocal nature of the innuendos, however, saved Eaton's case and made the whole court 'frequently convulsed with laughter' during the trial. As the defence argued, Eaton's fable – like many other fables from Aesop to Biblical stories – was to be seen as a representation of tyranny in general, rather than a specific allusion to 'our sovereign lord the king'. Furthermore, the tactic of the defence was to turn around the accusation and charge the prosecution with making the link between an allegorical tyrant and the imagined execution of George III. See Boyle C. Thelwall, *The Life of John Thelwall, by his Widow* (London: John Macrone, 1837) 110–11. For interpretations of Eaton's story see John Barrell, *Imagining the King's Death: Figurative Treason, Fantasies of Regicide 1793–1796* (Oxford: Oxford University Press, 2000) 103–8; Jon Mee, '"Examples of Safe Printing": Censorship and Popular Radical Literature in the 1790s', *Literature and Censorship*, ed. Nigel Smith (Woodbridge: D.S. Brewer, 1993) 81–95; and Mark Philp, 'The Fragmented Ideology of Reform', *The French Revolution and British Popular Politics*, ed. Mark Philp (Cambridge: Cambridge University Press, 1991) 50–77.

4. Thelwall, *The Life of John Thelwall*, 107–11.

5. Barrell, *Imagining the King's Death*, 106–7.

6. Philip Smith, 'Narrating the Guillotine: Punishment Technology as Myth and Symbol', *Theory Culture Society* 20.5 (2003): 35–6.

7. The guillotine as a means of capital punishment was last used in 1977. For twentieth-century experiments searching for life in severed heads see Daniel Arasse, *The Guillotine and the Terror*, trans. Christopher Miller (1987; London: Penguin, 1989) 37–8 and Philip Smith, 'Narrating the Guillotine', 46–7. Charlotte Corday was Jean-Paul Marat's assassin, guillotined in 1793. She was looked upon as a figure of beauty, sensibility and heroism in the period. See David Bindman, *The Shadow of the Guillotine: Britain and the French Revolution* (London: British Museum Publications, 1989) 146.

8. Soemmering quoted by Arasse, *The Guillotine and the Terror*, 38. For the medical debates surrounding the guillotine see Arasse, *The Guillotine and the Terror*, 38–46; Philip Smith, 'Narrating the Guillotine', 38–46; and Dorina Outram, *The Body and the French Revolution: Sex, Class and Political Culture* (New Haven and London: Yale University Press, 1989) 111–23.

9. Sue quoted by Arasse, *The Guillotine and the Terror*, 38.

10. Sédillot quoted by Philip Smith, 'Narrating the Guillotine', 40.

11. *Le Matin*, 3.3 (1907): 2. Dr Dassy de Lingères (a late-nineteenth-century experimenter) is quoted by Philip Smith, 'Narrating the Guillotine', 47.

12. Arasse, *The Guillotine and the Terror*, 42.

13. Thelwall's membership of the Physical Society did not last long, however. The open materialism of his second paper, 'On the Origin of Sensation' (also

written in 1793) got a hostile response by some members of the Society, and as a result Thelwall decided to give up his membership.

14. For iatromechanism and Boerhaave see Sergio Moravia, 'From Homme Machine to Homme Sensible: Changing Eighteenth-Century Models of Man's Image', *Journal of the History of Ideas* 39.1 (1978): 45–9 and John P. Wright, 'Materialism and the Life Soul in Eighteenth-Century Scottish Physiology', *The Scottish Enlightenment: Essays in Reinterpretation*, ed. Paul Wood (Rochester: University of Rochester Press, 2000) 179. For seventeenth-century theories of animal motion see Hubert Steinke, *Irritating Experiments: Haller's Concept and the European Controversy on Irritability and Sensibility, 1750–90* (Amsterdam and New York: Rodopi, 2005) 19–26.

15. Whytt made the first important introduction of the nervous system into Edinburgh medicine. According to Christopher Lawrence, Whytt was an important link between enlightenment medicine and the culture of sensibility, because moral theorists of sensibility and sympathy in the latter half of the century built heavily on the physiological concept of nervous sensibility as developed by Whytt and his followers. For Boerhaave's system and his influence in Europe and especially Scotland see Wright, 'Materialism', 178–9 and Andrew Cunningham, 'Medicine to Calm the Mind: Boerhaave's Medical System, and Why It Was Adopted in Edinburgh', *The Medical Enlightenment of the Eighteenth Century*, ed. Andrew Cunningham and Roger French (Cambridge: Cambridge University Press, 1990) 40. On Whytt and the Scottish Enlightenment see Christopher Lawrence, 'The Nervous System and Society in the Scottish Enlightenment', *Natural Order: Historical Studies of Scientific Culture*, eds. Barry Barnes and Steven Shapin (Beverley Hills and London: Sage, 1979) 19–40.

16. Maureen McNeil, *Under the Banner of Science: Erasmus Darwin and his Age* (Manchester: Manchester University Press, 1987) 160.

17. For Cullen's views and context see Steinke, *Irritating Experiments*, 212–13; McNeil, *Under the Banner of* Science, 149; and Wright, 'Materialism', 179. See also William Cullen, *Nosology* (Edinburgh: C. Stewart, 1800).

18. For Brown see McNeil, *Under the Banner of Science*, 150–1.

19. For Brunonianism and its intersections with radical politics see Tim Fulford, 'Radical Medicine and Romantic Politics', *Wordsworth Circle* 35.1 (2004): 20; Nicholas Roe, *John Keats and the Culture of Dissent* (Oxford: Clarendon Press, 1997) 174; Neil Vickers, 'Coleridge, Thomas Beddoes and Brunonian Medicine', *European Romantic Review* 8.1 (1997): 47–94; Michael Barfoot, 'Brunonianism under the Bed: An Alternative to University Medicine in Edinburgh in the 1780s', *Brunonianism in Britain and Europe*, ed. W. F. Bynum and Roy Porter (London: Wellcome Institute for the History of Medicine, 1988) 44; Christopher Lawrence, 'Cullen, Brown and the Poverty of Essentialism', *Brunonianism in Britain and Europe*, 1–21. For materialist ideas in the Romantic period see Alan Richardson, *British Romanticism and the Science of the Mind* (Cambridge: Cambridge University Press, 2001), esp. 1–38.

20. Steinke, *Irritating Experiments*, 234 and 20.

21. Sergio Moravia, 'From Homme Machine to Homme Sensible: Changing Eighteenth-Century Models of Man's Image', *Journal of the History of Ideas* 39.1 (1978): 45–60.

22. As Descartes writes in *Discourse on the Method*: 'From this aspect the body is regarded as a machine which, having been made by the hands of God, is incomparably better arranged, and possesses in itself movements which are much more admirable, than any of those which can be invented by man. Here I specially stopped to show that if there had been such machines, possessing the organs and outward form of a monkey or some other animal without reason, we should not have had any means of ascertaining that they were not of the same nature as those animals. On the other hand, if there were machines which bore a resemblance to our bodies and imitated our actions as far as it was morally possible to do so, we should always have two very certain tests by which to recognise that, for all that, they were not real men.' René Descartes, 'Discourse on the Method', *Key Philosophical Writings* (Ware: Wordsworth, 1997) 107. The two points of distinction are language and reason.

23. Aram Vartanian, *Diderot and Descartes: A Study of Scientific Naturalism in the Enlightenment* (Princeton, NJ: Princeton University Press, 1953) 211. For the philosophical debates and positions that develop in response to Descartes's animal-machine idea see also Leonora Cohen Rosenfield, *From Beast-Machine to Man-Machine: Animal Soul in French Letters from Descartes to La Mettrie* (New York: Octagon, 1968).

24. Kathleen Wellman, *La Mettrie: Medicine, Philosophy, and Enlightenment* (Durham, NC and London: Duke University Press, 1992) 174–5.

25. Descartes, 'Discourse on the Method', 108–9. In Part 5 of the *Discourse on the Method*, where Descartes describes the animal and human bodies as mechanisms, he refers to a previous work, *Le Monde*, in which he elaborates on these, but which he decided to suppress when hearing of the condemnation of Galileo. See Descartes, 'Discourse on the Method', 97.

26. Julien Offray de la Mettrie, *Machine Man and Other Writings*, trans. and ed. Ann Thomson (Cambridge: Cambridge University Press, 1996) 35. This and subsequent quotes by permission of Cambridge University Press.

27. On the importance of the polyp for the advancement of materialist ideas see Aram Vartanian, 'Trembley's Polyp, La Mettrie, and Eighteenth-Century French Materialism', *Journal of the History of Ideas* 11.3 (1950): 259–86; Philip C. Ritterbush, *Overtures to Biology: The Speculations of Eighteenth-Century Naturalists* (New Haven and London: Yale University Press, 1964) 122–41.

28. Vartanian, 'Trembley's Polyp', 259–60 and 265–8. Ann Thomson, introduction, *Machine Man and Other Writings*, by Julien Offray de La Mettrie (Cambridge: Cambridge University Press, 1996) xx. Evolutionist ideas, that is, the theory that complex organisms in the scale of being have evolved by certain natural processes from simpler ones, appear in La Mettrie's work starting with *L'Homme machine*. Cf. Vartanian, 'Trembley's Polyp', 276.

29. Vartanian, 'Trembley's Polyp', 264.

30. La Mettrie, 'Man as Plant', *Machine Man and Other Writings*, ed. Ann Thomson (Cambridge: Cambridge University Press, 1996) 75–88.

31. Ann Thomson, *Materialism and Society in the Mid-Eighteenth Century: La Mettrie's Discours Préliminaire* (Geneva and Paris: Librairie Droz, 1981) 39.

32. C.U.M. Smith, "Julien Offray de la Mettrie (1709–1751)", *Journal of the History of the Neurosciences* 11.2 (2002): 110–24.

33. Wellman, *La Mettrie*, 272–85. For the reception of La Mettrie's *L'Homme machine* and its later influence see also Aram Vartanian, *La Mettrie's L'Homme machine: A Study in the Origins of an Idea* (Princeton, NJ: Princeton University Press, 1960) 95–138. As Vartanian observes elsewhere, in the twentieth century attempts have been made to restore La Mettrie to his deserved place in the history of ideas. For La Mettrie's place in French materialism, his marginalisation and his reputation see Vartanian, 'Trembley's Polyp', 259–86. For La Mettrie's influence on other *philosophes* see also Rosenfield, *From Beast Machine*, 142. For La Mettrie's life and works see Thomson, *Materialism and Society* (5–20 for La Mettrie's life and 33–9 for the *Histoire naturelle de l'âme*).

34. The work was published in 1747 but is dated 1748. For the publication details of the treatise see Vartanian, *La Mettrie's L'Homme machine*, 6, 137–8. An eighteenth-century English translation, with the title *Man a Machine*, was published in London by W. Owen in 1749, attributing the authorship to Marquis d'Argens. It was reprinted in 1750 with La Mettrie as author. See Thomson, introduction, 2 for information on the English translation.

35. Julien Offray de la Mettrie, *Machine Man and Other Writings*, trans. and ed. Ann Thomson (Cambridge: Cambridge University Press, 1996) 5. Further references will be given in parentheses in the text.

36. Wellman, *La Mettrie*, 180–1; Thomson, *Materialism and Society*, 44.

37. Chyle, as defined by the *OED*, is 'the white milky fluid formed by the action of the pancreatic juice and the bile on the chyme, and contained in the lymphatics of the intestines, which are hence called lacteals. The term has been used to designate the fluid in the intestines just before absorption'.

38. For a discussion of La Mettrie's line of argument in *L'Homme machine* see Thomson, *Materialism and Society*, 39–45 and her introduction to *Machine Man*, ix–xix.

39. La Mettrie studied the reaction of irritability, and developed the concept further after Albrecht von Haller. Haller attributed irritability (autonomous contracting force) only to the muscle tissue, and distinguished it from the concept of sensibility, which was related to nerve functioning. Nerves, in Haller's theory, did not possess irritability, but were responsible for sensibility. La Mettrie, however, extended the idea of irritability to other parts of the body as well. It was with La Mettrie that irritability replaced the soul or the vital principle that was supposed to be responsible for the movements of the body. For La Mettrie's contribution to the concept of irritability see Vartanian, *La Mettrie's L'Homme machine*, 88–9.

40. According to Vartanian, it is very likely that La Mettrie borrowed this theory of soul–body connection from Jerome Gaub. He attended the lecture where Gaub presented the idea. Later on, Gaub accused La Mettrie of appropriating his ideas for a materialist philosophy, which was far from the original intention of Gaub, who was an orthodox religious believer. It is not only the ideas on the connection of body and mind that are analogous to those developed in Gaub's *De regimine mentis*, but La Mettrie uses some of Gaub's examples as well. See Vartanian, *La Mettrie's L'Homme Machine*, 90–1 and Jerome Gaub, 'De regimine mentis', *Mind and Body in Eighteenth-Century Medicine*, ed. L. J. Rather (London: Wellcome, 1965) 13, 115.

41. Much attention was devoted in the period to physiological impulses that do not respond to the conscious will and cannot be explained from mechanical

irritability either. The explanation of these states was always a challenge, and sympathy was often claimed to have a leading role in finding the solution. One such difficult-to-explain phenomenon in the Haller–Whytt debate on sensibility and irritability was the mystery of penile erection, when the muscles respond neither to spontaneous irritable impulse nor to the conscious force of the will. In Whytt's explanation, it is nervous sympathy that accounts for phenomena beyond consciousness and pure mechanism.

42. La Mettrie's medical experiences during the War of Austrian Succession serve for the basis of such examples. From 1742 through 1745 La Mettrie served as a military doctor. See Vartanian, *La Mettrie's L'Homme machine*, 4, and Thomson, *Materialism and Society*, 8.

43. La Mettrie, *Man a Machine* (London: W. Owen, 1749) 10.

44. Abel Boyer, *Dictionnaire royal françois et anglois* (La Haye, 1702); Abel Boyer, *Dictionnaire royal françois-anglois et anglois-françois* (London, 1748); Louis Chambaud, *Dictionnaire françois et anglois* (London, 1761); Abbé Brillant, *Dictionnaire universel françois et latin, vulgairement appelé Dictionnaire de Trévoux* (Paris, 1771). Here I would like to thank Alain Schorderet for drawing my attention to the documented existence of the phrase and its 1714 use by Claude Buffier in the following sense: 'To let one's spirit go, and let simple ideas appear to the imagination, without examining how these ideas are related to one another.' Also, I would like to thank Anne Birien for drawing my attention to the expression 'boire à la Suisse'.

45. 'On dit familièrement, Rêver à la Suisse, pour dire, avoir l'air de penser à quelque chose, et ne penser à rien.' *Dictionnaire de l'Académie françoise* (Paris, 1798).

46. Alain Rey, *Dictionnaire historique de la langue française* (Paris: Dictionnaires Le Robert, 1992). For a history of Swiss Guards and mercenaries see John McCormack, *One Million Mercenaries: Swiss Soldiers in the Armies of the World* (London: Leo Cooper, 1993).

47. Vartanian, *La Mettrie's L'Homme machine*, 199–200, n4. On the debate between La Mettrie and Haller see also Wright, 'Materialism', 182–3. Haller, like Boerhaave – and unlike La Mettrie – held a Cartesian conception of the soul, and argued for the necessity of an external cause and an immaterial substance.

48. The dedication to Haller is omitted from Ann Thomson's translation, but it is present in La Mettrie, *Man a Machine and Man a Plant*, trans. Richard A. Watson and Maya Rybalka (Indianapolis and Cambridge: Hackett, 1994) 20–6. The latter translation is based on the version of *L'Homme machine* as it appears in La Mettrie's *Oeuvres philosophiques* (Berlin, 1751). On the dedication see also Vartanian, *La Mettrie's L'Homme machine*, 104.

49. Vartanian, *La Mettrie's L'Homme machine*, 201–2, 82–5.

50. Sigmund Freud, 'The Method of Interpreting Dreams', *The Standard Edition of the Complete Psychological Works of Sigmund Freud*, ed. James Strachey et al., vol. 4, Interpretation of Dreams (London: Vintage, 2001) 102–3, hereafter *SE*.

51. Non-rational mental functioning was sometimes seen as a defect in our mechanism. George Cheyne, in *The Natural Method of Cureing the Diseases of the Body, and the Disorders of the Mind Depending on the Body* (1742), explains sleep and dreaming by 'the disability and incapacity of the bodily organs to

continue and perpetuate the active and rational voluntary functions'. Sleep signals that the body needs 'new repair and winding up', while dreaming is an imperfect state of waking caused by 'irritation from flatulence and obstructed perspiration' or by pain (Cheyne, *Natural Method*, 40). On Whytt's concept of sympathy see his *Observations on the Nature, Causes, and Cure of Those Disorders which have been Commonly Called Nervous, Hypochondriac, or Hysteric* (Edinburgh: T. Becket, 1765). On sympathy and non-conscious states see also James Rodgers, 'Sensibility, Sympathy, Benevolence: Physiology and Moral Philosophy in *Tristram Shandy*', *Languages of Nature: Critical Essays on Science and Literature*, ed. Ludmilla Jordanova (London: Free Association, 1986) 126 and 133, and G.S. Rousseau, 'Psychology', *The Ferment of Knowledge: Studies in the Historiography of Eighteenth-Century Science*, eds. G.S. Rousseau and Roy Porter (Cambridge: Cambridge University Press, 1980) 143–210.

52. Albrecht von Haller, *A Dissertation on the Sensible and Irritable Parts of Animals* (1752; London: Nourse, 1755) 4. Further references will be given in parentheses in the text. The *Dissertation* was originally published in Latin in 1752. My references are to the 1755 English translation.

53. For Haller's life, his relation to the doctrines of Boerhaave, and the intellectual context see Lester S. King, introduction, *First Lines of Physiology*, by Albrecht von Haller (New York and London: Johnson, 1966) ix–lxxii. This is a reprint of the 1786 English edition of Haller's treatise.

54. Whether his influence on the literature and morality of sensibility was direct or indirect is an object of debate. See R.F. Brissenden, *Virtue in Distress: Studies in the Novel of Sentiment from Richardson to Sade* (London: Macmillan, 1974) 42; G.S. Rousseau, 'Nerves, Spirits and Fibres: Toward the Origins of Sensibility' (1975), *Nervous Acts: Essays on Literature, Culture and Sensibility* (Basingstoke and New York: Palgrave Macmillan, 2004) 157–84; Anne C. Vila, *Enlightenment and Pathology: Sensibility in the Literature and Medicine of Eighteenth-Century France* (Baltimore and London: Johns Hopkins University Press, 1998) 13–14; Steinke, *Irritating Experiments*, 231–4. On the interrelatedness of the language of medicine and the literature of sensibility see also John Mullan, *Sentiment and Sociability*, 201–40; Ann Jessie Van Sant, *Eighteenth-Century Sensibility and the Novel: The Senses in Social Context* (Cambridge: Cambridge University Press, 1993); and G.S. Rousseau, ed., *The Languages of Psyche: Mind and Body in Enlightenment Thought* (Berkeley: University of California Press, 1990).

55. See Vila, 'Beyond Sympathy', 24.

56. Thomas Henry, *Memoirs of Albert de Haller, M. D.* (Warrington: Eyres and Johnson, 1783) 79–81.

57. In *Theaters of the Body*, the psychoanalyst Joyce McDougall talks about 'disaffected' states, by which she means pathological states resulting from a foreclosure of the psychic component of affects that are by nature psychosomatic. The foreclosure of feelings from consciousness is the result of an overwhelming emotional experience that threatens the identity. This, she observes, leads to a 're-somatisation' of affect, which manifests itself in repetitive actions or addictive behaviour. See Joyce McDougall, *Theaters of the Body: A Psychoanalytic Approach to Psychosomatic Illness* (New York: Norton, 1989) 90–105.

58. Cf. Pierre Klossowski, 'Nature as Destructive Principle', *The One Hundred and Twenty Days of Sodom and Other Writings*, by the Marquis de Sade, comp. and trans. Austryn Wainhouse and Richard Seaver (New York: Grove, 1966) 69–70.

59. Elaine Scarry, *The Body in Pain* (Oxford: Oxford University Press, 1985) 41–2.

60. Ibid., 4–6, 13–17, 27–8.

61. Francis Barker, *The Tremulous Private Body: Essays on Subjection* (Ann Arbor: University of Michigan Press, 1995) vii, 65–102.

62. The question of the possibility of 'living matter' was a highly debated issue among eighteenth-century Scottish writers. The question was whether the principle of life and animation could be inherent in matter itself, or whether an intelligent principle was necessary for life. The most sustained defence of the life soul was given by Robert Whytt in his *Essay on the Vital and Other Involuntary Motions of Animals* (1751). See Wright, "Materialism", 177.

63. Whytt refutes the Gassendist distinction between rational soul (animus) and life soul (anima). See Robert Whytt, *Essay on the Vital and Involuntary Motions of Animals* (1751; Edinburgh: Balfour, 1763) 307–16.

64. According to Whytt, the sentient principle is also the source of moral sense. Similarly to a faculty that immediately acts upon irritation or pain, 'the DEITY seems to have implanted in our minds a kind of SENSE respecting *Morals*, whence we approve of some actions, and disapprove of others, almost instantly, and without any previous reasoning about their fitness or unfitness [...]. Upon the whole, there seems to be in man one sentient and intelligent PRINCIPLE, which is equally the source of life, sense, and motion, as of reason [...].' Whytt, *Essay*, 318–19, 321. See also Wright, 'Materialism',184–7; Lawrence, 'Cullen, Brown and the Poverty of Essentialism", esp. 23–8; John P. Wright, 'Substance Versus Function Dualism in Eighteenth-Century Medicine', *Psyche and Soma: Physicians and Metaphysicians on the Mind–Body Problem from Antiquity to Enlightenment*, eds. John P Wright and Paul Potter (Oxford: Clarendon Press, 2000) 237–54. For the Haller–Whytt debate see also R.K. French, *Robert Whytt, the Soul, and Medicine* (London: The Wellcome Institute of the History of Medicine, 1969) 63–76.

65. Whytt, *Physiological Essays* (1755; Edinburgh: Hamilton, Balfour and Neill, 1761). Further references will be given in parentheses in the text. My references are to the 1761 edition. See also Wright, "Materialism",189.

66. For the meanings of motion see Ernest Klein, *A Comprehensive Etymological Dictionary of the English Language*, 2 vols (Amsterdam: Elsevier, 1966–7); Eric Partridge, *Origins: A Short Etymological Dictionary of Modern English* (London: Routledge, 1958). Cf. Peter Brooks' concept of plot as narrative desire, that is, a motor force of the narrative which, together with maintaining the act of narration, by being a desire for the end, is also a force that finally brings the narrative to a closure. The narrative, in order to move on, has to surpass its own desire for ending, which 'kills' the narrative. Brooks's theory is based on the description of the *fort/da* game and the repetition compulsion in Freud's *Beyond the Pleasure Principle*. Peter Brooks, *Reading for the Plot* (Cambridge, MA: Harvard University Press, 1993) esp. 37–61. A related study – based on Brooks's theory – is Carol Houlihan Flynn's 'Running out of Matter', *Languages of Psyche*, ed. G. S. Rousseau (Berkeley: University of California Press, 1990) 147–85, which emphasises the healing, curing aspect of painful

irritation, stimulation, motion and terror in eighteenth-century medical practices and techniques of narration.

67. Simon Richter, *Laocoon's Body and the Aesthetics of Pain* (Detroit: Wayne State University Press, 1992) 32.

68. The heart was an important point in Whytt's argument about the role of the mind in the involuntary motion of animals. Referring to the experiments described in Stephen Hales's *Statical Essays*, he claims that the perpetual motion of the heart is not explainable from mechanical principles only, and that a higher principle needs to be in operation. See Wright, 'Materialism', 184. Note also that in ancient physiologies the heart was considered to be the centre of all sensation. K. D. Keele points out that according to Aristotle, the sensibility of an organ was closely related to its content of blood. In Aristotle's theory, the heart creates the blood contained in it from food, and it possesses the highest degree of sensibility in the body: 'For the first sensory part is that which first has blood; that is to say, the heart which is the source of blood, and the first parts to contain it.' Keele finds the origin of metaphors such as 'hard-hearted' or 'soft-hearted' in the belief that the degree of the sensibility of the heart can vary in different animals dependent on the denseness or softness of the texture of the organ. K. D. Keele, *Anatomies of Pain* (Oxford: Blackwell, 1957) 32, 1–15, 16–40.

69. Paul de Man, 'Aesthetic Formalisation: Kleist's *Über das Marionettentheater*', *The Rhetoric of Romanticism* (New York: Columbia University Press, 1984) 285–6; Heinrich von Kleist, *On a Theatre of Marionettes*, trans. Gerti Wiford (London: Acorn, 1989).

70. *Russian Cruelty: Being the Substance of Several Letters from Sundry Clergymen in the New-Marck of Brandenburgh*, with a preface by G. Whitefield (London, 1760) 5, 8. Further references will be given in parentheses in the text.

71. Cf. André Green's distinction between two types of affect. The first one is integrated into the structures of signification in the unconscious and preconscious chain, and the second overflows from this chain and destroys sense-making structures, threatening to paralyse or lead to compulsive action. See his collection of essays, *On Private Madness* (London: Karnac, 1997) 206.

72. As Green writes, there are different degrees to the possibility of expressing affect. While affect can often be expressed in language, affects can resist linguistic representation: 'Language without affect is a dead language: and affect without language is uncommunicable. Language is situated between the cry and the silence. Silence often makes heard the cry of psychic pain and behind the cry the call of silence is like comfort.' See *Private Madness*, 205.

73. Cathy Caruth, *Unclaimed Experience: Trauma, Narrative, and History* (Baltimore: Johns Hopkins University Press, 1996) 1–9.

74. For language as a transmitter of the act of awakening to consciousness see Caruth's analysis related to Lacan's reading of the dream of the burning child mentioned in Freud's *Interpretation of Dreams*. In Lacan's reading, the words of the child addressed to the father are no longer mastered by the one who says them, but they are the means of transmission, of passing on the imperative of awakening to others. See Caruth, *Unclaimed Experience*, 91–113.

75. Jacques Derrida, *Without Alibi*, ed. and trans. Peggy Kamuf (Stanford, Stanford University Press, 2004) 238–304.

3   'I Will Not Weep': Tears of Sympathy in Henry Mackenzie's *The Man of Feeling*

1. Review of *The Man of Feeling*, by Anon. *Monthly Review* 44 (1771): 418.
2. Letter to Sir Walter Scott (4 September 1826), in *The Private Letter-Books of Sir Walter Scott*, ed. Wilfred Partington (London: Hodder & Stoughton, 1930) 273. Lady Louisa Stewart also points out the rather different effect Mackenzie's novel had on its readers a few decades later. When her circle of friends read aloud *The Man of Feeling*, 'the effect altogether failed. Nobody cried, and at some of the passages, the touches that I used to think so exquisite – Oh Dear! They laughed.' She goes on to observe that Rousseau's *La Nouvelle Heloise*, 'the book that all mothers prohibited and all daughters longed to read' in her youth, is found tiring and dull by the younger generations in the 1820s. See Partington, *Letter-Books*, 273. For changing reading – and weeping – practices in the eighteenth century see Anne Vincent-Buffault, *The History of Tears: Sensibility and Sentimentality in France* (Basingstoke and London: Macmillan, 1990).
3. Henry Mackenzie, *The Man of Feeling*, ed. Maureen Harkin (Plymouth: Broadview, 2005) 59. Further references to this edition are given in parentheses in the text.
4. John Dwyer, 'Enlightened Spectators and Classical Moralists: Sympathetic Relations in Eighteenth-Century Scotland', *Sociability and Society in Eighteenth-Century Scotland*, ed. John Dwyer and Richard B. Sher (Edinburgh: Mercat, 1993) 112.
5. John Mullan, *Sentiment and Sociability: The Language of Feeling in the Eighteenth Century* (Oxford: Clarendon, 1988) 118–19 and 'The Language of Sentiment: Hume, Smith, and Henry Mackenzie', *The History of Scottish Literature*, ed. Andrew Hook, vol. 2 (Aberdeen: Aberdeen University Press, 1987) 275. See also Janet Todd's chronology of the development of sensibility in the period in *Sensibility: An Introduction* (London: Methuen, 1986) 3. For the insistence of criticism on Harley's unfitness for the world see also David G. Spencer, 'Henry Mackenzie, a Practical Sentimentalist', *Papers on Language and Literature* 3 (1967): 314–26; G.J. Barker-Benfield, *The Culture of Sensibility* (Chicago and London: University of Chicago Press, 1992) 142 and 144; Gillian Skinner, *Sensibility and Economics in the Novel, 1740–1800* (London: Macmillan, 1999) 92.
6. Susan Manning, introduction, *Julia de Roubigné*, by Henry Mackenzie (East Linton: Tuckwell, 1999) ix; Stephen Bending and Stephen Bygrave, introduction, *The Man of Feeling*, by Henry Mackenzie, ed. Brian Vickers (Oxford: Oxford University Press, 2001) xvii.
7. Maureen Harkin, 'Mackenzie's *Man of Feeling*: Embalming Sensibility', *ELH* 61 (1994): 318–19 and 336. In the introduction to her edition of *The Man of Feeling* Harkin points out the emphasis in sentimental novels on 'instructing the reader how to react, how to feel'. But also, Harkin claims, Mackenzie is highly conscious about 'the futility of effort that emerges in sentimental fiction'. See Harkin, introduction, *The Man of Feeling*, by Henry Mackenzie (Plymouth: Broadview, 2005) 12–13.
8. For a history of tears and their role in the eighteenth century to represent true emotional response see Tom Lutz, *Crying: The Natural and Cultural History of*

Tears (London and New York: Norton, 1999) 50–2. For a variety of psychological views on tears see *Adult Crying: A Biopsychosocial Approach*, ed. Randolph R. Cornelius and J.J.M. Vingerhoets (Hove: Brunner-Routledge, 2001).

9. Henry Mackenzie, *Letters to Elizabeth Rose of Kilravock: On Literature, Events and People 1768–1815*, ed. Horst Drescher (Edinburgh and London: Oliver and Boyd, 1967) 17; further references to this edition are given after quotations in the text as *ER*. Mackenzie and Elizabeth Rose started to correspond in 1768, when the young Mackenzie settled down in Edinburgh after finishing his legal studies in London. His cousin, living in Kilravock castle, was his literary confidante to whom he sent finished chapters of *The Man of Feeling*, on which Elizabeth Rose commented. Mackenzie's correspondence with his cousin is discussed in detail in Chapter 1 of this monograph.

10. Letter to Henry Mackenzie (4 May 1771), *Literature and Literati: The Literary Correspondence and Notebooks of Henry Mackenzie*, ed. Horst Drescher, vol. 1, Letters 1766–1827 (Frankfurt am Main: Lang, 1989) 50–1. Drescher presents this letter in Elphinston's innovative spelling, which I here standardise, as Drescher also does later.

11. Mackenzie, *Man of Feeling*, 49.

12. In *A Treatise of Human Nature*, David Hume questions the existence of objects as distinct from our mind and perception. Moreover, in Hume's opinion, it is not only external existence that should be treated with doubt, but also our own body, which we similarly experience through sense perception. Ideas of doubt regarding the external world that is accessible to us only through the senses have also been advocated by earlier philosophers of the period. In the *Essay Towards a New Theory of Vision* (1709), George Berkeley argues that all we see is not the objects themselves, but a signifying system of the external world. The knowledge we can have of external objects is an interpretation given by the mind to the information gained by us via perception. In John Locke's theory, our knowledge of the world is entirely dependent on processes of sensation and reflection. See David Hume, *A Treatise of Human Nature*, ed. L.A. Selby-Bigge and P.H. Nidditch (Oxford: Clarendon Press, 1978) 66–8 and 187–218; George Berkeley, 'An Essay Towards a New Theory of Vision (1709)', *The Works of George Berkeley*, ed. Alexander Campbell Fraser, vol. 1 (Oxford: Clarendon, 1901) 127–210; John Locke, *An Essay Concerning Human Understanding* (London: Penguin, 1997) 109–10.

13. Smith and Hume were a direct influence on Mackenzie. Mackenzie knew and admired Hume. As a lawyer of aristocratic descent, he mixed with those literati who contributed to the lively intellectual scene of eighteenth-century Edinburgh, including, besides Hume and Smith, Henry Home (Lord Kames), Hugh Blair, William Robertson and Alexander Carlyle. Hume and Smith were founder members of the Select Society established in 1754. See Harold William Thompson, *A Scottish Man of Feeling: Some Account of Henry Mackenzie, Esq. of Edinburgh and of the Golden Age of Burns and Scott* (London and New York: Oxford University Press, 1931) 40, and Mullan, 'Language of Sentiment', 275. For the comparison of the human mind to a looking-glass in John Locke's philosophy see Locke, *Essay*, 25, where the metaphor implies a mechanical, passive receptivity of the mind to external ideas.

14. For an investigation of the period's fascination with exploring where feelings come from, how they are transmitted and to whom they belong, see

Adela Pinch, *Strange Fits of Passion: Epistemologies of Emotion, Hume to Austen* (Stanford, CA: Stanford University Press, 1996). As Pinch argues, many eighteenth- and early nineteenth-century writers discover that one's feelings may not really be one's own (2–3).

15. Adam Smith, *The Theory of Moral Sentiments*, ed. Knud Haakonssen (Cambridge: Cambridge University Press, 2002) 129. Further references to this edition are given after quotations in the text.

16. See, for instance, Yorick's pleasure in distributing his money among a group of beggars or his determination not to give anything to the Franciscan monk in Sterne's *Sentimental Journey* (1768). At one point, Yorick uses the scene of begging to expose female vanity, where the act of charity is performed in expectation of undeserved praises. See Laurence Sterne, *A Sentimental Journey*, ed. Ian Jack (Oxford: Oxford University Press, 1968) 6–7, 35–7 and 107–9.

17. Sarah Fielding, *The Adventures of David Simple*, ed. Malcolm Kelsall (Oxford and New York: Oxford University Press, 1994) 19.

18. Anthony Ashley Cooper, Third Earl of Shaftesbury, *Characteristics of Men, Manners, Opinions, Times*, ed. Lawrence E. Klein (Cambridge: Cambridge University Press, 1999) 204; Francis Hutcheson, *An Inquiry into the Original of Our Ideas of Beauty and Virtue; in Two Treatises* (London: J. Darby, 1725) 132.

19. Oliver Goldsmith, *The Vicar of Wakefield: A Tale. Supposed to be Written by Himself* (London: F. Newbery, 1766) 26–7. Further references to this edition are given after quotations in the text.

20. Jessica Benjamin, *Like Subjects, Love Objects: Essays on Recognition and Sexual Difference* (New Haven and London: Yale University Press, 1995) 30.

21. Jessica Benjamin, *The Bonds of Love: Psychoanalysis, Feminism, and the Problem of Domination* (New York: Pantheon Books, 1988) 7–8 and 32–3. See also Sigmund Freud, 'Group Psychology and the Analysis of the Ego' (1921), *The Standard Edition of the Complete Psychological Works of Sigmund Freud*, ed. James Strachey et al., vol. 18 (London: Vintage, 2001) 67–143, hereafter *SE*; Mikkel Borch-Jacobsen, *The Emotional Tie: Psychoanalysis, Mimesis and Affect*, trans. Douglas Brick et al. (Stanford: Stanford University Press, 1992) 1–14.

22. For the operation of transference in the process of reading see Peter Brooks, 'The Idea of a Psychoanalytic Criticism', *The Trial(s) of Psychoanalysis*, ed. Françoise Meltzer and Peter Rudnytsky (Chicago and London: University of Chicago Press, 1987) 152–5; and Jerre Collins et al., 'Questioning the Unconscious', *In Dora's Case*, ed. Charles Bernheimer and Claire Cahane (New York: Columbia University Press, 1990) 252.

23. Mary Wollstonecraft, *Mary; and The Wrongs of Woman*, ed. Gary Kelly (Oxford and New York: Oxford University Press, 1976) 135.

24. Sigmund Freud, *Delusions and Dreams in Jensen's Gradiva*, *SE*, vol. 9, 7–95; Wilhelm Jensen, *Gradiva*, trans. Helen M. Downey (Los Angeles: Sun and Moon, 1993).

25. For feminist readings of Freud's reading of *Gradiva* see Sarah Kofman, 'Summarize, Interpret (Gradiva)', *Freud and Fiction*, trans. Sarah Wykes (Cambridge: Polity, 1991) 85–117; Mary Jacobus, 'Is There a Woman in This Text?', *Reading Woman* (London: Methuen, 1986) 83–109; Rachel Bowlby, 'One Foot in the Grave', *Still Crazy After All These Years: Women, Writing and Psychoanalysis* (London: Routledge, 1992) 157–82.

26. Smith, *The Theory of Moral Sentiments*, 16.

27. For a list of the editions of Mackenzie's novel see Thompson, *A Scottish Man of Feeling*, 417–18. The latest editions are by Brian Vickers (Oxford University Press, 2001) and Maureen Harkin (Plymouth, UK: Broadview, 2005).
28. The index first appeared in Henry Morley's 1886 edition and is reproduced in Brian Vickers's 2001 edition. See Vickers 110–11.
29. Harkin, introduction, 20.
30. *Textual Practice* 22.1 (2008) has recently advocated a return to a feeling-based reading practice. See esp. Mason and Armstrong, 'Introduction: Feeling: "An Indefinite Dull Region of the Spirit"?', 1–19.

4 Women and the Negative: The Sentimental Swoon in Eighteenth-Century Fiction

1. Sarah Fielding, *The History of Ophelia*, ed. Peter Sabor (Plymouth, UK: Broadview, 2004) 224–5 and Elizabeth Inchbald, *A Simple Story*, ed. J. M. S. Tompkins (Oxford: Oxford University Press, 1998) 67.
2. For controversial attitudes to sensibility see R. F. Brissenden, *Virtue in Distress: Studies in the Novel of Sentiment from Richardson to Sade* (London: Macmillan, 1974) 56–64 and Chris Jones, *Radical Sensibility: Literature and Ideas in the 1790s* (London and New York: Routledge, 1993) 1–19.
3. Hannah More, *Sacred Dramas [. . .] To which it is added, Sensibility: A Poem*. 5th edn (1782; London: T. Cadell, 1787) 284, my emphasis.
4. Janet Todd discusses the character type of the 'woman of feeling' in *Sensibility: An Introduction* (London: Methuen, 1986). On female nerves, illness and fainting see also G.J. Barker-Benfield, *The Culture of Sensibility* (Chicago: University of Chicago Press, 1996) 23–36. The significance of the blush in nineteenth-century literature is explored by Mary Ann O'Farrell's *Telling Complexions: The Nineteenth-Century Novel and the Blush* (Durham and London: Duke University Press, 1997).
5. According to Janet Todd, tears, sighs and fainting fits constitute a 'vocabulary' of sensibility in the 'language of the heart'. See Todd, *Sensibility*, esp. 77–81, 65–128. The quote 'nerves, spirits and fibres' is from the title of G.S. Rousseau's essay, 'Nerves, Spirits and Fibres: Toward the Origins of Sensibility' (1975), *Nervous Acts: Essays on Literature, Culture and Sensibility* (Basingstoke and New York: Palgrave Macmillan, 2004) 157–84. This, of course, is not to say that swooning is an exclusively female characteristic in the eighteenth-century novel. The focus of this chapter, however, will be the female sentimental swoon only.
6. Julia Borossa, *Hysteria* (Cambridge: Icon, 2001) 70–1.
7. Otto Kernberg, introduction, *The Work of the Negative*, by André Green, trans. Andrew Weller (London and New York: Free Association, 1999) xiii–xiv and André Green, *The Work of the Negative*, esp. chapters 'An Introduction to the Negative in Psychoanalysis' (1–13) and 'Aspects of the Negative: Semantic, Linguistic and Psychic' (14–25).
8. See, for instance, George Cheyne's *The English Malady: or, a Treatise of Nervous Diseases of All Kinds, as Spleen, Vapours, Lowness of Spirits, Hypochondriachal, and Hysterical Distempers, etc.* (London: G. Strahan, 1733) 14–16. Cheyne considers loss of sensation, loss of voluntary motion, as well as hysteric and

epileptic fits, and even yawning and stretching as different grades of nervous disorders. Loss of sensation accompanies his first category of nervous disorders, which includes melancholy, apoplexy, and fainting fits.

9. John Quincy, *Lexicon Physico-Medicum; or, a New Medicinal Dictionary*, 5th edn (1719; London: Longman, 1736) 438–9. See also Stephen Blanchard's short, seventeenth-century definition: 'a sudden Prostration or Swooning with a very weak or no Pulse, and a Depravation of Sense and Motion'. *A Physical Dictionary* (London: J. D., 1684). His dictionary was re-edited in the 1720s.

10. Robert James, *A Medicinal Dictionary: Including Physic, Surgery, Anatomy, Chymistry, and Botany, in All Their Branches Relative to Medicine* (London: T. Osborne, 1743–5). See entries on '*syncope*' and '*lipothymy*'. Hereafter I will refer to the relevant dictionary entries in parentheses.

11. Lipothymy is characterised by a 'Paleness of the Face, Lips, and Cheeks, and a Stupor of all the Senses', followed by a dimness of sight, falling to the ground, and the patient's being 'Insensible to what is done to him' (James, '*syncope*'). For the distinction between syncope and lipothymy see also G. Motherby, *A New Medical Dictionary; or, General Repository of Physic* (London: Johnson, 1775). According to Motherby, in a state of lipothymy the patient perceives and understands but loses the power of speech. In syncope, the patient loses feeling and understanding.

12. Samuel Johnson, *A Dictionary of the English Language* (London: W. Strahan, 1755). Johnson gives the following meanings of syncope: to contract, to abbreviate by omission of part of a word, and to divide a note in music. See also the entries 'contraction', 'elision' and 'syncope' in J.A. Cuddon, *The Penguin Dictionary of Literary Terms and Literary Theory*, 4th edn (London: Penguin, 1992) 178, 255, 890.

13. In William Godwin's *Deloraine* (London: Richard Bentley, 1833) Margaret, Deloraine's second wife, literally wastes away during her constant efforts to please her father and to deny the desires of her heart. A victim of relentless obedience, she falls into a fit of asphyxia and dies when she suddenly finds out that William, her long-lost and long-mourned lover is alive.

14. Throughout the eighteenth century, syncope remains interpreted as a heart condition. Robert Hooper's *Compendious Medical Dictionary* (London: Murray and Highley, 1798), Hooper's more substantial *Medical Dictionary*, 4th edn (London: Longman, 1820), which had several re-editions in the early nineteenth century, and Robert Morris and James Kendrick's *The Edinburgh Medical Dictionary* (Edinburgh: Bell and Brandfute, 1807) place syncope in the class of 'neuroses', that is, illnesses pertaining to the nerves. In syncope, the respiration and the action of the heart either cease or become much weaker. All these dictionaries distinguish ordinary fainting from '*syncope cardiaca*', which is an organic, irremediable affection of the heart.

15. Eric Partridge, *Origins: A Short Etymological Dictionary of Modern English* (London: Routledge, 1958).

16. See William Battie, *A Treatise on Madness* (London: J. Whiston and B. White, 1758); William Rowley, *A Treatise on Female, Nervous, Hysterical, Hypochondriachal, Bilious, Convulsive Diseases, with Thoughts on Madness, Suicide [. . .]* (London: C. Nourse, 1788); Robert James, *A Medicinal Dictionary: Including Physic, Surgery, Anatomy, Chymistry, and Botany, in All Their Branches Relative to Medicine* (London: T. Osborne, 1743–5) and *A Treatise on Canine*

Madness (London: J. Newbery, 1760); William Perfect, *Cases of Insanity and Nervous Disorders Successfully Treated* (Rochester: T. Fisher, [1785?]) and *Select Cases in the Different Species of Insanity, Lunacy or Madness* (Rochester: W. Gillman, 1787); Robert Whytt, *Observations on the Nature, Causes, and Cure of Those Disorders which Have Been Commonly Called Nervous, Hypochondriac, or Hysteric.* (Edinburgh: T. Becket, 1765); and John Haslam, *Observations on Insanity* (London: F. and C. Rivington, 1798). For a detailed discussion of the close relationship between sensibility and hysteria in the eighteenth century see John Mullan, *Sentiment and Sociability: The Language of Feeling in the Eighteenth Century* (Oxford: Clarendon, 1988) 201–40.

17. For the subversive narrative techniques of the novel see Deborah Down-Miers, 'Springing the Trap: Subtexts and Subversions', *Fetter'd or Free? British Women Novelists, 1670–1815*, ed. Mary Anne Schofield and Cecilia Macheski (Athens: Ohio University Press, 1986) 308–23; Linda Bree, *Sarah Fielding* (New York: Twayne; London: Prentice Hall, 1996) 135 ff; Gillian Skinner, *Sensibility and Economics in the Novel, 1740–1800* (London: Macmillan; New York: St. Martin's, 1999) 57–8.

18. Bree, *Sarah Fielding*, 140–1.

19. As Moira Dearnley argues, Wales in *The History of Ophelia* represents a symbolic locale of absolute virtue and innocence. See Moira Dearnley, *Distant Fields: Eighteenth-Century Fictions of Wales* (Cardiff: University of Wales Press, 2001) 70–1. As Dearnley points out, following the poor performance of Welsh troops in the Civil War, satires of the Welsh began to proliferate in the popular presses in the 1640s, reinforcing stereotypes which remained influential throughout the eighteenth century. Besides the negative, abject image of the ridiculous, cowardly Welshman, another view also existed that idealised Wales as a place of uncorrupted nature and virtue distant from the life of English high society. Like Fielding's *Ophelia*, Jane Austen's *Love and Friendship* (1790) presents a similar encounter of the hero with an innocent Welsh girl. By the time of Austen's novel the theme of the retreat into Wales as a way of seclusion from 'civilisation' and a contrast between simple rustic life and London society, had already become a well-established motif. See Dearnley, *Distant Fields*, xiii–xxi.

20. Fielding, *Ophelia*, 55, 225, 258. Subsequent references to Fielding's novel will be given in parentheses in the text.

21. Peter Sabor, introduction, *The History of Ophelia*, by Sarah Fielding (Plymouth, UK: Broadview, 2004) 19.

22. Valerie Steele, *The Corset: A Cultural History* (New Haven and London: Yale University Press, 2001) 1, 21, 67–85. Stay-making was traditionally in the hands of men. The cutting and fitting of whalebone needed male strength, while sewing and stitching of stays could be done by women. By the late eighteenth-century stays had become less heavily boned, and the craft was gradually taken over by women. See Steele 18.

23. For the issue of female blankness related to Rousseau's *Émile*, Edgeworth's *Belinda*, and Burney's *Camilla*, see Jane Spencer, *The Rise of the Woman Novelist* (Oxford: Blackwell, 1986) 161–4.

24. Sigmund Freud, 'The Neuro-Psychoses of Defence', *The Standard Edition of the Complete Psychological Works of Sigmund Freud*, ed. James Strachey et al., vol. 3 (London: Vintage, 2001) 58–9, hereafter *SE*.

25. For the ways in which the hysteric symptom can signify see Sigmund Freud, 'Fragment of an Analysis of a Case of Hysteria' (1905), *SE*, vol. 7, esp. 41–8.
26. Nicola J. Watson, *Revolution and the Form of the British Novel 1790–1825: Intercepted Letters, Interrupted Seductions* (Oxford: Clarendon Press, 1994) 1–22. As Watson argues, the plot of seduction was understood after 1789 as one of the French Revolution's paradigms.
27. Philip Stewart and Jean Vaché, introduction, *Julie, or the New Heloise: Letters of Two Lovers Who Live in a Small Town at the Foot of the Alps*, by Jean-Jacques Rousseau, The Collected Writings of Rousseau, vol. 6 (Hanover and London: University Press of New England, 1997) ix–xxi. Hereafter I will quote from this edition by indicating part, letter and page number, by permission of the University Press of New England, Lebanon, NH. This is the latest unabridged English translation of the novel, which attempts to remain as close to the French original as possible. It also contains a reproduction of the twelve engravings by Gravelot, which appear in the first edition of Rousseau's novel.
28. The full title of the first edition consisted of a main title and two subtitles. The second subtitle, with the epigraph, occurred on a separate page. See Stewart and Vaché, introduction, xiii.
29. Stewart and Vaché, introduction, xvi. For a discussion of the novel's title and an editorial tendency to elide a woman's name see Peggy Kamuf, *Fictions of Feminine Desire: Disclosures of Heloise* (Lincoln and London: University of Nebraska Press, 1982) 97–100. For woman as a simulacrum in Rousseau, see Linda M. G. Zerilli, *Signifying Woman: Culture and Chaos in Rousseau, Burke, and Mill* (Ithaca and London: Cornell University Press, 1994) 16–59.
30. For a reading of Saint Preux's fantasy of the landscape in the mountains of Valais see Mary Jacobus, *Psychoanalysis and the Scene of Reading* (Oxford: Oxford University Press, 1999) 59–66.
31. It is Saint Preux's 'guilty pen' that Julie implicitly holds responsible for her loss of chastity and her mother's death after her discovery of their clandestine correspondence. As Nancy K. Miller argues, the pen is provided with a destructive phallic force in the novel. As she puts it, 'the pen/dagger/phallus that kills Julie's filial innocence thus indirectly destroys the maternal principle as well'. See Nancy K. Miller, *The Heroine's Text: Readings in the French and English Novel, 1722–1782* (New York: Columbia University Press, 1980) 106. And indeed, for Julie, the loss of innocence comes not with the actual sexual act, but with breaking her silence and writing her passion to Saint Preux. Saint Preux's 'guilty pen' is a creative and disintegrative force at the same time.
32. Tony Tanner, *Adultery in the Novel: Contract and Transgression* (Baltimore and London: The Johns Hopkins University Press, 1979) 122–3; Sigmund Freud, "Fetishism" (1927) *SE*, vol. 21, 148–57.
33. Cf. the scene in the mountains of Valais, where Saint Preux projects the image of Julie's body, again piecemeal, onto the female inhabitants of the village, and imagines her to be present wherever he goes. See 1, letter 23, 67–8.
34. David Marshall, 'Fatal Letters: Clarissa and the Death of Julie', *Clarissa and Her Readers: New Essays for the Clarissa Project*, eds. Carol Houlihan Flynn and Edward Copeland (New York: AMS, 1999) 213–53.

35. For a similar moment see Saint Preux's visit during Julie's life-threatening illness with smallpox, which Claire calls 'the image of death' (III, letter 14, 274). The meeting takes place while Julie is lying unconscious with high fever in the very chamber where she lost her virginity. While here Julie's face is disfigured by the marks of the smallpox, at her death the face is covered with a veil, as the body started to decompose. In the smallpox episode, even though she is unconscious, Julie seems to recognise him, and holds out her hand. Which Saint Preux covers with his kisses.

36. As Freud claims, in the analytic situation we never discover a 'no' in the unconscious. Recognition of an unconscious content by the ego is often expressed in a negative formula. See *SE*, vol. 19, 235–9.

37. Jean Starobinski reads Rousseau's novel in terms of a Hegelian dialectic, arguing that the novel is structured around the dynamics of immediacy and mediation, or, in other words, transparency and obstruction. This forms part of the dialectic of passionate love, virtuous abnegation, and a final synthesis of passion and virtue at the end of the novel. See Jean Starobinski, *Jean-Jacques Rousseau: Transparency and Obstruction*, trans. Arthur Goldhammer (Chicago and London: University of Chicago Press, 1971) 86–7. However, I think that Rousseau's construction of the woman of feeling challenges Starobinski's dialectic reading. The woman of feeling captures the exact point where Hegel and Freud essentially differ: the simultaneity of negation and affirmation as they are tied together through the event of repression. Unlike in Hegel, affirmation in Rousseau – as in Freud – does not come about through the negation of negation. Julie dies, and her transgressive desire can never be compatible with virtuous marriage. Julie's absences and death, and the simultaneous final reinstatement of her desire prove the impossibility of a Hegelian synthesis; they are tied into the work of the negative which operates according to a Freudian rather than a Hegelian dynamic. It is this dynamic – filled with discontent – that effectively contributes to the disruptive, radical undertones Watson attributes to Rousseau's text. For the meeting points and disjunctions of Hegel's and Freud's thought see Green, 'Hegel and Freud: Elements for an Improbable Comparison', *Work*, 26–49, esp. 46–9. Paul de Man critiques Starobinski's dialectical reading on different grounds, positing that the relationship which Starobinski understands as transparency is in fact a relationship of reading. See *Allegories of Reading* (New Haven and London: Yale University Press, 1979) 190–2.

38. Note how Julie constantly displaces the beginning of her misfortunes. Here she attributes it to the kiss, while at other times she blames it on confessing her passion to Saint Preux or on reading Saint Preux's first letter. The original place of seduction shifts constantly and becomes more and more elusive in the course of Julie's continuous re-reading of her own story.

39. Tanner, *Adultery in the Novel*, 116–17. See also Judith N. Shklar, 'Rousseau's Images of Authority (Especially in La Nouvelle Heloise)', *The Cambridge Companion to Jean-Jacques Rousseau*, ed. Patrick Riley (Cambridge: Cambridge University Press, 2001) 167–9.

40. Peter Mortensen, 'Rousseau's English Daughters: Female Desire and Male Guardianship in British Romantic Fiction', *English Studies* 83:4 (2004): 360.

41. Henry Mackenzie, *Julia de Roubigné*, ed. Susan Manning (East Linton: Tuckwell, 1999) I, letter 20, 70–1.

42. Adam Smith, *The Theory of Moral Sentiments*, ed. Knud Haakonssen (Cambridge: Cambridge University Press, 2002) 170, emphases added.
43. Letter from Maria Edgeworth to Elizabeth Inchbald, 14 January 1810. James Boaden, *Memoirs of Mrs Inchbald: Including Her Familiar Correspondence with the Most Distinguished Persons of Her Time*, vol. 2 (London: Bentley, 1833) 152–4, qtd. in Gary Kelly, *The English Jacobin Novel 1780–1805* (Oxford: Clarendon Press, 1976) 78.
44. Kelly, *The English Jacobin Novel*, 76, emphasis added.
45. Elizabeth Inchbald, *A Simple Story*, ed. J. M. S. Tompkins (Oxford: Oxford University Press, 1998) 39. Further references will be given in parentheses in the text. This and subsequent quotes by permission of Oxford University Press.
46. For an interpretation of Catholicism and Protestantism in the novel see Ian Balfour, 'Promises, Promises: Social and Other Contracts in the English Jacobins (Godwin/Inchbald)', *New Romanticisms: Theory and Critical Practice*, eds. David L. Clark and Donald C. Goellnicht (Toronto: University of Toronto Press, 1994) 239; Roger Manwell calls *A Simple Story* the first English Catholic novel. According to him, the character of the Catholic lord was perfectly new in the period. See Roger Manwell, *Elizabeth Inchbald* (Lanham: University Press of America, 1987) 72. As Annibel Jenkins points out, in Catholic households in the period the sons were reared as Catholics, but if the mother was a Protestant the daughter also became a Protestant. See Annibel Jenkins, *I'll Tell You What: The Life of Elizabeth Inchbald* (Lexington: The University Press of Kentucky, 2003) 280.
47. As Terry Castle points out in *Masquerade and Civilisation*, Miss Milner is unreadable to her environment, where she represents an alien principle. In Castle's interpretation, she is like a heroine from a French novel, who has strayed into the story from another tradition and whose inconsistencies and indecision, therefore, no one knows how to read. As Castle observes, even her closest companion, Miss Woodley misinterprets her according to the standards of French sentimental romances. When Miss Milner becomes melancholy, for instance, Miss Woodley assumes it is due to a moral struggle over being in love with the rakish Sir Frederick. Terry Castle, *Masquerade and Civilization: The Carnivalesque in Eighteenth-Century English Culture and Fiction* (London: Methuen, 1986) 301–2.
48. Freud, 'Negation' (1925) *SE*, vol. 19, 235–9.
49. André Green, *On Private Madness* (London: Karnac, 1997) 257.
50. Eleanor Ty, using Kristeva's terminology, claims that Miss Milner's communications remain in the field of the semiotic. See *Unsex'd Revolutionaries: Five Women Novelists of the 1790s* (Toronto: University of Toronto Press, 1993) 88–9. For the importance of gestures and non-verbal expressions in the novel see also Nora Nachumi, '"Those Simple Signs": The Performance of Emotion in Elizabeth Inchbald's *A Simple Story*', *Eighteenth-Century Fiction* 11.3 (1999): 317–38; Jane Spencer, introduction, *A Simple Story*, by Elizabeth Inchbald, ed. J. M. S. Tompkins (Oxford: Oxford University Press, 1998). As Spencer writes, 'Under the influence of her unmentionable passion for Dorriforth, the verbally aggressive Miss Milner is forced into communicating, like a sentimental heroine, through blushes and other body-language. The irony is

that the bodily signs which usually, in the literature of sensibility, speak more truly than words, are radically ambiguous in Inchbald's world.' Inchbald, she claims, exploits the cultural ambiguities behind such gestures, as they may indicate not just innocence, but guilt and sexual consciousness at the same time. See Spencer, introduction, xvi, by permission of Oxford University Press.

51. Inchbald first attempted to publish the novel in 1779, when the novel consisted only of the story of Dorriforth and Miss Milner. Since Inchbald could not get it published, she had to put it aside. She made modifications and added the second part, the story of Matilda, in the 1780s. After its publication in 1791, the novel brought unprecedented success to its author. Between the first version of 1777 and its publication in 1791, the draft was read by several friends, including Godwin, whose comments and revisions significantly changed the manuscript from its epistolary form into a third-person narrative. For the conception and publication of the novel see Jenkins, *I'll Tell You What*, 273–310; Ty, *Unsex'd Revolutionaries*, 88; and Manwell, *Elizabeth Inchbald*, 72–3.

52. 'Matilda's person, shape, and complection were so extremely like what her mother's once were, that at the first glance she appeared to have a still greater resemblance of her, than of her father – but her mind and manners were all Lord Elmwood's; softened by the delicacy of her sex, the extreme tenderness of her heart, and the melancholy of her situation' (220). Patricia Meyer Spacks comments on Lord Elmwood's identification of Matilda with her mother in *Desire and Truth: Functions of Plot in Eighteenth-Century English Novels* (Chicago: University of Chicago Press, 1990) 200.

53. In *Playing and Reality*, Winnicott mentions the importance of the 'negative side of relationships'. The traumatic experience of waiting for the mother's longed-for response when that response is never forthcoming, leads the child to a state where only what is negative is felt to be real. Such experiences result in a psychic structure where even the object's presence cannot modify the negative model that has become characteristic of the subject's experience. For this patient, Winnicott writes, the only real thing is the gap. As Green puts it, 'The negative has imposed itself as an organised object relationship quite independent of the object's presence or absence.' See Donald Winnicott, *Playing and Reality* (Hove: Brunner-Routledge, 2001) 20–5 and Green, *Work*, 5 and *Private Madness*, 274. Another, related pathology is what Green calls 'dead mother complex', caused by a depressed, ill, or otherwise preoccupied though present mother. The baby conceives such mother as dead, and as someone who needs to be brought back to life. See Green, *Private Madness*, 142–73.

54. Castle, *Masquerade and Civilization*, 324.

55. Review of *A Simple Story*, by Mary Wollstonecraft. *Analytical Review* 10 (May 1791): 101–2.

56. Following J. Schaeffer, Perelberg refers to hysteria as something that is fundamentally 'a mode of thinking about sexuality and the sexual object'. Rosine Jozef Perelberg, 'The Interplay of Identifications: Violence, Hysteria, and the Repudiation of Femininity', *The Dead Mother: The Work of André Green*, ed. Gregorio Kohon (London: Brunner-Routledge, 2001) 185.

5   Godwin's Case: Melancholy Mourning in the 'Empire of Feeling'

1. *Mary Wollstonecraft and William Godwin: A Short Residence in Sweden, Norway and Denmark, and Memoirs of the Author of The Rights of Woman*, ed. and int. Richard Holmes (Harmondsworth: Penguin, 1987) 268–9. Subsequent references are cited in the text as *Memoirs* and *Short Residence*, respectively.

2. For the publication and reception of the *Memoirs* see Ford K. Brown, *The Life of William Godwin* (London and Toronto: Dent, 1926) 133–4; Claire Tomalin, *The Life and Death of Mary Wollstonecraft* (1974; London: Penguin, 1992) 289 ff.; R. M. Janes, 'On the Reception of Mary Wollstonecraft's *A Vindication of the Rights of Woman*', *Journal of the History of Ideas* 39 (1978): 293–302; Mitzi Myers, 'Godwin's Memoirs of Wollstonecraft: The Shaping of Self and Subject', *Studies in Romanticism* 20:3 (1981): 299–316; William St. Clair, *The Godwins and the Shelleys: The Biography of a Family* (London: Faber, 1989) 184–6; Amy Rambow, '"Come Kick Me": Godwin's *Memoirs* and the Posthumous Infamy of Mary Wollstonecraft', *Keats–Shelley Review* 13 (1999): 24–30; Tilottama Rajan, 'Framing the Corpus: Godwin's "Editing" of Wollstonecraft in 1798', *Studies in Romanticism* 39:4 (2000): 511; Mary Jacobus, 'Intimate Connections: Scandalous Memoirs and Epistolary Indiscretion', *Women, Writing, and the Public Sphere: 1700–1830*, eds. Elizabeth Eger and Charlotte Grant (Cambridge: Cambridge University Press, 2001) 274–5.

3. Robert Southey to William Taylor, 1 July 1804, *A Memoir of the Life and Writings of the Late William Taylor of Norwich*, ed. J.W. Robberds, 2 vols (London: John Murray, 1843) vol. 1, 507; Roscoe's lines on Godwin's mourning of Wollstonecraft were 'written from memory' on a copy of the *Memoirs* by Dr William Shepherd:

   > Hard was thy fate in all the scenes of life,
   > As daughter, sister, mother, friend, and wife;
   > But harder still thy fate in death we own,
   > Thus mourn'd by Godwin with a heart of stone.

   See *Notes and Queries* III, 8 (1865): 66, qtd. in Ralph M. Wardle, *Mary Wollstonecraft: A Critical Biography* (London: Richards; Lawrence: University of Kansas Press, 1951) 357, n.17. See also Tomalin, *Mary Wollstonecraft*, 337, n.9.

4. Richard Polwhele, 'The Unsex'd Females: A Poem', ed. Gina Luria (New York and London: Garland, 1974) 29–30.

5. Myers notes that attitudes towards Godwin's *Memoirs* have been contradictory. While some praise the work as honest and sympathetic, other commentators 'find Godwin's vision of Wollstonecraft chauvinist and retrograde, a mere sexist stereotype of woman as all sentiment and no ideas' ('Godwin's Memoirs', 303).

6. Sigmund Freud, 'Mourning and Melancholia', *The Standard Edition of the Complete Psychological Works of Sigmund Freud*, ed. James Strachey et al., vol. 14 (London: Vintage, 2001), esp. 243–9. Subsequent references to the *Standard Edition* are cited as *SE*. See also Freud, 'The Ego and the Id', *SE*, vol. 19, 12–66.

7. *SE*, vol. 14, 244–5, 256; *SE*, vol. 19, 29; David L. Eng and David Kazanjian, introduction, *Loss: The Politics of Mourning* (Berkeley: University of California Press, 2003) 1–25; Judith Butler, 'Moral Sadism and Doubting One's Own Love: Kleinian Reflections on Melancholia', *Reading Melanie Klein*, ed. Lindsey Stonebridge and John Phillips (London and New York: Routledge, 1998) 179–89.

8. Godwin to [Hugh Skeys], 4 October 1797. Oxford, Bodleian Library, MS. Abinger c. 22, fols 55–7. [Peviously Dep.b. 227/8 (a)]. This and all subsequent material from the Abinger Collection is cited by permission of The Bodleian Libraries, University of Oxford. Godwin's papers have recently been rearranged under permanent shelfmarks and folio numbers. Here I cite the new, finalised catalogue numbers, with the old Dep. numbers given in brackets for reference. Regarding the reordering of letters from the former Dep. b. 227/8(a) (the folder of Godwin's letter-press copies of his outgoing correspondence) see Pamela Clemit, 'William Godwin and James Watt's Copying Machine: Wet-Transfer Copies in the Abinger Papers', *The Bodleian Library Record* 18. 5 (2005): 532–60. I rely on Clemit's identification of Godwin's correspondents in the cited letters. The square brackets are intended as an indication that the addressees' names, as identified by Clemit, are not present on the pieces of papers themselves. A conspectus that cross-references each item in the collection from the old Dep. shelfmarks to the new 'MS. Abinger' shelfmarks and folio numbers can be found here: http://www.bodley.ox.ac.uk/dept/scwmss/wmss/online/1500-1900/abinger/conspectus.html.

9. Sunday, 10 Sept. 1797. Oxford, Bodleian Library, MS. Abinger c. 22, fol. 42. [Previously Dep.b. 227/8 (a)].

10. Qtd. in Brown, *The Life of William Godwin*, 131.

11. Godwin to Inchbald, 10 Sept. 1797, Oxford, Bodleian Library, MS. Abinger c. 22, fol. 40. [Previously Dep. b. 227/8 (a)]; qtd. in Charles Kegan Paul, *William Godwin: His Friends and Contemporaries*, 2 vols. (London: Henry S. King, 1876) vol. 1, 276.

12. Roger Manvell, *Elizabeth Inchbald, England's Principal Woman Dramatist and Independent Woman of Letters in Eighteenth Century London: A Biographical Study* (New York; London: Lanham, 1987) 99–101; St. Clair, *The Godwins and the Shelleys*, 171–2. See also Rambow, 'Come Kick Me', 40.

13. [Inchbald] to Godwin, 10 Sept. 1797, Oxford, Bodleian Library, MS. Abinger c. 3, fols. 120–1. [Previously Dep. c. 509, item 2 of 39]; qtd. in Kegan Paul, *Godwin*, I: 277.

14. Godwin to [Inchbald], 13 Sept. 1797, Oxford, Bodleian Library, MS. Abinger c. 22, fols. 44–5. [Previously Dep. b. 227/8 (a)]; qtd. in Brown, *The Life of William Godwin*, 131 and Kegan Paul, *Godwin*, I: 278.

15. [Inchbald] to Godwin, 14 Sept. 1797, Oxford, Bodleian Library, MS. Abinger c. 3, fols. 89–90. [Previously Dep. c. 509, item 3 of 39]; qtd. in Kegan Paul, *Godwin*, I: 279.

16. Godwin did not have access to various sources and letters which could have shown perspectives other than Wollstonecraft's. Letters were withheld from Godwin by friends, family and relations: Everina Wollstonecraft and Henry Fuseli, for instance, refused to share the letters in their possession. Imlay's letters do not survive either. See Tomalin, *Mary Wollstonecraft*, 288. Wollstonecraft's letters to Fuseli were destroyed, probably to conceal the scandal, soon after Wollstonecraft's grandson, Sir Percy Florence Shelley, had bought them from

John Knowles. See Wardle, *Mary Wollstonecraft*, 350, n.8. See also Janet Todd, ed., *The Collected Letters of Mary Wollstonecraft* (London: Penguin-Allen Lane, 2003) 204–5 for an attempted reconstruction of the fragments. For Godwin's shaping of the image of Wollstonecraft see also Holmes, introduction, *Mary Wollstonecraft and William Godwin: A Short Residence in Sweden, Norway and Denmark, and Memoirs of the Author of The Rights of Woman* (Harmondsworth: Penguin, 1987) 53–4, as well as Rajan, 'Framing the Corpus', 511–31 and Myers, 'Godwin's Memoirs', 299–316.

17. For the details of the Wollstonecraft–Imlay relationship see; Tomalin, *Mary Wollstonecraft*, 210–44; Janet Todd, *Mary Wollstonecraft: A Revolutionary Life* (London: Weidenfeld & Nicolson, 2000) 231–87; Barbara Taylor, *Mary Wollstonecraft and the Feminist Imagination* (Cambridge: Cambridge University Press, 2003) 123–4; Charles Kegan Paul, 'Prefatory Memoir', *Letters to Imlay*, by Mary Wollstonecraft (London: Kegan Paul, 1879) xxxviii–xlviii.
18. Tomalin, *Mary Wollstonecraft*, 190.
19. London, Nov. 1795, Mary Wollstonecraft, *Letters to Imlay, with Prefatory Memoir by Charles Kegan Paul* (London: Kegan Paul, 1879) Letter 70, 187, hereafter cited as *LI*.
20. Gothenburg, 26 Aug. 1795. *LI*, letter 64, 171–2.
21. London, November 1795. *LI*, letter 73, 193, emphasis added.
22. London, 27 Nov. 1795, *LI*, letter 74, 198, 197. For the destructive, sado-masochistic dynamic of the Wollstonecraft–Imlay correspondence see Mary Jacobus, 'Intimate Connections', 281–6. Jacobus shows how the 'love letter metamorphoses into a scene of mutual torture'. Here love letters turn into 'hate letters', becoming the instruments of 'epistolary self-destruction' and of 'mingled self-torture and revenge' (285).
23. Hull, 27 May 1795, *LI*, letter 42, 116.
24. London, 27 Nov. 1795, *LI*, letter 74, 195–6.
25. Copenhagen, 6 Sept. 1795, *LI*, letter 65, 175, emphasis added.
26. Hamburg, 27 Sept. 1795, *LI*, letter 67, 177, emphasis added.
27. Hamburg, 25 Sept. 1795, *LI*, letter 66, 176, emphasis added.
28. For an interpretation of Wollstonecraft's melancholia see Mary Jacobus, 'In Love With a Cold Climate: Travelling With Mary Wollstonecraft', *First Things: The Maternal Imaginary in Literature, Art and Psychoanalysis* (New York and London: Routledge, 1995) 63–82.
29. Mary Wollstonecraft, *A Vindication of the Rights of Woman* (London: Penguin, 1992) 156, emphasis added.
30. Wollstonecraft, *Rights of Woman*, 153–4.
31. Daniel O'Quinn, 'Trembling: Wollstonecraft, Godwin and the Resistance to Literature', *ELH* 64 (1997): 771–2.
32. Havre, 7 Apr. 1795, *LI*, letter 38, 108.
33. London, 27 Nov. 1795, *LI*, letter 74, 198.
34. London, 22 May 1795, *LI*, letter 40, 113.
35. For the circumstances of Wollstonecraft's death see Vivien Jones, 'The Death of Mary Wollstonecraft', *British Journal for Eighteenth-Century Studies* 20 (1997): 187–205.
36. Godwin was reading Rousseau's *Julie* – among other works, such as *Confessions, Émile* and Goethe's *Werther* – at the time of writing the *Memoirs*

and around the time of Wollstonecraft's illness and death. See Godwin's diary, Oxford, Bodleian Library, MS. Abinger e. 8, fols. 1–48. [Previously Dep. e. 203 (No. 8)]. The punctuality of the diary is striking: even half-pages of what he reads or writes are indicated.

37. Imlay returned Wollstonecraft's letters after their final separation. Godwin could have seen these letters even before Wollstonecraft's death, and definitely had immediate access to them after her death and during the time of his own correspondence with Inchbald. He also knew about the details of the Wollstonecraft–Imlay relationship from private conversations with Wollstonecraft. See Kegan Paul, 'Prefatory Memoir', xli. See also Holmes, *Mary Wollstonecraft and William Godwin*, 53.

38. Melanie Klein, 'Mourning and Its Relation to Manic-Depressive States' (1940), *Love, Guilt and Reparation and Other Works by Melanie Klein* (London: Karnac and The Institute of Psychoanalysis, 1992) 355–6.

39. As Tilottama Rajan argues, Wollstonecraft, as presented in the *Memoirs*, is also a 'subject-in-process' – in that her life and ideas are seen by Godwin as unfinished ('Framing the Corpus', 513–14).

40. 1 July 1796, qtd. in Ralph M. Wardle, ed. *Godwin and Mary: Letters of William Godwin and Mary Wollstonecraft* (Lincoln and London: University of Nebraska Press, 1966) 4–5. Hereafter *Godwin and Mary*.

41. Gary Kelly, *The English Jacobin Novel 1780–1805* (Oxford: Clarendon, 1976) 225–6.

42. William Godwin, a schedule of literary projects, Sept. 1798, Oxford, Bodleian Library, MS. Abinger c. 38, fols. 1–2r. [Previously Dep. b. 228/9, item 2a of 5]. Qtd. in Kegan Paul, *Godwin*, I: 294.

43. William Godwin, *St. Leon* (London: G. G. and J. Robinson, 1799) viii–ix.

44. William Godwin, analysis of his own character, miscellaneous notes, 1798, Oxford, Bodleian Library, MS. Abinger c. 32, fols. 37–40. [Previously Dep. b. 228/9, item 1 of 5].

45. Godwin to ?Anthony Carlisle, 19 Sept. 1797, Oxford, Bodleian Library, MS. Abinger c. 22, fols. 50–2. [Previously Dep. b. 227/8 (a)].

46. [Godwin] to [Samuel Parr], 13 Sept. 1797, Oxford, Bodleian Library, MS. Abinger c. 22, fol. 46. [Previously Dep. b. 227/8 (a)].

47. 14 Sept. 1797, Oxford, Bodleian Library, MS. Abinger c. 22, fols. 48–9. [Previously Dep. b. 227/8 (a)]; qtd. in Kegan Paul, *Godwin*, I: 280.

48. Godwin to [Hugh Skeys], 4 Oct. 1797. Oxford, Bodleian Library, MS. Abinger c. 22, fols. 55–7. [Previously Dep. b. 227/8 (a)].

49. Godwin to Thomas Holcroft, 10 Sept. 1797, Oxford, Bodleian Library, MS. Abinger c. 22, fol. 39. [Previously Dep. b. 227/8 (a)]; Godwin to Hugh Skeys, 4 Oct. 1797.

50. Qtd. in St. Clair 180.

51. Godwin to ?Charlotte Smith, 24 Oct. 1797, Oxford, Bodleian Library, MS. Abinger c. 22, fols. 71–3. [Previously Dep. b. 227/8 (a)]. Emphasis added. Qtd. in Kegan Paul, *Godwin*, I: 280-81. Clemit differs from Kegan Paul here, who identified this correspondent as Mrs Cotton. See Clemit, 'William Godwin and James Watt', 541.

52. The small 'n' after names appears in the manuscript but I have not seen it transcribed in scholarship before. It probably means 'not at home' (confirmed by William St. Clair, oral communication, January 2007).

53. Oxford, Bodleian Library, MS. Abinger e. 8, fols. 1–48. [Previously Dep. e. 203 (No. 8)]. I noticed several errors in Kegan Paul's transcription of the diary (*Godwin*, I: 274–5). Here I cite the entries as I believe they appear in the original manuscript. Kegan Paul's citation is from 30 August to 10 September, but his last entry is incomplete. Godwin's diary was recently digitalised: *The Diary of William Godwin*, eds. Victoria Myers, David O'Shaughnessy and Mark Philp (Oxford: Oxford Digital Library, 2010). http://godwindiary. bodleian.ox.ac.uk.

54. Kegan Paul, *Godwin*, I: 274.

55. Julia Kristeva, *Black Sun: Depression and Melancholia*, trans. Leon S. Roudiez (New York: Columbia University Press, 1989) 11. See also *SE*, vol. 14, 246–8.

56. Kristeva, *Black Sun*, 12–13, 21–2.

57. Ibid., 24. For Klein's argument on mourning and depression see Melanie Klein, 'A Contribution to the Psychogenesis of Manic-Depressive States' (1935), *Love, Guilt and Reparation and Other Works by Melanie Klein* (London: Karnac and The Institute of Psychoanalysis, 1992) 262–89 and Melanie Klein, 'Mourning and Its Relation to Manic-Depressive States', 344–69. For the role of symbol formation in Kleinian psychoanalysis see Melanie Klein, 'The Importance of Symbol-Formation in the Development of the Ego' (1930), *Love, Guilt and Reparation*, 219–32; Hanna Segal, 'Notes on Symbol Formation' (1957), *The Work of Hanna Segal: A Kleinian Approach to Clinical Practice* (New York and London: Jason Aronson–Rowman & Littlefield, 1981) 49–65; Juliet Mitchell, introduction, *The Selected Melanie Klein* (New York: Free Press, 1986) 9–32.

58. This instantaneous affective communication re-surfaces in Godwin's 1833 novel, *Deloraine*, between Deloraine and his much-loved – and much-idealised – first wife, Emilia. Emilia dies of a fever before the birth of her second child. Many aspects of this sentimental relationship appear to recall the Godwin–Wollstonecraft correspondence and Godwin's *Memoirs*. See Godwin, *Deloraine*, 3 vols (London, 1833), esp. vol. 1, chapter 2.

59. 4 Oct. 1796, *Godwin and Mary*, letter 53, 41, emphases added.

60. 13 Sept. 1796, *Godwin and Mary*, letter 36, 33.

61. Nicolas Abraham and Maria Torok, *The Shell and the Kernel: Renewals of Psychoanalysis*, ed., trans., and int. Nicholas T. Rand (1987; Chicago and London: University of Chicago Press, 1994) vol. 1, 130, 136–7, see also 125–38.

62. I am grateful to Tilottama Rajan for drawing my attention to Godwin's later novels in this context.

Bibliography

Abraham, Nicholas and Maria Torok. *The Shell and the Kernel: Renewals of Psychoanalysis.* Ed., trans. and int. Nicholas T. Rand. Vol. 1. Chicago and London: University of Chicago Press, 1994.

Akenside, Mark. *Pleasures of the Imagination.* London: R. Dodsley, 1744.

Alford, C. Fred. *What Evil Means to Us.* Ithaca and London: Cornell University Press, 1997.

Allard, James Robert. *Romanticism, Medicine, and the Poet's Body.* Aldershot: Ashgate, 2007.

Andree, John. *Cases of the Epilepsy, Hysteric Fits, and St. Vitus Dance, Cases of the Bite of Mad Creatures.* London: W. Meadows and J. Clarke, 1746.

Andrews, Jonathan and Andrew Scull. *Undertaker of the Mind: John Monro and Mad-Doctoring in Eighteenth-Century England.* Berkeley: University of California Press, 2001.

Arasse, Daniel. *The Guillotine and the Terror.* Trans. Christopher Miller. 1987. London: Penguin, 1989.

Arendt, Hannah. *Eichmann in Jerusalem: A Report on the Banality of Evil.* London: Faber, 1963.

——. *On Revolution.* Harmondsworth: Penguin, 1973.

Ariés, Philippe. *The Hour of Our Death.* Trans. Helen Weaver. London: Penguin, 1981.

——. *Western Attitudes Toward Death: From the Middle Ages to the Present.* Trans. Patricia M. Ranum. Baltimore and London: Johns Hopkins University Press, 1974.

Armstrong, Isobel. 'Textual Harassment: The Ideology of Close Reading, or How Close is Close?' *Textual Practice* 9 (1995): 401–20.

Arnold, Thomas. *A Case of Hydrophobia, Commonly Called Canine Madness.* London: T. Chapman, 1793.

Austen, Jane, *Love and Friendship, and Other Writings.* Ed. Janet Todd. London: Phoenix, 1998.

——. *Persuasion.* Ed. Janet Todd and Antje Blank. Cambridge: Cambridge University Press, 2006.

——. *Sense and Sensibility.* Ed. Edward Copeland. Cambridge: Cambridge University Press, 2006.

Baier, Annette C. *A Progress of Sentiments: Reflections on Hume's Treatise.* Cambridge, MA: Harvard University Press, 1991.

——. *Death and Character: Further Reflections on Hume.* Cambridge, MA: Harvard University Press, 2008.

Balfour, Ian. 'Promises, Promises: Social and Other Contracts in the English Jacobins (Godwin/Inchbald)'. *New Romanticisms: Theory and Critical Practice.* Eds David L. Clark and Donald C. Goellnicht. Toronto: University of Toronto Press, 1994. 225–50.

Barfoot, Michael. 'Brunonianism under the Bed: An Alternative to University Medicine in Edinburgh in the 1780s'. *Brunonianism in Britain and Europe.*

Ed. W. F. Bynum and Roy Porter. London: Wellcome Institute for the History of Medicine, 1988. 22–45.

Barker, Francis. *The Tremulous Private Body: Essays on Subjection.* Ann Arbor, MI: The University of Michigan Press, 1995.

Barker-Benfield, G. J. *The Culture of Sensibility: Sex and Society in Eighteenth-Century Britain.* Chicago: University of Chicago Press, 1992.

Barrell, John. *Imagining the King's Death: Figurative Treason, Fantasies of Regicide 1793–1796.* Oxford: Oxford University Press, 2000.

Barry, Peter, 'An Academic Discipline Foresees its Death'. *PN Review* 33.3 (173) (2007): 16–20.

Barthes, Roland. *S/Z.* Trans. Richard Miller. London: Jonathan Cape, 1975.

Bate, Walter Jackson. 'The Sympathetic Imagination in Eighteenth-Century English Criticism'. *ELH* 12.2 (1945): 144–64.

Batson, C. Daniel. *The Altruism Question: Toward a Social-Psychological Answer.* Hillsdale, NJ: Lawrence Erlbaum, 1991.

Battestin, Martin C. and Clive T. Probyn, eds. *The Correspondence of Henry and Sarah Fielding.* Oxford: Clarendon Press, 1993.

Battie, William. *A Treatise on Madness.* London: J. Whiston and B. White, 1758.

Bell, Michael. *Sentimentalism, Ethics and the Culture of Feeling.* Basingstoke: Palgrave, 2000.

Bender, John. *Imagining the Penitentiary: Fiction and the Architecture of Mind in Eighteenth-Century England.* Chicago and London: University of Chicago Press, 1987.

Bending, Stephen and Stephen Bygrave. Introduction. *The Man of Feeling.* By Henry Mackenzie. Ed. Brian Vickers. Oxford: Oxford University Press, 2001. vii–xxiv.

Benedict, Barbara M. *Framing Feeling: Sentiment and Style in English Prose Fiction 1745–1800.* New York: AMS, 1994.

——. 'Reading Faces: Physiognomy and Epistemology in Late Eighteenth-Century Sentimental Novels'. *Studies in Philology* 92:3 (1995): 311–28.

Benjamin, Jessica. *Like Subjects, Love Objects. Essays on Recognition and Sexual Difference.* New Haven and London: Yale University Press, 1995.

——. *The Bonds of Love: Psychoanalysis, Feminism, and the Problem of Domination.* New York: Pantheon, 1988.

Bennett, Andrew, ed. *Readers and Reading.* Harlow: Longman, 1995.

——, ed. *Reading Reading: Essays on the Theory and Practice of Reading.* Tampere: University of Tampere, 1993.

Benstock, Shari. *Textualizing the Feminine: On the Limits of Genre.* Norman, OK and London: University of Oklahoma Press, 1991.

Berkeley, George. *The Works of George Berkeley.* Ed. Alexander Campbell Fraser. Vol. 1. Oxford: Clarendon Press, 1901.

Bindman, David. *The Shadow of the Guillotine: Britain and the French Revolution.* London: British Museum, 1989.

Blackstone, William. *Commentaries on the Laws of England.* Vol. 1. Oxford: Clarendon Press, 1765–9.

Blair, Hugh. *Lectures on Rhetoric and Belles Lettres.* 3 vols. Dublin: Whitestone, 1783.

Blancard, Stephen. *A Physical Dictionary.* London: J. D., 1684.

Boaden, James. *Memoirs of Mrs. Inchbald: Including Her Familiar Correspondence with the Most Distinguished Persons of Her Time.* 2 vols. London: Richard Bentley, 1833.

Boltanski, Luc. *Distant Suffering: Morality, Media and Politics*, trans. Graham Burchell. Cambridge: Cambridge University Press, 1999.

Bonds, Mark Evan. *Wordless Rhetoric: Musical Form and the Metaphor of the Oration.* Cambridge, MA: Harvard University Press, 1991.

Borch-Jacobsen, Mikkel. *The Emotional Tie: Psychoanalysis, Mimesis, and Affect.* Trans. Douglas Brick et al. Stanford, CA: Stanford University Press, 1992.

——. *The Freudian Subject.* Trans. Catherine Porter. Stanford, CA: Stanford University Press, 1988.

Borossa, Julia. *Hysteria.* Cambridge: Icon, 2001.

Bowlby, Rachel. 'One Foot in the Grave'. *Still Crazy After All These Years: Women, Writing and Psychoanalysis.* London: Routledge, 1992. 157–82.

Boyer, Abel. *Dictionnaire royal françois et anglois.* La Haye: Adrian Moetjens, 1702.

——. *Dictionnaire royal françois-anglois et anglois-françois.* London, 1748.

Bree, Linda. *Sarah Fielding.* New York: Twayne; London: Prentice Hall, 1996.

Brillant, Abbé. *Dictionnaire universel françois et latin, vulgairement appelé Dictionnaire de Trévoux.* Paris: Compagnie des libraires associés, 1771.

Brissenden, R. F. *Virtue in Distress: Studies in the Novel of Sentiment from Richardson to Sade.* London: Macmillan, 1974.

Brooks, Peter. *Body Work: Objects of Desire in Modern Narrative.* Cambridge, MA: Harvard University Press, 1993.

——. *Reading for the Plot.* Cambridge, MA: Harvard University Press, 1992.

——. 'The Idea of a Psychoanalytic Criticism'. *The Trial(s) of Psychoanalysis.* Eds. Françoise Meltzer and Peter Rudnytsky. Chicago and London: University of Chicago Press, 1987. 145–59.

Brown, Ford K. *The Life of William Godwin.* London and Toronto: Dent, 1926.

Brown, Stuart, ed. *British Philosophy and the Age of Enlightenment.* London and New York: Routledge, 1996.

Brown, Vivienne. *Adam Smith's Discourse: Canonicity, Commerce, and Conscience.* London and New York: Routledge, 1994.

Browne, Richard. *Medicina Musica: or, a Mechanical Essay on the Effects of Singing, Music, and Dancing on Human Bodies.* London: John Cooke, 1729.

Burke, Edmund. *A Philosophical Enquiry into the Origin of Our Ideas of the Sublime and Beautiful.* Ed. Adam Phillips. Oxford: Oxford University Press, 1990.

Burney, Fanny. *Evelina: or, a Young Lady's Entrance into the World.* London: T. Lowndes, 1779.

Burrows, J. F. and A. J. Hassall. 'Anna Boleyn and the Authenticity of Fielding's Feminine Narratives'. *Eighteenth Century Studies* 21 (1988): 427–53.

Burton, John Hill. *Life and Correspondence of David Hume.* Edinburgh: William Tait, 1846.

Butler, Judith. *Bodies that Matter: On the Discursive Limits of 'Sex'.* London: Routledge, 1993.

——. 'Moral Sadism and Doubting One's Own Love: Kleinian Reflections on Melancholia'. *Reading Melanie Klein.* Eds. Lyndsey Stonebridge and John Phillips. London and New York: Routledge, 1998. 179–89.

——. *The Psychic Life of Power: Theories in Subjection.* Stanford: Stanford University Press, 1997.

Butler, Marilyn, ed. *Burke, Paine, Godwin, and the Revolution Controversy.* Cambridge: Cambridge University Press, 1984.

Byrd, Max. *Visits to Bedlam. Madness and Literature in the Eighteenth Century.* Columbia, SC: University of South Carolina Press, 1974.

Campbell, Blair. 'La Mettrie: the Robot and the Automaton'. *Journal of the History of Ideas* 31.4 (1970): 555–72.

Canning, George. 'The New Morality'. *Anti-Jacobin* 36 (1798): 282–7.

Carey, Brycchan. *British Abolitionism and the Rhetoric of Sensibility.* Basingstoke: Palgrave Macmillan, 2005.

Caruth, Cathy. *Unclaimed Experience: Trauma, Narrative, and History.* Baltimore, MD: Johns Hopkins University Press, 1996.

Castle, Terry. *Masquerade and Civilization: The Carnivalesqe in Eighteenth-Century English Culture and Fiction.* London: Methuen, 1986.

Chambaud, Louis. *Dictionnaire françois et anglois.* London: A. Millar, 1761.

Chambers, Ephraim. *Cyclopaedia: or, an Universal Dictionary of Arts and Sciences.* 2nd edn. 2 vols. London: D. Midwinter, 1738.

——. *Cyclopaedia: or, an Universal Dictionary of Arts and Sciences.* 5th edn. 2 vols. London: D. Midwinter, 1741–3.

——. *Cyclopaedia; or, an Universal Dictionary of Arts and Sciences.* London: J. F. and C. Rivington, 1786.

——. *Supplement to Chambers's Cyclopaedia; or, an Universal Dictionary of Arts and Sciences,* 2 vols. London: W. Innys, 1753.

Chandler, James. 'The Languages of Sentiment'. *Textual Practice* 22.1 (2008): 21–39.

Chertok, Leon and Raymond De Saussure. *The Therapeutic Revolution: From Mesmer to Freud.* Trans. R.H. Ahrenfeldt. New York: Brunner-Mazel, 1979.

Cheyne, George. *The English Malady: or, a Treatise of Nervous Diseases of All Kinds, as Spleen, Vapours, Lowness of Spirits, Hypochondriacal, and Hysterical Distempers, etc.* London: G. Strahan, 1733.

——. *The Natural Method of Cureing the Diseases of the Body, and the Disorders of the Mind Depending on the Body.* London: G. Strahan, 1742.

Clemit, Pamela. 'William Godwin and James Watt's Copying Machine: Wet-Transfer Copies in the Abinger Papers'. *The Bodleian Library Record* 18.5 (2005): 532–60.

Collins, Jerre et al. 'Questioning the Unconscious'. *In Dora's Case.* Eds. Charles Bernheimer and Claire Cahane. New York: Columbia University Press, 1990. 243–53.

Conger, Syndy McMillen. *Mary Wollstonecraft and the Language of Sensibility.* Rutherford: Fairleigh Dickinson University Press; London and Toronto: Associated University Presses, 1994.

Cooper, Bransby Blake. *The Life of Sir Astley Cooper, Bart.* Vol. 1. London: John W. Parker, 1843.

Cornelius, Randolph R. and J. J. M. Vingerhoets, eds. *Adult Crying: A Biopsychosocial Approach.* Hove: Brunner-Routledge, 2001.

Cox, Stephen D. *'The Stranger Within Thee': Concepts of the Self in Late-Eighteenth-Century Literature.* Pittsburgh: University of Pittsburgh Press, 1980.

Cuddon, J. A. *The Penguin Dictionary of Literary Terms and Literary Theory.* 4th edn. London: Penguin, 1992.

Cullen, William. *Nosology.* Edinburgh: C. Stewart, 1800.

——. *The Works of William Cullen, M. D.* Edinburgh: Blackwood; London: T. and G. Underwood, 1827.

Cunningham, Andrew. 'Medicine to Calm the Mind: Boerhaave's Medical System, and Why It Was Adopted in Edinburgh'. *The Medical Enlightenment of the Eighteenth Century*. Ed. Andrew Cunningham and Roger French. Cambridge: Cambridge University Press, 1990. 40–66.

Daly, Macdonald. 'Vivisection in Eighteenth-Century Britain'. *British Journal for Eighteenth-Century Studies* 12 (1989): 57–68.

Darnton, Robert. 'The High Enlightenment and the Low-Life of Literature in Pre-Revolutionary France'. *Past and Present* 51 (1971): 81–115.

Davis, Mark H. *Empathy: A Social Psychological Approach*. Madison, WI: WCB Brown and Benchmark, 1994.

Dawson, Deidre. 'Is Sympathy so Surprising? Adam Smith and French Fictions of Sympathy'. *Eighteenth-Century Life* 15 (1991): 147–62.

Dawson, Virginia P. *Nature's Enigma: The Problem of the Polyp in the Letters of Bonnet, Trembley, and Réaumur*. Philadelphia: American Philosophical Society, 1987.

De Bolla, Peter. *The Discourse of the Sublime: Readings in History, Aesthetics and the Subject*. Oxford: Blackwell, 1989.

De Man, Paul. 'Aesthetic Formailzation: Kleist's *Über das Marionettentheater*'. *The Rhetoric of Romanticism*. New York: Columbia University Press, 1984. 263–90.

——. *Allegories of Reading*. New Haven: Yale University Press, 1979.

De Quincey, Thomas. 'The English Mail-Coach'. *Confessions of an English Opium-Eater and Other Writings*. Ed. Grevel Lindop. Oxford: Oxford University Press, 1998. 183–233.

Deane, Seamus. *The French Revolution and Enlightenment England 1789–1832*. Cambridge, MA, and London: Harvard University Press, 1988.

Dearney, Moira. *Distant Fields: Eighteenth-Century Fictions of Wales*. Cardiff: University of Wales Press, 2001.

Deleuze, Gilles. *Coldness and Cruelty*. New York: Zone, 1989.

—— and Félix Guattari. *Anti-Oedipus: Capitalism and Schizophrenia*. Trans. Robert Hurley, Mark Seem and Helen R. Lane. London: Athlone, 1983.

Derrida, Jacques. 'Cogito and the History of Madness'. *Writing and Difference*. Trans. Alan Bass. London and New York: Routledge, 2003. 36–76.

——. *Of Grammatology*. Trans. Gayatri Chakravorty Spivak. Baltimore and London: Johns Hopkins University Press, 1974.

——. 'Psyche: Inventions of the Other'. *Reading de Man Reading*. Eds. Lindsay Waters and Wlad Godzich. Minneapolis: University of Minnesota Press, 1989. 25–65.

——. *Without Alibi*. Ed. and trans. Peggy Kamuf. Stanford: Stanford University Press, 2004.

Descartes, René. 'Discourse on the Method'. *Key Philosophical Writings*. Ware: Wordsworth, 1997. 71–122.

Dictionnaire de l'Académie françoise. 5th edn. Paris, 1798.

Digby, Kenelm. *Of the Sympathetic Powder: A Discourse in Solemn Assembly at Montpellier*. London: John Williams, 1669.

Dixon, Thomas. *From Passions to Emotions: The Creation of a Secular Psychological Category*. Cambridge: Cambridge University Press, 2003.

Down-Miers, Deborah. 'Springing the Trap: Subtexts and Subversions'. *Fetter'd or Free? British Women Novelists, 1670–1815*. Eds. Mary Anne Schofield and Cecilia Macheski. Athens: Ohio University Press, 1986. 308–23.

Duffy, Edward. *Rousseau in England: The Context for Shelley's Critique of the Enlightenment*. Berkeley: University of California Press, 1979.

Dwyer, John. 'Enlightened Spectators and Classical Moralists: Sympathetic Relations in Eighteenth-Century Scotland'. *Sociability and Society in Eighteenth-Century Scotland*. Eds. John Dwyer and Richard B. Sher. Edinburgh: Mercat, 1993. 96–118.

——. 'Introduction – "A Peculiar Blessing": Social Converse in Scotland from Hutcheson to Burns'. *Sociability and Society in Eighteenth-Century Scotland*. Eds. John Dwyer and Richard B. Sher. Edinburgh: Mercat, 1993.1–22.

——. *The Age of the Passions: An Interpretation of Adam Smith and Scottish Enlightenment Culture*. East Linton: Tuckwell, 1998.

——. *Virtuous Discourse: Sensibility and Community in Late Eighteenth Century Scotland*. Edinburgh: Donald, 1987.

—— and Richard B. Sher, eds. *Sociability and Society in Eighteenth Century Scotland*. Edinburgh: Mercat, 1991.

Eales, Nellie B. 'A Satire on the Royal Society, Dated 1743, Attributed to Henry Fielding'. *Notes and Records of the Royal Society of London* 23.1 (1968): 65–7.

Eaton, Daniel Isaac. 'King Chauntclere; or, The Fate of Tyranny'. *Politics for the People; or, Hog's Wash* 8 (1793): 102–7.

Edgeworth, Maria. *Belinda*. London: J. Thomson, 1801.

Elkins, James. *Pictures and Tears: A History of People Who Have Cried in Front of Paintings*. New York and London: Routledge, 2001.

Ellenberger, Henri F. *The Discovery of the Unconscious: The History and Evolution of Dynamic Psychiatry*. London: Fontana, 1970.

Ellis, Havelock. *Studies in the Psychology of Sex*. Vol. 3. Philadelphia: Davis, 1920.

Ellis, Markman. *The Politics of Sensibility: Race, Gender, and Commerce in the Sentimental Novel*. Cambridge: Cambridge University Press, 1996.

Ellison, Julie. *Cato's Tears and the Making of Anglo-American Emotion*. Chicago and London: University of Chicago Press, 1999.

——. 'The Politics of Fancy in the Age of Sensibility'. *Re-Visioning Romanticism: British Women Writers, 1776–1837*. Eds. Carol Shiner Wilson and Joel Haefner. Philadelphia: University of Pennsylvania Press, 1994. 228–55.

Eng, David L. and David Kazanjian, eds. *Loss: The Politics of Mourning*. Berkeley: University of California Press, 2003.

Fairer, David. 'Sentimental Translation in Mackenzie and Sterne'. *Essays in Criticism* 49:2 (1999): 132–51.

Falco, Maria J., ed. *Feminist Interpretations of Mary Wollstonecraft*. University Park, PA: Pennsylvania State University Press, 1996.

Fara, Patricia. *Sympathetic Attractions: Magnetic Practices, Beliefs, and Symbolism in Eighteenth-Century England*. Princeton, NJ: Princeton University Press, 1996.

Felman, Shoshana. 'Rereading Femininty'. *Yale French Studies* 62 (1981): 19–44.

——. 'To Open the Question'. *Yale French Studies* 55–6 (1977): 5–10.

Ferenczi, Sándor. 'Confusion of Tongues between Adults and the Child'. *Final Contributions to the Problems and Methods of Psycho-Analysis*. Ed. Michael Balint. Trans. Eric Mosbacher et al. London: Karnac, 2002. 156–67.

——. 'Introjection and Transference'. *First Contributions to Psycho-Analysis*. Trans. Ernest Jones. London: Karnac, 2002. 35–93.

——. 'On the Definition of Introjection'. *Final Contributions to the Problems and Methods of Psycho-Analysis*. Ed. Michael Balint. Trans. Eric Mosbacher. London: Karnac, 2002. 316–18.

——. *The Clinical Diary of Sándor Ferenczi.* Ed. Judith Dupont. Trans. Michael Balint and Nicola Zarday Jackson. Cambridge, MA: Harvard University Press, 1995.

Ferguson, Adam. *Essay on the History of Civil Society.* Edinburgh: A. Millar, 1767.

Fielding, Henry. *An Apology for the Life of Mrs. Shamela Andrews.* London: A. Dodd, 1741.

Fielding, Sarah. *Remarks on Clarissa.* Ed. Peter Sabor. 1749. Los Angeles: William Andrews Clark Memorial Library, 1985.

——. *The Adventures of David Simple.* Dublin: William Smith, 1744.

——. *The Adventures of David Simple. With a Preface by Henry Fielding.* 2nd edn. London: A. Millar, 1744.

——. *The Adventures of David Simple,* ed. Malcolm Kelsall. Oxford and New York: Oxford University Press, 1994.

——. *The Governess, or the Little Female Academy.* London: T. Clarke, 1765.

——. *The History of Ophelia.* London: R. Baldwin, 1760.

——. *The History of Ophelia.* Ed. Peter Sabor. Plymouth, UK: Broadview, 2004.

Fiering, Norman S. 'Irresistible Compassion: An Aspect of Eighteenth-Century Sympathy and Humanitariansim'. *Journal of the History of Ideas* 37. 2 (1976): 195–218.

Finke, Michael C. and Carl Niekerk, eds. *One Hundred Years of Masochism: Literary Texts, Social and Cultural Contexts.* Amsterdam: Rodopi, 2000.

Flynn, Carol Houlihan. 'Running Out of Matter: The Body Exercised in Eighteenth-Century Fiction'. *Languages of Psyche: Mind and Body in Eighteenth-Century Thought.* Ed. G.S. Rousseau. Berkeley: University of California Press, 1990. 147–85.

Forrest, Derek. *The Evolution of Hypnotism.* Forfar: Black Ace, 1999.

Forrester, John. *Seductions of Psychoanalysis.* Cambridge: Cambridge University Press, 1990.

Foucault, Michel. *Discipline and Punish.* Trans. Alan Sheridan. London: Penguin, 1977.

——. *Madness and Civilization: A History of Insanity in the Age of Reason.* Trans. Richard Howard. New York: Vintage, 1965.

French, R. K. *Robert Whytt, the Soul, and Medicine.* London: The Wellcome Institute of the History of Medicine, 1969.

Frend, William. 'Peace and Union Recommended to the Associated Bodies of Republicans and Anti-Republicans'. *Political Writings of the 1790s.* Ed. Gregory Claeys. Vol. 1. London: Pickering & Chatto, 1995. 105–27.

Freud, Sigmund. *The Standard Edition of the Complete Psychological Works of Sigmund Freud.* 24 vols. Ed. James Strachey et al. London: Vintage, 2001.

Frith, Chris D. *Making Up the Mind.* Malden, MA: Blackwell, 2007.

Frye, Northrop. 'Towards Defining an Age of Sensibility'. *ELH* 23.2 (1956): 144–52.

Fulford, Tim. 'Radical Medicine and Romantic Politics'. *Wordsworth Circle* 35.1 (2004): 15–21.

Gaub, Jerome. 'De Regimine Mentis'. *Mind and Body in Eighteenth-Century Medicine.* Ed. L. J. Rather. London: Wellcome, 1965.

Gerard, Alexander. *Essay on Taste.* London: A. Millar, 1759.

Godwin, William. Analysis of his own character, miscellaneous notes, 1798. Oxford, Bodleian Library, MS. Abinger c. 32, fols. 37–40. [Previously Dep. b. 228/9, item 1 of 5].

——. A schedule of literary projects, Sept. 1798. Oxford, Bodleian Library, MS. Abinger c. 38, fols. 1–2r. [Previously Dep. b. 228/9, item 2a of 5].

——. *An Enquiry Concerning Political Justice, and Its Influence on General Virtue and Happiness.* 2 vols. London: G. G. and J. Robinson, 1793.

——. *An Enquiry Concerning Political Justice, and Its Influence on Morals and Happiness.* 2 vols. 3rd edn. London: G. G. and J. Robinson, 1798.

——. *Deloraine.* London: Richard Bentley, 1833.

——. Diary, 1795–1798. Oxford, Bodleian Library, MS. Abinger e. 8, fols. 1–48. [Previously Dep. e. 202 (No.7) and Dep. e. 203 (No. 8)].

——. *Fleetwood; or, The New Man of Feeling.* London: Richard Philips, 1805.

——. Letters. Oxford, Bodleian Library, MS. Abinger c. 22 and c. 3 [Previously Dep.b. 227/8 (a) and Dep. c. 509].

——. *Mandeville: A Tale of the Seventeenth Century.* Edinburgh and London, 1817.

——. *St Leon.* London: G. G. and J. Robinson, 1799.

Goldsmith, Oliver. *The Vicar of Wakefield: A Tale. Supposed to be Written by Himself.* London: B. Collins, 1766.

Goring, Paul. *The Rhetoric of Sensibility in the Eighteenth Century.* Cambridge: Cambridge University Press, 2005.

Graham, Henry Grey. *Scottish Men of Letters in the Eighteenth Century.* London: Black, 1901.

Green, André. *On Private Madness.* London: Karnac, 1997.

——. *The Fabric of Affect in the Psychoanalytic Discourse.* Trans. Alan Sheridan. London: Routledge, 1999.

——. *The Work of the Negative.* Trans. Andrew Weller. London and New York: Free Association, 1999.

Greene, Donald. 'Latitudinarianism and Sensibility: The Genealogy of the "Man of Feeling" Reconsidered'. *Modern Philology* 75 (1977–8): 159–83.

Griffiths, Paul and Mark S. R. Jenner. *Londinopolis: Essays in the Cultural and Social History of Early Modern London.* Manchester and New York: Manchester University Press, 2000.

Grinberg, Leon. 'On a Specific Aspect of Countertransference Due to the Patient's Projective Identification'. *International Journal of Psycho-Analysis* 43 (1962): 436–40.

Gross, Daniel M. *The Secret History of Emotion: From Aristotle's Rhetoric to Modern Brain Science.* Chicago: University of Chicago Press, 2006.

Grossman, Joyce. '"Sympathetic Visibility," Social Reform and the English Woman Writer: *The Histories of Some of the Penitents in the Magdalen-House*'. *Women's Writing* 7 (2000): 247–66.

Hagstrum, Jean H. *Sex and Sensibility: Ideal and Erotic Love from Milton to Mozart.* Chicago and London: University of Chicago Press, 1980.

Haller, Albrecht von. *A Dissertation on the Sensible and Irritable Parts of Animals.* London: Nourse, 1755.

——. *Letters from Baron Haller to His Daughter on the Truths of the Christian Religion.* London: J. Murray, 1780.

——. *Poems.* Trans. Mrs. Howorth. London: J. Bell, 1794.

Hamilton, Paul. *Historicism.* London: Routledge, 1996.

Hamilton, R.D. *The Principles of Medicine, on the Plan of the Baconian Philosophy.* Vol. 1. London: Thomas and George Underwood, 1822.

Hamlyn, D.W. *Sensation and Perception: A History of the Philosophy of Perception.* London: Routledge and Kegan Paul, 1961.

Harkin, Maureen. Introduction. *The Man of Feeling.* By Henry Mackenzie. Plymouth: Broadview, 2005. 9–38.

——. 'Mackenzie's *Man of Feeling*: Embalming Sensibility'. *ELH* 61 (1994): 317–40.

Harris, John. 'Coleridge's Reading in Medicine'. *Wordsworth Circle* 3 (1972): 85–95.

Hartley, David. *Observations on Man: His Frame, His Duty, and His Expectations.* London: S. Richardson, 1749.

Haslam, John. *Observations on Insanity.* London: F. and C. Rivington, 1798.

Hawley, Judith. 'The Anatomy of *Tristram Shandy*'. *Literature and Medicine During the Eighteenth Century.* Eds. Marie Mulvey Roberts and Roy Porter. London: Routledge, 1993. 84–100.

Hays, Mary. 'Memoirs of Mary Wollstonecraft'. *Annual Necrology, for 1797–8.* London, 1800. 411–60.

——. 'Obituary of Wollstonecraft'. *The Monthly Magazine* 4 (1797). *Lives of the Great Romantics III. Godwin, Wollstonecraft and Mary Shelley by Their Contemporaries.* Ed. Harriet Jump. Vol. 2. Wollstonecraft. London: Pickering & Chatto, 1999. 5–7.

——. *The Memoirs of Emma Courtney.* 1796. Ed. Eleanor Ty. Oxford: Oxford University Press, 1996.

Hazlitt, William. 'On Poetry in General' (1818). *Romantic Criticism 1800–1850.* Ed. R. A. Foakes. London: Edward Arnold, 1968. 108–17.

Heath, Eugene. 'The Commerce of Sympathy: Adam Smith on the Emergence of Morals'. *Journal of the History of Philosophy* 33.3 (1995): 447–66.

Hegel, G. W. F. *Aesthetics: Lectures on Fine Art.* Berlin Lectures, 1823–9. Trans. T. M. Knox. *German Aesthetic and Literary Criticism.* Ed. David Simpson. Cambridge: Cambridge University Press, 1984. 206–41.

Heimann, Paula. 'On Countertransference'. *International Journal of Psycho-Analysis* 31 (1950): 81–4.

Heller-Roazen, Daniel. *The Inner Touch: Archaeology of a Sensation.* New York: Zone Books, 2007.

Henry, Thomas. *Memoirs of Albert de Haller, M. D.* Warrington: Eyres and Johnson, 1783.

Hertz, Neil. 'Lurid Figures'. *Reading de Man Reading.* Eds. Lindsay Waters and Wlad Godzich. Minneapolis: University of Minnesota Press, 1989. 82–104.

Herwig, H. M. *The Art of Curing Sympathetically or Magnetically [...] With a Discourse Concerning the Cure of Madness, and An Appendix to Prove the Reality of Sympathy [...].* London: Tho. Newborough, 1700.

Hirschman, Albert O. *The Passions and the Interests: Political Arguments for Capitalism before Its Triumph.* Princeton, NJ: Princeton University Press, 1977.

Hobbes, Thomas. *Leviathan.* Ed. C. B. Macpherson. London: Penguin, 1985.

Hoeveler, Diane Long. 'Reading the Wound: Wollstonecraft's *Wrongs of Woman*; or, *Maria* and Trauma Theory'. *Studies in the Novel.* 1999 (31.4): 387–408.

Hoffmann, M. L. 'Is Altruism Part of Human Nature?' *Journal of Personality and Social Psychology* 40 (1981): 121–37.

Holmes, Richard, ed. and int. *Mary Wollstonecraft and William Godwin: A Short Residence in Sweden, Norway and Denmark, and Memoirs of the Author of The Rights of Woman.* Harmondsworth: Penguin, 1987.

Hont, István and Michael Ignatieff. *Wealth and Virtue: The Shaping of Political Economy in the Scottish Enlightenment*. Cambridge, Cambridge University Press, 1983.

Hooper, Robert. *A Compendious Medical Dictionary*. London: Murray and Highley, 1798.

——. *Medical Dictionary*. 4th edn. London: Longman, 1820.

Hope, Vincent. *Philosophers of the Scottish Enlightenment*. Edinburgh: Edinburgh University Press, 1984.

Horne, George. *A Letter to Adam Smith LL.D. on the Life, Death, and Philosophy of His Friend David Hume, Esq. By One of the People Called Christians*. Oxford: Clarendon, 1777.

Houlbrooke, Ralph. *Death, Religion, and the Family in England, 1480–1750*. Oxford: Clarendon, 1998.

Hume, David. *An Enquiry Concerning the Principles of Morals*. Ed. L.A. Selby-Bigge. Oxford: Clarendon Press, 1975.

——. *A Treatise of Human Nature*. Ed. L. A. Selby-Bigge and P. H. Nidditch. Oxford: Clarendon Press, 1978.

——. *The Life of David Hume, Esq. Written by Himself*. London: W. Strahan, 1777.

Hutcheson, Francis. *An Inquiry into the Original of Our Ideas of Beauty and Virtue; In Two Treatises*. London: J. Darby, 1725.

——. *On the Nature and Conduct of the Passions with Illustrations on the Moral Sense*. 1728. Ed. Andrew Ward. Manchester: Clinamen Press, 1999.

Ignatieff, Michael. *Just Measure of Pain: The Penitentiary in the Industrial Revolution 1750–1850*. Harmondsworth: Penguin, 1989.

——. *The Needs of Strangers*. London: Hogarth Press, 1984.

Ilie, Paul. *The Age of Minerva: Cognitive Discontinuities in Eighteenth-Century Thought. From Body to Mind in Physiology and the Arts*. 2 vols. Philadelphia: University of Pennsylvania Press, 1995.

Inchbald, Elizabeth. *A Simple Story*. London: G. G. and J. Robinson, 1791.

——. *A Simple Story*. Ed. J. M. S. Tompkins. Oxford: Oxford University Press, 1998.

Jackson, Stanley W. *Melancholia and Depression: From Hippocratic Times to Modern Times*. New Haven, CT and London: Yale University Press, 1986.

Jacobson, Edith. *Depression: Comparative Studies of Normal, Neurotic, and Psychotic Conditions*. New York: International Universities Press, 1971.

Jacobus, Mary. 'A Whole World in Your Head: Rereading the Landscape of Absence'. *Psychoanalysis and the Scene of Reading*. Oxford: Oxford University Press, 1999. 52–83.

——. 'In Love With a Cold Climate. Travelling With Mary Wollstonecraft'. *First Things. The Maternal Imaginary in Literature, Art, and Psychoanalysis*. New York: Routledge, 1995. 63–82.

——. 'Intimate Connections: Scandalous Memoirs and Epistolary Indiscretion'. *Women, Writing, and the Public Sphere: 1700–1830*. Eds. Elizabeth Eger and Charlotte Grant. Cambridge: Cambridge University Press, 2001. 274–89.

——. 'Is There a Woman in This Text?' *Reading Woman*. London: Methuen, 1986. 83–109.

——. '"The Science of Herself": Scenes of Female Enlightenment'. *Romanticism, History and the Possibilities of Genre: Re-Formation of Literature, 1789–1837*. Eds. Tilottama Rajan and Julia M. Wright. Cambridge: Cambridge University Press, 1998. 240–69.

James, Robert. *A Medicinal Dictionary: Including Physic, Surgery, Anatomy, Chymistry, and Botany, in All Their Branches Relative to Medicine*. 3 vols. London: T. Osborne, 1743–5.

——. *A Treatise on Canine Madness*. London: J. Newbery, 1760.

James, Susan. *Passion and Action: The Emotions in Seventeenth-Century Philosophy*. Oxford: Clarendon Press, 1997.

Janes, R. M. 'On the Reception of Mary Wollstonecraft's *A Vindication of the Rights of Woman*'. *Journal of the History of Ideas* 39 (1978): 293–302.

Jenkins, Annibel. *I'll Tell You What: The Life of Elizabeth Inchbald*. Lexington: The University Press of Kentucky, 2003.

Jensen, Wilhelm. *Gradiva*. Trans. Helen M. Downey. Los Angeles: Sun and Moon, 1993.

Jimack, Peter. 'The French Enlightenment I: Science, Materialism, and Determinism'. *British Philosophy in the Age of Enlightenment*. Ed. Stuart Brown. London: Routledge, 1996. 228–50.

Johnson, Barbara. 'The Critical Difference: BartheS/BalZac'. *The Critical Difference. Essays in the Contemporary Rhetoric of Reading*. Baltimore and London: Johns Hopkins University Press, 1980. 3–12.

Johnson, Claudia L. ed. *Equivocal Beings: Politics. Gender, and Sentimentality in the 1790s*. Chicago and London: University of Chicago Press, 1995.

——. *The Cambridge Companion to Mary Wollstonecraft*. Cambridge: Cambridge University Press, 2002.

Johnson, James. *Essay on Morbid Sensibility of the Stomach and Bowels*. London: T. and G. Underwood, 1827.

Johnson, Samuel. *A Dictionary of the English Language*. 2 vols. London: W. Strahan, 1755.

Jones, Chris. *Radical Sensibility: Literature and Ideas in the 1790s*. London and New York: Routledge, 1993.

Jones, Vivien. 'The Death of Mary Wollstonecraft'. *British Journal for Eighteenth-Century Studies* 20 (1997): 187–205.

Jordanova, L. J. ed. *Languages of Nature: Critical Essays on Science and Literature*. London: Free Association, 1986.

Jump, Harriet Devine. *Mary Wollstonecraft: Writer*. New York and London: Harvester Wheatsheaf, 1994.

Kahn, Victoria. *Wayward Contracts: The Crisis of Political Obligation in England, 1640–1674*. Princeton and Oxford: Princeton University Press, 2004.

Kames, Henry Home, Lord. *Elements of Criticism*. 2 vols. 1785. London: Routledge-Thoemmes, 1993.

Kamuf, Peggy. *Fictions of Feminine Desire: Disclosures of Heloise*. Lincoln and London: University of Nebraska Press, 1982.

Keele, K. D. *Anatomies of Pain*. Oxford: Blackwell, 1957.

Kelly, Gary. *Revolutionary Feminism: Mind and Career of Mary Wollstonecraft*. New York: St Martin's; London: Macmillan, 1996.

——. *The English Jacobin Novel 1780–1805*. Oxford: Clarendon Press, 1976.

Kernberg, Otto F. *Borderline Conditions and Pathological Narcissism*. Ed. Robert Langs. New York: Jason Aronson-Rowman & Littlefield, 1975.

King, Lester S. Introduction. *First Lines of Physiology*. By Albrecht von Haller. 1786. New York and London: Johnson, 1966. ix–lxxii.

——. 'Stahl and Hoffmann: A Study in Eighteenth Century Animism'. *Journal of the History of Medicine and Allied Sciences* 19 (1964): 118–30.

Kivy, Peter. *The Seventh Sense: Francis Hutcheson and Eighteenth-Century British Aesthetics*. Oxford: Clarendon Press, 2003.

Klein, Ernest. *A Comprehensive Etymological Dictionary of the English* Language. 2 vols. Amsterdam: Elsevier, 1966–7.

Klein, Melanie. 'A Contribution to the Psychogenesis of Manic-Depressive States'. 1935. *Love, Guilt and Reparation and Other Works by Melanie Klein*. London: Karnac and The Institute of Psychoanalysis, 1992. 262–89.

——. 'Mourning and Its Relation to Manic-Depressive States'. 1940. *Love, Guilt and Reparation and Other Works by Melanie Klein*. London: Karnac and The Institute of Psychoanalysis, 1992. 344–69.

——. 'The Importance of Symbol-Formation in the Development of the Ego'. 1930. *Love, Guilt and Reparation and Other Works by Melanie Klein*. London: Karnac and The Institute of Psychoanalysis, 1992. 219–32.

Kleist, Heinrich von. *On a Theatre of Marionettes*. Trans. Gerti Wilford. London: Acorn, 1989.

Klossowski, Pierre. 'Nature as Destructive Principle'. *The One Hundred and Twenty Days of Sodom and Other Writings*. By Marquis de Sade. Trans. Austryn Wainhouse and Richard Seaver. New York: Grove, 1966. 65–86.

Kofman, Sarah. 'Summarize, Interpret (Gradiva)'. *Freud and Fiction*. Trans. Sarah Wykes. Cambridge: Polity Press, 1991. 85–117.

Krafft-Ebing, Richard von. *Psychopathia Sexualis: With Especial Reference to the Antipathetic Sexual Instinct*. Trans. Franklin S. Klaf. London: Staples Press, 1965.

Kristeva, Julia. *Black Sun: Depression and Melancholia*. Trans. Leon S. Roudiez. New York: Columbia University Press, 1989.

——. *Powers of Horror: An Essay on Abjection*. Trans. Leon S. Roudiez. New York, Columbia University Press, 1982.

——. *Strangers to Ourselves*. Trans. Leon. S. Roudiez. New York and London: Harvester Wheatsheaf, 1991.

——. *Tales of Love*. Trans. Leon S. Roudinez. New York: Columbia University Press, 1987.

La Mettrie, Julien Offray de. *Machine Man and Other Writings*. Trans. and ed. Ann Thomson. Cambridge: Cambridge University Press, 1996.

——. *Man a Machine*. London: W. Owen, 1749.

——. *Man a Machine and Man a Plant*. Trans. Richard A. Watson and Maya Rybalka. Indianapolis and Cambridge: Hackett, 1994.

——. 'Man as Plant'. *Machine Man and Other Writings*. Ed. Ann Thomson. Cambridge: Cambridge UP, 1996. 75–88.

——. *Oeuvres philosophiques*. Berlin, 1751.

——. 'Treatise on the Soul'. *Machine Man and Other Writings*. Ed. Ann Thomson. Cambridge: Cambridge University Press, 1996. 41–74.

Lacan, Jacques. *The Four Fundamental Concepts of Psycho-Analysis*. Ed. Jacques-Alain Miller. Trans. Alan Sheridan. London: Penguin, 1979.

Laplanche, Jean and Jean-Bertrand Pontalis. *The Language of Psychoanalysis*. London: Karnac, 1988.

Lavater, Johann Caspar. *Essays on Physiognomy; for the Promotion of the Knowledge and the Love of Mankind. Abridged from Mr. Holcroft's Translation*. London: G. G. J. and J. Robinson, 1800.

Lawrence, Christopher. 'Cullen, Brown and the Poverty of Essentialism'. *Brunonianism in Britain and Europe*. Ed. W. F. Brynum and Roy Porter. London: Wellcome Institue for the History of Medicine, 1988. 1–21.

——. 'The Nervous System and Society in the Scottish Enlightenment'. *Natural Order: Historical Studies of Scientific Culture*. Eds. Barry Barnes and Steven Shapin. Beverley Hills and London: Sage, 1979. 19–40.

Le Bon, Gustave. *The Crowd*. Int. Robert K. Merton. Harmondsworth: Penguin, 1977.

Lechte, John. *Julia Kristeva*. London: Routledge, 1990.

Lepenies, Wolf. *Melancholy and Society*. Trans. Jeremy Gaines and Doris Jones. Cambridge, MA and London: Harvard University Press, 1992.

Locke, Don. *A Fantasy of Reason: The Life and Thought of William Godwin*. London: Routledge and Kegan Paul, 1980.

Locke, John. *An Essay Concerning Human Understanding*. London: Penguin, 1997.

London, April. 'Sarah Fielding'. *Dictionary of Literary Biography*. Ed. Martin C. Battestin. Vol. 39. British Novelists, 1660–1800. Detroit: Gale, 1985. 195–204.

Lutz, Tom. *Crying: The Natural and Cultural History of Tears*. London and New York: Norton, 1999.

MacDonald, Michael. 'The Secularization of Suicide in England 1660–1800'. *Past and Present* 11 (1986): 50–100.

Mackenzie, Henry. 'Criticism on the Character of Hamlet'. *The Works of Henry Mackenzie*. Vol. 4. 1808. London: Routledge-Thoemmes, 1996. 371–95. Rpt. of *The Mirror* 99–100 (1780).

——. 'Distresses of the Families of Soldiers: Story of Nancy Collins'. *Works*. Vol. 4. 208–16. Rpt. of *The Mirror* 44 (1779).

——. 'Effects of Sentiment and Sensibility on Happiness, from a Guardian'. *Works*. Vol. 5. 1–17. Rpt. of *The Mirror* 101 (1780).

——. *Julia de Roubigné*. Ed. Susan Manning. East Linton: Tuckwell, 1999.

——. *Letters to Elizabeth Rose of Kilravock. On Literature, Events and People. 1768–1815*. Ed. Horst W. Drescher. Edinburgh and London: Oliver and Boyd, 1967.

——. *Literature and Literati: The Literary Correspondence and Notebooks of Henry Mackenzie*. Ed. Horst Drescher. Vol. 1. Letters 1766–1827. Frankfurt am Main: Peter Lang, 1989.

——. *Literature and Literati: The Literary Correspondence and Notebooks of Henry Mackenzie*. Ed. Horst Dreshcer. Vol. 2. Notebooks 1763–1824. Frankfurt am Main: Peter Lang, 1999.

——. 'On Novel-Writing'. *Works*. Vol. 5. 176–87. Rpt. of *The Lounger* 20 (1785).

——. 'On the Moral Effects of Scenes of Sorrow'. *Works*. Vol. 4. 272–81. Rpt. of *The Mirror* 72 (1780).

——. 'Story of Louisa Venoni'. *Works*. Vol. 4. 55–77. Rpt. of *The Mirror* 108–9 (1780).

——. *The Anecdotes and Egotisms of Henry Mackenzie 1745–1831*. Ed. Harold William Thompson. London: Oxford University Press, 1927.

——. 'The Effects of Religion on Minds of Sensibility: Story of La Roche'. *Works*. Vol. 4. 175–207. Rpt. of *The Mirror* 42–4 (1779).

——. 'The Exile, an Elegy'. *Works*. Vol. 4. 325–31. Rpt. of *The Mirror* 85 (1780).

——. *The Man of Feeling*. Ed. Maureen Harkin. Plymouth: Broadview, 2005.

——. *The Man of Feeling*. Ed. Brian Vickers. Oxford: Oxford University Press, 2001.

——. *The Man of the World*. *Works*. Vols. 1–2.

——. *The Works of Henry Mackenzie*. 8 vols. 1808. London: Routledge-Thoemmes, 1996.

Mandeville, Bernard. *The Fable of the Bees*. Ed. Phillip Harth. Harmondsworth: Penguin, 1970.

Manning, Susan. Introduction. *Julia de Roubigné*. By Henry Mackenzie. East Linton: Tuckwell, 1999. vii–xxvi.

Manning, Susan. Introduction. *The Works of Henry Mackenzie*. 1808. London: Routledge-Thoemmes, 1996. v–xxvi.

Manvell, Roger. *Elizabeth Inchbald: England's Principal Woman Dramatist and Independent Woman of Letters in 18th Century London. A Biographical Study*. Lanham, New York and London: University Press of America, 1987.

Marivaux, Pierre Carlet de Chamblain. *Le Paysan Parvenu or, The Fortunate Peasant*. 1735. New York and London: Garland, 1979.

Marshall, David. 'Fatal Letters: Clarissa and the Death of Julie'. *Clarissa and Her Readers: New Essays for the Clarissa Project*. Eds. Carol Houlihan Flynn and Edward Copeland. New York: AMS, 1999. 213–53.

——. 'The Business of Tragedy: Accounting for Sentiment in Julie de Roubigné'. *Passionate Encounters in a Time of Sensibility*. Eds. Maximilian E. Novak and Anne Mellor. Newark: University of Delaware P; London: Associated University Presses, 2000. 150–73.

——. *The Figure of Theater: Shaftesbury, Defoe, Adam Smith and George Eliot*. New York: Columbia University Press, 1986.

——. *The Surprising Effects of Sympathy. Marivaux, Diderot, Rousseau, and Mary Shelley*. Chicago, London: University of Chicago Press, 1988.

Marshall, Dorothy. *Eighteenth Century England*. London: Longmans, 1962.

Mason, Emma. 'Feeling Dickensian Feeling'. *19: Interdisciplinary Studies in the Long Nineteenth Century* 4 (2007): 1–19. 31 October 2008. http://www.19.bbk.ac.uk.

—— and Isobel Armstrong. 'Introduction: Feeling: "An Indefinite Dull Region of the Spirit"?' *Textual Practice* 22.1 (2008): 1–19.

McCarthy, Thomas J. *Relationships of Sympathy: The Writer and the Reader in British Romanticism*. Aldershot: Scolar, 1997.

McCormack, John. *One Million Mercenaries: Swiss Soldiers in the Armies of the World*. London: Leo Cooper, 1993.

McDougall, Joyce. *Theaters of the Body: A Psychoanalytic Approach to Psychosomatic Illness*. New York: Norton, 1989.

McDougall, William. *The Group Mind*. Cambridge: Cambridge University Press, 1927.

McGuinness, Arthur E. *Henry Home, Lord Kames*. New York: Twayne, 1970.

McNeil, Maureen. *Under the Banner of Science: Erasmus Darwin and His Age*. Manchester: Manchester University Press, 1987.

Mee, Jon. '"Examples of Safe Printing": Censorship and Popular Radical Literature in the 1790s". *Literature and Censorship*. Ed. Nigel Smith. Woodbridge: D. S. Brewer, 1993. 81–95.

——. *Romanticism, Enthusiasm, and Religion*. Oxford: Oxford University Press, 2003.

Mellor, Anne K. 'Righting the Wrongs of Woman'. *Nineteenth Century Contexts* 19.4 (1996): 413–24.

Milgram, Stanley. *Obedience to Authority: An Experimental View*. 1974. London: Pinter & Martin, 2005.

Miller, Nancy K. *The Heroine's Text: Readings in the French and English Novel, 1722–1782*. New York: Columbia University Press, 1980.

Minois, George. *History of Suicide: Voluntary Death in Western Culture.* Trans. Lydia G. Cochrane. Baltimore and London: Johns Hopkins University Press, 1999.

Mintz, I. *The Hunting of Leviathan: Seventeenth-Century Reactions to the Materialism and Moral Philosophy of Thomas Hobbes.* Cambridge: Cambridge University Press, 1962.

Mitchell, Juliet, ed. *The Selected Melanie Klein.* New York: Free Press, 1986.

Mitchell, Robert. *Sympathy and the State in the Romantic Era.* New York and London: Routledge, 2007.

Molella, Arthur Philip. *Science of Sensibility and the French Revolution.* MA dissertation. Cornell University, 1968.

Monboddo, James Burnet. *Of the Origin and Progress of Language.* Edinburgh: A. Kincaid, 1773–6.

Money-Kyrle, R. E. 'Normal Counter-Transference and Some of its Deviations'. *International Journal of Psycho-Analysis* 37 (1956): 360–6.

Monro, John. *Remarks on Dr. Battie's Treatise on Madness.* London: John Clarke, 1758.

Moore, Jane. *Mary Wollstonecraft.* Plymouth: Northcote, 1999.

Moravia, Sergio. 'From Homme Machine to Homme Sensible: Changing Eighteenth-Century Models of Man's Image'. *Journal of the History of Ideas* 39.1 (1978): 45–60.

More, Hannah. *Sacred Dramas [. . .] To which it is added, Sensibility: A Poem.* 5th edn. 1782. London: T. Cadell, 1787.

Morillo, John D. *Uneasy Feelings. Literature, the Passions, and Class from Neoclassicism to Romanticism.* New York: AMS, 2001.

Morris, David B. 'Painful Pleasures: Beauty and Affliction'. *The Culture of Pain.* Berkeley: University of California Press, 1991. 198–223.

Morris, Robert and James Kendrick. *The Edinburgh Medical and Physical Dictionary.* 2 vols. Edinburgh: Bell and Brandfute, 1807.

Morrison, Sir Alexander. *The Physiognomy of Mental Diseases.* London: Longman, 1843.

Mortensen, Peter. 'Rousseau's English Daughters: Female Desire and Male Guardianship in British Romantic Fiction'. *English Studies* 83.4 (2002): 356–70.

Mossner, Ernest Campbell. *The Life of David Hume.* Oxford: Clarendon Press, 1980.

Motherby, G. *A New Medical Dictionary; or, General Repository of Physic.* London: J. Johnson, 1775.

Mullan, John. 'Sensibility and Literary Criticism'. *The Cambridge History of Literary Criticism.* Eds. H. B. Nisbet and Claude Rawson. Vol. 4 (Cambridge: Cambridge University Press, 1997) 419–33.

——. *Sentiment and Sociability: The Language of Feeling in the Eighteenth Century.* Oxford: Clarendon Press, 1988.

——. 'The Language of Sentiment: Hume, Smith, and Henry Mackenzie'. *The History of Scottish Literature.* Ed. Andrew Hook. Vol. 2. 1660–1800. Aberdeen: Aberdeen University Press, 1987. 273–88.

Myers, Milton L. *The Soul of the Modern Economic Man: Ideas of Self-Interest, Thomas Hobbes to Adam Smith.* Chicago and London: University of Chicago Press, 1983.

Myers, Mitzi. 'Godwin's Memoirs of Wollstonecraft: The Shaping of Self and Subject'. *Studies in Romanticism* 20 (1981): 299–316.

——. 'Unfinished Business: Wollstonecraft's *Maria*'. *Wordsworth Circle* 11.2 (1980): 107–14.

Nachumi, Nora. '"Those Simple Signs": The Performance of Emotion in Elizabeth Inchbald's *A Simple Story*'. *Eighteenth Century Fiction* 11:3 (1999): 317–38.

Neill, Anna. 'Civilization and the Rights of Woman: Liberty and Captivity in the Work of Mary Wollstonecraft'. *Women's Writing* 8.1 (2001): 99–117.

Norman, Robert. *Newe Attractive, Shewing the Nature, Propertie, and Manifold Vertues of the Loadstone.* London, 1720.

Novak, Maximillian E. and Anne Mellor, eds. *Passionate Encounters in a Time of Sensibility.* Newark: University of Delaware Press; London: Associated University Press, 2000.

Nugent, Christopher. *Essay on the Hydrophobia.* London: James Leake, 1753.

Nunberg, Herman. 'Transference and Reality'. *International Journal of Psycho-Analysis* 32 (1951): 1–9.

Nussbaum, Martha. *Upheavals of Thought: The Intelligence of Emotions.* Cambridge and New York: Cambridge University Press, 2001.

'Obituary of Mary Wollstonecraft'. *The Gentleman's Magazine*, 86.2 (1797); *Lives of the Great Romantics III. Godwin, Wollstonecraft, and Mary Shelley by Their Contemporaries.* Ed. Harriet Jump. Vol. 2. Wollstonecraft. London: Pickering and Chatto, 1999: 1–3.

O'Farrell, Mary Ann. *Telling Complexions: The Nineteenth-Century Novel and the Blush.* Durham and London: Duke University Press, 1997.

O'Hagan, Timothy. *Rousseau.* London and New York: Routledge, 1999.

O'Quinn, Daniel. 'Trembling: Wollstonecraft, Godwin, and the Resistance to Literature'. *ELH* 64 (1997): 761–88.

Outram, Dorina. *The Body and the French Revolution: Sex, Class and Political Culture.* New Haven and London: Yale University Press, 1989.

Partington, Wilfred, ed. *The Private Letter-Books of Sir Walter Scott.* London: Hodder and Stoughton, 1930.

Partridge, Eric. *Origins: A Short Etymological Dictionary of Modern English.* London: Routledge, 1958.

Pastore, Nicholas. *Selective History of Theories of Visual Perception: 1650–1950.* New York: Oxford University Press, 1971.

Paul, Charles Kegan. 'Prefatory Memoir'. *Letters to Imlay.* By Mary Wollstonecraft. London: Kegan Paul, 1879. v–lxiii.

——. *William Godwin: His Friends and Contemporaries.* Vol. 1. London: King, 1876.

Paulson, Ronald. *The Life of Henry Fielding: A Critical Biography.* Oxford: Blackwell, 2000.

Perelberg, Rosine Jozef. 'The Interplay of Identifications: Violence, Hysteria, and the Repudiation of Femininity'. *The Dead Mother: The Work of André Green.* Ed. Gregorio Kohon. London: Brunner-Routledge, 2001. 173–92.

Perfect, William. *Cases of Insanity and Nervous Disorders Successfully Treated.* Rochester, [1785?].

——. *Select Cases in the Different Species of Insanity, Lunacy or Madness.* Rochester: W. Gillman, 1787.

Pfau, Thomas. *Romantic Moods: Paranoia, Trauma, and Melancholy, 1790–1840.* Baltimore: Johns Hopkins University Press, 2005.

Phillips, Mark. *Society and Sentiment: Genres of Historical Writing in Britain, 1740-1820.* Princeton, NJ: Princeton University Press, 2000.

Philp, Mark. 'The Fragmented Ideology of Reform'. *The French Revolution and British Popular Politics*. Ed. Mark Philp. Cambridge: Cambridge University Press, 1991. 50–77.

Pinch, Adela. *Strange Fits of Passion: Epistemologies of Emotion, Hume to Austen*. Stanford, CA: Stanford Universoty Press, 1996.

Polwhele, Richard. *The Unsex'd Females. A Poem*. Ed. Gina Luria. New York and London: Garland, 1974.

Pontalis, Jean-Bertrand. *Frontiers in Psychoanalysis: Between the Dream and Psychic Pain*. London: Hogarth and the Institute of Psycho-Analysis, 1981.

Poovey, Mary. *The Proper Lady and the Woman Writer*. Chicago: University of Chicago Press, 1984.

——. 'The Social Constitution of "Class": Toward a History of Classificatory Thinking'. *Rethinking Class: Literary Studies and Social Formations*. Eds. Wai Chee Dimock and Michael T. Gilmore. New York: Columbia University Press, 1994. 15–56.

Pope, Alexander. *The Works of Alexander Pope, Esq; With Explanatory Notes Never Before Printed*. Vol. 1. London: B. Lintot, 1736.

Porter, Roy. *A Social History of Madness: Stories of the Insane*. London: Weidenfeld, 1987.

——. *Mind-Forg'd Manacles: A History of Madness in England from the Restoration to the Regency*. Cambridge, MA: Harvard University Press, 1987.

Pratt, Samuel Jackson. *Supplement to the Life of David Hume, Esq., Containing Genuine Anecdotes, and a Circumstantial Account of his Death and Funeral, to Which is Added, a Certified Copy of His Last Will and Testament*. London: J. Bew, 1777.

Quincy, John. *Lexicon Physico-Medicum; or, a New Medicinal Dictionary*. 1719. 5th edn. London: T. Longman, 1736.

Racker, Heinrich. *Transference and Counter-transference*. London: Hogarth, 1968.

Radcliffe, Ann. *The Romance of the Forest*. London, T. Hookham and J. Carpenter, 1791.

Radden, Jennifer, ed. *The Nature of Melancholy: From Aristotle to Kristeva*. Oxford: Oxford University Press, 2000.

Rai, Amit S. *Rule of Sympathy: Sentiment, Race, and Power 1750–1850*. New York and Basingstoke, Palgrave, 2002.

Rajan, Tilottama. 'Framing the Corpus: Godwin's Editing of Wollstonecraft in 1798'. *Studies in Romanticism* 39:4 (2000): 511–31.

——. 'Wollstonecraft and Godwin: Reading the Secrets of the Political Novel'. *Studies in Romanticism* 27 (1988): 221–51.

—— and Julia M. Wright, eds. *Romanticism, History, and the Possibilities of Genre*. Cambridge: Cambridge University Press, 1998.

Rambow, Amy. '"Come Kick Me": Godwin's *Memoirs* and the Posthumous Infamy of Mary Wollstonecraft'. *Keats–Shelley Review* 13 (1999): 24–57.

Rather, L. J. *Mind and Body in Enlightenment Medicine: A Study Based on Jerome Gaub's De Regimine Mentis*. London: Wellcome Historical Medicine Library, 1965.

Reddy, William M. *The Navigation of Feeling: A Framework for the History of Emotions*. Cambridge: Cambridge University Press, 2001.

Review of *A Simple Story*, by Mary Wollstonecraft. *Analytical Review* 10 (1791): 101–2.

Review of *The Man of Feeling*, by Anon. *Monthly Review* 44 (1771): 418.

Rey, Alain. *Dictionnaire historique de la langue française*. Paris: Dictionnaires Le Robert, 1992.

Richardson, Alan. *British Romanticism and the Science of the Mind*. Cambridge: Cambridge University Press, 2001.

Richardson, Samuel. *Clarissa; or, the History of a Young Lady*. London: S. Richardson, 1747–8.

——. *Pamela; or, Virtue Rewarded*. London: S. Richardson, 1740.

——. *The History of Sir Charles Grandison*. London: S. Richardson, 1754.

Richter, Simon. *Laocoon's Body and the Aesthetics of Pain*. Detroit: Wayne State University Press, 1992.

Riskin, Jessica. *Science in the Age of Sensibility: The Sentimental Empiricists of the French Enlightenment*. Chicago and London: University of Chicago Press, 2002.

Risse, Guenter B. *New Medical Challenges During the Scottish Enlightenment*. Amsterdam and New York: Rodopi, 2005.

Ritterbush, Philip C. *Overtures to Biology: The Speculations of Eighteenth-Century Naturalists*. New Haven and London: Yale University Press, 1964.

Rivers, Isabel. *Reason, Grace and Sentiment: A Study of the Language of Religion and Ethics in England, 1660–1780*. Vol. 2. Shaftesbury to Hume. Cambridge: Cambridge University Press, 2000.

Riviere, Joan. *The Inner World and Joan Riviere. Collected Papers 1920–1958*. Ed. Athol Hughes. London: Karnac, 1991.

Robberds, J. W., ed. *A Memoir of the Life and Writings of the Late William Taylor of Norwich*. 2 vols. London: John Murray, 1843.

Rodgers, James. 'Sensibility, Sympathy, Benevolence: Physiology and Moral Philosophy in *Tristram Shandy*'. *Languages of Nature: Critical Essays on Science and Literature*. Ed. Ludmilla Jordanova. London: Free Association, 1986. 116–58.

Roe, Nicholas. '"Atmospheric Air Itself": Medical Science, Politics and Poetry in Thelwall, Coleridge and Wordsworth'. *1798: The Year of the Lyrical Ballads*. Ed. Richard Cronin. Basingstoke: Macmillan; New York: St Martin's Press, 1998. 185–202.

——. *John Keats and the Culture of Dissent*. Oxford: Clarendon Press, 1997.

Rosenfield, Leonora Cohen. *From Beast-Machine to Man-Machine: Animal Soul in French Letters from Descartes to La Mettrie*. New York: Octagon, 1968.

Ross, Ian Simpson. *The Life of Adam Smith*. Oxford: Clarendon Press, 1995.

Roulston, Christine. *Virtue, Gender, and the Authentic Self in Eighteenth-Century Fiction: Richardson, Rousseau, and Laclos*. Gainesville: University Press of Florida, 1998.

Rousseau, G.S. 'Nerves, Spirits, and Fibres: Towards Defining the Origins of Sensibility'. *Nervous Acts: Essays on Literature, Culture and Sensibility*. Basingstoke and New York: Palgrave Macmillan, 2004. 157–84. Rpt. of *Studies in the Eighteenth Century III. Papers Presented at the Third David Nichol Smith Memorial Seminar, Canberra, 1973*. Eds. R.F. Brissenden and J.C. Eade. Canberra: Australian National University Press, 1976. 139–57.

——. *Nervous Acts: Essays on Literature, Culture and Sensibility*. Basingstoke and New York: Palgrave Macmillan, 2004.

——. 'Psychology'. *The Ferment of Knowledge: Studies in the Historiography of Eighteenth-Century Science*. Eds. G.S. Rousseau and Roy Porter. Cambridge: Cambridge University Press, 1980. 143–210.

——. 'Science Books and Their Readers in the Eighteenth Century'. *Books and Their Readers in Eighteenth-Century England.* Ed. Isabel Rivers. Leicester: Leicester University Press; New York: St Martin's Press, 1982. 197–225.

——, ed. *The Languages of Psyche: Mind and Body in Enlightenment Thought.* Berkeley: University of California Press, 1990.

Rousseau, Jean-Jacques. *Eloisa, or a Series of Original Letters, Collected and Published by Mr. J. J. Rousseau, Citizen of Geneva.* 4 vols. Trans. William Kenrick. London: R. Griffiths, 1761.

——. *Émile, or On Education.* Trans. Allan Bloom. Harmondsworth: Penguin, 1991.

——. *Julie, or the New Heloise. Letters of Two Lovers Who Live in a Small Town at the Foot of the Alps.* Trans. and annot. Philip Stewart and Jean Vaché. Hanover and London: The University Press of New England, 1997.

Rowley, William. *A Treatise on Female, Nervous, Hysterical, Hypochondriachal, Bilious, Convulsive Diseases... with Thoughts on Madness, Suicide [...].* London: C. Nourse, 1788.

Russian Cruelty: Being the Substance of Several Letters from Sundry Clergymen in the New-Marck of Brandenburgh. London, 1760.

Rutsky, R.L. *High Techné: Art and Technology from the Machine Aesthetic to the Posthuman.* Minneapolis: University of Minnesota Press, 1999.

Sabor, Peter. Introduction. *The History of Ophelia.* By Sarah Fielding. Plymouth, UK: Broadview, 2004. 7–30.

——. 'Richardson, Henry Fielding, and Sarah Fielding'. *The Cambridge Companion to English Literature 1740–1830.* Eds. Thomas Keymer and John Mee. Cambridge University Press, 2004. 39–156.

Sade, Marquis de. 'Reflections on the Novel'. *One Hundred and Twenty Days of Sodom and Other Writings.* Comp. and trans. Austryn Wainhouse and Richard Seaver. New York: Grove, 1966. 91–116.

——. *The One Hundred and Twenty Days of Sodom and Other Writings.* Comp. and trans. Austryn Wainhouse and Richard Seaver. New York, Grove, 1966.

Saint-Pierre, Bernardin de. *Paul and Virginia.* Trans. Helen Maria Williams. Paris [?], 1795.

Sánchez-Pardo, Esther. *Cultures of the Death Drive: Melanie Klein and Modernist Melancholia.* Durham and London: Duke University Press, 2003.

Santayana, George. *The Life of Reason; or, the Phases of Human Progress.* London: Constable, 1905.

Santner, Eric L. *Stranded Objects: Mourning, Memory and Film in Postwar Germany.* Ithaca and London: Cornell University Press, 1990.

Scarry, Elaine. *The Body in Pain.* Oxford: Oxford University Press, 1985.

Scheler, Max. *The Nature of Sympathy.* Trans. Peter Heath. London: Routledge and Kegan Paul, 1954.

Schofield, Mary Anne. *Masking and Unmasking the Female Mind: Disguising Romances in Feminine Fiction 1713–1799.* Newark: University of Delaware Press; London and Toronto: Associated University Presses, 1990.

Schofield, Robert E. *Mechanism and Materialism: British Natural Philosophy in an Age of Reason.* Princeton, NJ: Princeton University Press, 1970.

Schor, Esther. *Bearing the Dead: The British Culture of Mourning from the Enlightenment to Victoria.* Princeton, NJ: Princeton University Press, 1994.

Schor, Naomi. 'Female Paranoia: The Case for Psychoanalytic Feminist Criticism'. *Yale French Studies* 62 (1981): 204–19.

Segal, Hanna. *The Work of Hanna Segal: A Kleinian Approach to Clinical Practice.* New York and London: Jason Aronson-Rowman & Littlefield, 1981.

Shaftesbury, Anthony Ashley Cooper, Third Earl of. *Characteristics of Men, Manners, Opinions, and Times.* Ed. Lawrence Klein. Cambridge: Cambridge University Press, 1999.

Shapiro, Michael J. *Reading 'Adam Smith': Desire, History and Value.* London: Sage, 1993.

Sharma, Renuka. *Understanding the Concept of Empathy and Its Foundations in Psychoanalysis.* Lewinston: Edwin Mellen, 1993.

Sher, Richard B. 'Science and Medicine in the Scottish Enlightenment: The Lessons of Book History'. *The Scottish Enlightenment: Essays in Reinterpretation.* Ed. Paul Wood. Rochester: University of Rochester Press, 2000. 99–156.

Shklar, Judith. N. 'Rousseau's Images of Authority (Especially in La Nouvelle Heloise)'. *The Cambridge Companion to Jean-Jacques Rousseau.* Ed. Patrick Riley. Cambridge: Cambridge University Press, 2001. 154–92.

Shorter, Edward. *A History of Psychiatry from the Era of the Asylum to the Age of Prozac.* New York: John Wiley, 1997.

Singer, Tania et al. 'Empathic Neural Responses are Modulated by the Perceived Fairness of Others'. *Nature* 439 (26 January 2006): 466–9.

Siskin, Clifford. *The Historicity of Romantic Discourse.* New York and Oxford: Oxford University Press, 1988.

——. *The Work of Writing: Literature and Social Change in Britain, 1700–1830.* Baltimore and London: Johns Hopkins University Press, 1998.

Skinner, Gillian. *Sensibility and Economics in the Novel, 1740–1800: The Price of a Tear.* London: Macmillan; New York: St Martin's, 1999.

Smith, Adam. *An Inquiry into the Nature and Causes of the Wealth of Nations.* Eds. R. H. Campbell, Andrew S. Skinner, and William B. Todd. Oxford: Clarendon Press, 1976.

——. *Essays on Philosophical Subjects.* Dublin: Wogan, 1795.

——. 'Letter from Adam Smith LL.D. to William Strahan, Esq.' *The Life of David Hume, Esq. Written by Himself.* London: W. Strahan, 1777. 39–62.

——. *The Theory of Moral Sentiments.* Ed. Knut Haakonssen. Cambridge: Cambridge University Press, 2002.

Smith, C.U.M. 'Julien Offray de la Mettrie (1709–1751)'. *Journal of the History of the Neurosciences* 11.2 (2002): 110–24.

Smith, Philip. 'Narrating the Guillotine: Punishment Technology as Myth and Symbol'. *Theory Culture Society* 20.5 (2003): 27–51.

Smith, William. *A Dissertation Upon the Nerves.* London: W. Owen, 1768.

Solomon, Andrew. *The Noonday Demon: An Atlas of Depression.* New York: Simon and Schuster, 2001.

Spacks, Patricia Meyer. *Desire and Truth: Functions of Plot in Eighteenth-Century English Novels.* Chicago and London: University of Chicago Press, 1990.

Spencer, David. 'Henry Mackenzie, a Practical Sentimentalist'. *Papers on Language and Literature* 3 (1967): 314–26.

Spencer, Jane. Introduction. *Elizabeth Inchbald: A Simple Story.* Ed. J. M. S. Tompkins. Oxford: Oxford University Press, 1998. vii–xx.

——. *The Rise of the Woman Novelist: From Aphra Behn to Jane Austen*. Oxford: Blackwell, 1986.

Spink, J. S. *French Free-Thought from Gassendi to Voltaire*. London: Athlone, 1960.

Stafford, Barbara Maria. *Body Criticism: Imaging the Unseen in Enlightenment Art and Medicine*. Cambridge, MA: MIT Press, 1991.

Starobinski, Jean. *Jean-Jacques Rousseau: Transparency and Obstruction*. Trans. Arthur Goldhammer. Chicago and London: University of Chicago Press, 1971.

Starr, G. A. 'From Socrates to Sarah Fielding: Benevolence, Irony, and Conversation'. *Passionate Encounters in a Time of Sensibility*. Eds. Maximilian E. Novak and Anne Mellor. Newark: University of Delaware Press; London: Associated University Presses, 2000. 106–26.

St Clair, William. *The Godwins and the Shelleys: The Biography of a Family*. London: Faber, 1989.

Steele, Valerie. *The Corset: A Cultural History*. New Haven and London: Yale University Press, 2001.

Steinbrügge, Lieselotte. *The Moral Sex: Woman's Nature in the French Enlightenment*. New York: Oxford University Press, 1995.

Steinke, Hubert. *Irritating Experiments: Haller's Concept and the European Controversy on Irritability and Sensibility, 1750–90*. Amsterdam and New York: Rodopi, 2005.

Stephen, Leslie. *History of English Thought in the Eighteenth Century*. [S. I.]: Smith, Elder, 1876.

Sterne, Laurence. *A Sentimental Journey*. Ed. Ian Jack. Oxford: Oxford University Press, 1998.

——. *The Life and Opinions of Tristram Shandy, Gentleman*. Ed. Graham Petrie. London: Penguin, 1985.

Stewart, M.A. *Studies in the Philosophy of the Scottish Enlightenment*. Oxford: Clarendon Press, 1990.

Stonebridge, Lyndsey and John Phillips. *Reading Melanie Klein*. London and New York: Routledge, 1998.

Tanner, Tony. *Adultery in the Novel: Contract and Transgression*. Baltimore and London: Johns Hopkins University Press, 1979.

Taylor, Barbara. *Mary Wollstonecraft and the Feminist Imagination*. Cambridge: Cambridge University Press, 2003.

Terada, Rei. *Feeling in Theory: Emotion After the 'Death of the Subject'*. Cambridge, MA: Harvard University Press, 2001.

Tester, Keith. *Compassion, Morality and the Media*. Buckingham, PA: Open University Press, 2001.

Thelwall, Boyle C. *The Life of John Thelwall, by his Widow*. London: John Macrone, 1837.

Thelwall, John. *An Essay Towards a Definition of Animal Vitality*. London: G. G. J. and J. Robinson, 1793.

——. *The Tribune*, Vol.2. London, 1796.

Thompson, Harold William. *A Scottish Man of Feeling: Some Account of Henry Mackenzie, Esq. of Edinburgh and the Golden Age of Burns and Scott*. London and New York: Oxford University Press, 1931.

Thomson, Ann. Introduction. *Machine Man and Other Writings*. By Julien Offray de La Mettrie. Cambridge: Cambridge University Press, 1996. ix–xxvi.

———. *Materialism and Society in the Mid-Eighteenth Century: La Mettrie's Discours Préliminaire*. Geneva: Droz, 1981.

Thurshwell, Pamela. *Literature, Technology and Magical Thinking, 1880–1920*. Cambridge: Cambridge University Press, 2001.

Tilmouth, Christopher, *Passion's Triumph over Reason: The History of the Moral Imagination from Spencer to Rochester*. Oxford: Oxford University Press, 2007.

Todd, Janet. *A Wollstonecraft Anthology*. Cambridge: Polity Press, 1990.

———. *Mary Wollstonecraft: An Annotated Bibliography*. New York and London: Garland, 1976.

———. *Mary Wollstonecraft: A Revolutionary Life*. London: Weidenfeld & Nicolson, 2000.

———. *Sensibility: An Introduction*. London: Methuen, 1986.

———., ed. *The Collected Letters of Mary Wollstonecraft*. London: Penguin-Allen Lane, 2003.

Tomalin, Claire. *The Life and Death of Mary Wollstonecraft*. Rev. ed. London: Penguin, 1992.

Trenchard, John. *The Natural History of Superstition*. London: A. Baldwin, 1709.

Ty, Eleanor. *Unsex's Revolutionaries: Five Women Novelists of the 1790s*. Toronto: University of Toronto Press, 1993.

Van Sant, Ann Jessie. *Eighteenth-Century Sensibility and the Novel: The Senses in Social Context*. Cambridge: Cambridge University Press, 1993.

Vartanian, Aram. *Diderot and Descartes: A Study of Scientific Naturalism in the Enlightenment*. Princeton, NJ: Princeton University Press, 1953.

———. *La Mettrie's L'Homme Machine: A Study in the Origins of an Idea*. Critical Edition with an Introductory Monograph and Notes by Aram Vartanian. Princeton: Princeton University Press, 1960.

———. 'Trembley's Polyp, La Mettrie, and Eighteenth-Century French Materialism'. *Journal of the History of Ideas* 11 (1950): 259–86.

Vetlesen, Arne Johan. *Evil and Human Agency*. Cambridge: Cambridge University Press, 2005.

Vickers, Neil. 'Coleridge, Thomas Beddoes and Brunonian Medicine'. *European Romantic Review* 8.1 (1997): 47–94.

Vila, Anne C. 'Beyond Sympathy: Vapors, Melancholia, and the Pathologies of Sensibility in Tissot and Rousseau'. *Yale French Studies* 92 (1997): 88–101.

———. *Enlightenment and Pathology: Sensibility in the Literature and Medicine of Eighteenth-Century France*. Baltimore and London: Johns Hopkins University Press, 1998.

Vincent-Buffault, Anne. *The History of Tears: Sensibility and Sentimentality in France*. Basingstoke and London: Macmillan, 1990.

Wallen, Martin. *City of Health, Fields of Disease: Revolutions in the Poetry, Medicine, and Philosophy of Romanticism*. Aldershot: Ashgate, 2004.

Ward, Candace. 'Inordinate Desire: Schooling the Senses in Elizabeth Inchbald's *A Simple Story*'. *Studies in the Novel* 31.1 (1999): 1–18.

———. 'Sensibility, Tropical Disease, and the Eighteenth-Century Sentimental Novel'. *Discourses of Slavery and Abolition: Britain and Its Colonies, 1760–1838*. Eds. Brycchan Carey, Markman Ellis and Sarah Salih. Basingstoke: Palgrave Macmillan, 2004. 63–77.

Wardle, Ralph, ed. *Godwin and Mary: Letters of William Godwin and Mary Wollstonecraft*. Lincoln and London: University of Nebraska Press, 1966.

——. *Mary Wollstonecraft: A Critical Biography*. London: Richards; Lawrence: University of Kansas Press, 1951.

Watson, Nicola J. *Revolution and the Form of the British Novel 1790–1825: Intercepted Letters, Interrupted Seductions*. Oxford: Clarendon Press, 1994.

Wellman, Kathleen. *La Mettrie: Medicine, Philosophy, and Enlightenment*. Durham, NC; London: Duke University Press, 1992.

Whiston, William. *The Longitude and the Latitude Found by the Inclinatory or Dipping Needle; Wherein the Laws of Magnetism are Also Discovered*. London: J. Senex, 1721.

Whyte, Lancelot Law. *The Unconscious Before Freud*. London: Tavistock, 1962.

Whytt, Robert. *An Essay on the Vital and Involuntary Motions of Animals*. 1751. Edinburgh: John Balfour, 1763.

——. *Observations on the Nature, Causes, and Cure of Those Disorders Which Have Been Commonly Called Nervous, Hypochondriac, or Hysteric*. Edinburgh: T. Becket, 1765.

——. *Physiological Essays*. Edinburgh: Hamilton, Balfour and Neill, 1761.

Wilks, Samuel and G. T. Bettany. *A Biographical History of Guy's Hospital*. London: Ward, Lock, Bowden and Co., 1892.

Williams, Helen Maria. *Letters Written in France*. Eds. Neil Fraistat and Susan Lanser. Peterborough, ON: Broadview, 2001.

Wimsatt, William. *The Verbal Icon: Studies in the Meaning of Poetry*. Lexington, KY: University of Kentucky Press, 1954.

Wimsatt, W. K. and Monroe Beardsley. 'The Affective Fallacy'. *Twentieth Century Literary Criticism: A Reader*. Ed. David Lodge. London: Longman, 1972. 345–58. Rpt. of *Sewanee Review* 57 (1949): 31–55.

Winnicott, Donald. 'Hate in the Countertransference'. *International Journal of Psycho-Analysis* 30 (1949): 69–74.

——. *Playing and Reality*. Hove: Brunner-Routledge, 2001.

Winter, Alison. *Mesmerised*. Chicago and London: University of Chicago Press, 1998.

Wollstonecraft, Mary. *A Vindication of the Rights of Woman*. Ed. Miriam Brody. London: Penguin, 1992.

——. *Letters to Imlay, with Prefatory Memoir by Charles Kegan Paul*. London: Kegan Paul, 1879.

——. 'Maria, or the Wrongs of Woman'. *Mary; and The Wrongs of Woman*. Ed. Gary Kelly. Oxford: Oxford University Press, 1980. 71–204.

——. 'Mary, a Fiction'. *Mary; and The Wrongs of Woman*. Ed. Gary Kelly. Oxford: Oxford University Press, 1980. 1–68.

——. *Posthumous Works of the Author of a Vindication of the Rights of Woman*. Ed. William Godwin. 4 vols. London: Joseph Johnson, 1798.

——. *The Collected Letters of Mary Wollstonecraft*. Ed. Janet Todd. London: Allen Lane, 2003.

——. *The Works of Mary Wollstonecraft*. Ed. Janet Todd and Marilyn Butler. 7 vols. London: Pickering & Chatto, 1989.

Wood, Marcus. *Slavery, Empathy, and Pornography*. Oxford: Oxford University Press, 2002.

Wood, Paul, ed. *The Scottish Enlightenment: Essays in Reinterpretation*. Rochester: University of Rochester Press, 2000.

Wright, John. P. 'Materialism and the Life Soul in Eighteenth-Century Scottish Physiology'. *The Scottish Enlightenment: Essays in Reinterpretation*. Ed. Paul Wood. Rochester: University of Rochester Press, 2000. 177–97.

——. 'Substance Versus Function Dualism in Eighteenth-Century Medicine'. *Psyche and Soma: Physicians and Metaphysicians on the Mind-Body Problem from Antiquity to Enlightenment*. Eds. John P. Wright and Paul Potter. Oxford: Clarendon Press, 2000. 237–54.

Yeo, Eileen Janes. *Mary Wollstonecraft and 200 Years of Feminisms*. London and New York: Rivers Oram, 1997.

Yolton, John W. *Thinking Matter: Materialism in Eighteenth-Century Britain*. Minneapolis: University of Minnesota Press, 1983.

Zerilli, Linda M.G. '"Une Maitresse Imperieuse": Woman in Rousseau's Semiotic Republic'. *Signifying Woman: Culture and Chaos in Rousseau, Burke, and Mill*. Ithaca and London: Cornell University Press, 1994. 16–59.

Zimmermann, Everett. 'Fragments of History and *The Man of Feeling*: From Richard Bentley to Walter Scott'. *Eighteenth-Century Studies* 23:3 (1990): 283–300.

Index

The manufacturer's authorised representative in the EU is Springer
Nature Customer Service Centre GmbH, Europaplatz 3, 69115 Heidelberg,
Germany. If you have any concerns regarding our products, please
contact ProductSafety@springernature.com

Printed and bound by CPI Group (UK) Ltd, Croydon, CR0 4YY
19/05/2026
02113609-0007